A DESTINY OF Dragons

TJ Klune

This is a work of fiction. Names, characters, places, and incidents either are the product of the author's imagination or are used fictitiously, and any resemblance to actual persons, living or dead, business establishments, events, or locales is entirely coincidental.

A Destiny of Dragons

Copyright © 2017, 2019 by TJ Klune

Published by BOATK Books
http://tjklunebooks.com
tjklunebooks@yahoo.com

Cover Art by Paul Richmond   http://www.paulrichmondstudio.com
Cover content is for illustrative purposes only and any person depicted on the cover is a model.

Published 2019.
First Edition published 2017. Second edition 2019.
Printed in the United States of America

ISBN: 978-1-7340862-7-0 (paperback)
eBook edition available

For my eighth-grade creative writing teacher who told me that my stories would never amount to anything.

Suck it.

PROLOGUE
The Bird

I WAS SEVENTEEN YEARS OLD WHEN I brought a bird back to life.

I never told anyone about it.

I had felt particularly sorry for myself that day. There was a knight in the castle I'd been harboring a crush on, but he didn't even know I existed. And there was a rumor going around that he was dating the Prince. I thought (hoped) that was just gossip amongst the staff in the castle, but then I'd stumbled across the two of them in the library, heads bent close together. The Prince's hand had been on the knight's thigh, and the knight had this look on his face, this soft expression I'd never really seen on him before. It was directed at the Prince, and I'd felt this furious curl of jealousy in the pit of my stomach, acidic and hot. It rolled through me like nothing I'd ever felt before. I was young and stupid and had a crush on a man who had never looked at me, not even once. And why would he? The Prince was everything I wasn't: powerful and beautiful with a future that was certain.

I was this scrawny kid who'd been pulled from the slums because he accidentally turned a group of teenage douchebags to stone. I was grateful for everything I'd been given. My parents were living a life they never thought they could have. I had the best friends in a hornless unicorn and a half-giant. I thought my mentor was the best thing that had ever happened to me. I was healthy. I was happy. I was whole.

But there were also days when I was a little sad too. I was a teenager, so of course I thought the best thing for unrequited love was to mope about it. I kept a journal (*diary*, the unicorn would insist, *it's a diary where you write your depressing little teenage thoughts, Sam. Don't try to call it otherwise*) under my mattress filled with such asinine meanderings that only seventeen-year-olds are capable of, like *I would love him as deeply as the ocean* and *His eyes are as green as the grass in summer and I want to lay on that grass and rub my face in it and get grass stains on my face* and *S.H. + R.F. = TRUELOVE 4EVA.*

So, naturally, I was devastated and utterly convinced that I'd be alone for the rest of my days, having to watch the Prince and the knight grow more in love with each other and then eventually marry. I'd have to witness it every hour of every day because I was going to be the King's Wizard, and their love would bloom right in front of me for the rest of time. They would be happy together, eventually have a family, and I'd always be skulking in the background, emo as shit in a black robe, dyed black hair, and thick black eyeliner, giving enigmatic advice that wouldn't look out of place in a Gothic horror: *Oh, you want my opinion on the crops? I shall give it to you. The crow flies inverted to peck out the eyes of its enemies and lament its existence in the face of such bourgeois conformity. This is lame. Everything is lame.*

And since that was my inevitable future, I decided to start practicing by brooding along the edges of the Dark Woods outside of the City of Lockes. My mentor had sent me on an errand to collect something or other that he probably didn't even really need. My best friends volunteered to come along, but I flipped up my collar, thrust my hands in my pockets, and said I needed time to reflect on my own mortality and that it was best if I did that by myself, like I always did.

"Oh boy," the unicorn said. "You do that, Robert Smith."

I frowned at him. "Who?"

The unicorn shook his head. "This guy I knew. Crazy hair. Sad all the time. Used to sing about it. It got old real fast. Before your time."

Whatever. It was probably stupid old people music, anyway.

So there I was! Sad and despondent and alone and in the Dark Woods, which was a pretty terrible combination. *No one understands me*, I thought to myself as I kicked a rock into the trees. *No one appreciates me for who I am. My life is hard. I have deep feelings and everything hurts. I'm seventeen years old and everything I think matters and I will feel this way for the rest of my life.*

It probably would have gone on for quite a bit longer in that ridiculous teenage vein had I not stumbled across the bird.

I was about to kick another rock when I saw it.

It lay on its back in the grass beneath a tree, wings spread out underneath it, the left crooked at an odd angle. Its feet stuck in the air, yellowed and curled, little black talons at the end. Its plumage was white on its chest, with a gold stripe on the underside of its tail. From the wings and the top of its head, the rest of it was black, with little specks of white dotting the feathers. It must not have been dead long, as the ants hadn't yet found it. I didn't know if it'd hit a tree or if it'd been attacked by something larger than it, but it'd died here, in this spot.

I didn't know why I cared so much. I didn't know why it struck me as poignantly as it did. One moment I was sulking over something that would never be mine, and the next I was on my knees, hunched over this little bird, hesitating to reach out and touch it. In the grand scheme of things, this was nothing. Things died every day. It was the way of life. This was absolutely nothing.

But I reached for it anyway.

The bird wasn't stiff when I picked it up from the ground, meaning it'd died even more recently than I first thought. There was a little wetness on the back of my hands, and I felt the gash near its neck through the feathers where it'd been slashed by some creature that had left it here instead of swallowing it whole. It wasn't breathing. There was no heartbeat. It was dead.

I held that bird in my hand and I thought to myself, *It isn't fair. It isn't fair. It isn't fair.* And it was the thoughts of a seventeen-year-old boy who believed his heart to be broken, though in the grand scheme of things it might not have mattered. There was the sharp sting in my chest that only worsened when I saw his face, that happy smile when he looked upon the Prince, like the Prince was everything he could ever hope for.

And who was I to ever compare?

It isn't fair. This isn't fair.

I cupped my hands together, hiding the little bird away.

I didn't think of anything else.

No wishes upon the stars.

No ancient words in the tongue of those that came before me.

And there was this *pulse*, and I thought maybe I cracked, just a little, the pieces jagged and sharp. There was green and gold, the colors of the forest around me. It was almost effortless, really, more so than magic had ever been before. It started in my heart; I knew that for a fact. I felt lightning-struck, the beat erratic and heavy.

The colors whirled around me, a spinning corona of light that pooled between my cupped hands, so bright I almost had to look away. It began to cascade downward, like a waterfall, the drops of light spreading along the ground, pulsating slowly. The forest faded around me. The sky above darkened. Everything else melted away.

I thought, *It isn't fair.*

And then something hooked itself into my head and heart and *pulled.*

The air sizzled around me.

The lights grew brighter, and I had to—

There was a flutter of wings against my palm, the barest of touches.

I took in a great, gasping breath.

The magic around me began to fade, the light and sounds of the Dark Woods returning as if they'd never been silenced at all.

And from my closed hands came the smallest of chirps.

I looked down as I lifted my fingers away.

The bird blinked slowly up at me.

Its feet opened and closed.

The crooked wing moved back into place even as I watched, the feathers scraping against my fingers.

It took a moment, maybe two, before it righted itself, the talons digging lightly into my skin. There was a little smear of blood across my palm. The bird hopped around, looked up and down, to the left and the right. As it turned its head, I saw the ruffled feathers on its neck, but the skin looked intact. It chirped again.

And then it flew away into the trees, lost amongst the branches and leaves.

I sat there for a long time, in those Dark Woods.

Eventually I decided to head for home. My heart was still heavy, but it no longer felt shattered in my chest. I could do this. I could be who everyone wanted me to be. I didn't need the knight. He had the Prince, and I... well. One day I'd find someone made for me. And I would show them why I was made for them. It was going to be okay.

I put my hands in the grass to push myself up and—

I stopped, because the grass *crunched* under my fingers.

I looked down.

It was blackened. Burnt.

All around me. In a large circle. And everything in that circle was charred. The ground. The shrubbery. The trees. Everything. It was as if I'd burned the life out of it. To... to give—

I stood, my legs shaking, breath hitching in my chest. I took a step back. And another. And another. And then I turned and ran toward home.

I was seventeen years old when I brought a bird back to life.

I had taken life from the earth to do it.

And I never breathed a word of it to anyone.

I
CITY OF LOCKES

CHAPTER 1
Best Friends 5Eva

"Do I even want to know what we're doing?" Prince Justin asked me as we walked down a side street in the City of Lockes, trying to avoid detection.

"Absolutely," I said. *Probably not.* "I have the best ideas." There was plenty of evidence to the contrary, but it was usually spouted by excessively negative people, and I *hated* excessively negative people. "You can trust me." This was going to end in tears and death, most likely my own, but *he* didn't need to know that. At least not yet. I grinned my most trustworthy grin as I led him into an alley.

He stared at me.

I widened my smile so he'd understand.

"Are you… are you about to be ill? Because you look like you're about to be ill. Like you just ate a plate of bad beef and are entirely unsure of what end it's going to come out of. I suppose that's how you normally look, though, so I don't really think there's much of a difference."

"I'm *smiling* at you. To show my trustworthiness."

He grimaced. "Funny how that works. I still don't trust you at all."

"Lie. You trust me a *little* bit. Otherwise you wouldn't have snuck out of the castle with me without asking me why."

"I didn't do *anything* with you. You put your hand over my mouth and told me I had to come with you if I wanted to live. And I *repeatedly* demanded you tell me the reasons for—"

"We're the best of friends," I told a rather large alley rat as it scurried along down the cobblestones. "He hugged me once in the forest while a naked man with wings tried to get us to touch each other inappropriately." I frowned. "Huh. What does it say about my life that that sentence makes complete and total sense to me?"

"We're not anything of the sort," Justin snapped. "In fact, my first act as King will probably be to behead you. Fair warning. And the hug was against my will, like most of the things you do to me. And it was made worse by the fact that the King of Fairies kept telling you to lick my—"

"You can't kill me," I reminded him as I stopped us at the entrance of the alley. "You would miss me too much and would probably feel really bad." And I would also be dead, which would suck for me.

"I highly doubt I would feel anything at all but immense relief."

Okay, I could work with that. "The people would revolt."

"Or there would be celebrations in the streets as they would no longer need to hear your inane prattling."

My trump card! "Gary would come after you."

Justin sighed. "Now that I believe. He still looks at me like *I* wasn't the one left standing at the altar on my wedding day while my fiancé stared lovingly into the eyes of another man and spouted disgusting platitudes of jerking off your heart or whatever the hell else was said."

I glanced out the alley to make sure we hadn't been noticed. "I don't know if that's quite what happened."

His glare was rather ferocious. "Care for me to refresh your memory?"

Nope, not at all. "You're distracting yourself from what's important."

He gaped at me. "Your level of self-awareness would be remarkable if it wasn't so terrifying."

"Thank you."

"That wasn't—"

"Don't you want to know why we're here?" I asked.

"No."

"You did just a second ago."

"I've since changed my mind."

"Are you *sure* you don't want to know? Not even a little bit?"

"Sam, if you don't take me back to the castle this instant, I'm going to make sure you're miserable for the rest of our lives."

My heart swelled. It was inevitable.

He took a step back. "What. Why are you looking at me like that? Like you're having *feelings*?"

I needed to hug him very badly. "Because," I said, taking a step toward him. "You just said you wanted me to be miserable for the rest of *our* lives. Like we're going to live long and miserably together. *Forever*. As best friends."

He blanched as he held up his hands, back hitting the brick wall of the building behind him. "That's *not* what I meant. You stay back! You hear me? Godsdammit, Sam, you *stay back*—"

"We're going to hug," I demanded, taking another step.

"No, no we're *not.*"

"You can't stop it," I said, holding my arms out wide. "It's gonna happen."

"Godsdammit, I will kick you in the—"

But before he could move, I had him pressed up against the brick wall, arms wrapped tightly around him. His arms were trapped at his sides. I laid my head on his shoulder, tucking my nose against his neck. "Shh," I said. "Shh. It's okay. It's okay. Just let it happen."

"You are *hugging me against my will.*"

"There's no such thing," I whispered. It was a good hug. Maybe not the best, but we had time to get there. Justin had just all but admitted that. It was glorious. I would probably write a poem about this day when we got back home.

He sighed heavily, like he couldn't believe I could be so wonderful. "You really don't understand boundaries, do you?"

"Only that they're made to be broken," I said. "Also, I would let your arms go, but you've already proven you can't be trusted to hug me back."

"It's not *my* fault you bruise so easily," he muttered.

"Yet you still seem to try—"

"Are we done yet?"

"It hasn't even been a full minute. Everyone knows that hugs last for at *least* two minutes. It's mandatory."

"No one thinks that. Sam, literally *no one.*"

"Maybe we should," I said, squeezing him tighter. "Maybe there'd be no wars if people just hugged all the time. After all, you can't be armed if you have someone in your arms."

"Unless I stab you in the—"

I felt like that was a good time to end the hug.

I turned back toward the entrance to the alley as he grumbled what I was sure was nothing but compliments about my existence.

It was going on dusk, and the street ahead was busy as people scurried about. Shopkeepers working the stalls called out their wares in loud, boisterous voices, selling fresh fish from the port and handwoven baskets and jewels crafted by the fires of dragons. It stank of animal shit, cooking meat, and something so distinctly *Verania* that I couldn't help but love every single piece and part of it. These were *my* people; this was *my* city. As if in response, somewhere in the crowd, there came the sweet, sweet chords of a lute playing a song that had taken Verania by storm over the last several months after it'd spent close to a year circulating in the pubs.

"I swear to the gods," Justin muttered, "if I have to hear that godsdamned song about cheesy dicks *one more time*, I'm going to find out who started it and send them to the dungeons forever."

Since I had no desire to poop in a bucket for the rest of my life, I said, "I don't hear anything, so let's stop talking about it and focus on other things.

Like how I'm about to change your life. For the *better*."

"Anyone else, I might believe that. Coming from you, it sounds like a threat."

Since anything he had to say was, at this point, entirely without merit, I ignored him. I had a scene to set, after all. "Imagine," I said, waving my hands slowly in front of me, setting the shit out of that scene. "It's a lovely evening. There's music in the air. Everyone is happy. There's a feeling of joy in your heart."

He glared at me.

"Joy," I insisted. "You're feeling joy."

His eyes narrowed further.

"Okay," I said. "We'll come back to that part and work on it a little later. By the way, did you know that the skin under your eye twitches when I talk? I noticed that a long time ago. I wonder why that is. You may want to see the doctor in case it's a sign of illness or stress. Are you stressed? I can't imagine why. Where was I? Dammit. I forgot what we were talking about."

"Sam," Justin ground out.

"That's right," I said. "The scene. There's music and happiness—mostly—and joy in your heart, or there soon will be. The night stretches out in front of you, filled with promise. Your senses are tingling, and you're thinking, *Yes, this is going to be something magical. This is what I've been waiting for.*"

"That's not what I'm thinking right now."

"Regardless," I said, "you *will* be thinking it. And when you're thinking it, when you're caught up in the moment, when you feel like you're finally *alive*, what's the one thing you notice is missing?"

"The reason why your parents didn't sell you for the highest price they could the moment they realized you were nothing but an unmitigated tragedy?"

"Close," I said. "You're missing *love*."

He blinked at me, looking startled.

It didn't last long.

"Love," he repeated slowly, starting to frown.

"Love," I agreed.

"Sam, I mean this in the most succinct way possible. Okay?"

"Okay."

"What. The *fuck*. Are you talking about?"

I sighed. "Look, maybe, quite possibly, I feel bad for a certain knight coming to a dawning realization at the worst possible moment."

"Really," he said flatly. "You feel bad about that."

I did. Granted, it led to my virginity getting completely destroyed by the love of my young, albeit adventurous, life, but yes. I still felt slightly bad. It'd been years since I'd given my heart away but only thirteen months since I was sure it'd be protected enough for me to let it go. And I would always remember the look of betrayal on Justin's face when his husband-to-be looked him straight in the eye and said he loved another. "Mostly bad," I said. "Slightly giddy, but bad too. It's paradoxical, but then I am an enigma."

He rolled his eyes. "I still blame you. But mostly him."

"Because he's an idiot."

"Right? Such a fucking idiot."

"Seriously! Who *does* that? He literally waited until you were *getting married* to confess his undying love and admiration for me."

"I would have believed that more if you hadn't gotten that sappy look on your face."

I shrugged. "It's a by-product. Of the love and admiration."

"It's an *affliction*. A symptom of a festering disease that must be eradicated."

"Or one that we need to infect you with, which is why we're here. Gods, I love it when conversations come full circle. Don't you just love that? I do."

He stared at me with an expression on his face that suggested he did not love that.

"Anyway," I said hastily. "Let me get a good look at you before we proceed. I have to know what I'm working with."

"Working with? Why do I have a feeling I'm not going to like what you're making me do?"

"To be fair, you don't like anything I make you do, so. Now hush. Let me gaze upon you."

"Is this some freakish wizard thing?"

"Yes." It wasn't. "That's exactly it." That wasn't it at all.

I suppose if one liked frigid bitches hiding hearts laced with gold, one could reasonably say that Grand Prince Justin of Verania was an attractive man. Sure, he often looked like he'd bitten into the most bitter of lemons (something I'd tried to cure him of but only seemed to make worse), but men and women alike fawned over his porcelain skin, waxing poetically over his chocolate-brown curls. How *regal* he was, they exclaimed. How *beautiful*. It was as if the gods themselves had a hand in his making.

Even after I'd essentially princenapped him, he looked well put together. He was statuesque, broad shouldered with a narrow waist. He had elegant fingers and callused palms, a testament to how well-versed of a swordsman he was. His expensively embroidered tunic was stretched tightly across his arms and chest. His trousers had the right amount of pull along his thighs and—

"Holy crap," I breathed. "You're *dreamy*."

He said, "What." No inflection whatsoever.

"Like, no, just… give me a moment. My worldview just shifted and I'm struggling to go along with it."

"So… pretty much a normal day, then, for you."

"When did you get attractive?" I demanded.

"Are you *hitting* on me?" he asked incredulously.

"What! No! Of course not. At least, I don't think I am. Am I? I really need to sit down and think about this. What *am* I doing? With this? With my life? Oh my gods, what am I doing with my—"

Justin scoffed. "It wasn't enough that you swooped in and stole my fiancé right out from under me, but now you've taken me to a dark and dank alley to have your way with me? For shame, Sam of Wilds. For *shame*."

"I would *never* have my way with you in a dark and dank alley," I retorted. "I'm a *gentleman*. I would woo the shit out of you, wine and dine, the whole nine yards. And then we'd make sweet passionate love on a bed covered in roses and I would just go to *town* on your butt because apparently I'm a power top and—what the fuck are we *talking* about?"

He looked horrified. "I have no idea! You're the one that stole me away to try and power top me! I don't even know what that means!"

"That's not—" I took a deep breath and let it out slow. "Okay. Somehow, you've gotten us all off track. As usual."

"*Me*? Why you little—"

"We're here because we're going on a date."

"I don't *want* to date you! In fact, I would rather do *anything* else—"

"Not *me*. I found you a date with an awesome dude!"

It wasn't silent after that. No, it really couldn't have been, seeing as how we were in the middle of the City of Lockes. But Prince Justin *was* silent, like his mind had been blown at the thought of my extraordinary generosity, his synapses firing in the face of just how much I cared.

Which, honestly, contrasted heavily when he finally spoke. "You did *what*."

"Okay, so look. It's really rather terrible, but something I've learned is that when one falls in love and is *happy* about it, one wants nothing more than to spread that love to others, to see best friends—okay, okay, don't *growl* at me, *almost* best friends, gods—experience the same joy of falling for someone. I love love so much, that I want to shove it down your throat so you know what I'm going through."

"Sam."

"Yes, Justin."

"Are you telling me that right now, there is someone waiting for me to come to them to go on a date with them? Someone I've never met."

"Um. Yes?"

"How are you a real person?"

I frowned at him. "You know what? That's not the first time I've been asked that."

"Who is he?" Justin asked, sounding resigned (which possibly meant he was thrilled; I hadn't quite worked out all of Justin's facial expressions as of yet).

"Oh! You're going to *love* him. His name is William and he's a Sagittarius and he likes the same things you do."

"Like…."

"Um. You know. Stuff. Things. That everyone likes."

He cocked his head at me. "Sam."

"Yes, Justin."

"Where did you meet him?"

"At… the store."

"What store?"

I was feeling awfully sweaty because I really couldn't lie for shit. I suppose that was a good thing. Mostly. "The… hat. Store."

"The hat store."

"Yes," I said, swallowing. "Where I was buying a hat."

"What kind of hat?"

Why was it so warm in the dark and dank alley? "A pork pie."

He took a step toward me. "Really."

I nodded. "Gary says they're all the rage this season. And I trust his fashion sense. Because he's a unicorn. Unicorns are very fashionable, in case you hadn't noticed."

"And this man. This… *William*. What does he look like?"

And godsdamn his inquisitive mind! How neatly a trap it laid! "Like a… male… person."

"Sam."

"Yes, Justin." He was standing really close to me. I was uncomfortable.

"What—"

"Fine!" I cried. "You've *broken* me. I've withstood Dark wizards and really invasive corn, but I can't *take* the endless pools that are your eyes. I've never met him before. I've never even *seen* him before!"

"Aha!" Justin cried. Then, "Wait. What?"

"Ah, man. I feel better. That really was weighing on me."

"What do you *mean* you've never seen him?"

I blinked. "Just that. I've never seen him before." Was it that hard to understand?

"Then how do you know him?" he asked dangerously.

"He answered the ad."

Justin closed his eyes for a moment, breathing heavily through his nose. "What ad?"

Well, this was off to a very bad start. "Um. The one I placed in the back of *Lockes of Love*, the periodical for singles who are ready to mingle in the City of Lockes, under their man for man section?"

The skin under his eye twitched.

"It's okay," I said. "I made you sound really good. If there's one thing I'm good at, it's bullshitting."

Another twitch. Or maybe a more pronounced one. Like it was spreading.

"I'm serious! Look, I even cut it out and saved it, it was so good." I reached into the pocket under my robes and pulled out the folded piece of paper. I handed it over to Justin, who just glared at me. I poked it against his hand. "Come on. Come on, take it. *Take* it."

A man walked by the alley, staring at us with wide eyes.

I waved at him.

He walked away quickly.

Justin grabbed the paper from my hand and brought it up to his face. I didn't need to see what it said. I'd already had the genius of it memorized.

Looking For Love!

M4M. In position of power, would like someone else to take charge. Me: 20s Attractive w/ resting bitch face. Intelligent, slightly evil, ambitious. People think I'm cold, but it's really a front for a semisoft heart. I like rolling my eyes at wizards even though I secretly like them and think they're pretty cool. I also like deviled eggs.

"I know so much about you," I said helpfully.

You: Older? Maybe. Assertive attitude. Real go-getter. Takes what you want. Commanding, even. Must have eyebrows. Double jointed is a plus. No Darks or fairies named Dimitri.

Justin looked up at me slowly.

I smiled at him. "You're welcome. Some of them got really porny, but I took the high road. One talked about splitting you like a—"

"And someone responded to this," he said, voice strangely even.

"Yes! Well, actually, like a hundred people did, but I narrowed it down to the best one. And I've been sending notes back and forth posing as you so I could get a real sense of him. He seems like a nice guy. Maybe a little bossy, but I figured that's something you can work on when you marry him. Also, for some reason, he likes to call you boy and expects to be obeyed at all times, but hey, just roll with it. Could be fun."

"What part of you thought that this would be a good idea?"

"Most parts," I said. "But that's why I'm here. In case he turns out to be a raging psychopath—which I highly doubt because it seems like that's something you'd have to put down in the ad—I'll be there right by your side."

He said nothing for a long time. My jaw hurt from smiling so much.

Finally, "So let me get this straight. You impersonated the Prince of Verania to set up a date for me by using a personal ad in the back of a magazine that I usually see lying in the gutters and covered with bird feces. And not only that, but someone *responded* to said ad and now I'm on my way to meet him. Where you will also be in attendance."

"All the highlights," I said, suitably impressed.

Lots of twitching going on.

"Also," I said. "One more thing." I reached into my robe in the inner pocket and pulled out two matching beards from my old Mervin days. "Disguises. So we won't be recognized. If all goes well, then William will understand why you had to lie. Especially if it's for love. Do you want to put this on or should—you know what. I'll just do it. Just… hold still. You're kind of tense. Like really, really tense. It's not good for your back. And your hands are fists right now. So much tension. Sorry the beard is a little wet. And sticky. Tiggy spilled juice on it right before we left and I didn't have time to clean it. Just gonna hold it on your face for a moment to make sure it sticks… annnnd done."

He looked ridiculous.

"You look amazing," I said. "William won't know what hit him."

I had the best ideas.

I HAD THE WORST IDEAS.

Not that they started *out* that way, mind you, but for some reason, they tended to devolve quickly and out of my control. Dragons, truth corn, getting gay fairy married, turning boys to stone, and asking an important wizard to not explode my nipples. I'd like to think I have the best intentions in mind, but I lose the thread partway through.

Like today, for example.

I wanted Justin to find love.

And thought what if I brought love to *him*?

Ergo, I put out a search for love.

And then bring *him* to love.

Foolproof, right?

Almost. Except for the fact that William seemed to be almost as big as Tiggy, wore an entire herd's worth of leather, and made us call him Sir.

Justin and I sat side by side in the open-air café that William had suggested we meet at. (Though, if I was remembering correctly, he'd said *negotiate* rather than meet, but I had a lot going on at the time, so I couldn't be faulted for not remembering *every little detail*.) I wore a beard similar to Justin's, something that Sir hadn't missed, given that he'd raised an eyebrow as we approached and said, "I'm down for twins."

I should have known it was going to go downhill from there.

"Now, I understand you're looking to be dominated," Sir said.

Justin squeaked.

"Uhh," I said. "I don't think that's quite what I—"

"Did I say you could speak, boy?" Sir asked sharply.

"No, Sir. Sorry, Sir."

He waited a beat, as if making sure I wouldn't step out of line again. I didn't, because I didn't want to get fisted or have something shoved up my pee hole.

"Now. We should probably discuss hard limits," Sir said. "I'm okay with most things, even the... *fluids*... some others might have problems with. Even the more solid ones."

"So unbelievably gross," I breathed in awe.

"Also, after you sign the contract, you will become my personal property, and I like to share. I have a lot of friends who will want to tear off a piece for themselves while I watch. You will treat them with respect while they treat you like a piece of meat. It's how these things go. Also, I have this kink where I treat my subs like footstools."

"I will see you *castrated* for this," Justin whispered furiously at me.

"Stop saying things he might like!" I whispered back.

Sir coughed in warning.

We stared at him with wide eyes.

"Are you two quite finished?"

"You have no idea," Justin said.

"Absolutely none," I agreed.

"Good. Tell me. How do you feel about puppy play?"

Before I could answer that (*Ooh, I like puppies!*), we were interrupted by a shrill, grating, and dare I say *shriekish* voice. "Well eat me up and shit me out. Just what do we have here?"

·   I sighed. "Crap. I am never going to hear the end of this."

I turned slowly, already knowing what I would find.

Sure enough, there on the street only a few feet away (how had I not heard them approach!) stood a hornless unicorn, a half-giant, a dragon, and a knight with a resigned look on his face, something that I was extraordinarily used to being directed at my person, even after all this time.

"Heyyy," I said with a wave. "What. Is. *Up*."

"*Hey*, he says," Gary snapped, flipping his mane prettily. "Can you believe this? You raise a child most of his life, watch him go through *painful* years of puberty to become a reasonably attractive man, only to find him negotiating kink contracts with a leather Dom and saying *hey*." He sniffled. "I've never been more proud of anything in my life."

Tiggy frowned. "Sam a pain slut?"

"I highly doubt that, kitten. You know how he gets when he stubs a toe. He doesn't pop a boner, that's for sure."

"He's growing up so fast," the dragon named Kevin rumbled. "I remember when he was just a wee slip of a lad. Now he's this young man finding his way in the world. A sexy way that I will probably actively participate in because that's just who I am. No judgments. We're all gods' creatures, right? Just writhing on top of each—"

"Do I even want to know what you're doing?" the knight asked, cocking a devastatingly unfair eyebrow.

Knight Commander Ryan Foxheart, the dreamiest dream to have ever been dreamed.

And probably currently not very happy with me.

"It's not what it looks like?" I tried.

They all stared at me.

"Okay, it probably *is* what it looks like, but not for me. I'm not some kind of pain slut like Justin is. I'm here for moral support and nothing else."

"Really," Sir said. "You sure about that?"

"Wow," I said. "Your voice is deeply intimidating. That's impressive. I'm impressed." I turned back to the others. "Did you hear that? He makes us call him Sir. This is fun. I'm having such a good time. Please save me."

"Sam put a personal ad in the newspaper to try and make up for the fact that he is a home-wrecker," Justin said.

"See, that makes sense," Gary said.

"Hey! What about what *I* said?"

"Sam," Gary said, sounding disappointed. "Honestly, what do you expect me to believe? I *know* Justin's not a pain slut, because I've never seen him at the club getting flogged by Honest Helga."

"That's not a club I want to go to," I said. "Because of Honest Helga."

"She certainly knows how to pack a punch," Kevin agreed.

"*And*," Gary said, "I know you're a home-wrecker because I witnessed it with my own eyes. Remember that? Sam? Do you? When you wrecked their home? *I* remember when you wrecked their home."

Tiggy crossed his arms over his considerable chest. "That's not nice, Sam. Even if Knight Delicious Face ate your flower."

"He most certainly did," Kevin said. "We all heard it too. The acoustics in the castle are just extraordinary. Raise your hand if you thought Sam would be a screamer."

Tiggy raised his hand. Kevin raised a claw. Gary stood on three legs.

"I didn't *scream*," I said, scowling at all of them. "I was providing encouragement to my boo so he knew he was doing a good job. It's called positive reinforcement."

Ryan turned his face toward the heavens and sighed. He was either silently agreeing with me or deciding now was a good time to study up on constellations.

Kevin snorted a little lick of fire. "It sure sounded like you were positively reinforcing his—"

"Dear," Gary said. "We've talked about this. It's not polite to discuss other people's sex lives when one or more of them is a prude."

"I'm not a *prude*. Do you know how many things Ryan has *done* to me? Like, seventeen things."

"Name three," Gary said rather gleefully as he pranced in place.

"Easily," I said. "This one time, he put his toes in my—"

"That's probably enough of that," Ryan said.

I mimed the rest to Gary. It was the most accurate thing I'd ever done.

Gary squinted at me. "Are you pretending to eat a watermelon covered in peanut butter?"

"Close enough. I couldn't walk straight for like three days."

"I bet I could make it four," Sir said as he leered at me.

"I like him," Kevin announced. "We should all be sex friends and go on team-building retreats where none of us wear clothing and we all lay on top of each other."

"Yep," I said. "Time to go. This has just been lovely. Justin, will you be signing any contract or having any follow-up with Sir? I take it by the way you're squeezing my hand to the point of excruciating pain, that's a no. Sorry, Sir. Looks like the date was a bust. Next time, huh?"

"Or maybe," Sir said slowly, "you owe me for wasting my time." He glanced at Ryan. "He your bitch?"

"Oh, girl, that was a bad idea," Gary muttered.

"I smash?" Tiggy growled.

"Kind of my bitch," Ryan said.

"No shit," Justin said.

"Ha," Kevin said. "I knew it. That's so hot."

"Hey! Okay, I *am*, but that's still rude. Or maybe I'm my *own* man, and I can speak for myself. Maybe I *want* to go with him." I looked back at Sir. "I really don't want to go with you. I'm just trying to prove a point."

"Autonomy is very important," Sir said. "Unless I take it from you and cover you with my semen."

"You are the greatest man alive," Kevin said. "Teach me all your secrets."

"One day," Ryan said, "we're going to meet someone new who *doesn't* want to capture and/or have sex with you."

"I never did," Gary said. "He's a little too stringy for my tastes. Not enough meat on dem bones, if you know what I mean. Unicorns need a little more *oomph* since we're such voracious lovers."

"*Stringy?*" I gasped.

"It okay," Tiggy said, reaching down and patting me roughly on the head. "I do you."

"Aw. Really?"

"No."

"Dammit."

"I can't comment on this," Kevin said. "Given my position as his stepfather."

"You're not my—"

"I'd hit that so hard," Kevin told Sir.

"This did not turn out how I thought it would," I said.

"Does it ever?" Justin asked. "That was a legitimate question, by the way. Does *anything* ever turn out like you think it will?"

I nodded toward Ryan. "Locked that shit down, didn't I?"

"Oh snap," Tiggy said.

"Fist-bump me, babe," I said to Ryan, holding out my hand.

"Yeah, I'm not going to do that," Ryan said.

"Watch," Gary whispered to Tiggy. "It'll take five to ten seconds for him to give in. I've been teaching Sam how to unicorn."

I widened my eyes as much as possible and fluttered my eyelashes. "But, I *want* you to. For me? Please?"

Ryan sighed and fist-bumped me.

"Works every time," Gary said.

"I can hear you," Ryan said. "You're standing right next to me and not trying to hide the fact that you're talking about me."

"I thought we talked about how stalking me is wrong now that you're in a monogamous relationship with one of my best friends," Gary said. "Get a grip, Ryan. This obsession you have with me is going to ruin the best thing that's ever happened to you."

"*You* talked about that," Ryan reminded him. "Loudly and repeatedly. Once you woke me up at three in the morning by standing above me and breathing on my face, only to tell me to stop following you."

"Maybe you should listen!"

"You were in *my room*."

"I'll find you true love," I told Justin. "If it's the last thing I do."

"That feels like a threat," he said slowly.

"A threat of love," I agreed. "Now, I think it's time we head back to the castle. I'm famished and I'm probably going to get yelled at by four or five different people for sneaking you out to meet with a leather daddy."

"The *castle*?" Sir said.

"Oh, right," I said. "Yeah, this is Justin, the Prince of Verania, that you just tried to violate with your existence. Good job."

"Holy shit," he said, paling considerably. "The *Prince*? That means—" He looked from Gary to Tiggy. From Kevin to Ryan. Then back to me. "That means you're—"

I grinned at him. "Damn right. I'm Sam of Wilds, King's Wizard."

"Apprentice," Gary coughed.

"Don't explode my nipples!" Sir said as he stood up quickly, knocking his chair back. "I didn't know it was you!"

"Wow," I said. "That's *still* a thing? And now it's said about *me*?

Sweet molasses."

"Oh boy," Ryan sighed. "This is something I'm never going to hear
the end of."

This might have been the greatest day of my life. "Babe! Did you *hear*
that? He said—"

"Still standing right here."

"But—"

"Don't need to repeat it. Heard it enough the first time."

And that's when Tiggy decided to smash the table. But that was okay.
He'd earned it.

"How'd you figure out we were gone?" I asked Ryan as we
walked side by side toward the castle. The others were ahead of us, Gary
and Justin bickering back and forth as Kevin tried to get them to agree
to a threesome, Tiggy muttering to himself about his broom collection.

Ryan bumped his shoulder against mine. "Hadn't seen you in ten minutes or so. I figured you were probably getting into trouble."

Huh. That was… probably more accurate than I cared to think about.
"I could have handled it."

"Oh, I know."

"Do you?"

He shrugged. "Doesn't hurt to have backup." He blushed a little at
that, and I struggled to not launch myself at him and potentially be arrested
for lewd and lascivious conduct in the streets of the city.

"You're my backup?"

"Shut up, Sam."

"Nah, it's out there, dude. You can never take it back now."

"I regret everything."

And I doubted that quite a bit. I could see the way he was fighting a
losing battle against smiling, his lips quirking, eyes crinkling. To the world,
Knight Commander Ryan Foxheart was strong and brave, dashing and immaculate. And he *was* all those things, even to me. But he was so much more
than that, more than what the people of Verania thought he was. For one, he
was the world's sappiest dork, something I never expected and would lord
over him for the rest of our days.

"Came riding in to my rescue," I teased him. "Someone might think
you're a knight or something."

"I always have to rescue you."

"Pfft. I think you've got that a bit backward there."

"Probably. But that's okay."

"How'd you know where we were?"

He reached up and wrapped an arm around my shoulders, pulling me close. My arm went around his waist and he tilted his forehead against me as we walked. "I always know where you are," he murmured against my hair.

And my heart absolutely did not trip all over itself at that. Not at all, no sir. "Yeah, Gary was right. That does sound stalkery. You might want to curb that a little before someone gets the wrong idea that you want to put them in a hole in the basement. Pete told you, didn't he."

"Didn't even hesitate when he narced on you."

"That bastard. He needs to hurry up and retire so I can get away with things. I don't know why he decided to stay on. I think it was probably just to stop me from doing amazing things."

Ryan laughed in my ear. I didn't think I'd ever heard a sound so wondrous.

"You guys coming, or are you going to be grossly in love some more and make everyone hate you?" Gary called back, sounding appropriately disgusted.

"HaveHeart forever, motherfuckers," Tiggy said.

"We need to have a name like that," Kevin said to Gary. "So everyone will know our love is real. Something wicked. Like... Kery. Or Gavin. Oooh. Or *Dragoncorn*."

I can't say that I was really listening to them. No, I was getting kissed within an inch of my life and thinking, *Nothing can get better than this. This is my happy ending.*

But it wasn't, though.

Because things were just getting started.

CHAPTER 2
A Vision and a Warning

ONCE UPON A TIME IN THE Kingdom of Verania, there was a kickass boy born in the slums of the City of Lockes. His parents were hardworking, and at times life could be difficult, but they were alive and had all their teeth. Which was very important.

Now for the remix.

The kickass boy was apparently magic, turned his future boyfriend (who, at the time, was the world's biggest asshole) into stone, and was taken away from the life of poverty by a magical man in pink shoes to a castle where he met a wonderful King and a not-so-wonderful Prince. His parents came along for the ride and cheered and fretted like most parents do. The boy was sent into the Dark Woods one day and came back, unexpectedly having made friends with a hornless unicorn and a half-giant. He was given his first wizarding name of Sam of Wilds.

From there, the boy had many adventures as a wizard's apprentice, knowing one day all of Verania would depend upon him as the King's Wizard. Sure, he thought that was the coolest thing he'd ever heard, but it was *years* and *years* away. He had plenty of time to worry about things such as responsibility to King and Crown. So, during those first years, he did magic (somewhat successfully—though, as was pointed out on a regular basis, the magic he *did* do was never what he started out *trying* to do; the boy was of the belief that it was the thought that counted). He was captured a lot for some unknown reason, and villains tended to monologue whenever they were around him, as if they couldn't help but broadcast their plans in addition to spilling their life's stories while he usually was bound to a chair or a wall (or, on one notable occasion, the front of a pirate ship as a group of lesbian pirates called the Tuna Fishes were trying to use his magic to force mermaids into revealing their treasures—but never mind that now. It's a long story that involves a sea chanty about scissoring that the pirates insisted the boy learn and he has never forgotten).

But through it all, with his friends and parents and a great wizard named Morgan of Shadows by his side, he was happy. He looked upon the stars and found he could wish for nothing more, given all that he had.

Sure, maybe he was lonely every now and then, but it was a small thing, a negligible thing that he could ignore if he tried hard enough. He didn't allow himself to dwell upon it. There were too many things to see. New magic to explore. Obstacles to overcome. One day he would face the Trials to become a true wizard. He had his Grimoire he needed to complete. His friend, the unicorn, needed to find his horn. All of these things came first. Because that's just who the boy was.

But.

The boy was still human, regardless of his elevated station and lot in life. He was still prone to that humanity just like everyone else.

For you see, one day there came a knight to the castle. A knight unlike anyone the boy had ever seen before. He was beautiful and kind and smiled like sunshine, and the boy said to his friends, "I might be super gay right now."

His friends were not surprised.

Yes, he was a wizard and had many things to do. But he was human, and with it came the longing for something more. He was embarrassed by this feeling, after all he'd been given, but he couldn't help but dream about green eyes and locks of blond hair and wish that he could have what he felt in his heart.

Of course, things like that rarely work out, and the knight began to date the Prince, for which the King was happy, so the boy suffered in silence, resolutely not attempting to put together a spell to give said Prince the disposition of a flatulent selkie, even if he already had the personality to match.

But fate is a funny thing. It weaves its threads through the loom with steady hands. At first, the result is seemingly a distorted mess, but if one can wait long enough, the full picture comes into focus, the threads tightly intertwined, strong and true.

Maybe it's too grand a thought to think the boy had a fate beyond what he'd already been given, but he was *still* a boy and prone to boyish thoughts and wishes.

He was sure the knight never even knew his name.

The boy was wrong. So very, very wrong.

The boy was loved as much as he loved in return.

But it's a known fact that boys are stupid, stupid creatures without nary a lick of common sense between them, and so it took *ages* for anything to come of it. It also required the presence of a ridiculous amount of Dark wizards, a date with a man who had wonderful ears (though the knight didn't quite understand what the big deal was, if the scowl on his face meant anything), a dragon kidnapping the Prince, a forest full of secrets, an extraordinarily perverted disgruntled ex who was six inches tall with wings, a fairy drag mother with eyes and tongue as sharp as a knife, an elf who wanted to relieve the boy of all vestiges of his virginity, and a crazy corn cult who felt the need to build a religion around the dragon in fifty-seven days. (The boy *still* marvels at the tenacity of insanity.)

And then the boy stood atop the dragon's keep and a secret was revealed, something he'd kept locked away in his heart in hopes that it would never be discovered. The pain he felt then matched the look on the knight's face.

For the boy was powerful, maybe more powerful than anyone who had ever come before. The caveat to all the extent of his magic was this: he must find the person in the world who could stabilize his magic. A person who could hold the foundation for his magic together. A person who, without them, the boy could descend into darkness.

The cornerstone.

To a wizard, the cornerstone is the most precious thing in the world. Something revered, something treasured. Those that have forsaken the idea of a cornerstone have done so knowing they will be consumed by the darkness inherent in all magic.

The boy didn't know the extent of his magic. Neither did his mentor, though the boy thought Morgan of Shadows knew more than he was saying. As did the man even higher up, the grand wizard known as Randall, a terrifying man whose nose the boy had once turned into a dick. The boy could see the concern when he returned to the castle after making the knight choose between himself and the Prince. The knight had chosen to follow his oath rather than his heart.

He threw himself back into living. He told himself he would never forget, and if there was one person for him, then there could be another. He was stronger than he'd given himself credit for, and while it cracked his heart, he was not broken.

But he hadn't seen the full picture woven by fate.

Because sometimes, the power of love is greater than an oath could ever be. And as soon as the knight saw the boy standing near him on his wedding day, he realized that some things were meant to be broken so that others could be made whole.

And then they fucked.

Holy shit, did they fuck. In so many godsdamned positions, it wasn't even funny. It shouldn't have been *possible*, some of the ways they were able to bend. This one time, the boy took the knight up against a wall and just *railed* into him and—

"REALLY, SAM?" MORGAN OF SHADOWS said, face in his hands. "This is what you've spent your time on?"

I looked up from where I'd been reading to him from my Grimoire.

He sat across from me in our laboratories underneath Castle Lockes in his old rocking chair that he'd had for a century or two. I thought it'd been a gift from someone important, possibly even *her*, the one who'd helped him build his magic, but I'd never gotten the courage to ask. All I knew was that no one aside from Morgan could sit in that chair for fear of having their fingers turned to spiders (a threat I wasn't sure I wanted to see if would be carried out).

I sat opposite him, resting my Grimoire in my lap, carefully turning the thick pages as I read off my condensed (and highly accurate) biography, something Morgan said was necessary. A wizard's Grimoire wasn't just for ingredients for potions or steps to a spell. It was a wizard's history, both personal and professional. Morgan had tasked me with writing down my history in order to make sure that anyone who followed me understood the steps I'd taken to become the person I was. Granted, he'd been kind of vague when giving me this assignment, but I could admit to taking a few creative liberties. To be fair, though, I thought future generations should be aware of just how much sex I was having and who I was having it with so they could completely understand me as a person and realize how awesome I was. There were even pornographic stick figure drawings in the margins that illustrated my prowess.

"Yes, well, there's nothing wrong with having a healthy libido," I said, trying to figure out if I should write the time I sat on Ryan's face or if I should maybe go to church a little bit more. It really could have gone either way.

"I'm sure there isn't," Morgan said. "Not that I would know anything about that."

"Oh, right. The asexual thing."

"Yes, the *asexual thing*."

"So, how does that work, honestly? You didn't find anything about what I just wrote titillating?"

There was the side-eye I knew and loved so well. "You might have lost me at the part of Ryan getting… how did you so eloquently put it? Oh yes. Getting *railed*."

I frowned. "Huh. Well, to each his own, I guess. I am so happy that you know that about yourself. It truly shows a mark of a great man when he knows who he is through and through. Personally, I am so okay with the sex, you don't even know."

"Oh, I think I do, given that I hear about it all the time."

"We're bros. I'm supposed to tell you stuff like that."

"Bros," Morgan repeated.

"Exactly. Bros tell each other everything. It's the bro-code. Everyone knows that."

"Maybe *bros* should learn to practice some restraint."

"That doesn't sound like a very bro thing to do. As a matter of fact, that might be anti-bro, and I would never do that to you. Now, should I continue, or…?"

He didn't look pleased at such a prospect. "How much more does it go on?"

Pages upon pages. "Oh. Um. Not long."

"Sam." Only he could say my name with so much exasperation and fondness all at the same time. It was really quite remarkable.

"I might have written an ode to his penis in iambic pentameter that goes on for forty-seven stanzas," I admitted. "I feel better now that I've said that out loud."

"Of course you did." Morgan sighed.

"Did you know that *penis* doesn't rhyme with as many things as one might think? That was a lesson I learned far too late."

"Oddly enough, I don't spend time trying to rhyme words with *penis*."

"Wow," I said. "You put a lot of disdain in such a short sentence. I wish I could do that."

"It comes with recent experience," he said dryly.

"I'll get there, I'm sure."

"Of that I have no doubt."

"Did you hear that one part, though? About the secrets? It might have been easy to miss. I can read it again if you'd like."

He leveled me with a flat look. "How could I miss it? You are many, many things, Sam, but subtle is not one of them. I don't know if you even have a passing familiarity with the concept."

"I'm choosing to take that as a compliment," I decided. "Because I have a fragile sense of self and must do such things to protect my ego."

He snorted before scrubbing his hands over his face. "I tell you things when you need to know them. Anything more will distract you from what's truly important. Sam, I need to know that you're taking this seriously. That everything we're working toward is something you can face head-on without disruption."

That might have stung more than I thought it would. "I do my best," I said, trying to not sound as small as I felt.

He sighed and sat up in his chair. His long black beard trailed in his lap and hung over his knees. He wore magenta robes today, with periwinkle clogs sticking out underneath. I had asked him once if he was color blind. He told me he was old enough that he could wear whatever he wanted. And when someone had been alive for nearly three centuries, it's hard to try and find any argument against that.

But what I noticed even more than his eccentric clothing was how tired he looked. He had shadows like bruises under his eyes; and his shoulders were slightly slumped. His beard was shaggier than normal, and his hair was sticking up every which way, like he'd been running his fingers through it.

I glanced around the lab, trying to see any evidence of what he might be up to in my absence, but everything seemed to be in its place. The only thing unkempt was Morgan himself, and that was only noticeable if you knew him as well as I did. I wondered if he—

"I know you do," he said. "Your tenacity in all things has never been found to be lacking. And I'm not trying to scold you. I know that all of... *this* can be overwhelming."

"All of *this*," I said slowly, tasting the words, trying to find meaning in the enigmatic.

"You're a wizard, Sam. Possibly the most powerful one in an age. The fact that we haven't yet even begun to scratch the surface of what you're capable of would be overwhelming even for someone with far more experience. It's not a detriment, but merely an observation."

But I *wasn't* overwhelmed. Disconcerted maybe. Slightly fearful, sure. But I wouldn't let it become my sole focus. I'd been taught there was a ceiling to all magic, a point where it could go no further. Just because we hadn't yet found that ceiling for me didn't mean it didn't exist. I just chose not to dwell on it. "I'm okay," I told him, hoping that if this was what was bothering him, I could attempt to put his mind at ease. "Really. I've got you and Ryan and everyone else. I'm handling things all right." Then a thought struck me. "Wait a minute. Did *Randall* say something? He did, didn't he? Of *course* he did, that old bastard, I *knew* he had it in for me!"

After the debacle of the wedding and the deflowering of my body, Randall hadn't stuck around very long. "Castle Lockes is too loud, and people here smell bad," he'd said, glaring at anyone that tried to come within ten feet of him. "And absolutely nothing is made of ice! How can you people *exist* like this?"

He was gone a day later, either by foot or horseback or some ancient magic that I would probably never understand. Morgan had said he'd gone back to Castle Freeze Your Ass Off ("It's Castle Freesias, Sam. I've told you that a *thousand* times.") in the snowy lands of the North, but I had spent weeks following his supposed departure jumping at shadows, sure that this was just another test and that Randall was watching me from everywhere, waiting for any sign of weakness to turn some part of me into a gigantic dick as revenge.

I still didn't necessarily believe that wasn't the case. For all I knew, Morgan was scheming along with Randall to enact some revenge for something I deserved. The sting of possible betrayal was bitter indeed.

Morgan sighed. "Randall doesn't have it out for you."

"That's what *you* think. You don't see the way he stares at me sometimes."

"I'll bite," he said. "How does he stare at you?"

"Like I'm an idiot."

"Sam. You *are* an idiot."

"Oh. Things suddenly make much more sense right now."

"Funny how that works, isn't it?"

"Eye-opening to say the least. I might have to course correct a few things in my life. Or just keep them as they are to see how much shit I can get into."

Morgan folded his hands in his lap. "Randall's just… concerned."

That didn't sound good. "About?"

"You," Morgan said. He hesitated for a moment, like he was trying to pick and choose his words. That didn't sit right with me. "The last year has been a whirlwind for you."

"But everything turned out all right," I said. "Right? We rescued Justin, Kevin followed us home and can only talk when I'm near, and has somehow formed a weird psychosexual bond with Gary, and now, for reasons we don't quite understand, they think they're my pseudoparents. I found my cornerstone, and he loves me just as much as I love him. Justin is on his way to tolerating my existence, even though we're already total BFFs. We may have a viable lead to track down Gary's horn for the first time in years. What's there to be concerned about?"

"Whirlwind," he said again. "Things have changed greatly for you."

Which, okay. Fair point. "But it's all been for the better…?"

"Is that a question?"

"Yes. Wait. No. Things *are* better." And they were. I couldn't remember a time that I'd been happier. I'd found what I was looking for, what I'd been waiting for. This wasn't an end. This was only the beginning. "Where is this coming from?"

"We just want you to succeed," Morgan said. "I'm not going to be around forever, Sam. Neither will Randall. One day we'll both cross the veil into whatever waits beyond it. I need to know you'll be okay when that happens."

And maybe I started panicking a little at the thought. "Are you *dying*?" I said, sounding rather shrill. "Is that what all this is? A lead-up to where you tell me you're wasting away and will vomit profusely and then fall over and convulse obscenely in your death throes? You know I don't like it when people die, and I *really* don't like it when people vomit. Why would you do that to me—oh my gods, are you *insane*?"

"And of course that's what you took away from that," Morgan said, shaking his head. "Dear gods, Sam, take a breath before you pass out. You're turning blue."

I did as he said because breathing was good. "You can't die!" I demanded. "I won't allow it. If you even *think* of doing it, I will hunt you down and kill you myself. Are we clear?"

He smiled at me then, as rare as it was beautiful. "Crystal. And I'm not dying, Sam. Neither is Randall. We'll be around a long time yet."

"Either that or Randall will outlive us all just to spite me," I muttered.

"I wouldn't put it past him."

"You're mocking me, aren't you."

"Why, where would you ever get an idea like that?"

I eyed him up and down, trying to find any evidence of impending death. Aside from the tiredness, there wasn't any. "You sure there's nothing wrong with you?"

He didn't hesitate. "I'm sure."

"And you would tell me if there was."

"When the time came—and if you needed to know—yes."

"Morgan."

He wouldn't budge an inch. "Sam."

I groaned. "Gods, you're infuriating sometimes."

"You're infuriating all the time."

"When I tell people you're sassy," I told him, "no one believes me. They just look at me like I'm the weird one."

"So, how they always look at you, then."

I scowled at him.

He looked rather pleased with himself.

"I guess we're stuck with each other," I said, trying to make it sound like it was the absolute worst thing in the world but not fooling anyone.

There was that smile again. "I guess we are."

I hesitated, trying to find the right words to put his mind at ease. Words were never a problem for me. I could speak about anything and everything, though sometimes I tended to use them as a distraction or a shield. The more I talked, the less anyone would be able to see what I was really feeling. It worked, mostly.

But this was Morgan. He didn't deserve that from me. Not now. "You know I'll make you proud, right? Like, I know I can do stupid things sometimes. And maybe I don't always think things through. But I'm going to be a good wizard. For you."

He didn't say anything for a long time, just sat there watching me. I tried not to squirm while I waited. Then, "You already make me proud, Sam of Wilds. Every day."

"Should we hug now?"

"I'd prefer if we didn't."

"Are you sure? Because I feel like we should hug."

"Sometimes," he said, "we shouldn't act on feelings, no matter how strong they may be. Now, since I'm sure I will not escape it, I suppose I should hear your epic ode to penises."

"It's long," I warned him.

"So you've said."

"And hard."

"I am regretting so much already."

MORGAN LEFT ME ALONE WITH SPECIFIC instructions to keep going as I was, no distractions. "Your Grimoire isn't going to finish itself, Sam." Which, of course, gave me the idea of making a spell in which my Grimoire *would* complete itself, which, you know. *Genius.* But I obviously spent too much time around Morgan because he must have seen my entire train of thought coming a mile away and threatened me with bodily harm if I even *considered* cheating in such a way. Oh, and no more dick poems, because his heart could only take so much before it stopped itself just to get away from me.

He was such a drama queen.

He'd said he'd thought it was almost time to begin considering a binding for my Grimoire, either the skin of a fallen enemy defeated in battle or a material hard-won in the face of adversity. It would probably be years, he warned me, before I found such a thing, but the fact that he thought I was ready was monumental. I hadn't expected such a thing to fall from his lips for another five years at least, or even as much as a decade. It meant that my plan to be the youngest wizard to take the Trials would be within my reach. I had wanted to attempt them (*complete* them, I reminded myself) by the time I was thirty. If things kept going the way they were, maybe I could get to them sooner. Of course, that would be only if Randall would let me, seeing as how he administered the Trials. He was an obstacle that I was sure would find some way to muck up my plans, just because he could.

I was lost in a fantasy of finding a way to banish Randall to the far reaches of the earth, and I didn't hear the door to the labs open. Probably not the best idea, given my propensity for having trouble find me at the most random of times.

But then there were hands on my waist and lips trailing along my neck, and my magic said *yes* and *home* and *mineminemine.* I tilted my head back, letting it lie on his shoulder as he pressed himself against my back.

"Hey," Ryan Foxheart murmured against my skin.

"Hi," I said, closing my eyes and relaxing.

"You didn't hear me come in, did you?"

I scoffed. "Of course I did."

I felt his smile. "Liar."

"I was busy doing very important things."

"Uh-huh. So, do we need to talk about why your Grimoire is open to a page that says *His shaft is thick and epic / without it I feel apoplectic?*"

"Nope," I said hurriedly, reaching forward and slamming the Grimoire shut. "Nothing for you to see here. Secret wizarding stuff. Very hush-hush. Ancient and all that. Why, even seeing the words could cause your eyes to melt right out of your face."

"Really," he said, gripping my hips. "Is that what you're going with?"

"It wasn't even *about* you," I said. "Not everything is about you, you know. Gods, how self-centered can you get? I'm a *wizard*, Ryan. I will have *secrets.* You're tearing us apart."

"Uh-huh." He moved his hands from my hips, trailing them along to the front of my trousers.

"Ngh," I said, because I had no blood left in my brain.

"Eloquent as always. Maybe I should just jack you off right here. Think that'll help you become vocal again?"

Yes. Yes it would. He had the best ideas. I always thought so.

"Except," he said, sounding regretful. He gripped my dick through my trousers with his big hand, holding it tight. "*Except*, didn't Morgan say that if he ever caught us having sex in the labs again, he'd curse us both and make it so the thought of touching each other was the most disgusting thing that could ever happen?"

"I don't remember that at all," I said, arching into him. I brought my hand up to the back of his head, trying to hold it in place. "You must have dreamed it."

"I don't know if I did," he said, teeth scraping against my neck. "In fact, I'm pretty sure we were standing right about here when it happened. And you squeaked a little bit, just like—"

His grip tightened, and the noise that came from my mouth was something I would never be proud of.

"—that," he finished, sounding unbearably smug. "*Now*, I remember it."

He laughed as I turned around and shoved him away, but he grabbed on to my hand and wouldn't let me go.

"You're an ass," I said.

He shrugged. "Probably. But then, you are too. It's why we go so well together."

"I've obviously made a very big mistake. You should go and see if Justin will take you back and I will find someone who isn't a cock tease and who is also vascular and has nicer nipples."

He rolled his eyes as he tugged me forward. "Because that's going to happen. You're stuck with me and my average nipples. I mean, who else is going to be my own personal Foxy Lady?"

He kissed me, and I bit his lip just this side of too hard. He didn't seem to mind, if his tongue had anything to say about it. I let him mack on my face (because I *was* a nice person) for a little bit, before he pulled away, eyes crinkling in the corners. Somehow, my hands had found their way to his chest and were curled into the leather jerkin he wore. He smelled like sun and sweat and grass. He had a smudge of dirt on his cheek and a thin, clotted cut on his bicep that I'd have to look at to make sure it didn't need stitching.

"Training went well, then?" I asked.

He nodded. "For the most part."

"Still getting shit?"

"Daily." Which, really, I should have felt bad about, what with the Castle Guard firmly planted in my corner and their rah-rah Go Sam mentality. They hadn't been too happy with him for waiting until the last (and worst) possible second to finally own up to his feelings for me. Don't get me wrong, knights were strong and hardworking and some of the fiercest people I had ever known. But they could also be the bitchiest, especially when they or someone they cared about had been wronged. How I'd come to foster that level of devotion, I had no idea, but I wasn't going to question it.

Honestly, though, I felt bad. I really did. I grinned at him. "Shouldn't have fucked up, then, huh?"

"Or maybe," he said, arching an eyebrow, "you could go and tell them they no longer need to defend your honor, given that I realized the error of my ways over a year ago."

"Nah," I said, poking him in the chest. "You chose not to jerk me off. I choose to let them jerk you around."

"I don't know that the punishment fits the crime," he said.

"You're welcome. Not that I mind, but what're you doing here? I thought we were supposed to meet for dinner."

"Yeah," he said. "We were. About an hour ago."

I winced. "Shit. My bad, dude. I got caught up in... uh. Working. On stuff."

"What kind of stuff?"

"Magic stuff. You wouldn't understand."

"That's odd, because I already got stopped by Morgan on my way down here," he said, looking smug again. "He said something entirely different. And he wouldn't stop looking at my crotch with a rather fearful expression on his face."

"Godsdammit," I muttered.

"You couldn't have gotten to fifty stanzas?"

I laughed and punched him lightly on the shoulder. "Bastard."

He leaned forward, lips trailing along my cheek until he reached my ear. "Bring it with you," he whispered. "You can read it to me later."

Hell fucking yeah I was going to do that. I was going to read it the fuck all over him.

WE WERE UP THE STAIRS, LAUGHING quietly to ourselves, shoulders bumping, hands clasped between us. It was easy, this thing between us, easier than it had any right to be given all the shit we'd gone through to get to this point. It'd hurt when I thought I could never have it. When we'd danced the night he was promoted to Knight Commander and became engaged to the Prince, I'd told myself that that was all I was going to have. That was all I was going to *let* myself have. It'd been too much to pine away in silent misery wanting something that I could never call my own. I wallowed, sure, but I knew the difference between the fantasy in my head and the reality in front of me.

But it's a funny thing, life is. No matter what you have planned, there's always going to be that one thing that comes along and says, *ha ha, fuck you, this is what's going to happen now.*

I could admit to being worried that, after all was said and done, if it'd be the same between us. That without being chased by Darks or cults or rabid fangirls, if we could just be Ryan and Sam without any of the bullshit.

Turns out we could.

Quite well in fact.

Sure, I grated on his nerves every now and then, and he *really* needed to learn not to be a douchebag all the time, but it was working for us. Mom and Dad had been hinting that they'd like to see something come of it before long, but I'd made sure to shut that shit down right away before Ryan could hear anything and before the idea could take root in my head. I had too much on my plate already as it was. Besides, we had time for all of that later.

Aside from an overzealous manticore that thought I would look better if my skin had been burnt to a crisp, everything had been quiet.

The Darks stayed away after their ill-advised attack on the castle.

Verania was safe.

People were happy.

Eventually, I just stopped waiting for the other shoe to drop. And even if it *had*, I was surrounded by people who would do everything for me, much like I'd do anything for them.

So there we were, jostling each other back and forth, only paying attention to each other, the way it should have been. We were young and in love and stupid, but we were *allowed* to be. After everything we'd been through, this was our happy ending.

I didn't see the woman in front of us. Didn't see her until I crashed into her.

I tried to apologize, but she slapped her hand over my mouth and dragged me into the shadows of the flickering torch on the wall. She was old, the lines and crags on her face pronounced, like a map to all her years. Her eyes shone darkly, her raven hair falling on her shoulders. Her wrinkled hand was warm against my face, her grip strong and sure for such an old thing. She had large metal bangles on her wrists that clanged together as she pressed me up against the wall.

"What the hell are you doing?" Ryan demanded, taking a step toward us.

The woman paid him no mind, like he wasn't even there. And for all intents and purposes, maybe he wasn't for her, because she only had eyes for *me*.

For the briefest of moments, I thought she was a Dark and that they were trying to take me yet again. I almost wanted to laugh at her audacity if that was the case, given how thoroughly we'd beaten the Darks last time we faced them and how there was a pissed-off Knight Commander standing right behind her in *Castle Lockes*, of all places. But there was something familiar about her, something in the way she looked at me that told me I wasn't quite right. Out of the corner of my eye, I saw flashes of green and gold as I pulled my magic toward me, ready to knock her on her ass, when her other hand came up in front of my face, her thumb and middle finger rubbing together briefly before she snapped.

"Insolent," she hissed. "Sneaking with your sneaks. *Dilo*. And here of all places. Like your *dook* could touch me, *chava*."

My eyes widened over her hand.

Because I literally had no idea what she was talking about. Her voice was low and smoky, her accent thick and melodious, the words falling from her lips like musical notes to a song I swore I'd heard before. It was like she had *felt* my magic, which could only mean she had some kind of magic herself. Normal people could feel it if there was an extreme concentration of it, like the static in the air before a storm. But this had been subtle, low, just beginning to pull itself together. I was impressed. I was going to kick her ass, sure, if she meant to do me and mine any harm, but still. Impressed.

Ryan drew his sword. "Let him go. I won't tell you again."

Her eye softened slightly, like the threat was something sweet to her. "You are not what I expected. I don't know why I thought you would be. There may be hope for us all yet. But I am sorry for this. I hope you remember that. In the end." She leaned forward and pressed a kiss against my cheek. It felt almost like it was *scalding*.

And then she was just *gone*, like she hadn't been there at all.

One moment she was pressed up against me, and then she *wasn't*.

I stumbled forward, unable to catch myself before falling to my knees.

Except the ground wasn't made of stone, like all the floors in the castle were.

No, my knees hit earth and leaves, wet and clumped together. The air was humid and thick, every breath I drew in harder than the one before it. From all around me came the sounds of wind blowing through trees, but that was *impossible*, because I *wasn't in the woods*, I *wasn't in the*—

I opened my eyes.

It was dark.

And I was in the woods.

"Well, fuck," I muttered, pushing myself to my feet. I wiped my hands off on my trousers as I looked around, trying to get my bearings. The sky above was obscured by the canopy of the trees. I couldn't see any landmark I was familiar with.

It seemed as if an old lady had transported me into the middle of nowhere.

"Oh my gods," I growled to no one in particular. "I am so going to punch her in the godsdamned *tit* the next time I see her."

The only response I got was the calling of birds in the trees, the singing of crickets in the tall grass that swayed back and forth.

There was a large hill in front of me, rising up and out of the forest floor, trees having grown around it. I thought it'd be best to climb it to get above the canopy and hopefully see the lights of the City, or at least some town or village where I could go to find out exactly where she'd sent me. Maybe I was closer than I thought I was. I hoped that was the case. The Dark Woods were an expansive thing right in the heart of Verania. I don't know that any human had actually ever reached the true middle, though many had claimed to. And with those claims came stories of Dark creatures that caused insanity if one but laid eyes upon them. Bullshit, probably, but compelling bullshit nonetheless. Maybe I could ask Dimitri the next time he tried to make me marry him.

The hill, though. I would get to the hill and find a way to get the hell out of here.

If I hurried, it had absolutely nothing to do with being in some unknown part of the Dark Woods in the middle of the night. I just wanted to go home.

The closer I got to the hill, the more the wind groaned through the trees.

The more gooseflesh prickled along my skin.

The more I had the uneasy feeling of being watched by *something*.

The air felt lightning-struck, like electricity crackling unseen.

Like magic was building.

From the ground rose pinpricks of light, green and gold and *white*, and it felt like *mine*, it felt like it belonged to *me*. The lights flitted around me, slow and heavy like cumbersome fireflies late in summer. I raised my hand to them, and they brushed along my fingers, warm and weighted.

But it was *more* than that. This was magic, purer than I'd ever felt before, and it wasn't coming from just me. If it was my magic, it was reacting to something already there. If it *wasn't* mine, I was reacting to *it*.

I looked back behind me to see the lights trailing after me. Each footstep I'd left in the soft earth was illuminated and flickering, the little lights landing upon them one by one.

I felt... safe, oddly enough.

Like nothing here could hurt me.

Like I had no reason to worry. These lights, whatever they were, wouldn't allow any harm to come to me. I didn't know how I knew that. I just did.

And so of course, that's when the little lights began to tremble and dim.

The wind picked up until it sounded like it was *growling* through the trees, like the Dark Woods were a thing that was *alive*.

Except... that didn't sound like the wind.

I turned back around.

For a long second, nothing happened.

Then the large hill in front of me moved up.

Then down.

Up and down. Up and down. Slowly and with great deliberation, like the very ground beneath my feet was taking in a lumbering breath and—

A chill crawled down my spine like ice.

"What is that?" I whispered as I took a step back.

Because the *earth* wasn't breathing. No. That wasn't possible.

But the gigantic thing in front of me was.

And now that I was closer, I could see it wasn't a hill at all. What rose from the ground wasn't made up entirely of dirt and grass and brush. There was growth upon it, as if it'd lain where it had for centuries and the forest had continued on around it. But through the vegetation there was something else, something mottled white.

Something *scaled*.

The hill moved.

Trees crashed down off it.

The earth groaned beneath it as roots snapped and broke apart.

I couldn't move. I couldn't *think*. All I could do was take in what was rising in front of me, larger than anything I'd ever seen before. There were brief flashes, impressions that broke through the haze that had fallen over my eyes and mind—*claws* and *teeth* and *wing, oh my gods that was a* wing—until a great eye turned toward me.

It blinked, slow and unfocused. The eye was bigger than I was, the skin around it cracked deeply. The iris itself was heterochromous, shoots of red and green and blue. Even as I watched, the colors seemed to swirl together, moving around the iris like waves crashing.

The eye itself moved left to right, and the little lights around me flew forward, running along the hardened skin.

The creature groaned, a deep rumbling thing that I felt vibrate from the ground up through my legs and hips until it buried itself in my chest, wrapping around my heart and *squeezing*.

The eye focused now, sharper, the gaze knowing.

And it was centered on me.

I took another step back.

I opened my mouth once, twice, but no sound came out.

Because I was at a loss. I had all the pieces to put together what I was seeing in front of me, but they were all jumbled in my head. I couldn't find or sense the pattern in them.

Finally, I did the only thing a person *could* do if they were in my position and faced with a gigantic hill monster after having been bad-touched by an old lady into the middle of the woods.

I waved and said, "Heeeyyy there."

The eye blinked.

"I'm just gonna back away slowly," I told it. "We can pretend this never happened. You… you just go back to sleep. Or whatever you were doing. I didn't mean to wake you up, and I promise it'll never happen again. Don't mind me at all."

It started to growl.

"Okay, so you *do* mind me. That's just swell. I'm going to get out of your hair. Not that you have any hair. No, you just have scales and teeth the size of Tiggy, and oh my gods, why are you *moving* toward me, you fucking psycho! I'm going to punch *both* her tits, I swear to—"

The eye tilted away.

Only to have a great gaping maw pointed at me instead.

And even though I was whiting out in terror, I had a vague understanding of the *shape* of the *head* in front of me, the way the reptilian lips curled around teeth, the twin slits at the end of the *snout* that were its nostrils. A hard ridge rose on the top of its head, fanning out in a half-spherical protrusion, like a bony crown. Sharp, pointed juts of bone stuck out from the top of the crown, gleaming brightly in the starlight.

I knew what this was.

It was a dragon.

Bigger than any other I'd seen before.

In the Dark Woods, which meant it was—

It opened its jaws and—

"Sam!"

I jerked my head left. Ryan was there. I was in the castle, staring up at the ceiling. I was in the—

I looked right. The dragon took a step toward me that caused the earth to quake under my feet. Its foot was gigantic, easily the size of a carriage, with wicked sharp claws digging into the ground.

"Sam, wake up!"

"I am," I said in the castle.

"I am," I said in the woods.

I said, "I am, I am, *I am*—"

And then all the sounds in all the world fell away as the dragon spoke. His voice was a deep rumble, as if the words were heaving from the very depths of him. I felt every word vibrating down into my bones.

The great dragon said, "I have awoken, O human child. In this forest deep, in the dark of the wild. And I have seen what is in your heart. Take heed of my warning: *you are not ready.*"

And then everything was *melting*, the dragon, the forest, the colors bleeding together as I took in a gasping breath. The ground split apart beneath my feet and I was falling, I was *falling*, I was—

A sharp crack across my face. My head rocked to the side.

"Mother*fucker*," I groaned.

"Oh, *now* you wake up?" Ryan growled above me. "You *asshole.*

Don't you ever scare me like that again!"

I opened my eyes as I clutched my cheek. I was on my back on the floor in Castle Lockes, in the same hallway we'd been in before... *whatever* had just happened. I glared up at Ryan, who was at my side, leaning over me, an annoyed look on his face.

"You hit me!"

"No shit," he said. "I couldn't think of anything else to do!"

"So you *hit* me? Who *does* that?"

"Your eyes were rolling back in your head, and you were *shaking*."

I pushed myself up as he fell back on his knees. There were a couple of guards standing a little farther down the hall, watching us warily, but I ignored them. "So the first thing you think of when you see me having a seizure is to *hit* me?"

"I said your name first," he said with a frown. "Like... three times."

"Oh, *that* makes it better. Sam, Sam, Sam, oh it's not working. I should probably domestically violence my boyfriend by punching him in the *mouth*. For shame. We need couples therapy if we're ever going to survive this."

He rolled his eyes. "Glad to know you're just as you always are."

"Amazing?"

"Maybe not quite the word I was going to use."

"Yes, well, abusers probably *don't*."

"I didn't *abuse*—you know what, no. You are *not* going to distract me. What the hell was that about?"

And I could see it then, the pinched look on his face, the way the corners of his mouth were drawn down. He looked scared and worried, and even if he beat me, I swore I could change him and make him love me. "I'm fine," I said. "Your forehead is doing that wrinkle thing when I've done something dumb and you don't know whether to hug me or yell at me."

"It is not," he muttered, forehead wrinkling further. "I wasn't even worried. And fair warning, I am going to probably hug *and* yell at you."

I snorted. "I see no problem with any of that. How long was I down for?"

"Five minutes? Maybe a little more. What happened?"

"And I was always here? I didn't... disappear or anything?"

That certainly didn't make the expression on his face go away. If anything, his eyes narrowed further. "Disappeared *where*?"

"Fuck if I know," I said, scrubbing my hand over my face. "I was in the middle of the Dark Woods, I think. Some place I didn't recognize. After she—wait. Where is she?"

"I don't know," Ryan said. "One minute she had you up against a wall, and the next it was like she wasn't *there*. You fell and you wouldn't wake up. You were shaking and I couldn't—"

I reached up and cupped his face. "I'm okay," I said.

"I know," he said, but he leaned into my hands. "It's just that—fuck. Don't do that again, okay?"

"Sure," I said. "I won't let old women press me against walls and make me have weird visions. Got it."

"Asshole," he said, sounding disgustingly fond.

Gods, I loved the fuck out of him.

And I was about to tell him as much when another thought hit me, one far more important. "The King," I said. "Oh fuck, we have to get to the King."

Ryan's eyes hardened because he immediately went to the same thought I had: *assassin*. A change overcame him, skin thrumming, hands tightening. I wasn't dealing with a concerned boyfriend anymore. This was the Knight Commander of the Castle Guard, whose one job was to protect the Crown and all its extensions.

And he was fucking *pissed*.

Knight Commander Ryan Foxheart looked up at the guards down the hall and barked, "Sound the alarm. *Now.*"

CHAPTER 3
The King is Such a KILF

BELLS WERE CLANGING THROUGHOUT THE CASTLE as Ryan and I raced toward the King's offices above the throne room. A section of the knights were already in motion to take any member of the King's Court to the lower levels where the dungeons were fortified against any outside attack. My parents and Tiggy and Gary would have been corralled either way, depending upon where they were in the castle. I tried not to think of them too much, instead focusing my attention on the job in front of me: protecting the Grand Prince and Good King Anthony of Verania.

It was one of the first lessons Morgan had taught me when he had taken us away from the slums: the walls could crumble around us, the floor might shake beneath our feet, the stars could rain down atop our heads in blazing bursts of rock and fire, but nothing would matter more than protecting the King. "He's the reason Verania stands tall and proud," Morgan had said as I'd stared at him with wide eyes. "Without him, or without someone to take his place like the Prince, Verania could fall into darkness. The people are what make Verania great. But it's the King that holds us all together."

Granted, the King wasn't one to just stand aside and let others protect him without lifting a finger, much to Morgan's consternation. It certainly didn't help matters when the King would rather be in the thick of things than standing on the sidelines. He knew of his own importance, but he wouldn't let others fight his battles for him. He'd be side by side with his people if at all possible.

And so it was that I had to trust Ryan's knights to take care of my family if they weren't going to be with us. I had a job to do, one job, and that was to make sure the King and Justin were safe. Morgan would be doing the same.

We hit the second floor of the castle and turned left, running down a long hallway with high ceilings. Flags decorated the walls on either side of us, symbolizing the major cities of Verania. Maids and butlers were scurrying around us, trying to make their way to the throne room where they'd be surrounded by the Castle Guards.

A group of Ryan's knights stood in front of the doors leading to the King's offices, Pete, who had known me even before I'd come to the castle, amongst them. He looked wary as we approached, sensing that something wasn't quite right. "Report," Ryan snapped as we got within hearing distance.

"Secured, sir," Pete said. "Nothing in or out except for known personnel. King and Prince in the safe room."

"Morgan?" I asked.

"Already here," Pete said. "Just appeared out of nowhere, like he usually does."

"One day he's going to teach me how to do that," I muttered.

Pete smiled at me. "Don't rightly know if that'd be something we'd want, you being able to sneak up behind us."

"I'm a de*light*," I told him.

"Is now really the time for this?" Ryan growled.

I rolled my eyes. "Sorry, Pete. You know how he gets when he's all worked up over something."

"Oh boy, do I ever."

"I don't get like *anything*—"

"You kind of do," one of the knights said, voice muffled through the armored helmet over his head. "Mostly." He withered under Ryan's glare.

Gods, I loved the knights.

I turned at the sound of hooves on stone and immediately had a weight lifted off my shoulders.

Gary was trotting toward us, followed by Tiggy, who carried a person under either arm as carefully as he could.

Rosemary and Joshua Haversford.

My mother and father.

"Do you *hear* this ruckus?" Gary said, standing in front of me, nostrils flaring. "There I was, partway through my beauty bedtime regimen, which you *know* I don't need because I am beautiful and always have been, when what should I hear? *Alarms*, Sam. *Alarms*. And I would say that my first thought would have been for you or the safety of the King, but that would be a lie. No, my first thought was about me. How this would affect *me*. Sam. *Sam*. I have come to the startling realization that I am a self-centered bitch and even *better*, that I would do nothing to change it."

I rolled my eyes at him. "Whose idea was it to grab my parents and make sure they were safe?"

"Mine, of course," Gary said.

"Ah. Not as self-centered as you might think, then."

Gary frowned at that. "Godsdammit. I care too much. It is my gift. It is my curse."

"I helped," Tiggy said. "I have feelings too. Many, many feelings." He squeezed my parents tighter to him. "I have feelings right now."

"He does," my mother said, patting an olive-skinned hand against his chest. "He told us that he would smash anything that would try and hurt us."

My father looked grumpy. "I don't see why *I* had to be carried. Especially in front of all the knights. This is so embarrassing. I can smash things too. I'm almost as big as Tiggy." Which really wasn't too much of a stretch. My father's people came from the snowy North, and it showed by the sheer bulk my father carried with him.

"I love you, tiny human," Tiggy told my father.

"Gah," Dad said. "I can't even with your face right now. It's unfair. I'm trying to be cross and you're just sitting here looking like you do. I don't even care if the boys saw this now. You can carry me all you want to."

Tiggy looked inordinately pleased at such a prospect.

"Where's Kevin?" I asked.

Gary rolled his eyes. "Said something about defending my honor and blah, blah, blah. He's probably circling above the castle right now, snapping at nothing and calling it a success. I love him with a fire that burns within me. Now, are you going to tell me what's going on, or do I have to choke the life out of you?"

"That escalated quickly," Pete said.

"It usually does with them," Ryan said. "Let's just be thankful Gary isn't glittering yet."

"Do I *need* to glitter?" Gary asked him, narrowing his eyes. "Does Gary need to bring the—"

"Nope," Ryan said. "Absolutely not. Everything is fine. There's nothing—"

And since I felt just awful about this whole thing (and was probably not the most sensible person to have existed), I blurted, "A strange woman broke into the castle and bad-touched me and I had a vision about a white dragon in the middle of the Dark Woods and then Ryan domestically violenced me back to reality and now we think there's an assassin trying to murder all of our faces."

It was rather quiet after this pronouncement.

Then:

"You got to third base with a *woman*?" Gary screeched.

"I didn't domestically violence you. *Stop saying that*," Ryan snapped.

"I smash Knight Delicious Face?" Tiggy said, frowning at Ryan.

"Assassins?" Dad asked. "I hope they don't try and assassinate anyone I know. Why, that would just be rude and uncalled-for. And cool, because I've never seen an assassin before."

"Visions of white dragons?" Mom repeated. "That's not ominous or anything. And why can't you have visions of white *weddings* like I want you to have? You would look so *good* in white."

"What woman?" Pete asked, and since he was the only sane one out of the bunch (mostly), I turned to him.

"I don't know. I've never seen her before." I glanced at Ryan, who shrugged. "She was old. Dark skin, dark hair. Bracelets on her wrist." There was something else. Something that she'd— "She called me *chava*."

"*Chava*?" Mom said, sounding slightly choked.

"And *dook*?" I said. "She said it couldn't touch her? I don't know what that—"

Dad paled as he looked back at Mom. "You don't think…?"

She shook her head. "I don't know. It's—I suppose it's possible. Why here? Why now?"

That didn't bode well for me. "What are you—"

The door to the offices opened behind us. The knights spun on their heels, drawing their swords, closing in around me. While my focus was Justin and the King, theirs included me, which was touching but extraordinarily uncomfortable.

But it was just Morgan, glaring at all of us, though it softened slightly when his gaze fell upon me. "Do I even want to know why you're all just standing around out here? Let them through. Quickly, if you please."

"We were *trying*, you old codger," Pete said. "Except we learned now that Ryan beats Sam or white dragon assassins or something. Who even knows anymore."

"I don't *beat* him, oh my gods, that's how *rumors* start—"

"He punched me in the face," I said morosely. "But he's gonna change for the baby, I swear."

"I taught him that," Gary said quite loudly. "In case you didn't know."

"Would you get in here," Morgan said as he pushed through the knights. He grabbed me by the scruff of the neck and started pulling me toward the offices of the King. It was meant to be rough, his grip harsh, but as soon as his hand touched my neck, I felt calmer. Stronger. The tripping of my heart slowed, and I thought maybe I could finally catch my breath. Morgan was like that for me. He always had been, ever since the beginning. He knew it too, if the way he gently squeezed my neck meant anything. "Knight Commander, make sure your knights are prepared and then join us inside if you please. Gary, Tiggy, bring Joshua and Rosemary. Step to it."

When Morgan spoke, everyone obeyed.

Or at least it sounded as if they did. I wouldn't know, because Morgan wouldn't let me turn around and look behind us. He kept a firm hand on me, pushing me inside the offices.

Inside, there were three more knights that I recognized, shields and swords drawn, standing in front of a large, ornate bookcase. They nodded at me, relief palpable on their faces.

The office was large, the walls and floors made of stone, the ceiling high, a massive candle chandelier hanging from the middle. There were two fireplaces, one at either end of the room, both roaring. The far wall was adorned with an intricately drawn map of Verania, which had been a gift from the elves upon his coronation. It was supposed to show when the country of Verania herself was in danger, imbued with some sort of elven magic that not even Randall understood completely. It'd never moved, not even once, since the King had received it, not that we knew of. Sure, there may have been a blip when the Darks had tried to take the castle last year, but no one had been in the room to see it. I glanced over it now, just to be safe. It looked the same as always. The frozen mountains of the north. The Luri Desert in the west. The jungles of the east. The coastal south. The Port. City of Lockes. Meridian City. All the villages, no matter how small.

Still, it didn't move. Not even now. Which, if there was a threat upon the King, I would have hoped it would have done *something*. But it hadn't even done anything when Justin had been taken by Kevin. For all we knew, the elves were full of shit, which wouldn't surprise me.

There was a desk made from trees in the Dark Woods, heavy and foreboding, sitting in front of the wall of bookcases. Scrolls lay strewn across it, the King's feather pen discarded hastily across the top. Like he'd been in the middle of something and pulled away as soon as the alarms rang, which was probably exactly what happened. It's what *should* have happened.

"He's probably really annoyed," I said, staring at the bookcase. Behind it, there was a room encased with magic that only Morgan or I could break through. In the event that something happened to the both of us, the King would wait for a sign from Randall before attempting to leave. He didn't like hiding away very much, but he knew the reasons behind it. Especially in the face of the unknown.

"Undoubtedly," Morgan said, moving toward the bookcase.

"Do you think he's—" I started to say but was cut off when Morgan pressed the spines of seven books in quick succession, leaving behind green glowing fingerprints that flared, then faded. There was a large click and the sound of gears grinding together. The bookcase shifted forward, the large hinges groaning as it opened.

"What's he doing?" Ryan asked, coming into the office and closing the door behind him. "Why's he letting them out? We don't even know what's happening yet."

"I don't know," I said. My mother and father stood off to the side near one of the fireplaces, whispering furiously at each other. They must have felt me staring at them, because they immediately stopped talking and waved at me frantically. "You ever get the feeling that people know more than they're saying?"

Ryan snorted. "Hate to break it to you, but that's pretty much the life I lead these days."

I glanced at him, only to find him watching my parents with a small smile on his face. It did traitorous things to my heart, to see him watching them as he did. After the whole… debacle that was our fucked-up courtship, my mother and father had invited Ryan out to lunch, telling me in no uncertain terms that I was not allowed to join them. Four hours later, they returned to the castle looking smug, whereas Ryan was pale. None of them would tell me what they spoke about, only that Ryan said my mother was the scariest woman he'd ever met in his entire life, and that it also had turned him on a little bit.

"Damn right it did," my father had said. "Why, I bet even Sam—"

"Nope," I'd said, cutting that off before it went too far. "Absolutely not."

But since then, there'd seemed to be an understanding between the three of them. Sure, Ryan still stuttered and blushed his way through conversations with them, like he was nervous and was still trying to find out the best way to impress them. But they treated him just like they'd treated Tiggy and Gary when I'd brought them back from the Dark Woods: like he already belonged to them. He didn't have anyone else to call his family. His mother was gone, his father only gods know where. He never had any brothers or sisters. And my parents knew this, which is why they loved him the way they did. It gave me *feelings* that I didn't even know what to do with.

Like right now.

I sighed dreamily.

"You've got that expression on your face again," Ryan said. "I don't even have to look at you to know."

"I would have so many of your babies," I whispered fervently. "You don't even know."

Ryan started choking quite loudly, but everyone ignored him, used to his weirdness by now.

There was a door on the other side of the bookcase made from the wood of an ash tree. It was said that it'd been given by the Meliae, a sort-of wood nymph, hundreds of years before when the castle had been constructed. The Meliae had disappeared into the realm with the elves, leaving behind little tendrils of magic. Dimitri and his fairies were descendants of the Meliae, though they refused to ever talk about it. Fairies were secretive assholes, and I didn't expect that to change anytime soon.

There was an ancient sigil carved into the door, even older than the tongue of magic in which we spoke. Morgan said it'd come from a time when people lived only in the trees, reading bones and stones like they were able to tell the future. It was two lines forming a peak like a mountain, with an off-centered *S* shape in the middle, bisected by three slashes. I did my best not to touch it, as it always made my skin feel like it was vibrating unpleasantly.

Morgan traced the sigil, the same green glow following his fingertip. Once he'd completed the sigil, another lock clicked and the door swung open.

Inside was Good King Anthony of Verania and his son, the Grand Prince.

Both of whom did not look very impressed.

The King was a barrel-chested man with long flowing white hair that fell on his broad shoulders and a kickass mustache that I had to hear Gary wax poetically about at least once or twice a week. Granted, it wasn't that much of a hardship, and if I'd met the King in another life, I'd probably have no problem in calling him Daddy.

Not that I told anyone that.

Ever.

Except for Gary and Tiggy, because let's be honest, I told them everything.

Which, of course, meant they told the King. In the middle of him hosting a dinner with all his heads of state. To say the silence that followed was shocking would be an understatement. Morgan's face had been in his hands, Justin had been disgusted, the King smiled widely, all while Ryan looked like he was conflicted about his duty to protect the King versus wanting to demand they fight for my honor right then and there. The sex had been really damn good that night. With Ryan. Not with the King. I couldn't even look at the King without blushing for the six weeks that followed, especially when he would wink at me every time he saw me.

He wasn't winking now, though.

"I don't know why I have to get shoved in that blasted room like that," he said, looking adorably irate. "I have a sword, Morgan. A *sword*. It's very large, I'll have you know. Many people think so."

"I bet he does," Gary whispered near my ear. "Probably takes two hands just to hold it up and everything."

"It does seem like it'd be pretty big," I mused.

"Mine's bigger," Ryan said with a frown. "I measured."

Gary snickered as I patted Ryan on the shoulder. "Of course it is."

Morgan sighed. "Anthony, we've been over this. As the King of Verania, you have *one* job when there are possible attempts on your life. You *hide*. The fact that you fought Darks in your own throne room was enough to send your court into a tizzy. The heads of state *demanded* you never again do such a thing. *I* know you can protect yourself and others, and so do they. But it doesn't matter to the King's Court."

The King waved Morgan's words away. "A bunch of ninnies," he said. "Just because I have a crown doesn't mean I can't pick up a sword. Why, kings of old would lead their armies into battle, sleeping and eating and fighting alongside their soldiers."

"We aren't at war," Morgan said.

"We're at *something*. Why are the alarm *bells* ringing if we're—"

The bells stopped ringing.

"Well," the King said. "This is certainly awkward. Am I to assume this has been a false alarm?" He glanced over at Ryan. "Perhaps a training drill I wasn't made aware of? *Again*?"

"My liege," Ryan started, only to be interrupted when Gary sneezed a sound remarkably close to "Kiss-ass."

I punched Gary in the throat. "Let him do his job," I hissed at him.

"Oh please," Gary said. "You just like it when he acts all Knight Commander-y. Forgive me if I don't want to stand next to your power boner for the next ten minutes."

I said, "I don't get a *power boner*, what the hell," even though it sounded like something I would get rather easily.

Ryan brought a closed fist to his chest and bowed low toward the King. "If the King wishes, I can provide a situation report immediately."

"Oh my gods," I said to Gary. "I get a boner for power."

"Do you think he knows he's not really whispering that?" Mom asked Dad. "Because it seems like he thinks he's whispering."

"I'm pretty sure he doesn't know he does a lot of things he probably shouldn't," Dad said. "We're not to blame for that at all. We're wonderful parents."

"Hi, Sam," the King said, smiling broadly.

I waved. "Hey. Don't mind me. I'm just standing over here with my uncomfortable realizations about certain kinks I have."

"Sam a kinky bitch," Tiggy said.

"Too right," I said. "It's moments like these that I try and—"

"Sam," Ryan said in that tone of voice he got sometimes.

"Uh-oh," I said to Gary. "He's getting growly."

"And his eyebrows are doing that thing," Gary said.

"Well maybe if you would stop *talking*—"

"*Me*? I'm not the one here sporting half a chub because—"

"This is the future of the kingdom," Justin said to the King. "This is seriously what you want to leave me with. I will go down in the annals of history and these people will be my legacy."

"Heh," Gary said. "He wants to go down in annals. Gross."

"Don't get it," Tiggy said.

"That's because my humor is sophisticated," Gary said with a haughty sniff. "It plays to a higher crowd."

"I think you're doing a good job," I whisper-shouted to Ryan, giving him a thumbs-up. "You give the best status reports out of anyone I've ever met."

"You mean I'm *trying* to give a status report," Ryan said. "But *someone* keeps interrupting me."

"Rude," I said to Gary. "Try to give a man a compliment after he gives you a probable black eye, and this is the thanks I get."

"That's what happens in all long-term relationships," Gary said. "Face it, kitten. The magic is gone because you've let yourself go."

"I did what now?" I said, wondering if the courts would believe my defense of justifiable homicide toward a magical creature.

He smiled sticky sweet. "Love you."

Tiggy bent over until we were face to face, his nose nearly touching mine. "You look nice," he decided after a moment.

"*Thank* you, Tiggy."

"Maybe tired in your face."

"You know *nothing*, you tall freak of nature!"

He patted me on the head with a big hand.

"You're very lucky," the King told Justin, reaching out and squeezing his shoulder. "Most people would kill to have this support behind them."

"Can't I just kill my support?" Justin asked. "It seems like it'd be easier. And I'd be happier about it."

"He doesn't mean that," I told the King. "He respects us. Maybe even loves us a little."

Justin glared at me.

"Begrudgingly," I amended.

The glare lessened. Slightly. Probably not at all. "Why do I have a feeling that this little incident involved you somehow?"

"Because you leap to conclusions based upon past experiences which have no basis on our current situation?" I asked, hoping that would be the end of it.

"Uh-huh," Justin said. "Knight Commander, report."

"There was a woman," Ryan said. "She... attacked Sam."

"And there it is," Justin said.

"Attacked," Morgan said. "Attacked *how*?"

"Actually—" Mom said.

"I wasn't *attacked*," I said. "She was just... forceful in her conviction that she should be pressing me up against a wall."

"She had her hand around your throat," Ryan snapped. "And she *spoke* to you. She said that you couldn't touch her. And then she disappeared and you *collapsed*."

"Is that true?" the King asked, taking a step toward me. "Are you all right?"

"Maybe we should—" Dad said.

"Yeah," I said. "Except for all the parts where he made it sound like I sucked. I *had* her. If she hadn't done her little disappearing trick, everything would have been *fine*."

"Yeah, okay," Ryan said. "What about the part where you thought you were in the Dark Woods with a white dragon?"

"I haven't quite figured that out yet," I admitted, though it pained me to do so. "But I *will*. I just need to think about it. So thank you for spilling the beans like that. You jerk."

Ryan shook his head. "You didn't see it, okay? One minute she was there and the next she was gone and you just *collapsed*. I thought she'd—"

His jaw tensed as he swallowed thickly. "You didn't see what I saw."

Godsdammit. Leave it to Knight Delicious Face to get sentimental while I was trying to get fired up. Any argument that I had left as quickly as it'd come.

"I think we might know—" Mom said.

"I'm sorry," I said to Ryan. "I didn't... I just.... Dammit. I'm sorry, okay?"

He nodded but wouldn't look at me.

"What they talkin' 'bout?" Tiggy asked Gary.

"Their feelings," Gary said, sounding teary-eyed. "Their awful and wonderful feelings. Stupid, stupid boys. Hug me, Tiggy, and never let me go."

Tiggy did just that.

"Stupid is right," Justin muttered. "Gods, this is painful. Glad I got out of that while I still could."

"Did she hurt you?" the King asked, checking me up and down.

I pushed his hands away. "I'm *fine*. It was just... look. I don't know what she wanted or who she is, but we'll find her, okay? Anything else we can deal with after we know where she is."

The King didn't look appeased by this.

There was one person who'd been remarkably silent, especially since I should have heard a *be quiet, Sam* by now. I turned to Morgan, ready to be scolded for actively derailing the conversation yet again. Anything I was about to say died in my mouth as Morgan stood with his eyes closed, taking deep, slow breaths. His hands were fists at his sides, and he looked paler than I'd ever seen him before. I frowned as I took a step toward him. "Morgan?"

He opened his eyes, and there was something there, something I couldn't quite make out. It looked painful, whatever it was, like the thoughts in his head were physically hurting him. It was gone before I could nail it down. But his words were hushed when he spoke. "What did she say to you?"

The room fell quiet.

This wasn't my friend speaking. This was Morgan of Shadows, my mentor.

I thought on it, wanting to get as close as possible. "Sneaking with your sneaks. *Dilo*. And here of all places. Like your *dook* could touch me, *chava*. She said that we weren't what she expected, and that it was a good thing. And that she was sorry for what was to come."

He surprised me then, by turning toward my parents. "Is it she?"

My mother's shoulders sagged as my father wrapped an arm around her. "It would seem so."

"We didn't know," Dad said. "She hasn't... contacted us. Not since...."

"Uh, guys?"

They all turned to look at me.

"What are you talking about?"

My mother sighed. "*Dilo* means fool. *Dook* is magic. *Chava* means boy. It's from the old tongue."

"Gypsies," I breathed. "You—you know who it is?"

She opened her mouth, then closed it, like she couldn't find the words. She glanced at my father, who gave her a resigned nod. She looked back at me and said, "Vadoma Tshilaba. *Mamia.*"

A memory then. From the day in the alley so very long ago:

And you, dearie? Surely you haven't always been Rosemary Haversford.

It is a name I adopted when I chose to leave the clan and marry my love. I was born Dika Tshilaba.

Ah. I see. Your mamia *was Vadoma, then.*

Yes, my lord. You've heard of her?

Perhaps.

"*Mamia*," I said faintly.

"Yes," Mom said. "The elder of my clan. The *phuro.* My… mother. Your grandmother, Sam. She's finally come for—"

The door to the offices burst open. Ryan whirled around, pulling his sword, but it was just Pete, who only had eyes for the King. "Word has been sent from the gates," he said, sounding rather breathless. "There are gypsies here, requesting an audience with the King and his wizard. And they asked for Sam specifically."

Well shit.

CHAPTER 4
The Wolf of Bari Lavuta

WHEN ONE'S LONG-LOST GRANDMOTHER POPS OUT of the blue demanding an audience after essentially assaulting one in front of one's boyfriend before sending one on a mind-bending trip to face a dragon believed to be only legend, it's probably understandable if one is *slightly* wary at the prospect.

The problem with that?

One has really stupid friends.

"A real live *gypsy*," Gary said as we made our way down to the throne room. "Can you *imagine* it? Oh my gods, what will she be *wearing*? What will *I* wear? I'm not even ready for this right now. Sam, *Sam*. Look at me. You look at me right now!"

I looked at him.

His eyes were wide as he leaned in close, breathing right onto my face. I almost went cross-eyed. "Do I have your attention?"

"Yes, Gary."

"*Good.* Now, should I pose like this when I meet the queen of the gypsies?" He froze in the middle of the hallway, nostrils flaring, chest puffed out, one leg up off the floor and bent, a ridiculous smile stretched across his face. He looked like a manic unicorn clown on mushrooms. "Or like *this*?" He flipped his head back, shaking his mane, the white hair dyed with red stripes because didn't I know that *crimson* was in this season, was I a *charlatan*, honestly, Sam, you are just a living, breathing *tragedy*. His eyelashes fluttered, and there was a hint of sparkles in the air, shimmering ever so lightly around him.

I stared at him.

"Bah," he said. "I don't even know why I ask you. Gods only know that you wouldn't have even landed yourself a man if it hadn't been for me. You used to dress like a freshly outed lesbian, not that there's anything wrong with being a lesbian. I love lesbians because they *get me*. We are *kindred spirits*. You, however, are useless to me! *Useless!* Tiggy, oh *Tiggy darling*. I need your assistance. You must tell me how I should stand when I meet the queen of the gypsies." And he was off again, that whirlwind of sass and sparkles that I loved so much I couldn't even muster up the strength to strangle.

"What's this all about, you think?" Ryan muttered next to me.

"I don't know," I admitted. "She…. I've never met her."

"But she's your grandmother?"

"Right."

"So why wouldn't you have seen her?"

"Because my mother fell in love with my father."

Ryan frowned. "What does that have to do with anything?"

"It's part of their culture," I said. "Gypsies are betrothed to gypsies. Loving someone outside of that is frowned upon. My mother was given a choice. She could renounce my father and marry her intended or love him and be shunned from her clan."

"And she chose your father," Ryan said, looking up at my parents, who walked in front of us. Dad's arm was around her waist, holding her close as he whispered in her ear. Her shoulders were tense, but she was nodding to whatever Dad was saying to her.

"She loved him," I said with a shrug. "She's told me that she couldn't imagine a world without him in it. That even though the choice meant losing part of herself, she would rather that than lose him."

"I know the feeling," he said, then immediately blushed.

I stopped. He made it another step or two before he turned back around to see me gaping at him. The flush crawled its way up his neck, splotching his cheeks.

"You *do*?" I managed to say.

He reached up and scratched the back of his neck, gaze darting everywhere but me. "I, uh. Okay, so, the thing is—"

"Sam? Ryan? What's the holdup?"

My eyes were wide when I turned to Morgan, who was waiting for us at the end of the hall. He must have seen something on my face because he sighed that sigh usually reserved for me. "Now? Really?"

"I am about to have so many feelings," I told him. "And I will probably kiss my boyfriend so much that it looks like I'm eating his face. Unless you want to stay and watch that, you should leave right now. Unless you *do* want to stay and watch. Then we'll need to have a conversation about boundaries. Really, Morgan. Learn some propriety—"

"Five minutes," he said. "If you're not in the throne room in five minutes, I will send you to Randall *tomorrow* and make Ryan stay here."

"But… but *feelings*."

"Five minutes, Sam of Wilds."

And he was gone around the corner.

Since I didn't want to scar some unsuspecting maid with some good old-fashioned homoerotic face sucking, I grabbed Ryan by the hand and pulled him toward the nearest door I could find. I opened it, shoved him inside, followed him in, and closed the door behind us.

It was a broom closet.

A small dark broom closet that smelled like feet and floor cleaner.

It was perfect.

"So," I said. "Hi."

"Hi, Sam," he said, sounding amused.

"Okay, enough foreplay. Explain."

"Enough *foreplay*? We haven't even *done* any—"

"Ryan Foxheart, I swear to the gods if you don't explain right now, I'll do… something… terrible, okay I don't even know what the hell is wrong with me. Oh my gods, *explain*."

I felt more than saw his hands come to mine, squeezing my fingers. I could barely make out his features in the dark, and he licked his lips nervously. "It's just…."

I waited.

"It's *just*…."

I was done waiting. "It's just hard for you to form even the simplest of words at a crucial moment?"

He scowled at me. "Give me a minute."

"We only have *four* now. Morgan will *banish* me to Castle Freeze Your Ass Off. With *Randall*. Without *you*. What would I do without you?"

He started to smile. "Ah, that's so—"

"I mean, there are a billion things I could do without you, but still."

"—like you," he said. He shook his head. "Look, Sam. It's just… you know how important being a knight is to me."

I nodded, because I did. For the longest time, it'd been the *most* important thing to him, something he'd been working toward for years.

"And the oath I made," he said. "It was… everything. For a long time." As it should have been. Because an oath to a knight is the promise of their life for another's.

"I know," I said. "And I know why you did it. I know who you did it for." His mother, even though she had passed before she could ever see what he would become. "But I don't—"

"It *was* the most important thing, Sam," Ryan said, reaching up to cup my face. "Until you."

And what the hell does one say in the face of that?

Nothing, apparently.

Because I was gaping at him again.

Also with a boner in my heart.

"I chose you, Sam," he said quietly. "And I would do it again and again, over anything else. My duty and fealty is to the King of Verania. But my heart belongs to you."

"Bastard," I whispered.

He smiled softly, thumbs brushing my cheeks. "So I know why your mother did what she did. She made her choice, like I've made mine. Because I can't imagine a world without you in it. And I hope I never have to. I would follow you anywhere."

"I am going to kiss you so hard in a few seconds," I warned him. "There's going to be tongue and spit and everything."

"Tongue and spit and everything," he repeated.

"And you're going to enjoy it."

He shrugged. "Probably."

And so I surged forward and kissed him, knocking him against the wall behind him. It was awkward and messy what with the tongue and spit and the fact that he was laughing, laughing, *laughing* at me, his smile pressed against mine, his grip firm on my face.

Eventually, I just rested my forehead on his, breathing him in, feeling the heat and weight of him against me, familiar and sweet.

"I'm worried," he finally said.

"About?" I asked as I kissed his nose and cheek. The corner of his mouth.

"What if…?"

"What if what?"

He sighed, breath hot on my face. "What if she tries to take you away? To her clan?"

I snorted. "Not gonna happen."

"We don't know why she's here."

"No, we don't. But I'm not leaving Castle Lockes. I'm not leaving my parents. Or the King. Or Gary and Tiggy. And I'm not leaving you. Ryan, there are things more important in this world than where I come from. And that's where I'm going. With them and with you. You're my cornerstone. If she says I have to go with her, if she tries to make me, she's going to have a fight on her hands, because I won't let anything tear us apart. I promise."

"Yeah?" he said, arching against me, sounding rather breathless.

"Yeah," I said.

"I'm going to kiss you now," he said. "There's going to be tongue and spit and everything."

I grinned at him. "Fuck yeah. I'm totally down with that. This was hella romantic. Even if it smells like feet in here."

He rolled his eyes but kissed the hell out of me anyway. So that was okay.

TWELVE MINUTES LATER, WE STUMBLED THROUGH the Great Doors into the throne room, where everyone was waiting for us. I brushed my hands over my hair, trying to smooth it back down, knowing I couldn't do a damn thing about how swollen my lips were or the stubble burn on my chin. If I looked anywhere near as debauched as Ryan did, then I was going to get so much shit.

"I said five minutes," Morgan reminded me as we approached the throne where the King was seated. The throne itself was a massive thing, forged from black stone, inlaid with veins of silver and gold and quartz. It was ostentatious, like the heavy crown the King wore upon his head, and he preferred not to have anything to do with them at all. But for appearance's sake, it was required every so often.

Like now.

"Did you?" I said to Morgan. "I could have sworn you said to let our young love fly free."

"Sam got kissy face," Tiggy whispered to Gary.

"Of course he does, kitten," Gary said. "That's what happens when you're a slut."

"You get that too."

"Well, yes," Gary said patiently. "Because I'm a slut."

"Oh," Tiggy said. "Tiggy no slut. I love my flower."

"Of course you do. And one day, you'll meet a nice boy or girl giant and there will probably be a lot of grunting and monosyllabic wordplay and then your flower will be shredded."

"Or I can have more brooms," Tiggy said.

"Or that," Gary agreed. "Because all that matters is that you're happy and that Sam's a slut."

Mom and Dad stood off next to Justin's smaller throne. Mom looked rather stricken, Dad's arm still firmly around her, holding her close. I squeezed Ryan's hand before letting it go and walking over to them. Mom's dark eyes were trained on me, watching every step I took. She made the smallest of sounds as I hugged her, like she was surprised. Her arms came up and around my back, clutching tightly. She was strong, this woman I adored, even if she only came up to my chin. She was the fiercest of people, who loved with her whole heart. She was kind and good and never had a cross word for anyone. I couldn't stand the look on her face.

"We're going to be okay," I murmured as my dad rubbed a hand up and down her back. "I promise."

She sighed and nodded against my chest. I held on for a moment longer before pulling away. She had steel in her eyes when she looked back up at me. "She's good," she said. "She's a good *phuro*. A firm hand when she needs to be, the softest of touches when she doesn't. But that was long ago. I do not know who she is now or why she's come here. She is my *mamia*, but you are my son. I don't know what she wants, but if it's not something you're willing to give, then don't. Do you understand?"

I nodded, unsure of what else to say.

She gave a small smile. "I know you do."

I kissed her forehead and took my place next to Morgan on the right side of the King, Ryan on my other side, with Gary and Tiggy a step or two down the raised dais where the throne sat.

"Sam," Gary hissed up at me. "*Sam.*"

"What?"

"Hi."

"Hi, Gary."

"I've decided on my pose when I meet the queen of the gypsies."

"That's nice, Gary."

"Yeah. Just thought you should know."

"Kind of serious here, Gary."

"Is it? Is that why you all look so dour?"

"Probably, Gary. Family business and all that."

"Ah. That's a good reason."

"Exactly."

"Why are you still talking to me, Sam? This is *serious*. I can't believe that you'd—"

And that's when the window near the dais burst open and a dragon stuck his head inside.

"My love!" Kevin cried. "You are safe because I have *saved* you!"

"It's like it never ends," Justin muttered, sinking down in his seat.

"This is how you know you're having fun," the King said, patting his hand.

"Saved me from what?" Gary asked, prancing over to Kevin, tail swishing back and forth.

"And he calls *me* a slut," I said to Ryan. "Look at him. Tail all up in the air like he wants everyone to see his business."

"There are things I can't unsee when you say them aloud," Ryan said with a grimace. "Why would you do that to me?"

"The most *ferocious* of creatures," Kevin said, preening under the attention. "They snapped and they *snarled*. They had *wings* and teeth the size of my face! They came here with the sole intention of stealing my loves away from me, but I rose against them in battle with a mighty roar. They squeaked when they saw just how *big* my... wingspan was." He scrunched up his face and raised his voice, in approximation of exactly what, I had no idea. "Oh no! It is the fearsome Beast from the East! We didn't know *he* was here! Retreat, *retreat*!" His voice lowered to his usual grumble. "But did I allow them to flee? Of *course* not. I said, 'You came here to steal the most magnificent of creatures who climbs upon my junk and take said creature away from me? How *dare* you.' And then I said, 'You have made a mistake this day, one that will echo into *eternity*.'"

"Oh my gods," Gary said. "I'm *swooning*. Sam. Sam, are you *hearing* this?"

"I don't know if that's exactly what happened," I said slowly.

Gary snapped his head toward me and glared. "Shut up. Just because *my* man went out and took on an entire army of evil while *yours* just stood there posing with his sword—"

"Hey! I don't *pose*—"

"—doesn't give you the right to try and emasculate our savior."

"Yeah," Kevin said. "Don't immaculate me. And he's exactly right. There was an entire *army* of evil that I vanquished so no one could take Gary away from me. They also might have wanted Sam and Justin and Ryan too, but I told them there was too much sexual tension there that I was waiting to see if it would combust into a ménage of sexual *thrusting*, just this wild and crazy orgiastic—sorry, what was that?"

"No one said anything," I said. "They never do when you get gross."

"Oh, I could have sworn I heard either you or Ryan or Justin agree with me on the erotic tension thrumming between the three of you." He stared at us.

We stared back.

"Nothing? Well. I guess my ears deceived—Justin, your mouth is moving. Are you asking if I want to watch you have sexual relations with your former lover and his new lover? No? That's not what you were saying if that look means anything. Okay. Where was I? Ah yes!" His eyes narrowed and he bared his fangs. "There I was, protecting all of Castle Lockes from sexual deviants who wanted nothing more than to take what was mine away from me. But I destroyed them all with my love for Dragoncorn. They fled from whence they came, back into the dark abyss, and once again, the world was saved thanks to *Kevin*. No, *please*, I absolutely *don't* need a life-sized statue of me made of gold *erected* in the city center so that others may bask upon me. And if I can't convince you otherwise, I will promise not to steal it to hoard, even if I should have it because it looks like me and is shiny and probably has eyes made of rubies. Hold the applause. I *shan't* need it."

We held our applause. Just barely.

"My *hero*," Gary sighed. "You are going to get so much muffin tonight."

"Ooh," Kevin said. "An appropriate reward for my valor. What kind of muffin?"

"Banana nut," Gary purred.

Kevin gasped. "My *favorite*."

"You don't want to eat his banana nut muffin," I whispered to Morgan. "It actually means—"

"I *know* what it means," Morgan snapped. "You gave me a list of their entire *bakery*. In all the years I've lived, I have *never* read such depravity."

"Did you read the part about their scones and—"

"And that's where I think this should end," Morgan said firmly. "Because the gods only know how much longer this will go on if I don't shut you up now."

He had a point. "The gypsies are on their way in," I told Kevin. "We need to be ready."

The ridge above Kevin's eyes furrowed. "Gypsies? Aren't they mostly peaceable people?"

"Mostly."

"So we're not under attack."

"Not that we know of."

"And you just let me tell that mostly false but true story of how I defended everyone because of my amazingness."

"Pretty much."

Gary was nickering near his ear, and Kevin's eyes rolled back in his head. "I am gonna get so laid tonight. Thank you, Sam. I'll take you out to toss the ball around later and you can tell me about the project for science class that you're doing. We'll get you first place yet, just you wait and see. No boy of mine is gonna get a damn participation ribbon. Those things are only given to first-place *losers*."

"Remember what you said in the foot-smelling closet?" I asked Ryan. He nodded. "You can't take it back now."

"Already did," he assured me. "You're on your own with this one. Hell, I might see if *I* can go with the gypsies."

And before I could come up with the appropriately devastating retort, the Great Doors opened and the announcer walked into the throne room. "Your Majesty," he said. "The *phuro* of the Bari Lavuta Clan requests an audience. Vadoma Tshilaba extends her greetings of peace from her people to those in the City of Lockes. She wishes to see the faces of her daughter and grandson."

The King looked from me to my mother, then back toward the Great Doors. "The *phuro* may enter in the spirit of peace."

The announcer nodded and went back through the Great Doors.

"Sam," Morgan said quietly. "You must listen to me. Are you listening?"

I glanced over at him to find him watching the doors. "Yes."

"Whatever Vadoma says, you must know that having you by my side has been one of the greatest joys in my long life. That I wouldn't have changed it for anything. Do you understand?"

A chill went down my spine. "What are you—"

"Do you understand?"

No. No I didn't. "Morgan."

"There is much I haven't told you," he said, finally looking at me. There were lines around his eyes and mouth. He looked tired, more so than I'd ever seen him. Like he was an old man. He *was* an old man, close to three centuries, but he never *looked* it. He smiled tightly. "All I ever wanted was to keep you safe and whole."

"You *have*. Why are you—"

The Great Doors groaned as they parted, the Castle Guards pushing against them.

At first, nothing else happened.

Then I felt a prickle along the back of my neck, like the softest of whispers, as if *something* was reaching out for me. It felt familiar, as if I'd somehow known it before.

A man came first, barefoot, each step deliberate and soft. He was shirtless, the shadows from the flickering candlelight crawling along his muscular torso. His trousers were tight at the waist but billowed along his thighs and legs. His arms were heavily tattooed, colorful lines etched into his skin seemingly without pattern. A gold band was wrapped around his right bicep. His skin was darker than my mother's, his black hair pulled back and tied in short ponytail. His eyes were dusky, with what looked to be black coal smudged around them.

Dude was hot.

"Um," Gary whispered. "Can I have him, please? For science."

"I would also like to partake in said science," Kevin whispered back. "If the science we are speaking of involves an experiment where I cover him in my dragon juice."

And what made matters worse was that even in the presence of the King of Verania, the King's Wizard, even the Prince, this man never once looked away from me as he approached.

"Uh-oh," Gary said.

"Why uh-oh?" Tiggy asked.

"We're probably about to see unnecessary displays of testosterone," Gary said. "And it's going to be *glorious*."

I wondered what the hell they were talking about until Ryan muttered, "He could have at least put on more clothes before coming in. And why can't he walk like a normal person? Is he *trying* to have sex with the air? Who does that?"

Oh boy.

The man stopped a respectable distance away from the dais. He cocked his head at me, that unnerving stare unwavering. Now that he was closer, I could see just how young he was, probably around my age. I felt off-center at that watchful gaze. It only lasted a moment before he dropped to his knees. Gary let out a slightly pained noise at the sight, but I ignored him.

The man leaned forward, hunched over, arms extended out in front of him. His hands touched the ground, palms flat on the floor as he bowed down.

The muscles in his back rippled as he held the pose for almost a full minute. There was that prickle of familiarity again, something that teased along my senses, just out of reach.

The throne room was silent. I thought to speak first, but it wasn't my place. The King would know when it was time.

The man finally pushed himself back up to his feet in one fluid and *slow* motion. "My Good King," he said, voice raspy. It was almost startling to hear. "It is an honor to stand before you." He had an accent much like my mother's, musical and light, except far thicker, like his tongue curled around each word deliberately.

"The honor is mine," the King said, bowing his head. "It has been far too long for your people to stand in Castle Lockes."

The man grinned suddenly, wide and blinding. "I'm sure there were reasons for that, don't you think? Certain... circumstances." His gaze flickered to me before returning to the King. "But no matter. My name is Ruv. I am the Wolf of Bari Lavuta."

"The Wolf?" the King asked, glancing at my mother.

"It means he's the enforcer of the *phuro*," Mom said quietly. "The Wolf is to her what the Castle Guard is to you. He protects her at all costs. With his life if called upon."

Ruv snapped his attention away from me and looked upon my mother. His smile took on a softer edge at the sight of her. "Dika Tshilaba," he said, bowing in her direction. "I have heard many wonderful things about you."

"Is that right?" Mom said. "How strange. I'd thought my name would have been banished for all days given the path I followed."

"A good path too," my dad said, puffing out his chest. "The best path, even."

"Perhaps you're not as lost to them as you think," Ruv said. "The paths we take may lead us from home, but they always return us to where we started in the end."

He turned back toward the King but kept glancing at me, like he was assessing. I didn't know what he saw when he looked at me, and I tried not to squirm under his watchful gaze. Ryan must have seen it too, because he inched closer in what was I'm sure an attempt for subtlety but probably missed the mark by a good distance.

"I'm not going to whip it out and demand he suck it," I whispered to him.

"Thank the gods for small favors," he whispered back.

"Hey! I'm not *small*, you asshole."

"I didn't say you *were*. And why would you even be thinking of whipping it out?"

"Maybe because you look like you're going to piss on me just to mark your—"

"Ahem," Morgan said pointedly.

Ruv glanced between Ryan and me, brow furrowing, but the look was gone before I could even place it.

"Your *phuro* is here, is she not?" asked the King.

"She is," Ruv said. "But it is customary for the Wolf to enter first to avoid any... complications."

"And what complications might that be?"

The answering smile was razor sharp. "We are not always welcome when we leave the desert. Precautions must be taken. You understand."

"There is nothing to fear here," the King said lightly. "Your *phuro* is safe."

"Oh, I don't know about that," Ruv said, glancing at me again. "The power in this room is *satarma*. Like a star to be wished upon."

"But your *phuro* has already entered," Morgan said, speaking for the first time to Ruv. "Has she not?"

"Old one," Ruv said with another bow. "You are a legend amongst my people."

"A legend would imply I don't exist."

"And yet here you are," Ruv said.

"I notice you didn't answer my question."

Ruv grinned. It really was a nice smile, if one cared about such things. "I did not."

"He's sassy," Gary hissed at me. "We need to keep him."

"He's not *that* sassy," Ryan muttered.

"Sam, can you tell the Knight Commander to calm the fuck down? He's harshing my new boy-crush buzz and I won't tolerate it a moment more."

Because Gary was a unicorn and my best friend, I said, "Ryan, stop harshing Gary's buzz."

"My *boy*-crush buzz, Sam, get it right. It is so hard to find good help these days."

"I good help," Tiggy said.

"The best, really," Gary agreed.

"Stop harshing his boy-crush buzz," I said to Ryan.

Ryan scowled.

Ruv looked amused. "I see we are well met. She will be pleased by all of you, as I am. The *phuro* will enter."

He turned on his heel and walked back through the Great Doors.

CHAPTER 5
Vadoma Tshilaba

"Okay," Gary said as soon as he disappeared. "I feel like we should have real talk right now. Because seriously? Dat. *Ass*. Do you know how many coins you could bounce off of that thing?"

"I have many coins in my horde," Kevin said. "Perhaps we should invite him to see."

"I don't like him," Ryan said. "He's suspicious. Coming in here all... suspiciously."

Justin snorted. "Yeah, because that's the reason."

"What?" Ryan asked, eyes narrowed. "There's no other reason. I don't *need* another reason. There was *suspiciousness*. That should be enough reason for everyone!"

"Uh-huh," Justin said, sounding bored. "And it had absolutely nothing to do with how he was like a starving man and Sam was a four-course meal. Which, honestly. What is with people and their incredibly bad taste in this kingdom? I know attraction is subjective, but come *on*."

"Hey!"

"You have a strange eyebrow-to-face ratio," Justin said with a shrug.

"Feeling self-conscious now," I said, covering my eyebrows with my hand and glaring at Gary. "You should have *told* me I had weirdness going on!"

Gary blinked. "I thought it was just something we didn't talk about. You know, like how we don't talk about your nose."

"*What's wrong with my nose?*"

"Eep," Gary said.

"There's nothing wrong with your nose," Ryan said, pulling my hand away from my face. "And I like your bushy eyebrows."

I gaped at him. "They're not *bushy*."

"Like my taint before I get waxed," Gary said, which I ignored because oh my fucking gods, I could *never* go out in public again.

"He doesn't want to sex me up," I said to Ryan. "And even if he did, you know you're my one and only. You remember when we shattered my virginity? Well, I latched on to you like a barnacle after that. I'm slowly sucking the life out of you, because I'm never going to let you go."

"Do you ever get the feeling like we failed as parents?" Dad asked Mom.

"Either that or we did something really right," Mom said. "I don't know which is worse."

"I don't trust this," the King said to Morgan. "He did seem to have eyes for Sam."

Morgan hesitated. Then, "Sam's… notoriety is well-known throughout Verania. We don't rightly know what has fallen upon gypsy ears."

"I'm taking that as a good thing," I told Gary. "They call me Notorious S.A.M."

"Nobody calls you that."

"Well maybe they should start."

"Look at you with your head in the sand," Gary said. "Nice."

"We should hear what she has to say," Mom said. "She never does anything without reason. The fact that she left the desert is enough to raise concern."

The King nodded but said nothing.

"It always seems to center around you, doesn't it?" Justin said to me, though he didn't sound particularly spiteful. "Funny how that works."

I blanched. "I didn't ask for it." Though, I couldn't disagree with him. Somehow, it always did seem to concern me somehow. And that wasn't something I particularly enjoyed.

"No, I suppose you don't. Yet here we are. Again."

"We'll still be best friends even if it *is* about me, right?"

"We're not best friends now."

"He's in denial," I said to Gary.

"Eh, keep chipping away," Gary said. "Pretty soon we'll be inviting him to our hair-braiding parties where we have pillow fights in our underwear and gossip about boys."

"I don't do that," I said.

"Yes, you do," Gary said. "We did it just last week, remember? And you talked about how curved Ryan's—"

"—knee is when he bends it," I said quickly (and smartly, if I do say so myself; it was *genius*). "That's all. Nothing else."

"Says the guy who went to fan clubs about Ryan in disguise," Justin said.

"Oooh," everyone else said.

Including Ryan.

That bitch.

But whatever witty rejoinder I might have had was cut off when my grandmother, Vadoma Tshilaba, entered the throne room.

It was like the air around me stuttered, and I saw offshoots of green and gold skirting along the edges of my vision. There was a buzzing sensation racing along my arms and curling around my fingertips that almost *itched* for me to take action, though what *type* of action, I didn't know. Morgan dropped a hand on my shoulder and Ryan crowded against me, and it was enough to stop me from taking a step forward.

The woman that entered was the same as the apparition that had disappeared after accosting me in the hallway. She held her head high as she walked, standing tall and proud. Her hair fell upon her shoulders, streaked with the lightest of gray. She wore a blue dress that left her thin shoulders exposed. Around her waist was tied a tan shawl, the fringes of which hung down her sides. She wore a crown of sorts, more a headband than anything else. It was thin and gold, with little trinkets hanging down onto her forehead. She was old, as evidenced by the lines and wrinkles around her face, but she moved with an economic grace, almost like a waltz, counted and measured, nary a step out of place.

And she was magic, that much I could tell.

It absolutely *poured* off her in waves, as if her aura was shedding magenta and fuchsia and crimson. It was intrusive but not invasive. If anything, I felt the need to allow it to push against mine, even as Morgan's hand tightened on my shoulder, as Ryan gripped my forearm. And again it was *familiar*, like I'd known it before, and the only thing I could think of that made any sense was that it was familial, that my magic recognized hers because of the blood that ran through both of us. I was not a gypsy, but I'd come from them. Northern blood had diluted the pureness, but only by a generation. I knew her because I'd descended from her. It didn't feel like Morgan's. Or Randall's. It felt *earthy* somehow.

She stopped in the same place Ruv had, a respectable distance and to make herself seem like a nonthreat. I had the idea, though, that it didn't matter how close or far away she was. If she wanted something to happen, it would.

Ruv stood at her right, standing on one foot, stretching the other out behind him, curving it up toward his back. He reached his arms behind his head and grabbed on to his foot. The muscles in his stomach clenched. His eyes never left me.

"I don't know if that's creepy or erotic," Gary whispered to Kevin.

"Can't things be both?" Kevin rumbled. "I mean, I'm scared, but I could easily get an erection if called upon to do so."

Vadoma didn't even acknowledge me. No. Her eyes were on her

daughter.

Mom clutched Dad's hand but didn't speak.

After what felt like an age, this great and powerful woman named Vadoma said, "Dika. You have aged poorly. All that processed meat you're eating, I'm sure."

That... was not what I expected. I stared at my grandmother with wide eyes.

Mom, however, said, "*Daj*, Mother. It's a wonder you're still alive. Tell me. How does the cold dead thing you call a heart still beat in your chest?"

My jaw dropped.

"Oh my gods," Gary whispered. "This shit is gonna get *cray-cray*. Tonight, on *Castle Lockes*, watch as families reunite as a crazy old lady with awesome taste in jewelry sees her daughter again for the first time. Will eyes be scratched out? Find out... on *Castle Lockes*."

"Bah," Vadoma said, seemingly dropping all pretense. She slouched a little, her forehead wrinkling even more. "My heart will stop when it needs to stop, little *kanny*."

"I am not your little chicken," Mom snapped, dropping my father's hand and pushing her shoulders back.

"I made you," Vadoma said. "You took forty-seven hours to come out of me because I wasn't ready to let you go yet. You are little *kanny* until I say so."

"I want to be her when I grow up," Gary said to Tiggy. "Forty-seven *hours*? My gods, the thigh control alone."

"Gary gonna have babies?" Tiggy asked.

"Probably," Gary said. "But most likely not."

"I be Uncle Tiggy," the half-giant decided.

Vadoma turned her disdainful gaze to my father. "Still here, I see. *Dilo*. You got fat. You like processed meats, fat man? Probably put them in your fat mouth."

Dad sighed. "Hi, Vadoma. Lovely to see you again, Vadoma. Thanks for coming, Vadoma."

"Your parents ate sass for breakfast," Gary said.

I was still gaping. Because out of all the things that I thought *could* happen, this was certainly not it.

"You come to *posta*, fat man," Vadoma said with a nod. "I feed you good food."

My dad snorted. "It hasn't been long enough for me to forget the first time you invited me to a *posta*. You forgot to tell me that it was a sacrificial ritual and that I was to be the sacrifice."

"Spoils surprise," Vadoma said. "Very bad. Vadoma doesn't like spoiling surprises."

"Crazy lady sacrifice Josh-pop?" Tiggy asked Gary.

"It seems like," Gary said, sounding impressed. "*And* she can pull off a shoulderless dress at her age? Sign me up for that shit right the fuck now. Gypsy queen who can sacrifice people when she wants to? That's what I was *born* for."

"I smash crazy lady?" Tiggy asked.

"If you do, make sure you don't get blood on the clothes. You know how hard it is for me to find good vintage these days. Also, we'll want to ensure that I'm installed somehow as the new figurehead. Queen Gary the Magnificent. No. Queen Gary the *Supreme* Magnificent."

"I smash crazy lady," Tiggy said, taking a step forward.

"I don't know if that's the best course of action," Morgan said mildly.

Tiggy pouted. I could see Morgan struggling against that look to give the go-ahead to smash my grandmother. Greater men than anyone in this room had fallen to the power of Tiggy's pout. But somehow, Morgan was able to withstand it.

The King stood from his throne and bowed toward Vadoma. "It is an honor."

Vadoma said, "Of course it is. I am here, am I not?"

He didn't even blink at that. "So you are. Though I must admit to being a bit mystified as to the reason for this visit."

"You would be," Vadoma said.

"How many of your people am I to be expecting in the City of Lockes?"

She snorted. "Just me and the boy."

The King frowned. "I didn't expect the *phuro* to travel without an entourage."

She ignored his unspoken question. "Is that your son?"

"Yes," the King said. "Prince—"

"Stand up," Vadoma said to Justin.

Justin did.

"Hmm," Vadoma said. "You'll do."

"For what?" Justin asked, sounding annoyed.

"You may sit back down," Vadoma said. "I am done with you now."

Justin scowled at her but did as he was told. Which honestly shocked the hell out of me, so much so that I still hadn't been able to find my voice to say a single thing. I thought maybe that was a good thing and hoped that if I didn't speak, she wouldn't know that I was here and then would go back to the desert and not say anything about my eyebrows.

She moved on. "You there. Gigantic man. What is your name?"

Tiggy pointed at himself before looking around to see if there were any other gigantic men around him. "Me?"

"Yes, you. Speak now."

"I Tiggy."

"Tiggy."

"Yes?"

"I like you," Vadoma said. "You may live."

Tiggy looked pleased and confused.

Vadoma turned to Gary.

"My Gypsy Queen," Gary said, bowing low. "I am Gary the Supreme Magnificent. But you can just call me Gary. It is truly a blessing to be in—"

"I don't like you at all," Vadoma said.

Gary stood up from his bow slowly, eyes narrowing. "I'm sorry?"

"You're a unicorn, yes?"

"Yes?"

"Is that a question? You either are or aren't. Make up your mind."

"Yes. I am a unicorn."

"Then I don't like you," Vadoma said.

"But—"

"No talking! Vadoma has no time for magical talking unicorns."

The air started to sparkle around Gary.

"That's never a good sign," Kevin said. "Dear, maybe you should just calm down a little bit? You know how things turn out when you feel stabby."

"Calm down?" Gary said dangerously. "*Calm down*? Oh, it is *on* now. Does Gary have to bring the motherfucking *pain* up in here?"

"Bah," Vadoma said. "Useless creatures with your prancing and your fluffy tails. Dragon. You there. Dragon!"

"Me?" Kevin said. "Please don't say anything that could damage my self-esteem. I am very softhearted, and I would hate to cry in front of you."

"How long you been able to talk?" Vadoma asked.

Kevin looked confused, or as much as a dragon with his head shoved through a window *could* look confused. "I've *always* been able to talk. I do have a tongue, you know. Granted, I don't use my tongue for just talking. Sometimes I use it for—"

"How long have you been able to talk so that others understand you?"

Kevin said, "Oh. Since Sam showed up at my keep and forced me to come along with him and leave my horde behind. He was really rather militant about it. All like, *Dragon, you must leave your invaluable treasure behind because me and my tight little ass and whiny voice are telling you to do. I'm Sam of Wilds. I tell people to do things and expect them to do it because I'm a bossy fucking twink.*"

"That's not what happened!"

"Close enough," Gary said.

"I'm actually going to agree with Gary on that one," Justin said.

"Betrayer!" I gasped. "After everything I've done for you!"

"And what is it exactly you've done for me?"

"Well, there was that… um. Hold on. I'll think of something. Aha! There was that time that I—wait. No. That was a tree."

Everyone turned to stare at me.

And if there is one thing that can be counted on, it's that when I become the center of attention, I tend to make things awkward.

"I didn't do it," I blurted out.

Morgan face-palmed. I didn't blame him.

"What didn't you do?" Vadoma asked.

I swallowed thickly. "Whatever it is you think I did?"

"Good job in landing that one," Gary said to Ryan. "All your choices have led you to this moment. Really makes you think, doesn't it?"

"I make good choices," Ryan said. He glanced at me. "Mostly."

"Hmm," Vadoma said.

Which, obviously, I didn't know what to do with. Because when one *hmms*, one could be saying a multitude of things. For example:

Hmm: *You are so cool, Sam.*

Hmm: *I had high hopes for meeting you. All of which have been exceeded.*

Hmm: *Your dimples are adorable and I don't think your eyebrows are bushy.*

Hmm: *I am going to murder your face and then bathe in your blood as part of a gypsy ritual where I ask a goddess to damn you for all eternity while I curse everyone you love. Oh, and by the way, your eyebrows are terrible, and you are neither as adorable nor as quick-witted as you think you are. Most people hate you. Like I do. I hate you so much.*

"What does that even *mean*?" I demanded of Vadoma.

"A little high-strung, isn't he?" Vadoma asked.

"Yes," everyone else in the room said.

Which, you know. Fuck them all.

"See if I get you guys any presents for your birthdays ever again," I muttered.

"Sam, last year you painted me a picture of, and I quote, *an accurate representation of what our friendship means to me*," Gary said.

"Which was *fantastic*," I retorted. "Because everyone knows that homemade gifts are better than anything you can buy at the store."

"It looked like you had murdered defenseless animals on a blank canvas."

"Because I feel violent towards you sometimes. Like now, for instance."

"Oh," Gary said. "That makes more sense. I get it now. I wish I hadn't thrown it—I mean, I'm glad I hung it up in my room for everyone to see whenever they like. Except for Sam. Because he's not allowed in my room. For reasons. That have nothing to do with the painting."

I frowned at him.

"And you must be Knight Commander," Vadoma said to Ryan.

"I am," Ryan said, posing slightly because he still couldn't help himself. "I have pledged an oath to the King of Verania to protect the Crown at all—"

"Why you stand so close to my grandson?"

Ryan opened and closed his mouth a couple of times. He wasn't used to anyone interrupting his ridiculously dashing and immaculate speech about his oath and fealty, even if most people in the room had heard it a hundred times. And I was fine with hearing it again, if I was being honest. First, because I was proud of him and how far he'd come. Second, because I had this weird kink where I found it to be ridiculously hot when he talked about loyalty to the Crown and would usually try to find the nearest available surface to pound him into.

"Why... what?" he eventually said.

"You stand on top of my grandson," Vadoma said slowly, like she was speaking to an idiot. "Because...."

"Oh!" I said. "I can answer that one. Because he's my boo."

Ryan groaned.

"Don't act like you don't like it," I said, rolling my eyes. "Everyone knows you do."

"Literally everyone," Justin said. "Because that's all we had to hear about for months. *Sam said this* and *Sam did that* and *isn't Sam just the best thing to happen in the history of anything?*" Justin made a face. "I honestly gave thought to having myself executed to escape hearing anything else."

"You talk about me?" I asked Ryan.

Ryan flushed. "No," he said, sounding petulant.

"Yes," everyone else said. Including the knights along the walls.

"Wow," I said in awe. "You think I'm incredible. Having validation is pretty much the best feeling ever."

"I just like your face," Ryan mumbled, shuffling his feet on the floor. "And stuff."

"I am going to do so many things to you later," I said. "Things I can't talk about right now because my parents and my long-lost grandma are standing right near us and I want them to think I'm still a virgin."

"We don't think that," Dad said. "Especially since you came to us the day after you lost it and announced it at breakfast."

"He was so proud," Mom said fondly. "Like that time he was nine and brought home a bug he'd found under a log."

"Not quite the same thing," Dad said, squeezing Mom tighter. "But we'll count it as close enough."

Ruv *finally* dropped his pose and leaned toward Vadoma, mouth near her ear. He spoke to her in a clipped foreign tongue that reminded me of my mother. Vadoma nodded along with whatever he was saying until she held up a hand, cutting him off.

"You are together?" she asked me, nodding over at Ryan.

"Yes," Ryan said, taking my hand in his.

"In sin, even," I said, waggling my eyebrows, because if there is one thing I apparently could not do, it was to not brag that I'd somehow snagged Ryan Foxheart.

"Sam," Ryan chided gently, but I'm sure everyone in the room could see the smile quirking along his lips. I might have exasperated him and been more than frustrating, but for some reason, he loved me. And I would have done anything for him. We were kind of disgusting that way. "Maybe not tell that to your grandmother who you're meeting for the first time."

I sighed the sigh of the weary. "Whatever you say, babe."

"And don't call me that when I'm working."

"Whatever you say, *Knight Commander*."

He squeaked a little at that and started coughing, because he liked it as much as I did.

"Ugh," Gary said, his nose wrinkling. "It's like watching your mentally incapacitated great-aunt eating nothing but a jar of mayonnaise."

"That's…," I said. "Huh. I don't know quite how to take that."

"Badly," Gary said. "Preferably. Stop being so disgustingly precious in front of me. I'm going to vomit in the throne room, and no one wants to see that again."

"It look like rainbows," Tiggy said.

"Most things that come out of me look like rainbows," Gary said.

"Seriously," Kevin said. "By the time we finish our rigorous bouts of athletically tantric lovemaking, I look like the end result of a paint-by-numbers avant-garde tragedy done by a toddler."

"And he says *we're* gross," I said, trying not to gag.

It was then that Vadoma addressed Morgan for the first time. But her tone had changed into something fiery, something *angry*. "And you allowed this, wizard?"

That irked me because I was *standing right there*. "Hey," I snapped. "He doesn't have to *allow* me to do—"

"Sam," Morgan said, cutting me off. "That was not a question for you."

"But she—"

"Sam."

I knew that voice. That voice said I'd better shut my mouth before I was in trouble. I'd heard it more than I probably should have.

He waited just a beat more to make sure I'd heard him. Then he turned back to Vadoma. "He's more than capable of making his own choices, Vadoma. If they lead to mistakes, I can only hope that he learns from them. The Knight Commander was his own choice in the end. And I believe there was never a mistake in that."

She scoffed. "Foolish man. You know nothing. We had a deal."

Wait. What. "I'm sorry," I said. "I think I misheard you. You had a *what* now?"

"A deal," Vadoma said. "Tell him, Wizard. Tell him how you know of him from the moment of birth. Tell him what the *satarma* called out the night he came to this world. You knew him as I did. And you agreed to be his mentor until the day I came for him."

The room was ominously silent after that.

And it couldn't be— "Morgan?"

He looked stricken. "It's not as you're thinking, Sam. Anything I have done, anything I agreed to was only to protect you. You are not bound by the promises of a foolish old man."

That memory. That godsdamned memory.

Ah. I see. Your mamia *was Vadoma, then.*

Yes, my lord. You've heard of her?

Perhaps.

"You knew me," I breathed. "That day in the alley. The first time. You knew who I was."

"Yes," Morgan of Shadows said. "I knew you."

I couldn't form my thoughts in a proper order. All I could think about were the times I'd felt Morgan was holding something back from me, was keeping his secrets held close to his heart. Wizarding is *always* about secrets, but hadn't some part of me known that Morgan knew more than he had always said? I'd written it off as just him being Morgan. I'd trusted him when he said he'd tell me the things I needed to know when I needed to know them.

"What about him?" I snapped, jerking my head toward Ryan. "Did you know it was him too, then?"

Everyone looked confused. "Sam," Morgan said slowly. "Ryan wasn't in the alley that day. How could I have known him?"

I laughed bitterly. "Of course he was there. He was—" And I stopped myself because holy *fuck* was I an asshole. I closed my eyes. "Shit."

Because Ryan Foxheart wasn't always Ryan Foxheart.

Once upon a time, Ryan Foxheart had been a teenage douchebag named Nox with a penchant for kicking my ass whenever he could. There were only a handful of people in this world who knew Ryan had come from the slums, and I had effectively just outed him. It wasn't as if he was *ashamed* of it, it was just that in the history of the Veranian Knights, no one had *ever* risen to the position of Knight Commander after having come from the slums.

So imagine my surprise when, instead of being rightly furious with me, he squeezed my hand gently and said, "Sam."

I opened my eyes, shame burning on my face. He didn't look angry, just concerned. "I didn't mean—" I managed to choke out.

But he was already shaking his head. "It doesn't matter," he said, and he *meant* it. "We're in this together, yeah?"

I nodded, not trusting myself to speak.

"Then that's how we'll do it," he said. He leaned forward and kissed my cheek, a lingering thing, warm and dry. When he pulled back, I could see the resolve in his eyes and knew immediately where this was going to go. "Together."

"You don't have to—" I tried.

"I was there," he told Morgan. "The day in the alley. I was one of those turned to stone. I'm from the slums. Like Sam. Ryan Foxheart is a name I adopted for myself. My real name is Nox."

"Well fuck me silly," Gary said. "Did anybody else's nipples just get hard?"

"Mine did," Kevin said. "Wait. Do I even have nipples?"

"Nox?" Tiggy said. "Mean guy who hurt Sam?"

"Easy there, big guy," I said. "It was a long time ago."

Tiggy didn't look very appeased at that. And so maybe Ryan took a step closer to me, like I would protect him if Tiggy decided he needed to be smashed.

"Nox?" Dad said. "That little shithead whose ass I was going to kick but Rose said I couldn't because a grown man beating a child is never all right, even if said child is an asshole?"

"I think I did say most of that," Mom said, sounding equally shocked. "But for the life of me, I can't say why I would have stopped him now. Good thing he's not a child anymore."

Morgan sighed. "The two of you…." He shook his head. "The gods must really have a sense of humor."

"It's like a godsdamned romance novel," Justin said. "Because of course that's how Sam's life works out."

"I'll lay down my sword," Ryan said to the King. "I haven't acted as a Knight of Verania should. I lied to get to where I am. And for that, I am not worthy of the title Knight Commander. Or even a knight at all. I will accept any punishment you see fit to bestow upon me."

The King rolled his eyes. "You've got that martyr thing down, haven't you? Do you really think I would've promoted you to the Castle Guard if I hadn't known everything I could about you?"

Ryan looked shocked. "You *knew*?"

"I didn't tell him a damn thing," Justin said. "If that's what you're thinking."

"Of course I did," the King said. "I *am* pretty good at what I do, in case you haven't noticed. Request to resign denied. You will stay in the position you're in and you will like it until I say otherwise."

Ryan bowed again. "Yes, my King."

"Just don't be a douchebag to Sam anymore."

"Yes, my King."

"And this isn't something you felt you should have made known to me?" Morgan asked. "I could have vetted him further had you but asked."

"Really?" I asked. "You're gonna lecture him on secrets? You, of all people. Right now."

"Oh snap," Tiggy said.

Morgan flinched. Barely, but it was still there. "I didn't know it was him, Sam. Not with you then. Though I suppose it does make a bit of sense. And whatever machinations you think me capable of, I assure you you're wrong. Every decision I have made regarding you has been in your best interest."

"Would you have told me?" I asked bitterly. "If your hand hadn't been forced?"

"I had hoped I wouldn't have to. It was my wish that you live your life free of the chains of destiny. If I had any say in it, you would be safely tucked away where nothing could ever touch you." He rubbed a hand over his face. "All I ever wanted for you was for your happiness. It's what a mentor does. We teach you all that we can in hopes that it will be enough."

I understood what he was saying. But it wasn't enough. "Did you know?" I asked the King.

"No, Sam," he said softly. "I didn't. But even if I had, I would have trusted Morgan to know what he was doing. He has been around far longer than you or I. And he has always loved you as if you were his own. If he kept things away from you, it was because he thought he was doing the right thing."

"I don't know about that," Vadoma said. "Because it seems as if he has gone against what we discussed. *Dilo*. Never trust a wizard to do a woman's job. For all you know, he was trying to keep you to himself."

Morgan's eyes flashed. "Now see here, lady of the desert. You think yourself immune as a visiting dignitary. I assure you that's not the case."

She chuckled dryly. "*Bakla*. Liar. You have withheld long-hidden truths from the *chava*. You think he'll trust you now?"

"Regardless of what he did or didn't do," I said, "the fact remains I know him. I don't know you. Why should I trust anything you say?"

"Blood," she said.

I snorted. "Lady, look around you. The majority of the people here aren't related to me, but this is still my family. And I don't care just how thick the blood may be. If I think you're going to touch one hair on their heads, I will do everything I can to stop you. And as it turns out, I can do quite a lot."

Her eyes narrowed. "The knight. Do you care for him?"

"Yes." More than she could ever know.

"Do you treasure him?"

"Yes."

"Would you lay down your life for him?"

"Yes."

"Would you let him go if it was for the greater good?"

"*Yes*" was out before I could stop it. And even though it burned, I meant it. There was nothing that I wouldn't do for Ryan Foxheart.

"Good," she said, and a chill arced down my spine, because the look on her face was akin to *victory*. "Because you are being called upon for something greater than yourself. I have seen what you carry inside of you, Sam of Wilds. The lightning-struck heart that beats within your chest. I have known about you long before you were even a *thought*. I knew the day you were born, though my daughter was far from me by her own choice. I've seen what it is you'll become without the guidance I offer. There is a darkness rising in the corners of Verania, and it *calls for you*. You must not answer, no matter what it says." She clapped her hands once. It was a sharp crack that echoed in the throne room. "Ruv."

The Wolf of Bari Lavuta stepped forward and bowed again, eyes on me.

"I bring to you my Wolf," Vadoma Tshilaba said. "For he is the one thing the Knight Commander cannot be for you. Which is why, though difficult it may be, you must let Ryan Foxheart go. And you must do it now while we still have time."

"Really?" Ryan said, taking a step forward, shoulders tensed, angrier than I'd seen him in a long time. "And why should he do anything you say?"

"Because, *chava*," my grandmother said, not unkindly. "The Wolf is Sam's cornerstone."

"Ohhhhh *dayyyum*," Gary hissed. "To find out what happens after this stunning revelation, tune in next week on… *Castle Lockes*. Annnnnd… we're clear. Okay, what the *fuck* did that bitch just say?"

I didn't really remember much after that.

CHAPTER 6
Shit Just Got Real

WHEN I WAS TWELVE YEARS OLD, MORGAN of Shadows told me the most remarkable thing. Up until that point, I had been starry-eyed by the idea that I could do *magic*, that a man who seemed more myth than anything else could have come for *me*, that he saw something in *me*. I was just a boy from the slums with no prospects. I could read, sure, and I could write, even though it resembled chicken scratch. I was smart (probably too smart for my own good, according to my parents), but I wasn't much more than that. I would either work in the mills like my father or at the flower stand like my mother, and no matter the number of stars I wished upon, nothing would change my destiny. Some people, I knew, were meant for greater things. I wasn't one of them.

Until I was.

And in that first year, I didn't think I blinked even once, too busy staring at anything and everything I could. There was the *castle*, of course, and the *King* who knew my name. There were the Castle Guards, gruff men who would lay their life down for the Crown. There were the kitchens, with the cooks who made meals from sunup to sundown, covered in flour and flickering shadows from the fires in the ovens.

There were classes too, so many *classes* that I had to go to that sometimes, at my laziest, made me wish that I'd never stood in the alley and shouted *Flora Bora Slam*. There was proper etiquette I had to learn that didn't involve magic: how to bow in front of the King ("But he doesn't *care*! He *winks* at me and wriggles his mustache!"), which fork to use for which course at dinner ("They're *all* forks! Why does it matter how many prongs this one has? It'll still put food in my mouth!"), how to waltz ("*Dancing*? Send me back to the slums. I don't even care!"). I was measured for new clothes, my hair was cut, and fingernails were hardly ever dirty. Morgan knew it could be overwhelming, and there were days I didn't have to worry about any of it, days we'd spend holed up in the labs and I could watch him conjure spells with a wave of his hand, learning ancient words like *fie* and *twe* and *ain* that would cause the hairs on my arms to stand on end.

It was one of these times that he said he had something very important to discuss with me. I sat on the counter in front of him, my legs dangling. He didn't like when I sat there but never made me move once I had already jumped up.

I nodded solemnly and stared at him with wide eyes. "Is it how to blow something up in a fiery explosion with nothing but the power of my mind?"

He frowned. "What? No, of course not."

"Oh," I said. "That's… disappointing. I really thought today was going to be the day when you would teach me Fiery Mind Explosion of Doom."

Morgan sighed, a sound I was getting quickly used to. "You capitalized that in your head, didn't you?"

I grinned at him. "That's how you know it's real."

"Sam, there is no such thing as Fiery Mind Explosion of Doom."

"A wizard is only restrained by the limits of his imagination," I recited dutifully.

"I will regret ever having taught you that," he said. "Mark my words."

I reached over and patted his hand. "Probably. But if it's not exploding things, then what is it?"

"I need you to listen to me, Sam. Because this may be the most important thing you could learn as a wizard."

And didn't *that* just send my heart racing.

"Do you know what a cornerstone is?" he asked me.

I shook my head, because I still didn't know a lot of things. "Is it important?"

"Oh yes," he said. "It might just be the most important thing. You see, Sam, when a foundation is laid, the first stone placed atop it is called the cornerstone. It is important because all other stones will be set in reference to it. It helps to determine the position of the entire structure. Do you understand?"

I nodded.

"Magic works the same way. It builds upon itself after the foundation is laid. A cornerstone is needed to direct how the magic will grow. Without it, the magic would be shapeless. Or worse, it could grow out of control into something wicked. Something dark."

"Like the Dark wizards?" I asked quietly.

"Yes, little one," Morgan said. "Like the Dark wizards. Their magic is a misshapen thing, something grotesque and flawed. They think themselves above structure. Above a cornerstone. They see it as a hindrance. A restraint. Something that could hold them back."

"But it isn't."

"No. It's not."

I scrunched up my forehead in thought. "But… I don't want to carry a stone with me forever. It'd get heavy."

There was a smile on my mentor's face, and how my heart thumped at the sight of it. This man, this strange, strange man who had come out of nowhere to rescue my family from a life they didn't deserve, had become very important to me. I don't know that I was old enough to understand the specifics of love. I knew I loved my mother. I knew I loved my father. And I knew I loved Morgan of Shadows equally, but in a category all his own. I didn't understand it, but I wouldn't question it.

"You won't have to carry anything physical, little one. Though there are times the weight of it will seem like a burden."

I squinted at him. "Is this a riddle? I'm not very good at riddles. But I'm good at telling jokes. Everyone says so."

He shook his head. "No. No riddles. Not about this. Sam, a cornerstone isn't a thing. It's a person."

"A… person?"

"Yes," he said. "A person who will come to mean more to you than almost any other. One day your magic will recognize them. It may not happen right away. You may know this person for years before it happens. But one day your magic will say, *Here they are. Here is the person that will help us become more than we ever thought we could be.*"

I understood, but only in that way that twelve-year-old boys understand things. "But… but what if it's a *girl*?"

"Then so it will be."

"But I don't *like* girls," I said. And I really didn't. Most girls I dealt with in the castle that were my age didn't have time for a boy who sometimes forgot that you couldn't put your elbows on the table and that it's *not polite to blow your nose into a napkin, Sam, not everyone wants to see that.*

"Would you rather it be a boy?" Morgan asked, arching an eyebrow.

"Can't it just be you?" I asked. "You already make me happy."

Something stuttered across his face, something I was too young to understand. He moved until he was leaning against the counter at my side, arm wrapped around me, holding me close. I lay my head on his shoulder, feeling our magic mingle as it always did when we were together. Little stray hairs from his beard tickled my nose as he laid his head atop mine. "And you make me happy too," he said quietly. "More than you could possibly know. But no, Sam. I don't think it's me. But don't you worry. You'll find them."

"But… but how do I find one person out of the whole *world*?"

He chuckled. "There's more than one, Sam. It's about fate and the ties that bind you together. Maybe you already know this person. Maybe you have yet to meet. But until fate is ready to reveal them to you, you'll just have to wait. It'll happen."

"You promise? I don't want to be a Dark. I like it here with you."

He hesitated. But then he said, "I promise," and I believed him.

There was a moment then, years later, when I stood in a restaurant, a hush falling on the people in the room. Behind me sat a man named Todd with the most adorable ears. In front of me was a group of Dark wizards, monologuing their intentions for revenge after the death of Lartin the Dark Leaf.

And beside me?

Beside me stood Ryan Foxheart, sword drawn and at the ready. He hadn't even hesitated to stand with me at my side. He didn't question me. He didn't tell me to stand down. All it took was for a threat to rise against us before he prepared himself to fight at my side.

And there, in that moment, my magic *sang*.

There was no ritual. There was no process. He just *was*. We didn't have to paint runes on our skin out of sheep's blood and dance naked around a fire under a Hunter's Moon. There was no archaic spell that had to be performed that created ties between us that would bind us together. Every cornerstone was different to every wizard. Some were romantic. Some were platonic. Some were even familial.

But the fact remained that there was no one way to find your cornerstone. There was no one way to *act* with your cornerstone. Ryan was enough because he was *there*. He kept me away from the dark. He led me toward the light. It was the way he smiled at me, eyes crinkling, a hint of teeth. It was the way he trailed his fingers along my bare skin as we lay side by side, the room only lit with faint candlelight. It was the way he trusted me to take care of myself, but also trusted me to have his back. It was the way he knew I would never take him for granted.

That was what it meant to be a cornerstone.

And in the time I'd accepted him as such, I'd only grown stronger.

There are limits to magic.

But I didn't know if there were limits to me.

AND NOW I STOOD WITH MY arms crossed, glaring at Morgan. He leaned against a stone counter in the labs, a far-off look on his face. Ryan was next to me, twitching like he wanted to stab the problem to death. Which, honestly, I didn't blame him for. The others were upstairs after Vadoma's announcement had dissolved the tense conversation into utter chaos, with Gary asking if he had to choke a bitch, Tiggy threatening to smash everything in sight, Kevin suggesting all the men in the room solve their problems with an orgy, my mother having to be held back by my father, Justin looking supremely annoyed (which, in retrospect, wasn't really any different), and the King proclaiming no one would come into *his* castle and tell his wizard (*Apprentice*, Gary had coughed obnoxiously) what to do.

Morgan, however, had gotten the same look on his face that he had right now. Like he was thinking back on all the mistakes in his life that had led to this point and was getting ready to apologize for everything he'd done so we could hug it out like bros and move past this.

"I'm not apologizing for anything," he said, "if that's what you're thinking."

"What?" I said, sufficiently outraged. "I wasn't thinking that *at all*. And why not? You totally owe me! You practically had me wedded off to someone I don't even know! Did you sell me for some chickens? I swear to the gods, Morgan, if you didn't hold off for at least a goat, we're going to have a fucking problem here."

"Really, Sam?" Ryan growled. "A goat? *That's* going to be the problem here?"

"Relax, babe," I said, relaxing my scowl so I could kiss Ryan on the cheek. "You know you're my one and only. I don't care if it was *two* goats. You're stuck with me forever."

"It'd better at least been two goats and a pig or something," Ryan mumbled. "You're worth at least that much."

"Wow," I said. "I don't know how I feel about that at all."

Morgan sighed. "Can we focus here? Please? If that's not too much to ask."

I glared at him again. "Right. Because you're in so much trouble, you don't even know. What the hell was she talking about? I don't *have* another cornerstone. And even if I did, I choose Ryan. I will *always* choose Ryan."

"Damn right," Ryan said. "Because I'm awesome. I don't stand and pose like that asshole—"

"Not the best argument," I muttered to him under my breath. "You do that all the time."

"—I mean call myself the Wolf. You know who does that? Jackasses do that."

"Fist-pound me," I demanded.

Ryan didn't even hesitate. Like a *boss*.

We were a godsdamned united front against the tyranny of outside forces who wanted to do nothing more than to break our epic love apart. Well, we wouldn't stand for it! We would rise up against—

"You're narrating in your head, aren't you?" Morgan asked.

"What? No. Of course not. Who does that? That's stupid. But enough about me, let's get back to *you* and how much trouble you're in. After, of course, you tell me everything and why you sold me for chickens and not two goats and a pig like I'm *obviously worth*."

"I've never hidden from you what a cornerstone is, Sam," Morgan said. "Not once. You knew from the very beginning that there was the potential for there to be more than one. Fate doesn't deal in absolutes. There is always going to be some obscurity behind it."

"Gods," I muttered. "I hate it when you get philosophical."

"But even if that's the case," Ryan said, "it doesn't matter. *I'm* Sam's cornerstone. He felt drawn to me. He didn't feel anything for *Ruv*, which, by the way, who names their child *Ruv*?"

"Gypsies do, babe," I said. "It's actually a pretty common name."

"Oh. Right. Well. Okay, then."

"Also," I said, wincing slightly. "I don't know that it's *completely* accurate that I didn't feel anything when he came into the room."

"What," Ryan said without any inflection to signify punctuation, which made it that much worse.

"Yeah, um. See? So. Maybe. My magic? Might have jumped. Just a little."

"Your magic jumped," Ryan repeated in that same flat tone.

"Just a little," I reassured him, giving him the best smile I could.

"Okay," Ryan said.

"Okay?" That was easier than I thought it would be. I was sure he'd—

"Okay," Ryan said. "I'm going to go stab him with my sword."

And there it was.

He started to unsheathe his weapon and turned toward the door before I snagged him by the arm, pulling him back. "You can't murder him just because you feel like it."

"He made your *magic* jump," Ryan argued. "That's how it starts. First it's your magic, and then it's your dick, and then you're staring at me, wondering why *I* don't make your magic or dick jump anymore. And then you'll get really bitter toward me and wonder why I can't bend and touch my foot to the back of my head like *he* can, and then you'll run away with *Ruv*—seriously, what is *up* with that name?—and get married and have little gypsy babies or some shit."

I gaped at him.

He glared at the floor, hand still clutching his sword.

"I'm not going to do *any* of that," I finally said. "But wow. That was impressive. Dude. I am im*pressed*."

He rolled his eyes. "It doesn't take much to impress you, Sam."

"Lucky you, then."

"Hey!"

But I was already turning back to Morgan, who watched us with a fond look on his face. "He's not my cornerstone," I said. "Ryan is. And nothing is going to change that."

"Oh, I'm aware," Morgan said. "And I'm pretty sure everyone else in the castle is too if the way you bellowed exactly that was as loud as I think it was."

"Why is she here?" I asked, suddenly very, very tired. By now, Ryan and I should have been curled up together in my bed, his hands on me, skin slick with sweat. The fact that I was dealing with this instead was not doing anything for my mood. "And what deal did you make with her? No bullshit here, Morgan. And I swear to the gods, if I hear the word *destiny* out of your mouth again, I will kick you in the nutsac. I really will."

He sighed. "You have a destiny, Sam."

Ryan managed to pull me back just in time.

"I do *not*," I snapped at him. "I don't have *anything* aside from what's right here. I don't *want* anything else but what's right—what are you doing? Who are you calling?"

Morgan had pulled out his summoning crystal from a pocket in his robes, a thin piece of quartz that caught the candlelight in the labs. A bright spark shot off in the middle of the crystal and faded almost immediately. A second passed. And then another. And then—

"Do you know what *time* it is?" an angry voice said.

I groaned. This day was getting worse by the second.

"It's half past nine," Morgan said.

And the wizard known as Randall harrumphed. "*I* know what time it is. I was making sure *you* did. Seeing as how you *do*, I will move on to the next question. Why are you summoning me at such an ungodly hour?"

"Summoning," I said, elbowing Ryan. "Old people these days. Why can't he just say calling like everyone else?"

Ryan looked adorably confused. "Isn't it called a summoning crystal?"

"Shut up."

"Is that Sam I hear?" Randall asked sharply.

I frantically waved my arms at Morgan, shaking my head and mouthing *no, no, no*.

"Yes," Morgan said. "And Ryan Foxheart."

"What did they do now?" Randall asked. "They get stuck together like dogs in heat and can't handle it? Back in *my* day, we wouldn't break apart for *hours* if we could help it."

I choked on my tongue.

"It all started with the Sweeney cousins. There were five of them, and we each took turns—"

"Whyyy," I moaned, covering my ears, trying to block out everything I could. Still, certain things filtered in like, *and then he put it up my* and *we didn't have time to add spicy mustard* and *it ended up being stickier than I imagined*.

"—and that's how we ended up in a daisy chain for the entire week-end," Randall finished a few minutes later. "Those were different times. Men were men and did manly things. None of this fancy poof stuff like Sam here."

"Fancy poof stuff?" I exclaimed. "I'm going to turn your *eyes* into dicks! And then everyone is going to call you dick... eyes. Okay, I didn't think that through, but I reserve the right to come back to it when I think of a name that will scar you forever."

"Yes, yes, I'm sure it will be devastating. You still haven't explained why you've summoned me and won't stop talking."

Before I could remind him that *he*'d been the one going on for at least five minutes about cousin-loving, Morgan said, "Vadoma Tshilaba has come to Castle Lockes."

There was a beat of silence. Then, "Shit."

"Wait, he knew too?" I asked. "Of course he did. Because assholes stick together."

"He probably hasn't shut up about it, eh?" Randall asked.

"Not even the slightest," Morgan said. "Irate is probably the best description."

"You're damn *right* I'm ir—"

"Give me a minute," Randall grunted. "These old bones don't move as quickly as they used to. Hip, especially. Apparently, being almost seven hundred years old makes your body ache more than usual. Who would have thought?"

"Maybe you should just die, then," I muttered darkly.

"Certainly not I," Morgan said mildly, like he had all the time in the world.

"You'll find out soon enough," Randall said. "Pissing every five minutes, hands shaking, erectile dysfunction. Getting old is the worst."

"He's coming *here*?" I asked. "But that'll take weeks. We don't have time for—"

"You're still kind of stupid, aren't you?" Randall said from directly behind me.

The noise that came out of me was *not* a high-pitched scream, no matter what any of them said. It *wasn't*.

I whirled around, and sure enough, the most powerful wizard in the known world stood there, looking as grumpy and decrepit as always. His eyebrows looked like they had finally won the Battle of the Forehead and had begun to spread out in thick, wiry white hairs that seemed to reach his ears and nostrils. He was still in his pajamas, a striped onesie that was blown out on one knobby knee. On his feet were a pair of bunny slippers that I was sure wriggled their noses and whiskers, eyes blinking slowly. Randall himself watched me with a look of mild disdain with a dash of disgust and exasperation mixed in. He must have found me lacking as usual, because he clucked his tongue and shook his head.

"Sam," he said. "I had hoped I wouldn't have to see you for at least another year or so. I don't know that I'm mentally prepared for more of your inane prattling. But of course, this is just another fine mess you've gotten yourself into."

My heart was still beating wildly in my chest. "How did you *do* that?"

He rolled his rheumy eyes. "I'm a wizard, Sam. If you didn't know that, I will suggest to Morgan that he find a more appropriate job for you. Possibly in the kitchens. Or on your back in Meridian City."

"You just teleported from Castle Freeze Your Ass Off all the way here?

That's not possible!"

"Still slow on the uptake, I see," Randall said to Morgan as he shuffled his way to the stuffed high-back chair Morgan had set aside for him near the fireplace. "Do you think that'll ever go away, or is he going to be like that forever?"

"I seem to remember you saying the same thing about me," Morgan said. "In that same tone of voice, even."

"Yes, well," Randall said. "You learned quickly that I was always right and that you should do whatever I say. By a combination of dumb luck and sheer stupidity, your protégé has somehow found himself alive without learning anything at all. It would be rather remarkable if it wasn't so maddening."

"Why didn't anyone tell me about teleportation?" I demanded. "Do you know how much *easier* things would have been going after Justin? Or *any* time I've been captured?"

"I didn't tell you because you won't be able to do it," Randall said. "Only I can. It takes a discipline that you can't even begin to understand. Also, I'm old and it's easier. You're young and stupid, so it's your own fault you get captured. It's best to let you stew on it so you can hopefully learn from your mistakes. Hasn't happened yet, though I've still got some hope."

"He's got a point," Morgan said.

"Victim-blaming," I accused them.

Randall ignored me. "Knight Commander Foxheart, I see you haven't yet escaped the mindless babble. I'm still not convinced that you weren't coerced into this somehow."

"Yes, sir," Ryan said, tripping over his words. "I mean, no, sir. I mean, I don't know what to say to that, sir."

"You're supposed to be on *my* side," I hissed at him.

"I *am*," he said. "But that's *Randall*. Do you know what he could *do* to me?"

"Ah," Randall said. "Fear. What a beautiful motivator. But enough of this. Where is Vadoma? We might as well get this over with and done with. I'm sure Sam is going to do that thing where he gets really loud sooner rather than later, and I'd like to not be here for that part if at all possible."

"She's under the watch of the Castle Guard," Ryan said. "Along with that... that *man*."

Randall arched one of the eyebrows that was eating his face. "I take it we're not a fan of that *man*, whoever he may be."

"He's the Wolf to the *phuro*," Morgan said, sounding resigned. "And she brought him here to become Sam's cornerstone."

Randall cackled. "Oh, the *look* that must have been on his face. What I would have given to see that."

"I'm glad you find this all so amusing," I said, grinding my teeth together. "Seeing as how a woman I've never met came out of nowhere to tell me I had to break up with Ryan and do what she said. And only to find out that you both *knew* about this. Don't even get me started on the fact that she thinks I'm going to do anything with Ruv. I don't *care* how good he looks without his shirt on or how bendy he seems to be. It doesn't matter if that shit is erotic, or that he has dusky nipples, or—"

"I think we get it," Ryan snapped. "And dusky nipples? *My* nipples are like—"

"Hush, babe," I said. "I'm talking. Also, your nipples are wonderful and I am merely just trying to make a point."

"Which is?" he asked, crossing his arms over his chest and flexing unfairly.

My mouth dried a little. "Holy biceps," I whispered feverishly.

Ryan might have looked rather smug at that.

I shook my head, trying to rid myself of the image of licking Ryan's biceps. I could do that later. "It's not even *about* him. I don't care if he has the potential to be a cornerstone. Morgan told me there could be more than one a long time ago, but I've already made my choice. Nothing you or she or anyone else could say will change my mind on that. I don't care what sort of deal you made with her. It's not happening. Not now. Not ever."

Ryan's hand found my own, palm to palm, fingers entwined. He gave a gentle squeeze, and I did the same right back.

"I told you, Sam," Morgan said. "I didn't make a deal with her. Not over this."

"Then why is she so—"

"Oh, for heaven's sake," Randall said. "Just tell him. Or I could. I probably wouldn't sugarcoat it like you're going to. We don't agree on much, but even I can see the boy is tenacious. The gods only know why you insist on coddling the boy. I never did that for you."

Ah, and there it was again. Yet another reference to Randall as Morgan's mentor that they would probably tell me jack shit about. Much of Randall's past was shrouded in secret. At first I thought it was because he was at a level of magic my tiny little brain couldn't understand. But as I grew older, I came to realize it was just because he was a dick. There were stories told, of the madness of a king brought back to sanity by Randall's force of will and of his cornerstone, Myrin, who had been hidden in shadow. Myrin, who had built up Randall's magic to allow it to be where it was today.

I had so many questions about this, but now wasn't the time. "You knew me," I said. I was tired, exhausted really, and it was evident in my voice. "Before the day in the alley. Both of you."

"Yes," Morgan said simply.

"Because of her. Vadoma."

"Yes."

I looked back and forth between them, using Ryan's hand as an anchor. "Was any of this real, then? Or was everything that's happened to me, everything that has made me who I am... was it all planned from the start?"

There was a pained look on Morgan's face. "Sam, *everything* that you've been through, the lessons you've learned, both on your own and taught to you, have been real. I swear to you on all that I have."

"The paths we take are divergent," Randall said without his usual ire. "The choices we make cause them to splinter off in different directions. No one could have foreseen you becoming exactly the person you are today. It doesn't work like that. And Morgan's right. You have always had free will, Sam. You've been guided, but not controlled."

"Then what is this?" I asked. "What is all of this?"

"Gypsies have magic," Morgan said. "But it's different than what you or I know. The rules that govern the wizarding world do not apply to them. They can do things we cannot. The same can be said about us against them. They don't deal in the physical magic, but esoteric. Mystical. It's a—"

"Bunch of horse crap, if you ask me," Randall grunted. "Reading tea leaves and bones and wailing up at the heavens in front of a bonfire to show them the future."

"It felt real when she had me pressed up against a wall," I said.

Randall waved me off. "Sleight of hand. A distraction. Hardly civilized. I could stand outside under the stars and spout a hundred different predictions about the future and have the same success as the gypsies. The difference being I *know* it's a crock. The fact remains, most of it never ends up coming true. And even if it *does*, it's only because it was inevitable."

"Except me," I said.

"Except you," Morgan agreed. "But then, you have always been the exception. She came to me shortly before your birth under the cover of darkness. I was on the road between here and Meridian City, returning to the castle. I hadn't stopped, because I could see the lights of the City of Lockes, and I wanted to be home. I was alone on the road until I wasn't. She told me her name was Vadoma, that she hailed from the desert, and she had a message for me."

"And what was the message?" I asked slowly.

"That a boy would be born to one who was banished from her clan to live in poverty in a city at the seat of power. The banished one made a choice between the love of a man and the love of her people and suffered the consequences. And in her suffering, the boy would be born who would bring great change upon the world and rise against a tide of darkness that rose in opposition."

And that… was pretty fucking stupid. "Seriously," I said. "That's what she said."

"Yes," Morgan said.

"Okay, but. Like. That was so *vague*."

"Right?" Randall said. "Horse crap. Of course, after she got done with her hippy-dippy bullshit, she flat-out told Morgan that her daughter was pregnant and she thought the demon spawn was going to have some kind of magic. Her words, not mine, so you get that look off your face. You look like your huffing glue again."

"That was *one* time! I was *eleven*."

"Drugs are bad," Ryan said.

"Thank you for that contribution," I said. "You are the light of my life."

"Even though that was said sarcastically, it's true," Ryan said, and I fought hard not to swoon. Because fuck yeah, that was true.

"So she told you about an awesome kid being born—"

Randall coughed.

"A magical prodigy being born—"

Randall sneezed.

I glared at him. "A demon spawn being born—"

Randall smiled.

"—and you just bought whatever she had to say?"

"Of course not," Morgan said.

"Pretty much," Randall said.

"Pretty much," Morgan agreed. "To be fair, she was very convincing. Gypsies usually are with their outfits and wrist bangles. And even if that wasn't the case, Vadoma was well known for her predictions. People travel far and wide to have her read them."

"She also charges them for everything they're worth," Randall said. "And then tells them anything they want to hear. It's a scam, if you ask me."

"She's a *fortune-teller*?" I gasped. I couldn't think of anything worse than *fortune-tellers*. Most of it was bullshit, their little stands set up in festivals behind velvety purple curtains, peering into their crystal balls or reading lines on palms and gasping over just how *amazing* things were going to be. They weren't really prevalent in the City of Lockes outside of celebrations. But there was one on practically every corner in Meridian City, the signs in the windows promising to *TELL YOUR FUTURE!! CHEAP!!!!!!!* "But— but that's *terrible*."

"If you think about it," Randall said, "it's hardly surprising that would be your background."

"Hey! That was surprisingly effective in breaking me down emotionally. Nice job. Also, you bastard."

Randall looked rather pleased with himself.

"What does Ruv have to do with any of this?" Ryan asked. "Because I really feel that we should be talking about him more. Like, what kind of a name is Ruv? And how I'm obviously more muscular than he is, as everyone can probably tell. Also, does he not know how to put on shoes? *I* know how to put on shoes."

"And you do it very well," I said, leaning over and kissing him on the cheek. "In fact, no one puts on shoes like you do."

"Damn right," he mumbled, blushing slightly under the praise.

"I assume it's for the same reason she didn't want your mother to mar-ry your father," Morgan said. "Gypsies don't take to outsiders kindly, and as evidenced by their willingness to shun their loved ones, they like marriages outside of the clan even less. I imagine Ruv is meant to entice Sam back into the fold."

"I'm not going into *anyone's* folds except for Ryan's," I said.

"Yes!" Ryan said. Then, "Wait. What?"

"And so because a crazy woman came up to you in the middle of the night and put her fortune-teller nonsense all over you," I said, "you agreed to exchange me for two goats and a pig when the time came. What the fuck, Morgan?"

"I don't think that's a fair exchange," Randall said. "Too much goat for such a measly return."

Morgan sighed. "I didn't agree to anything, Sam."

"She seems to think you did. For all we know, she's going to try and enact some ancient gypsy law to try and claim I'm already betrothed to Ruv and must let him take me carnally under the light of the half-moon in a field of fireflies. I won't do it, Morgan. I really won't!"

"Is that true?" Ryan growled. "Is he going to be carnally taken sur-rounded by fireflies? You *know* Sam hates fireflies!"

"They're literally bugs that glow," I exclaimed. "Why does no one else see the problem here?"

"And *I'm* the only one that gets to carnally take *anything* from him," Ryan said.

"You're mostly a bottom, though," I said thoughtfully. "So I suppose it's mostly me carnally taking."

Ryan choked and started stuttering.

"This is what you woke me up for?" Randall asked Morgan.

"If I have to deal with this, then so do you," Morgan said.

"And all because Morgan agreed to this!" I said.

"I didn't."

I glared at him.

He stared right back.

"Fine," I said, conceding. "I believe you. Mostly."

He rolled his eyes. "How fortunate for us all."

"But don't think you're off the hook yet for lying to me all this time," I said, pointing my finger at him. "Because we're gonna have some words. You can count on that."

"I look forward to it with bated breath," Morgan said, a smile twitch-ing on his face.

"Good. So. Why is she here? Why now? And I will remind everyone in this room that no one is allowed to use the word *destiny* at any point. Ever. Or a *euphemism* for it either. Vocation. Calling. Purpose. None of it, because that's stupid and I hate it, and you should all hate it too. If you persist, I won't be held responsible for my actions."

I didn't miss the look exchanged between Morgan and Randall. Neither did Ryan, as he stiffened beside me. He was a warm line of comfort at my side, and even though our hands were slightly sweaty, there was no way I was going to let him go.

"There have been… whispers," Morgan finally said.

"Whispers," I repeated. "That's what you're going with."

"My gods," Randall said. "Remind me to give you more credit for everything, Morgan. I don't know how you haven't murdered him by now."

"Rumors, mostly," Morgan said. "Of a man. Superseding all ranks of the Darks."

I was confused. "The Darks don't *have* ranks," I said. "Isn't that kind of what makes them the Darks? They're scattershot."

"They seemed rather united in coming after *you*," Randall pointed out. Which, okay. That was fair. But the ones that *had* were either vanquished or imprisoned, spread out all over Verania.

"Like Lartin, then?" I said. "Is that who he is?"

"We don't know," Morgan said. "No one does. Again, Sam, this could all be nothing."

I watched him closely. "But you don't think it's nothing."

"I think," Morgan said slowly, "that Vadoma wouldn't be here if she didn't think it was important."

"Do you trust her?"

"No," Morgan said. "But that doesn't mean I don't believe her."

"And why should we believe her?" Ryan asked. "Why should we be doing anything she wants us to do?"

"When she touched Sam," Morgan said, "against the wall, he said he had a vision."

"Did I?" I said, playing dumb.

"Of a white dragon. A *great* white dragon."

Randall's eyes widened slightly before he schooled his face. It was quick, barely there. But I caught it. It didn't make me feel any better.

"Maybe," I conceded.

"And then there's Kevin. Who is also a dragon."

"Kevin," I snorted, trying to cover my unease. "If you could even call him that. He's more like a perverted lizard with wings."

"Be that as it may," Randall said, "before you, no one could speak with dragons."

"Dragon," I said. I was slowly losing control of this conversation. I knew the dreaded *D* word was on the tip of someone's tongue. "As in singular, not plural. Nothing else. And for all we know, it's just a byproduct of my magic. Like you teleporting or Morgan's eternal patience in having to deal with you."

"You can't know it's just the one," Randall said, ignoring my jibe completely. "Because you've never come face to face with the others."

"The dragon in the desert," Morgan said.

"The mated pair in the Northern Mountains," Randall said.

"And the Great White in the Dark Woods," Morgan said, "who you already seem to have made contact with."

"Don't you dare say it," I ground out.

"Holy shit," Ryan said, sounding breathless. "You have a Destiny of Dragons!"

"He capitalized it," Randall said.

"It must be true now," Morgan agreed.

Fuck my life.

CHAPTER 7
The Boner Carriage to Holy Fuck Me Town

TWO DAYS LATER, I'D STILL REFUSED to come out of my room. The door was locked, a chair shoved up underneath the handle, and I was pretty sure I was leaking enough magic to create a barricade I didn't even think about making on my own. All in all, it was very effective in keeping out the riffraff, which was essentially everyone I knew. It also meant I didn't have to hear about any destiny of dragons (*not capitalized*, thank you very much!). It wasn't the most mature way of dealing with things, but it was the only thing I could think of where I could avoid everyone and just *focus*.

The *problem* with trying to focus was that it was Gary and Tiggy's turn to try and get me to come out. They traded out in shifts that usually lasted a few hours. Each had their own specific tactic. Randall said he would give me another day before he teleported inside my room nude. Morgan told me that *he* hadn't even said the word, so I should just let *him* in. Mom and Dad laughed at me, then apologized for laughing, then laughed some more, reminiscing about how I used to lock myself in my room whenever I got mad at them, and how reassuring it was that I acted the same at twenty-one as I did when I was six. The King told me that I could stay in there as long as I needed to, but then in the next breath said that *he* would decide how long that should be, and if we disagreed, I'd be pooping in a bucket in the dungeons for at least a month. Justin would bitch that he didn't even *care* if I ever came out, that I could stay in there forever as far as he was concerned, which touched me deeply, as it felt like we were brothers from different mothers. Kevin tried to fly up to the windows in my room, but I shuttered them all while he scolded me that no sexy son of *his* would treat him like that.

Ryan had been conspicuously absent. As had Vadoma and her Wolf.

Gary and Tiggy, though?

I was going to murder them.

"—and *then* she said— You're not going to believe this, kitten. You want to know what that bitch said to me?"

"What she say?" Tiggy asked.

"She said, *Bitch, you ain't gonna get* my *man.* And then *I* said, *Bitch, I ain't even goin' after your man, but if I was, I'm sure I could totally get him because, girl, you nasty.* And then *she* said, *I ain't nasty,* you're *nasty.*"

"She a nasty girl," Tiggy agreed.

"Right? But get *this.* While she was saying *I* was nasty, I noticed that her *roots* were showing, so *I* said, *Girl, your hair looks like a* tragedy *up in here,* and she said, *Oh, I know, it's so embarrassing. My stylist died from a combination of gangrene and getting caught in a stampede of manticores.* So I said, *Listen. Just.* Listen. *You go down to Ming Win and she'll take care of you. She'll do your hair and your nails, and you tell her that Gary sent you because then she'll give me a five percent discount on my next visit because money doesn't grow on trees, if you know what I mean.* So she was all like, *Really, that's sounds awesome, thank you so much.* And I said, *Of course, that's why I'm here, and if you* ever *call me nasty again, I will fucking* cut *you.* And now we have tea once a month."

"I like tea," Tiggy said. "And pencils. And rocks and cats. And friendship stories."

"Of course you do, dear heart," Gary said. "You are precious, and I love you so. Now, on the forty-*second* time I got called a bitch, I deserved it, seeing as how I *had* been with her man. But did *I* know that he was married? Of *course* I did. But only because he needed unicorn jizz in order to free himself from the entrapment spell she'd put him under. And who was *I* to say no to that? He had *hair* on the back of his knuckles. You *know* how I feel about that."

"You feel good about that," Tiggy said.

"Exactly. So of course I called her a bitch back and—"

It'd been going on.

For two hours.

In very, *very* loud voices.

My *everything* was twitching.

"Bathe in your blood," I hissed under my breath. "Just *bathe*, motherfuckers."

I could outlast them.

I could.

I *would.*

Two minutes and sixteen seconds later, I threw open the door, ready to choke the life out of two of my closest friends.

Who immediately broke off when they saw me.

"Oh good," Gary said. "It worked."

"What worked?" I snapped at him, trying to resist the urge to reach out and *squeeze*.

"I knew there was only so much of my bitch stories you could take before you came out," he said, tossing his mane prettily. "Those amateurs before me don't know how to get under your skin as quickly as I do."

"I came out here to murder you," I admitted, because it was the right thing to do.

"Oh, tiny human," Tiggy said, patting me on the head with a big hand. "You try. You just try."

I knocked his hand away, but not before Gary was crowding me against the wall, his snout pressed against my face, eyes inches from my own.

"Sam," he said, breathing rather heavily. He didn't blink.

It was terrifying. "What?"

"How are you?"

"I've... been better?"

He nodded, which, given the fact that he was smashing his face against mine, caused me to nod too. "I understand," he said. "Now repeat after me. I am Sam of Wilds."

"I am Sam of Wilds."

"Not some punk-ass bitch."

"Not some punk-ass bitch."

"Gary is awesome."

"Gary is awesome—oh godsdammit."

Gary preened as he took a step back. "*Thank* you. It's about time I get the recognition I so obviously deserve. Tiggy, oh *Tiggy*, please take note of this date. The apprentice to the King's Wizard has declared me awesome."

Tiggy tapped the side of his head and winked at Gary. "Noted."

"Good," Gary said. "Now that that's out of the way—" He turned and snarled at me, eyes blazing.

"Eep!" I said, because even though it was scary, it was still a scary *unicorn*, and I couldn't help but fall in love just a little bit more.

"If you *ever* lock yourself in a room like a spoiled brat again, I will track down my horn, go on a quest to get said horn, defeat whatever creature *has* the horn, restore it to its rightful place atop my head, come back to the City of Lockes, march in a parade in my honor, and then come up to your room and *gore you to death. Do you understand?*"

"Your eyelashes are made of stars," I whispered reverently.

"I know," he hissed angrily. "It's because I'm beautiful. Now are we clear?"

"I understand," I said, because I did. Even without the overtly plotted threat of being gored, he was right. I couldn't lock myself away. Not with the threat of a destiny hanging over me. I had to face it head-on.

Like a *man*.

"Oh goodie," Gary said, dropping the rage façade like it was nothing. "Because you just *have* to see how Ryan is acting around Ruv. It's positively *adorable*. But mostly embarrassing. I'm embarrassed for him. And for you."

I sighed dreamily. Like a *man*. "He does posture whenever his masculinity is threatened."

"Knight Delicious Face threatened all the time," Tiggy said wisely.

"This is true," Gary said. "Why, even before we left, Ryan was challenging Ruv to a shirtless pull-up contest in the gym."

That… made my mouth a little dry. "And you didn't stay to *watch*?"

"Now you see what I do for you," Gary said. "I could have been watching sweaty muscled torsos, but instead I was up here saving your *life*." His eyes glistened suddenly with tears. "Why would you do this to me?" he asked, lip trembling.

I knew then what was the right thing to do. "To the gym!" I cried.

I SHOULD HAVE REALIZED THAT WE weren't the only ones who would have found a Ryan versus Ruv shirtless pull-up contest to be the event of the season. The castle was eerily quiet as we made our way down the stairs toward the labs.

"Where the hell is everyone?" I asked, wondering what would have caused the guards to mostly abandon their posts and the maids to leave their cleaning supplies haphazardly strewn across the floor. Even the kitchen was empty, large mixing bowls left on countertops, the smell of something burning slightly coming from the oven.

"Oh, my young, naïve little boy," Gary said. "I don't know if it's a good thing that you still have some innocence left. On one hand, it means you're still starry-eyed. On the other, it means that I need to work that much harder in corrupting you."

The closer we got to the gym, the louder it got, until it hit me where everyone was. And that… was both amazing and annoying. "Everyone is *ogling* my man?" I asked incredulously.

"To be fair," Gary said, "Ryan is the owner of dat ass. And even if he is sometimes the star of the stage show Douchetacular Douchetacular, he at least looks like a masturbatory wet dream while doing so. I know *I've* masturbated to thoughts of him before. Why, just last week even, I had this extended fantasy involving Ryan, a jar of bubbles, and an original dance number choreographed by an elf midget. Can I say midget or is that racist? Little person? I don't even know anymore. You say one thing and someone's offended, you say something else and another person is offended. People should probably just calm the fuck down."

I was too busy thinking about dat ass to defend my one true love against Gary's weird barb, even if it was sort of true about Ryan being douchetacular. Granted, I was sure the same thing could be said about me, so I figured it was probably better that we were together so no one else had to be subjected to us.

We reached the entrance to the gym, a large stone room where the Knights of Verania worked out on a daily basis. I usually avoided this place, given that it stank of sweat and I had an aversion to doing anything that required me to stand in place for an hour and try to lift weights over my head. Ryan wanted to make working out together a thing we did, because it could *bring us closer together, Sam, just stop complaining and do it.* But after a disaster that somehow ended up with me strung up upside-down from the ceiling due to a combination of a jump rope, a twenty-five-pound free weight, and the laws of physics, he never made me go down there again. I found another way to bring us closer together by giving him a sloppy blow job whenever he got back from working out. He couldn't find a reason to complain when I was choking on his dick, so. Win-win.

I was an expert at conflict resolution.

It didn't mean, however, that I couldn't appreciate the results of his strict regimen that found him here once, if not twice daily. Ryan Foxheart took the role of Knight Commander very seriously, even if the knights under him constantly gave him shit. He was good at what he did, and I was proud of him. And of his abs. And chest. And arms. And thighs.

Especially his thighs.

The crowd that had gathered spilled out of the entrance to the gym, people buzzing excitedly as they tried to peer over one another to get a glimpse of whatever was happening inside. I tried to push my way through, but the crowd was too thick, and no one seemed to give a damn that I wanted to ogle Ryan just like they were.

"This is some bullshit right here," I said, giving every consideration to using my magic to knock everyone down. Morgan wouldn't be very happy with me, but given that he was probably in the front, I could take whatever shit he threw at me. I heard a group of women talking about how they wanted to just hold Ryan down and ride him like a show pony, to which I almost blurted out Ryan preferred to be the one doing the riding. But regardless of what else could be said about me, sometimes I *did* have a filter.

"I don't have *time* for this," Gary said. "There are *mens* waiting for me to objectify them with my invasive and salacious gaze. Tiggy! Charging sack of potatoes!"

"Wait!" I said. "*No* charging sack of—"

"There are *mens*," Tiggy rumbled before picking me up and throwing me over his shoulder. He growled loudly as he pushed his way forward, people scattering out of his way so they didn't get crushed. Gary pranced along in the wake, head high, tail swishing back and forth.

"Excuse us," he said. "Priority package coming through to stare at the other priority packages."

I glared at him as I hung over Tiggy's shoulder, but he just winked at me like the asshole he was. "I will have my revenge," I snarled at him.

"Squealed the sad, tiny little man," he said. "Honestly, Sam. I thought you were actively trying to work on your threats. That was pathetic, and I am ashamed to say I know you."

It only took seconds before we reached the front of the crowd, every-one pushing to dive out of the way from what appeared to be a rampaging half-giant. Tiggy looked rather proud of himself as he set me back down on the ground. He ruffled my hair and said, "You're welcome," and even though I could have easily found a way through without having to be carried, I still hugged him just a little so he knew he was appreciated.

And then Gary choked and said, "Hot motherfucking damn, that is some good shit right there."

So I turned around.

And immediately realized I was wearing the wrong kind of pants to be on the boner carriage to Holy Fuck Me Town.

"Sweet molasses," I managed to say.

Because even though I knew what we'd be walking into, it still didn't prepare me for the sight in front of us.

Ryan Foxheart and the Wolf of Bari Lavuta at the chin-up bars, yes. And they were certainly shirtless, oh yes. There were miles of skin on display as the muscles in their backs tensed and flexed. I had no idea how long they'd been at it, but their arms were bulging as they pulled themselves up again and again.

Ryan was the bigger of the two, bulky muscle and sheer strength. Ruv was wiry, less built, but matching Ryan pull-up for pull-up.

The Castle Guard stood around them cheering, egging them on, count-ing out some ridiculous number (*three twelve! three thirteen! three four-teen!*). Ryan's teeth were gritted together, and I *knew* that expression. That expression said he was tired and sore but he didn't give a shit, because he was going to kick Ruv's ass.

Ruv, for his part, kept his face blank, as if he were unaffected by any-thing around him. It was rather disconcerting to see how effortless it seemed for him, even if he was covered in a sheen of sweat.

"I've been to orgies that started just like this," Gary whispered in my ear.

"What! When have you been to orgies? How many? Where was *I*?"

Gary rolled his eyes. "Like, two times. No wait, like. Fourteen times. And I told you I was going to church so you wouldn't get suspicious."

"Wait, so that entire *year* when you told me that you needed religion like air, you were actually getting jizzed on by multiple parties?"

"Pretty much. I blasphemed all over the place. But I will say that my soul felt clean afterward."

"I still can't believe people think unicorns are pristine and virginish creatures," I muttered. "All the ones I know are *whores*."

"I thought you only knew me," Gary said, sounding confused.

"Exactly."

"Boom," Tiggy said.

"Damn right, holla at your boy," I said as he fist-bumped me.

"That made me quiver all over," Gary admitted. He pressed a wet, sucking kiss against my ear. "Proud of you."

The King was there, standing next to Morgan and Randall, all of them whispering and obviously conspiring together. As if they could all feel my gaze, they turned to look at me, stared for a moment, then went back to whispering heatedly.

Justin stood off to the side, looking slightly disgusted as he watched Ryan and Ruv. Since I was convinced that all he needed was love to bring out his inner sunshine, I immediately started plotting ways that he and Ruv could be alone, fall in love, bone, and live happily ever after. Two birds with one stone. The planning was still in its earliest stages (seeing as how I'd just starting thinking of it six seconds before), and I didn't want to get ahead of myself (they would get *married* and have *babies* and—), so I put it on the back burner to let it simmer. I would find Justin true love if it was the last thing I did.

Mom and Dad were there too, and Mom was fanning herself for reasons I didn't understand while my father looked grumpy standing next to her. "I think Mom is getting a little too warm with all these people in here," I said to Gary.

"Yes," Gary said. "That's exactly the reason."

"Where's Kevin? This seems like it'd be right up his alley. Shouldn't he be here making everyone feel extremely uncomfortable?"

"Chasing sheep," Gary said. "You know how it is."

"He just likes to hear them scream in terror even though he'll never eat them. He's very strange."

Gary sighed. "He says it helps him sleep better at night. You know. After getting unicorned."

I grimaced, completely done with that conversation. I still wasn't quite sure how things... fit... between them, but it was a topic of conversation I wasn't prepared to have.

I didn't see Vadoma, but that didn't mean she wasn't there. It just meant she was probably slinking around in the shadows trying to make my life even more miserable than she already had. It didn't seem possible that I'd only known her for a few days and had actually only been face to face with her for an hour, and she'd been able to cause this much of a fuckup.

However, the display in front of me wasn't too bad to look at.

And it really *was* only for Ryan. Ruv might be a cornerstone. And maybe my magic recognized him as one. But it didn't matter to me. After everything we'd been through, nothing was going to take Ryan away from me.

And so I ogled.

I ogled *hard*.

"I am going to wreck him so bad," I promised to everyone within hearing distance.

A lot of people heard me, apparently, if the way they took a few steps away from me meant anything. I rolled my eyes at them. "I didn't mean right *now*."

"I have earplugs," Tiggy said. "And toast."

"You'd better," Gary said. "If he's walking straight tomorrow, then you have failed at homosexuality and I will mock you mercilessly. You are being called upon for a great task. This is why you were made. It is your *destiny*."

I scowled at him. "That's not funny."

"Kind of funny," Tiggy said. "A lot funny."

"Fuck dragons," Gary said. "You've got a destiny of *dick* ahead of you."

And, really. As much as I wanted to punch him in the eye, I couldn't argue with that. I turned back toward them and watched as Ryan pulled himself up again. His arms were shaking and I knew he had to be getting tired, but I also knew he would push himself until he collapsed if it meant beating Ruv. I didn't know what thoughts were going through his head, what he felt he needed to prove. Like this stranger could ever mean anything to me the way he did. As if anyone could.

He must have felt a change in the room, a little twist of *something*. It was unnerving really, how quickly we could find each other in a crowd. Morgan said it was because of the bond between us, those little threads that held us together. I didn't know that I was certain I understood how a cornerstone worked exactly, but Morgan assured me that we were as we should be, and even I couldn't deny the way I'd felt more settled into my own skin. It'd only built over the last year until it was something tangible, something strong. Sure, we had our moments when I'm sure he wanted to strangle me and I wanted to hex him to the ends of the known world, but we always found our way back to each other. And I thought maybe we always would.

Even in the middle of a crowd.

Ryan glanced over in our direction, eyes finding me almost instantly.

I rolled my eyes at him, because I knew what he was trying to do.

He winked at me. And immediately redoubled his efforts to kick Ruv's ass. It really shouldn't have been as endearing as it was, the bastard. But now that he knew I was there, he wouldn't lose. Either that or he'd keep going until he passed out. "Men," I huffed.

"We are pretty stupid," Gary agreed.

Probably. But fuck a destiny of dragons. I had a destiny of dick ahead of me. I didn't need anything else. Especially from—

you think this but you have no idea what's coming

I stopped. Took a staggering step.

"Sam?" Gary asked. "Are you—"

i've seen what lies in the future

The crowd around me was cheering even as they began to slow down, like they were moving underwater. It was like we were in a *painting*, the colors dripping and wet, bleeding together as it *melted*. I took a great gasping breath and—

  i've seen the darkness that burns at the heart of the world

  —tried to focus, but my blood was rushing in my ears, and there was green and gold and it was mine (*not* mine), and I took another step toward the King, because I had to protect the King, I had to keep him safe, it's what I'd been taught, it was my *duty* to make sure—

  it calls for you sam of wilds it calls for you because it needs you

  —he was protected in case we were under attack. There was a sharp burst in my head, colors exploding like a kaleidoscope, and I'd never *felt* this before. Never felt this out of control, that my magic could spill forth at any moment and destroy everyone and everything in this castle, in this *city*, and it—

  i have come because the gods have shown me the truth of all things

  —couldn't be. It *couldn't* be. I didn't want this. I didn't *need* this. Things were *fine* the way they were, and *she* had come here, into *my* home to try and take this all away from me like it's—

  Vadoma Tshilaba whispered in my ear. She said, "The stars will fall from the sky and chaos will consume this world unless you accept what it is you are being called on to do."

  I opened my eyes.

  I stood in the gym in the bowels of Castle Lockes.

  Gary and Tiggy were to my right.

  Morgan, Randall, and the King were off to my left. My parents were too. And Justin.

  Ryan and Ruv were on the chin-up bars.

  The crowd still stood around me.

  But they were all frozen, stuck with smiles on their faces, shouting and jeering silently. The women were swooning. The men were laughing. But not a sound was made. Not a single movement occurred.

  I croaked out, "You've got my attention."

  "Do I?" Vadoma asked from somewhere behind me.

  I whirled around. All I could see were the faces of the crowd behind me, twisted and unmoving. There were shadows encroaching along the edges of the gym, crawling along the stone walls.

  "Because your attention is not what I need," she said, and it was like she was *above* me. I jerked my head up, but there was nothing there. "I need your cooperation."

  "Why are you doing this?" I asked, gathering the green and the gold, discarding the old words from my thoughts because I didn't *need* them. I'd shown that before. Magic didn't have to be recitation. It could be will alone. Vadoma thought she knew me.

  But she had no idea what I was capable of.

"Because you wouldn't listen any other way," she said from some-where in the crowd. They stood like flesh-covered statues, and I fought to keep from looking at those I loved. And then, like she could read my thoughts, "They are distractions, aren't they?"

"No," I said, taking a step into the crowd, ducking under an arm raised here, stepping over a leg raised there. "They can't be. Not ever."

"Oh, *chava*," she said, sounding disappointed. "There is much for you to learn."

"I'm not like you," I told her, stepping around Pete, my old friend Pete, a small smile stuck on his lifeless face. I shuddered as his shoulder brushed mine. "I don't just banish those I love because they don't follow the path I lay out in front of them."

"And yet here you are, hoping I would be banished for a path I've laid before you."

"I don't love you. I don't *know* you."

"I am your blood."

My skin itched. "There is so much more to this world than blood."

"*Chava*," she said. "There will not *be* a world. The things I will show you. What is to come. You will be *begging* me to lead you. Because the only way to keep them safe is to leave them all behind. They will burn in the fire of a thousand suns unless you accept your destiny."

There was a moment of tense silence, and then the world snapped back into place. The crowd erupted around me, cheering wildly. I spun in circles, trying to find Vadoma in the throngs of people. She was nowhere to be seen.

"Sam?" Gary called above the noise. "How the hell did you get all the way over there?"

The raucous jeering around me gave way to groans and sounds of con-fusion. I turned back toward the front to see Ryan had dropped from the bar, eyes wide as he pushed through the crowd toward me. "What happened?" he asked when he stood before me. He gripped my shoulders tightly, fingers digging in almost enough to hurt. "You're… I felt it. Something."

I smiled weakly at him. "Nothing," I said. "It was nothing. Just thought I heard… it was nothing."

He frowned like he didn't quite believe me. "Sam, are you—"

"And what was happening in here?" I asked, deflecting as best I could. "You look like you're showing our guest the assets of Verania."

"Um," he said, flustered enough that his grip on me loosened. "Would you believe me if I said I had no idea?"

I watched as a droplet of sweat trickled down his neck to the hair on his chest. "Not at all," I said, though I might have squeaked it out just a little bit. I kept reminding myself that pretty much everyone in the castle was star-ing at us right now, including my parents, so it probably wasn't a good idea for me to lick my boyfriend's chest, no matter how much I wanted to. Even if it was *right there*. With *nipples* and everything.

"You sure about that?" he said, moving close enough that I could *smell* his skin. That swagger was back, that infuriating, sexy-as-hell *swagger* that made me want to punch him in the nuts as much as suck on them. Vadoma's voice was echoing in the back of my mind, but this was *Ryan*. Not even her thinly veiled threats could wash the sight of him from me.

I glared at him, standing my ground as he tried to crowd me. "It looked to me like you trying to prove something you don't even need to worry about."

"Oh, I'm not worried."

"No?"

He shook his head. "I've got it on good authority that you're a sure thing."

I rolled my eyes at him. "Keep talking like that, Knight Commander, and you might find yourself with pull-ups as the only form of physical release you'll get for a long, long time."

He laughed at me openly. Gods, how I loved that sound so much. Because when I heard it, it wasn't from a dashing and immaculate Knight Commander with a chip on his shoulder, but a green-eyed boy who I wanted everything with. "You sure about that?" he asked again, but it was soft and playful.

"Oh my gods," Gary groaned from behind us. "Would you two just go *fuck* already? This is so godsdamned disturbing to watch. It's like you're face-fucking me with a dick made of sugar. Stop it. You stop it right now and go fornicate before the rest of us get sucked into your black hole of love."

I pulled away from Ryan to find everyone in the gym staring at us with varying looks of lust and disgust on their faces. I was pretty sure the elderly man next to me had an erection that he kept trying to touch me with.

"I like you," he whispered to me.

"Uhh," I said. "That's sweet. And also terrible. We're gonna go somewhere else that's not where you are."

Ryan grabbed my hand and started pulling me toward the exit. I heard his knights hooting and hollering after us. "Get some, Knight Commander!" one of them yelled. "You've got that shit!" He didn't even turn around but raised a fist in victory to acknowledge he'd heard.

Of course he tripped over his feet when my mother said, quite loudly, "Young man, no one has *gotten that shit*, because that shit is my *son*. Let me tell you a little bit about *respecting* your partner—"

I squeezed his hand as I laughed. I could see the blush on the back of his neck.

I stopped laughing when I saw Vadoma out of the corner of my eye, standing near the back of the crowd.

Soon, she said, mouthing the word.

It felt like things were starting to spiral.

Ryan glanced back at me. I smiled at him as best I could.

He believed me, though.

That's what was important.

IT STARTED IN THE EMPTY HALLWAY near the top of the stairs. I'd been trailing behind him the whole way, barely taking my eyes off his ass in front of me. He wore low-slung trousers, the tip-top crack of his ass visible with every step he took. The muscles in his back rippled, and he didn't let me go.

I almost crashed into his back when he came to a stop. "What are we—*mmgh*—"

His mouth was on mine as he pressed me up against the wall. Keeping in mind that sexy is as sexy does, I just sort of sagged against him as his tongue swiped over mine. He rolled his hips against me, a quick, practiced move that never failed to make my knees a little weak. His hands were on my hips, his sweat-slick chest bumping mine. He broke the kiss and trailed his lips along my jaw. I turned my head to give him better access to my neck.

"You know," I said, slightly strangled, "I'm totally on board with this plan, but maybe we could—" And then he did that one thing he did so well involving his teeth and my ear. I jerked my head back, smacking it against the wall. "Ow. Motherfucking *ow*."

He chuckled against my face, reaching up to put a big hand between my head and the wall. "You've got to be more careful," he chided gently.

"Yeah, well, maybe you shouldn't be so good at eating my ear."

"Eating your ear. Gods, Sam, way to make that sound erotic."

"I didn't know we were going for erotic. I can do that if you like. I've been practicing. Oh, side of beef, put your mouth hole back on my hearing hole and eat it out. That's the ticket."

He leaned back, face twisted up in a grimace. "Mouth hole?"

I shrugged. "My erotic writings are intended for a specific audience."

"A dead one?"

"Whoa," I said. "Look who's got jokes while I've got a boner. One of those things should stop. I'll give you a hint. It's not my boner."

He reached between us and gripped me tight. I refused to let my eyes flutter shut, only because having him this close, sharing breaths, was a heady thing. "I'm going to take care of this," he said, jerking me through my trousers once, then twice. "And you're going to take care of me. And then we're going to talk about how you're deflecting again and how I won't stand for it. Are we clear?"

Right then, I probably would have agreed to about anything. "Crystal," I managed to say.

"Good," he said before leaning in for a lingering kiss. "Now come on. You've got some work to do."

"Why does even *that* sound hot?" I mumbled, letting him pull me along again.

"You're twenty-one years old," he said, glancing back at me. "Everything makes you hot."

"Only *your* everything," I said. "Which apparently I need to remind you of before you try and do even more pull-ups. Because you're that ridiculous."

"Did more than him," he muttered under his breath. "And besides, I had to do *something* to get you out of our room that you locked me out of for two days."

And shit. I felt bad about that. Because Ryan had essentially moved in with me a few months ago, abandoning his small single room down in the barracks. It'd been strange at first having someone in my space all the time, but then he'd pointed out he hadn't actually spent a night in his own room in almost a month beforehand, and I got over whatever weirdness I had going on. "Yeah, about that. Um. I'm sorry? I didn't…. Shit." I stopped walking, pulling on his arm until he turned around and faced me. "That wasn't fair of me," I said when he looked at me. "I'm sorry. I shouldn't have— Did you do a shirtless pull-up contest *just* to get me out of the room?"

He grinned at me. "I've got brains *and* brawns. Felt like a good time to put them together. And since you're a Foxy Lady, I knew you wouldn't be able to resist."

I gaped at him. "That was… devious. In a completely sexual manner. I approve, Sir Foxheart. Well played."

The grin softened on his face. "Next time," he said, leaning forward and kissing me on the tip of my nose, "don't cut me out, okay? It's rough, Sam. I know it is. But you can't just push me away. We're a team. And it sucks when I don't know what you're thinking."

I absolutely did not get choked up at that. "Yeah. A team."

"For all I knew, you were trying to figure out ways to break up with me to run away with Ruv," he said, laughing. But his eyes darted away for a split second, and even though he *knew* that was a ridiculous thing to say, it was still coming from a place that held a kernel of truth for him.

But I chose to follow his lead. "Like I could ever do that," I said. "Dude, I've put so much work into you, you have no idea. The idea of starting over with someone else just sounds exhausting."

He made a face at that. "Good to know."

"Where did you sleep the last couple of days?"

"Down in the barracks with the boys. I told them it was for morale. They didn't believe me and were convinced you'd kicked me out because I'd pissed you off somehow. It was an uncomfortable time for everyone."

"Did they try and shave your eyebrows again?"

"They weren't even subtle about it."

I shrugged. "What can I say? They love me. If you ever leave me, they'll make your life a living hell."

He rolled his eyes even as he leaned forward to kiss me again. "All the incentive I'll ever need."

"Okay, so are we gonna sit here and continue talking about feelings and junk, or are we going to get to the boning? I have needs."

He leveled me with a flat look. "Boning, Sam? Really?"

I leaned forward and kissed his cheeks and nose and chin. "Sorry, baby. Are you going to let me make sweet, sweet love to your mouth and butt holes with my throbbing member?"

He laughed as he shoved my face away. "That's it. You are *not* allowed to dirty talk ever again. I have never been more turned off in my life."

But his eyes were darkening, the green going from spring to a summer storm. He was still sweaty, little goose bumps on his shoulders. I didn't move, just let my gaze crawl all over him, starting from his bare feet and moving *slowly* up. He swallowed with an audible click, flexing his hands at his sides.

"Here's what I think we should do," I said, taking a step toward him, closing the distance between us. My knees knocked against his. We were almost chest to chest. He was breathing a little heavier, gaze never leaving my face. "I think we should go back to our room." I leaned forward and kissed him softly. "And I think you should remove the rest of your clothes." I trailed my hands up his arms. His breath hitched in his chest. "And you can get yourself ready while I watch. And when you've gotten three fingers in you, I'll come take care of the rest. That sound all right?"

He nodded once, sharp and quick.

"Good," I said. "Go."

He went, glancing back at me to make sure I was following.

I did, because it's what he expected of me.

We learned this about us as we navigated our relationship. Out there in the real world, Knight Commander Ryan Foxheart was in charge. He carried the weight of his knights and the Crown on his shoulders. He did it well. People respected him. They feared him. They mocked him mercilessly for almost fucking up our relationship before it even started. He took all of it with a cocked eyebrow and regal stance. He was dashing and immaculate. He was of the people, by the people, for the people. Verania loved him. The women wanted to sleep with him. The men wanted to be him (and some wanted to sleep with him too). The children wanted to grow up to *be* him. He was everything anybody could ever want.

And that was all well and good. He didn't let it go to his head (well, not *too* much, anyway—he was still a cocky bastard, after all). He'd worked hard to get where he was, gave a up a lot to become a Knight Commander. And it'd almost doomed us, given the oaths he'd made.

But a funny thing happened after all that was said and done.

I learned that I, Sam of Wilds, was a sex god.

And that's meant to be as humble as possible. You see, Ryan was in charge in most things of his life. As the Knight Commander for the Eighth Battalion, he oversaw a hundred knights as part of the Castle Guard. He ran their training sessions. He was their teacher, their instructor, their therapist, their punching bag, their bro, their dude, the man. He was calm, assertive.

He was also a big fucking bottom who liked it when I took charge in the bedroom.

"Holy shit," I'd said after the fourth time we'd had sex (which turned out to be the day after he was an asshole and almost got married but waited until the last second to confess his undying love for me). "I'm a sex god."

"Oh my gods," he'd muttered. "That's not—"

"I'm so good at this. You *like* it when I tell you what to do, and I'm *so* good at that."

"It's good, yeah, but we have to—"

"And I'm just a natural at being in charge. Right? Like, you're all *grr rawr* swinging dick when you're with the knights, but in here, you're all, *take me up against the wall, you savage brute.*"

"That's *not* what I said—"

"Not that I have a problem with that," I'd assured him, just in case he was worried. "I'm finding that I rather enjoy being in charge. I was doing some research, and it's come to my attention that I'm probably a power top."

"*Research*? When the hell would you have had time to do *research*? We haven't even left the room!"

"Obviously the sex we just had counted as research."

"Obviously."

I'd turned over on my side to face him, reaching over to trace a finger over his eyebrows. He'd hummed a little and leaned into the touch, and I thought, *I can't believe this is mine, I can't believe I get to have this.* "It's okay, you know," I'd said lightly.

"What is?"

"That we do this here. You and me?"

He'd flushed, refusing to look at me. "It's not... I don't... I just." He'd bitten his bottom lip. "I just like it, is all," he'd finally said quietly. "I don't have to think. With you. I know it'll be okay. That you'll take care of me. I don't have to worry about anything else."

I'd grinned at him. "Ergo, sex god."

He'd rolled his eyes, but he'd also been fighting a smile, and that was pretty much my undoing. The fifth time had been spectacular.

And we'd refined it over the last year, turning it into something more. Sure, I was still a sex god and said sex was hot. But there was a familiarity to it now. I knew him as well as he knew me. I knew what made him tick, the little things he liked. I knew what it meant when his eyes glazed over as he panted below me. And he knew what it meant when I started trembling, how close I was. I had something that he never gave to anyone else, something to call my own, and I protected it at all costs. It wasn't something I even really talked about with Gary and Tiggy. For all the bluster, for all the shit I could talk, there were some things that needed to be protected.

I figured I'd given him enough time. I made my way to our room, the door cracked, candlelight flickering inside. I took a breath and pushed it open.

And promptly lost said breath like I'd been punched in the stomach.

Ryan Foxheart was on our bed on his back, trousers discarded and forgotten on the floor. His hand was shiny with oil as he jerked himself off, head rocking back. But it was his other hand that caught my attention. *That* hand was between his legs, moving slowly as he fingered himself, stretching himself open as he pressed his feet flat against the bed, pushing up to try and get a better angle. From where I stood, it looked like he was already two or three fingers deep. It normally took longer than that; I'd only been in the hall a few minutes or so. Ruv must have really gotten under his skin if he was this worked up.

I watched his toes curl into the comforter as he arched his back slightly, bowing up and off the bed. He groaned my name, long and drawn-out, and it was all I could do to keep from running over and pouncing on him. This was going to be fast and messy, and I wanted to let it build just a little bit more before I took him.

My magic was singing underneath my skin, rushing through my blood. The thousands of tiny little strands that connected us, the facets of the cornerstone we'd built so far, were thrumming. It was a heady thing. Not just the sight of him, even though that was enough to almost knock me off my feet. But the *threads* that built between us, the little offshoots of green and gold and blue that sparked off in the corner of my eyes, just out of reach. It made me feel more powerful than I'd ever felt before. Sex didn't always need to be a component for cornerstones; Morgan was proof of that. But it *was* for Ryan and me, and I had no problem with that whatsoever.

"You ready?" I asked him in a low voice as I locked the door behind me. His hips jerked a little at the sound of the lock clicking.

He shook his head frantically. "Not yet," he said hoarsely. "Can't reach. Can't get where I—"

"You're getting close, though. Aren't you?"

"Yeah." He jacked himself another time or two. "Yeah, Sam. I'm close."

"Can't have that, can we? Put your hands above your head."

He groaned in frustration but did as I asked, pulling his fingers out of his ass with an obscenely *wet* sound. He rested his hands against the headboard, biceps flexing, fingers shiny in the candlelight. His dick twitched against his stomach.

"That's real good," I said lightly. "Keep them there."

He turned toward the sound of my voice, eyes wide. I waited until his focus was on me before I stalked toward him slowly, first pulling my jerkin off. I might have been a born sex god, but even sex gods could be insecure. It had taken a while for me to feel comfortable under his scrutiny. He was chiseled out of stone by the gods. I was a stick that had fallen out of a tree. But Ryan didn't seem to mind, seemed to like it in fact. I didn't know what that said about him, but I wasn't going to complain.

I let the jerkin fall to the floor, and he made an abortive movement with his hands. He caught himself, though, and let out a long, slow breath, trying to maintain some semblance of control. It was a sight to behold, the Knight Commander of Castle Lockes all spread out and wanting in our bed. No one else got to see him like this. This was only for me.

I popped the button to my trousers, wondering how much longer I could string him along. I was already half hard and itching to close the distance between us. But sex gods couldn't show they were affected. Sex gods played it cool and collected and sexy.

"You're thinking about being a sex god again, aren't you?" he asked, voice rough.

I snapped my head back toward him. His eyes were a little clearer than they'd been just a moment before, and he had that fond and exasperated look on his face that I knew so well. His cock was still hard, and his arms were still above his head. His legs were drawn up, feet down on the mattress. He was exposed but comfortable. He trusted me.

So of course I lied. "No, I wasn't thinking about that at all. I was thinking about what I was going to do to you."

"Really," he said. "That's what you're going with."

"Do you want to be ravaged or not?"

"When you put it like that, I might need a moment to think about it."

"You're impossible," I said with a scowl.

"Sam," Ryan said. "I am naked in our bed waiting for you to screw me. I'm pretty sure we shouldn't be talking right now."

"What about dirty talking?"

"I don't want to know what you want me to do to your ear hole."

I shoved my trousers and underpants to the ground. "Sex god," I said.

"Yeah, yeah," he said. "Come on, sex god. Let's get this show on the road."

"Bossy fucking bottom," I grumbled as I kicked my feet out of my trousers.

"Sam," he said, and he sounded a little desperate again. "Come over here and *screw me*."

When Knight Commander Ryan Foxheart makes such a demand, one does not hesitate. And no, I didn't trip and almost fall into the bed, no matter what anyone said. And if Ryan *did* say anything like that, he was a fucking liar and I would spank the shit out of him later.

He was laughing by the time I pulled myself on top of him, his arms still above his head. He spread his legs a little more, just enough to make room for me to lie on top of him. His eyes fluttered shut as I pressed my weight against him, cock to cock, chest to chest. I reached up and grabbed both of his wrists with one hand, holding him in place, and his breaths came in short little bursts. We were under no illusions that I could hold him in place; if he wanted to get up from under me, he would. But he *didn't*, and that was key. He *wanted* to be held down, *wanted* to feel like someone else was in control. He'd told me this in fumbling fits and starts, blushing terribly as he looked down at his hands. "We don't have to do it," he'd mumbled. "I'm just happy I get to have you at all."

And what the hell was I supposed to do in the face of *that*?

Everything I could, obviously.

And it just so happened our kinks lined up for the most part, no matter how vanilla they were. We weren't Gary and Kevin (oh my *gods* how we weren't Gary and Kevin), but we did okay.

And there was the fact that I would have given Ryan just about anything he could ask for. I could admit to still being a little starry-eyed when the thought crossed my mind that, out of everyone in the world, he wanted *me* the most, enough to break an oath he made in the name of his mother.

I kissed him, and he made this little noise in the back of his throat, soft and wounded, pressing his hands up against mine, testing how far I'd let him go. I tightened my grip as I controlled the kiss, grinding my hips down against his, letting the slick friction from the oil on his dick rub against my own. He gasped into my mouth, and I swallowed it down, my tongue against his.

I pulled away, watching as he lifted his head, trying to chase the kiss. He frowned when he couldn't get very far, pupils dilated until there was only the faintest ring of green. "Come on, Sam, please," he said. "Come on."

"Not yet," I said, pushing my hips forward again. "You can hold on for just a little bit longer, can't you?"

He shook his head back and forth.

"I think you can," I said, squeezing his wrists tighter, the way I knew he liked.

He tried to buck his hips up, but I pushed them back again, his dick sliding against my stomach as I rolled myself down again.

"I'm ready," he panted. "I promise. I'm ready."

I leaned forward and brushed my lips against his. I kissed my way down his jaw to his neck. He turned his head to allow me better access. I sucked on the skin near his collarbone, just low enough that I knew any mark would be hidden by his uniform. That was a lesson learned the first time we started this thing between us. Not only was it unprofessional (which Morgan scolded me for while the King just laughed at me), but Ryan's knights weren't exactly a subtle bunch, and they gave him as much crap as they possibly could.

He was begging me for more, begging me to fuck him, to just *fuck him godsdammit*, and I knew he'd reached his breaking point. The lovely flush had crawled down his neck to his chest and stomach, skin overheating as he tried to wriggle against the friction.

"Just fucking get on with it," he snarled at me, teeth bared. "Just fucking do it if you're going to do it, gods."

And oh. *Oh.* That's how it was going to be. He was goading me, and he knew I knew, but I was too far gone to care. It gave me something back, lording over him like this, making him squirm until he was pleading for me to fuck him. I don't know why, and I certainly hadn't expected anything between us to bloom like this.

But it did, and he was provoking me.

There was green and gold, and my magic said, *mineminemine*. He let out a happy groan when I dropped my grip on his wrists and flipped him over. He went willingly, knowing what he'd been working me toward. I knocked his legs apart with my knees while he pulled himself up on all fours, resting his weight on his elbows, face pressed to the side against the pillow.

He jerked his head forward when I breached him with my fingers, two, then three, working them in and out of his hole. "I'm good," he chanted. "I'm good, Sam, I'm *good*," and I slapped his ass, just once, in warning and he stopped. He breathed into the pillow, letting me do what I wanted.

There was a fourth finger, but it only lasted a moment before he growled at me to get on with it. I pulled my hand out and lined myself up, pushing down on his back, causing his chest to hit the bed and his hips to cant up toward me. The muscles in his back twitched as I pushed my cock into him. He sighed and closed his eyes, pushing his hips back toward me slowly until I was pressed flush against him. I waited a beat, and then another one. And another. Then he nodded, just once, a barely there thing as he breathed through his nose. I brought my hips back out and in again, fucking into him as I held him down.

It didn't take long for him to start those little sounds again, those little noises of grunts and *please* and *more, I can take more*. He gasped, eyes flying open, as I angled my hips differently.

"I bet he can hear you," I said through gritted teeth. "Ruv. You think he can hear you? I bet he can. Groaning like that. Saying my name. Acting like my *cornerstone*."

Ryan growled low in his throat, probably a little pissed that I would even *say* that name while we were fucking. He pushed himself up onto his hands and bowed his back, meeting me thrust for thrust. I slowed down my own movements, letting him fuck himself on my dick. I ran my hand up his back until I reached his hair, curling my fingers into it, getting a good solid grip. I pulled, arching his back even further and fucked into him again. The muscles in his arm bulged as he dug his fingers into the blankets.

I felt a little drunk, a side effect of the magic and the bond between us. It always hit hard in moments like this, making me feel detached and floating but like I was still tethered to him. His grunts were becoming louder, careening us both toward the end. I tugged on his hair sharply, and he pushed himself up until his back was flush against my chest. The angle was awkward, the mattress too soft to allow me to do anything but thrust shallowly.

But it was enough. As soon as my hand was around his dick, still sticky with oil, I only had to fuck into him two or three more times before he was coming over my hand, a strangled moan falling from his mouth. His ass squeezed around my cock, and I pushed up into him as deep as I could, sank my teeth into the meat of his shoulder, and shot off inside him.

All that green. All that gold.

How it sang.

I CLEANED HIM UP AS BEST I could, knowing he'd be sore and sticky still in the morning. He didn't seem to care, a blissed-out look on his face as I stripped the comforter off the bed and threw it to the floor. The fireplace kept away the worst of the chill, but one learned to ignore the cold when living in a castle. The drafts were always there, even during the summer. When the snows came in winter around All Hallowed Day, the fires never went out.

I pulled the blankets up and over us, tucking into his side. His leg came up and over mine, arm around me pulling me close. I rested my head on his shoulder, face pressed against his neck. I was drawing circles on his chest, and I felt his heart beating underneath my touch. I loved that heart, almost more than anything else in the world. It was important to me.

I said, "You know you have nothing to worry about, right?"

"There are always things to worry about," he said quietly.

"Maybe. But not this."

"This?"

He hissed when I pinched his nipple. "Knock it off. You know what I'm talking about."

"I'm not worried," he said, pulling me just a little bit tighter against him.

He was lying, and we both knew it. "Sure," I said. "Because you normally have middle-of-the-day shirtless pull-up contests that draw large crowds and end up in hardcore gay sex."

I didn't even need to look up to know he had a smug smile on his face. "Didn't seem like you had much to complain about there."

I rolled my eyes. "You're stupid sometimes."

"Probably," he agreed. "But I beat him, didn't I?"

"Did you?" I asked innocently. "From where I stood, you stopped right in the middle of it."

"Only because you were— Speaking of that."

Well, fuck. That was something I had been hoping to avoid. Maybe if I pretended I wasn't there, he wouldn't push it. "Gosh, I'm sore. Are you sore? I am a sex god, after all—"

"You're deflecting. Again."

Bastard. "I have no idea what you're talking about."

He shook me a little, jostling me at his side. "Sam. I know something was wrong. We don't keep things from each other. Ever."

"Lies. I have secrets. I'm a wizard. I'm *supposed* to be secretive."

"Sam, the one time you tried to keep a wizarding secret from me, you told me that you had a secret and couldn't tell me, and then told me anyway two minutes later."

"Secrets are hard. You don't even know."

"Sam."

I sighed, knowing he wasn't going to let this go. "Vadoma," I admitted. "She's getting in my head."

He tensed. "What? What did she say? Was it about Ruv again? God, I hate that guy. You just have to ignore her, Sam, I mean she's gotta be—"

"No, I mean she is *literally* getting in my head. Like, we were standing there, and then everyone was frozen except for me and her. I don't know what was real and what wasn't, if this was a mind game or if she actually froze everyone in that room."

"Oh," Ryan said.

"Yeah. Oh."

"How can she do that? I thought her magic wasn't supposed to be that great."

Good question. "I have no idea. It felt... I don't know. Fake, somehow. Like it wasn't real."

He pushed me off him gently, laying my head on my pillow so he could turn on his side and face me. Our foreheads were almost touching, and I could feel his breath on my face. He reached up and traced his thumb across my bottom lip. "You know I'd never let anything happen to you, right? You're a sex god, after all."

And I tried. I really did. I tried to hold in my laughter because I *was* scared. I *was* worried. But when faced with the earnestness of Ryan Foxheart trying to get a smile on my face, I was helpless. I burst out laughing and didn't miss the way he looked pleased with himself.

"So dumb," I said. "It's true, but you're dumb."

"Probably," he agreed. "But you wouldn't have it any other way."

"Nah," I said. "I wouldn't."

"We'll figure it out, okay?" he said. "I promise. We'll figure out what this is, this destiny or whatever. And I'll be with you every step of the way."

"I really hate that word."

"I know. But if you think about it, who else is going to have one beside you? Isn't that the sort of thing that happens to us? I'd say it's something we should have expected."

Us. Not *happens to you. Us.* Like there was no question that we were a team. "Why?" I asked, suddenly curious.

"Why what?"

"Why are you with me? After all this bullshit, after everything we've been through, why are you still here?"

He rolled his eyes. "Are you serious? Are you that stupid?"

"There's the romance I needed. My gods, the heart boner I've got is throbbing like you don't even know. Put your mouth hole on me and let me feel your insides."

He flicked the tip of my nose. I squawked and batted his hand away because I *hated* when people did that.

"You know why."

"I do?"

"Remember? Atop the tower?"

"The dragon's keep."

"Yeah. You and me."

"All those stars."

"I only saw you."

"Sap," I said, even though it made me feel warm. "Probably because you were breaking my heart."

"Yeah," he said. "Mine too. But do you remember what I said?"

But you have to believe me that it's always been you. I promise. I promise. I promise, because when I look upon these stars, there is nothing I wish for more than you.

"I remember," I said. As if I could ever forget. As if those words weren't etched upon my very soul. "That was... smooth. In retrospect. At the time, I thought you were an asshole, but now? Way to go."

He chuckled. "I *am* pretty good."

"Mostly."

He sobered when he said, "I meant it, Sam. Every word. It's always been you for me. I loved you even before I knew what it meant. That's why."

"Yeah?"

"Yeah."

"Me too."

"Good. Also, I feel it should be said that I will still stab Ruv if he so much as looks at you funny. That's not jealousy. It's practicality. And I just don't like his face."

"Eh," I said. "I'll allow it."

He leaned in and kissed me, slow and sweet as molasses. And I took everything he was giving me and gave back as much as I could. Because that's what we did for each other. He might have been my cornerstone, but I wanted to be the same for him, even if he didn't have the magic I did.

"It's going to be all right, you know?" he said. "You'll see. Everything is going to be just fine. I promise."

And I believed him.

CHAPTER 8
Getting Bad-Touched by Grandma

"So," RANDALL SAID. "YOU DECIDED TO stop being a chickenshit and face your destiny like a real man?"

I looked at Ryan. "Is it too late to go back into our sex den?"

He made a face at me. "Yes, because you called it a sex den."

"That's what it is," I muttered.

It was the next day after the shirtless pull-up contest, and Ryan had forced me out of the room, with no amount of promises of unlimited blowjays dissuading him from dragging me back out into the real world to face all the problems I would rather ignore. He had training to go to, and I had people to studiously avoid while I made my way down to the labs.

The problem with that was Randall loitering outside of the throne room. He had feigned surprise at running into us ("Oh, well, isn't *this* positively fortuitous!"), which led me to believe he'd been *waiting* for us, like some old crazed stalker wanting to drag us to his basement where he'd dug a hole to keep us in. Knowing Randall, that wasn't probably too far from the truth. I was convinced that one day, we would either finally understand each other or one of us would murder the other. I was leaning toward the murder side.

"Both of you need to follow me," Randall said.

"That's ominous," Ryan said. "Please don't hex me."

"He's going to put us in his hole," I hissed at Ryan.

"He's going to put us *where*?"

"No, not like that. Gross! Get your mind of the gutter."

"I wasn't even thinking about that until you said it!"

"Oh, so now you're blaming *me* for your depraved mind? I'll have you know I was *innocent* until I met you!"

"You're friends with Gary," Ryan said. "There's nothing innocent about you."

"Rude," I said. "Also the truth. I'll allow it."

"Please," Randall said. "Continue to waste my time. This will only better my mood."

"Sorry, Randall," Ryan said, bowing low. "I know your time is valuable."

"I know your time is valuable," I mocked under my breath.

"At least *one* of you respects me enough to say so," Randall said. "Thank you, Knight Commander."

"I'm sorry," I said. "I must have not gotten the invitation to the Randall and Ryan Mutual Jerkoff Society."

Ryan stared at me, horrified.

Randall's ancient liver lips twitched briefly.

"He's not going to hex you," I told Ryan. "He would have to face my wrath."

"Wailed the tiny, insignificant speck of dust," Randall said.

"Please forgive Sam," Ryan said. "He's had a… troubling couple of days."

"Really," Randall said. "And how do you explain everything else?"

"Um," Ryan said. "He's had a… troubling life?"

"I really have," I said. "Though, I blame a lot of other people rather than myself. It's easier that way."

"As enlightening as this has been," Randall said, "and it truly has been in ways I did not anticipate, we have places to be."

"See?" Ryan whispered to me. "Ominous."

I was in complete agreement. "And where are we going?"

"Why," Randall said, "to face your destiny, of course."

"You're doing that on purpose," I accused.

"Probably," Randall said. "But then, I've never met someone with a destiny before. Gods only know what this is going to do to your ego. I shiver at such a thought."

"And I have to go too?" Ryan asked nervously. "Surely Sam will be just fine on his own."

"Traitor!" I gasped, outraged. "Thrown me to the wolves already? What happened to all the promises of love and fealty after I fucked your butt?"

"Randall scares me," Ryan said.

"This makes me happy," Randall said.

"I also have knights to train. It's Wednesday. On Wednesdays, we attach seventy-five-pound packs to our backs and run around an obstacle course in full armor. It's actually a lot of fun. It boosts morale when we make it a contest."

"Right," I said. "Ryan has to go do that thing that just sounds terrible, and I'm sure Morgan needs me to work on my Grimoire in silence without anyone else around talking about things like fate and destiny and blah, blah, blah."

"Pete's overseeing the knights," Randall said. "And Morgan's waiting for us."

"Oh," Ryan said. "Crap. Okay, but. Why do *I* have to go?"

"You're Sam's cornerstone, are you not?" Randall asked. "Though, I suppose if you're too busy, we can always ask Ruv to stand in on your behalf. I'm sure he and Sam won't gaze into each other's eyes at all."

I couldn't help but be impressed at Randall's blatant manipulation of the bastard standing next to me. It was really rather devious, and he knew *exactly* what buttons to press.

"Ruv's going to be there?" Ryan growled.

"Absolutely," Randall said. "Probably wearing less than he did yesterday too. You know, when he won the pull-up contest."

"He didn't *win*—"

"I hope you realize you can't control me that easily," I told Randall. "I will never fall for your schemes."

"I'm the only person standing in the way of you becoming a full-fledged wizard," Randall said.

"Yep," I said. "Do you want us to follow you now or...?"

AND OF COURSE VADOMA WAS WAITING for us in the labs. Because that's how my life worked. She barely even looked up at me as we passed through the door. Randall shut it behind us and clicked the lock, an action wholly unnecessary but probably done on purpose to make the situation that much more awkward.

And it didn't make the situation any easier to see Ruv standing at her side. He wore a pair of loose-fitting pants cinched at the waist and a vest open at the chest with no shirt underneath.

"Doesn't he own full sets of clothing?" Ryan muttered. "No one wants to see any of that."

Far be it from me to argue with him, even if Ruv was of an attractive sort. I felt that old familiar tug at the sight of him, my magic recognizing him as the potential for something more. But it was muted, distant in comparison with the man standing next to me. It felt almost like an afterthought, the pang of something that could have been and nothing more.

Morgan stood at the opposite end of the labs, looking as tired as I'd ever seen him. Vadoma was standing at his side, hunched over the counter, flipping through—

"Hey!" I snapped, rushing forward. "What the hell do you think you're doing? That's *my* Grimoire!"

She didn't even try and stop me as I pulled it away from her, slammed it closed, and cradled it against my chest. It wasn't that I was *ashamed* about anything in there, but it was *private*. A wizard's Grimoire was his legacy to the world, all his accomplishments and triumphs and mistakes written down into one tome for future generations to study when the time came. That didn't mean I wanted anyone to read it *now*, especially since I tended to be a bit... descriptive about certain... things.

"That's not a Grimoire, *chava*," she said, sounding disgusted. "That is your diary. You write in pretty pink pen in your diary, little girl?"

"I told you," Morgan said, an edge to his voice. "Every Grimoire is different. And it's nothing you would understand, seeing as how you're not a wizard. Sam is young, and his Grimoire reflects that. But it is still his. Not yours."

It was almost enough to make me forgive him for being a liar and keeping shit from me for years. Close, but not quite.

"I'm not a wizard," she agreed. "But I've known these books. I know what they hold. *That* is not the book of a man with a calling. That is the meanderings of a child."

"I'm not a *child*."

"In a corner on one page, you wrote Mrs. Sam Foxheart," Vadoma said.

"Yes, well, I just wanted to see how it *sounded—*"

"Seven times."

"I had to practice my signature, obviously—"

"And surrounded it with hearts."

"It was romantic!"

"And then you did it on ten more pages."

"Yeah, I might have gotten a little carried away. I can admit that. I have a problem, okay? But I can *change*. I'm not addicted to it! I swear!"

"You hear that?" Ryan said to Ruv. "He wants to be my *wife*. Not yours. *Mine*. Ryan Foxheart for the win!" He stopped just short of fist-pumping when he started to frown. "Wait a minute. My *wife*?"

"I trust Sam," Morgan said, "to do what he's supposed to do. Yes, he is young. And yes, he is sometimes prone to distraction. But he is still my apprentice. And I will stand by him until the end of my days."

"Wow," I said. "That was pretty close to getting you off my shit list. Well played, Morgan. It almost was enough to make up for the fact that you've lied to me since you've known me."

"He can also be a vindictive little bastard," Randall said. "Turned my nose into a penis once, can you believe that? All because I had the temerity to criticize him the barest amounts."

I scowled at him. "You told me I was a waste of space and that Morgan would be better off with a doorknob as an apprentice."

"The barest amounts," Randall repeated.

"It's a work in progress," Morgan said to Vadoma. "And if you have as much experience as you claim, then you'll know that's how it goes. My own still isn't completed, and I doubt it ever will be. It's a living document, something that grows with every life experience."

"Not the same," Vadoma said, pointing a finger at Morgan. "You *know* this. The both of you do. He is not like you. He is not like the others. He is *different*. And your complacency will either end in his death or all of ours."

"That certainly sucked the fun out of the room," I muttered. "We can't possibly be related."

She narrowed her eyes at me. "I assure you we are. Even if I couldn't see the gypsy in your skin, I would know it from the magic that leaks from you with every step you take. The *dook* you have in your blood is not mine. I have sight. I see the shapes of things to come. Yours is *zor*. Strength. In the earth. In the heart. But you lack these things. The focus. You are careless. A *budjo*. A showman, not a shaman. But we are the same, regardless. You have come from Dika. And Dika comes from me. Which means *you* come from me. And I have known you for a long, long time."

"I still don't see what that has to do with—"

"What will you do?" Vadoma asked me. "When your cornerstone dies and you still walk amongst your people? Will you still believe the path you took was of the righteous?"

And that—

That was not okay.

That was *never* okay.

I took a step forward. "Are you threatening me or Ryan? Because if it was me, I could stand for that. I could *deal*... with that. But if you're threatening him, then we're about to have a fucking problem."

Her dark eyes flashed with something I didn't recognize. "You care for him," she said.

"More than anything."

"Because he's yours."

"And I'm his."

"For how long?"

I blinked. Because I didn't— "What do you mean?"

"Yes, *Vadoma*," Morgan said, sounding bitchier than I'd ever heard him before. It was really rather remarkable for a man of his age and stature to sound like he was ready to scratch a motherfucker's eyes out. "What exactly do you mean?"

She didn't even flinch. Steel balls, that one. I gave her a little more credit than I had at first. If Morgan had used that tone on me, I probably would have been running in the opposite direction.

"I have seen the stars," she said. "I have followed the bones where they've fallen. Unless Sam of Wilds gathers the dragons of Verania, the world will fall into darkness and all will be lost."

I laughed. "Get the fuck outta here."

She wasn't laughing.

Neither was anyone else. Even Ryan looked a little spooked.

"Guys," I tried. "Look. She's a *fortune*-teller. I don't care what she's known for. I don't care where she came from. I don't care who she is to me. She's an old kook, and this is bullshit. All of this is bullshit."

"What did he say to you?" she asked, cocking her head. "When you appeared before him?"

"Who?" I was so done with this shit. Maybe I could get the King to banish her from the City of Lockes and I could go back to living my life the way *I* wanted it to be. The way *I* wanted—

"The Great White," she said softly. "The Father of Dragons. The oldest in all of creation. He who created the world on his back. What did he say to you when you stood before him?"

I have awoken, O human child. In this forest deep, in the dark of the wild. And I have seen what is in your heart. Take heed of my warning: you are not ready.

"Nothing," I said. "He didn't say anything because it wasn't real. None of it was real. You tricked me. Somehow. Poisoned me. Made me hallucinate. I don't know what you're planning. I don't know why you're here. But it's not going to work. The dragon said nothing. He said nothing because it *wasn't real*. No one has seen the Great White in *centuries*. He's long dead. His bones are somewhere that will never be found."

"Not a word?"

I didn't look away. "Not a word."

"Morgan," she said.

"I've told you, Sam," Morgan said. "About the rumors. About a dark man rising."

"Have they been substantiated? By *anything*?"

"No," he said. "Nothing that can be considered concrete. But if there is a threat against the Crown, if there's the *smallest* chance that she's right, we owe it to Verania to investigate. Sam, we are the hands of the King, and sometimes the hand must make a fist even if the threat is hidden in shadow."

"So we're supposed to take her word on it?" I asked angrily. "This woman who banished my mother as if she was *nothing*? She took away *everything* because who she fell in love with didn't have the same skin color."

"Dika made her choice—"

"Only because you didn't give her anything else *to* choose!"

"Your ire comes quickly," Vadoma said. "Is this because you are frightened, or is this how you are? Does your fury flow through you at the slightest of provocations?"

"No," I said.

"No to which? *Chava*, we are governed by thousands of years of tradition. You may think it archaic. You may think it unfair. But this is the way it has *always* been. Just because she is my daughter did not give me the right to ignore what my ancestors had given me."

"She didn't need you," I said. "Look where she is. She's happy. She's healthy. She has a *family*. She is *loved*. If she had stayed with you, if she had forsaken my father, could she have said the same?"

"Her path split," Vadoma said simply. "Because she chose to follow her heart. Like yours. I have seen the path you are taking, Sam of Wilds. I have seen the possibilities that lie before you. He will come for you and take all that you hold dear."

A hand fell on my shoulder. I thought it'd be Ryan or Morgan, offering the smallest of comforts the way they did best. Imagine my surprise, then, when I glanced over and saw it was Randall. "Sam," he said. "We wouldn't ask you this if we didn't think it was important."

I swallowed back the sharp retort. "You haven't asked me anything yet."

"And I'm not going to," Vadoma said.

Randall's hand tightened on my shoulder.

The *phuro* began to smile. "I'm going to show you."

"ARE YOU SURE ABOUT THIS?" GARY asked me. "I mean, the last time you were mostly nude, covered in ancient symbols, and about to have weird powder blown in your face, you woke up after having been randomly adopted by cave trolls in the middle of the Dark Woods."

"Oh yeah," I said, wincing as Vadoma slathered more green paste on my back, muttering in an ancient tongue as she drew on my bare skin. The only thing keeping me from a public indecency charge was a thin cotton wrap around my hips, but even that almost wasn't enough. I was pretty sure if anyone looked hard enough, they'd be able to see my balls. "I'd forgotten about that. Sometimes I wish our adventures weren't so zany. Why can't we have *normal* adventures?"

"I can see your balls," Gary said, looking hard enough.

"Godsdammit," I said.

Gary looked away from my testicles like a true friend. "And we *do* have normal adventures. It's everyone else that's weird and boring and stupid. Also, don't use the word zany. It sounds stupid, and you should be ashamed of yourself."

"Last month we went to the Port," I reminded him. "And somehow found a magic mirror that wanted to imprison us forever in a realm where everything was some kind of opposite."

"It wasn't *that* bad."

"I was a butch lesbian! You were a heterosexual virgin pigeon. Tiggy was a *flower*. A *flower*, Gary."

"About that," Gary said. "I still haven't figured out how that was an opposite of what we already were."

"It was a talking mirror," I said. "It wasn't *supposed* to make sense."

"I mean, your opposite being a bull dyke makes sense, but the rest? Not so much."

"How does the opposite of me being a bull dyke make sense?"

Gary looked at me with a blank expression.

"You're insulting me, aren't you."

"Well I'm certainly not insulting bull dykes. I love them too much. They give me things like self-esteem and fancy woodwork."

"Hey," I snapped at Vadoma. "I don't care if I don't know you. You are still my grandmother. Get your hands out from my inner thigh. I swear to the gods. You don't need to draw symbols there, you pervert."

"I can still see your balls," Gary whispered.

"Today is terrible," I grumbled. "Absolutely terrible."

"He never shuts up, does he?" Randall asked Morgan.

"Not even when he's sleeping," Morgan said.

I glared over at them, using my hand to shield my eyes from the warm sunlight. We were outside in the middle of the fields to the east of the City of Lockes. We stood inside the fenced grounds that the knights used for training. The wooden dummies were anchored into the earth, slashed and chipped from repeated sword strikes.

Kevin was currently standing over by a rebuilt shed, laughing with Justin as they reenacted the time that Kevin had kidnapped the Prince and knocked me through the weapons' storage. I glared at the both of them as Kevin gave a whiny shriek I was sure was supposed to be me as he flailed backward toward the shed. Justin roared with laughter until they caught me watching them. Then they pointed at me and started all over again, because they were assholes and I hated the both of them.

Tiggy sat on the ground, my parents in his lap, petting each of them in turn as they lay against his chest. Mom looked a little tense, watching Vadoma as she moved around me, trying to cover my skin with the disgusting concoction that she wouldn't tell me the ingredients of. ("It's best if you don't know—I don't want to see a grown man cry. Again.")

The King stood with Morgan and Randall, all of them muttering to each other, probably telling more secrets that I would find out later and be super pissed about. I had decided as I was being dragged out of the city that I didn't like any of them anymore, especially when they wouldn't tell me what they were talking about. I didn't have time for maturity after hearing my grandmother tell me that she was going to need me to get mostly naked so she could rub me with her paste. It wasn't what I had expected anytime I had envisioned a family reunion. So I let the old farts mutter amongst each other, probably discussing destinies that I wanted nothing to do with, and that would probably end up with me getting killed or, at the very least, mildly aggravated.

Ryan, of course, stood near Ruv, who watched me passively, like he didn't have a care in the world. Ryan was posturing, because that's just who he was. He had his sword drawn and was hacking away at one of the dummies. There were unnecessary sword flourishes that looked like he was trying to twirl a baton, manly grunts that would not have been out of place at an all-male bordello, and posing so perfectly that the sun fell on the sweat on his exposed biceps, making him glisten as if he were being kissed by the gods. If it were anyone else, I would have thought it was slightly dashing and immaculate. But now that I knew him as well as I did, I thought something entirely different.

"My boyfriend's a douchebag," I said, sounding resigned. "He's hot, but still a douchebag."

"Pretty much," Gary said. "Mine's a dragon who we once tried to kill, and then he tongue-fucked my butt, and now we're married or something."

"You win," I said, because it was pointless to try and get one up on a unicorn.

"I usually do. Are you done getting bad-touched by your grandma?"

"That sentence vexes me," I said. "If I'm being honest."

"It should. I'm vexed, and I'm not being bad-touched, nor am I related to you. Though I suppose if there is inbreeding in your family history, it would make sense that you are the finished product of such."

"I would murder you if I wasn't almost covered in slime."

"Your balls are still hanging out."

"Yeah."

"I see you took my advice and started manscaping."

"Yeah."

"It looks nice."

"Thank you."

"I'm done," Vadoma said.

"Oh thank the gods," I said, taking a step away from her, trying to put as much distance between us as possible. "I'm pretty sure that I'm going to need therapy after this."

"Are you always this dramatic?" she asked me, wiping her hands with an embroidered towel.

"Mostly," Gary said. "That would be my doing."

"I still don't like you," Vadoma said.

"Ow," Gary said, dry as dust. "My heart. Whatever shall I do. If it makes you feel any better, I wouldn't put my smooth and youthful skin next to your craggy old face anyway."

"Unicorns," she growled. "Never has there been more useless creatures. Be gone with you, horse."

"Uh-oh," I said.

"Horse?" Gary snapped. "*Horse*? Oh, girl, you gone and done it *now*.

Watch this! Watch what's gonna happen! You watching? Are you *watching*?" He started prancing in place, working himself up into a fine glitter rage, jerking his head back and forth. "You see that pretty sparkle? That pretty sparkle is coming for *you*, you old bag. Gary's gonna bring the *pain* down on you like you wouldn't even *believe*."

"It's true," Vadoma insisted. "You are a horse with a horn. Oops. Not even that, are you?"

"*GAAAAAH!*" Gary screamed.

"Fear not, my love!" Kevin bellowed, the ground shaking beneath our feet as he barreled toward us. "For it is I, Kevin! And I shall save you from whatever it is that causes you pain!"

Ruv moved then, quicker than a human had any right to. One moment he was standing near Ryan, who continued beating the shit out of the wooden statue, and the next, he was in front of Vadoma, a long knife with a wicked curve pulled from *somewhere*. His teeth were bared, and he was crouched in front of Vadoma, shielding her. Her hand was on his shoulder, holding him in place.

Not to be outdone, Ryan ran over and tried to crowd in front of *me*, sword at the ready, as if he were expecting Ruv to attack at any moment.

So I smacked him on the back of the head.

"Ow," he said, glaring back at me.

"Stop it," I scolded him.

"Stop *what*?"

"You're trying to protect me."

"Well, *yeah*. This guy just pulled a *knife* on you!"

"And you don't think I can protect myself?"

"It's not *about* that. It's about making sure you're *safe*. I'm doing my job, Sam. And the sooner you remember that, the better off we'll both be."

I bristled at that. "I'm not—"

"Are they fighting?" Kevin whispered quite loudly.

"I think so," Gary whisper-shouted back. "Do you think we should tell them that now is not the time?"

"Why are we yelling quietly!" Tiggy yelled quietly.

I bit back whatever retort I had when Ryan took a deep breath. Because Gary was right, not that I would ever say that out loud to him ever. "Why don't we all just take a step back," I said, keeping my voice even. "In case you didn't notice, I'm mostly naked after being manhandled by my grandma. I would like today to be over so I can go get drunk and repress all the feelings I'm having right now."

There was a moment when I thought they wouldn't, that we were just going to square off right here and now, but then Vadoma squeezed Ruv's shoulder and he stood up slowly, bringing his knife down to his side.

It took Ryan just a beat longer to stand down, but he did. I noticed he didn't sheathe his sword, nor did he step away from me. I don't know where any of this was coming from, seeing as how we'd talked about him and me and how Ruv didn't mean a thing. Apparently I needed to bash it into his thick skull more than I already had.

I didn't have time for that now. The symbols she'd drawn on my skin were starting to buzz unpleasantly, not because of the paste itself, but deeper, underneath my skin. It felt like it was crawling inside of me, and I was practically vibrating because of it. It wasn't like any magic I'd ever felt before. Everything I'd known came from the earth. All those golds and greens were inherent in the air around me, in the ground beneath my feet.

This felt different. Cerebral. Like it was in my head, a thought that I couldn't shake. I wanted it off me as soon as possible.

I hadn't let her do this on a whim. She'd talked with Morgan and Randall first, explaining the runes she was to draw. I knew both of them had kept an eye on her while they whispered to each other, making sure she did exactly what she'd said. But I didn't know how much they knew of gypsy magic, though I had to trust their knowledge was far more extensive than my own.

"Are you okay?" Ryan asked.

I hadn't even realized I'd closed my eyes. I opened them, only to find Ryan standing in front of me, sword sheathed, a worried look on his face. I blinked at him, trying to clear my vision of the brighter colors that had begun to swirl around him.

"Whoa," I said. "That's fucking weird. You're so *colorful*."

His brow wrinkled. "Huh? Sam, your pupils are really blown out."

"Yeah," I said. "Sometimes I want to blow *you* out."

There was a choking sound right next to me. I turned and looked and saw what was possibly the most amazing creature in all of existence.

"Oh my gods," Gary said. "He's tripping *balls*."

"I'm not tripping balls," I said, wondering when my voice had gotten so deep. "*You're* tripping balls. I love you. You have no idea how much."

A gigantic head came into my vision, a nose almost pressed against mine. "Sam really high?" the gigantic head asked.

"Tiggy," I breathed. "Your very name is like a balm on my beleaguered soul. We should do a choreographed dance every time we enter a room so everyone will know how wonderful we are."

"I will remember this forever," Gary said. "I have been given no greater gift than this. Make him do funny shit so we can make fun of him forever! Sam, what do you think of Ryan?"

"His face," I said. "I like that shit." I bopped him on the nose.

"Yassss," Gary hissed.

"Enough," another voice said. I didn't like that voice at all. "We do not have much time. It has already started."

"Someone needs to take a chill pill," I said. "We're all just hanging out, man. You know? Just hanging out and chilling. My balls are cold, but it ain't no thing. Ryan likes them a lot. He puts them in his—"

Ryan slapped a hand over my mouth, and my eyes widened at the contrails it left behind, like his fingers were leaking every color possible. "That's probably enough of that."

"I love you so hard," I said, but it came out *mghmghshhgh*.

"I know," he said, eyes crinkling because he could understand me like no one else did.

"Step back," the voice I didn't like said. "We must hurry."

Ryan's hand tensed on my face before it dropped away. "You said this wouldn't hurt him."

"And it won't. Physically. But the longer we wait, the less of a chance I have to show him what he needs to see. Now step away."

"Ryan," another voice said. *That* voice I knew, even if I was a little mad at it right now. "I know you don't trust her. But you can trust me. I wouldn't let this happen if I thought it was going to harm him in any way."

Ryan didn't look very appeased at that. "And I'm supposed to believe you, Morgan? You've kept things from him all his life. What else haven't you told us? Told him? Do you know what it means to grow up in the slums? What it does to a person? You could have saved him. You could have *helped him.*"

"It's not as easy as you think."

"It's easier than you—"

"Knight Commander."

"My King."

"I give you my word. No harm will come to him."

And even then, Ryan hesitated. Then he bowed. "My King." It was said begrudgingly, as if it came at great expense. But before I could follow it, before I could chide the man I loved for being his usual self (and possibly fawn over him disgustingly for having my back as he did), I became distracted by these bright and shining threads that burst from my chest.

"Sweet molasses," I managed to say. "This is some fucked-up shit right here. I'm made of glowing *strings*."

"Yeah," Gary said. "Really fucking tripping balls. Everyone watch out for pirate ships."

The first strings were white and shining, thick and strong. There were a couple of them, and they curved through the air until they latched on to two different people.

My mother and father. There was a love to them, a bond that I didn't think could ever be broken.

The next set of strings was red and powerful. There was a sense of duty in them, of loyalty that came from responsibility. There was love in them too, but it was of a different sort. It latched on to the King and the Prince. The King's thread was like that of my parents in that I knew it would hold. The one with Justin was more tenuous, but I knew it would get stronger if we let it.

Randall's string was yellowed, like the pages in an old book. It was stiffer than the others, but it held.

Morgan's was a swirling green, and it came from just below my throat. It shook with magic that curled with my own, slow and familiar. It almost felt like my parents', but there were minute differences to it, differences that I couldn't quite parse out. For a moment, I thought I felt his sadness, his hurt over a perceived betrayal, but before I could follow it, it was gone.

Three more strings came forth, centered around my heart. They were blue, like the sky in the height of summer. Each one was firmly anchored within me, and they led to Gary and Tiggy and Kevin. It was friendship and brotherhood, the sense that I would die for these fools, if there was need for it. Gary's and Tiggy's were stronger than Kevin's, the years between us binding us together in ways it couldn't with the dragon. But the dragon's had something else mixed into it that no other string had, a shot of heterochromia, the colors shifting so quickly that I couldn't name a single one. It was at the core of his thread, and I felt it call to me, saying *here, here, here, this is why you are here, this is providence, this is the future.*

I didn't like that part very much.

Nor did I like the threads, weak as they were, that reached toward Vadoma and Ruv. Vadoma's was sickly in color, a pale orange that pulsed faintly. The thread to Ruv was a little stronger, a little healthier, though not by much, yellow like a muted sun. My magic reached for it tentatively but shied away before the connection could be made.

But it was the last thread that commanded my attention. It came from the center of my heart, bright gold and fibrous. I felt the pull of it, the way it tugged against the bonds in my chest. It had fastened itself securely in me, and even as I watched, little arcs of electricity shot through the thread like lightning in a storm. It crackled down the length of the thread until it reached Ryan Foxheart. My magic was not shy here. It didn't pull away. No, it *sang* as the runes on my skin burned, as the world began to melt around me, the colors all bleeding together.

And even though my mind was a blurry place, where specific thoughts eluded me, I knew one thing to be fact above all others: that if these were the threads that tied us together, then Ryan was the tether that held me earthbound. This was the cornerstone, the building block, and I marveled how bright it was.

"It's so much," I whispered in awe. "It's all so much, oh my gods, if you could only *see how much this is*—"

But everything else faded when Vadoma stepped in front of me, hand raised in front of her, palm up. Her eyes were dark and deep, and when she spoke, it came in crisp and clear, as if we were the only people left in the world.

She said, "I'm sorry for what it is I am about to show you."

Then she pursed her lips and exhaled sharply. Her breath hit a pile of lavender powder in the palm of her hand. It covered my face, and I inhaled in surprise, a low gasp. The granules hit my nose and mouth and tongue, and I was *breathing*, I was *breathing*, I was—

CHAPTER 9
The Vision

IT WAS NIGHT. THE STARS ABOVE were shining, brighter than I'd ever seen them before. I could see the Lightning-Struck Man. The Pegasus. Vhan's Fury. David's Dragon.

And it was this last that was the brightest of them all.

I knew the story that came with the constellation. How David had found the dragon as a hatchling. How he raised it as his own. How they leaned on each other. How they loved each other, inseparable for all their days.

And how David was taken from the dragon by death. It was said the dragon mourned so loudly that the stars trembled above until they changed into a dragon, permanently etched into the heavens to scour the skies for his lost friend.

Like most legends, there was a romantic notion to it. A bittersweet longing. Whether it was true or not, I didn't know. I'd never really considered it before.

Now? Now I could believe.

I could believe because the stars began to move.

The dragon began to move.

It was slow at first, as if awaking from a great slumber.

It stretched its wings, the tips brushing against Vhan's Fury, causing it to pulse.

The dragon began to move across the sky, and it—

It *fell*.

I cried out as the star dragon plummeted toward the earth, wings folded at its sides. At first it was just made of stars, but as it fell, lightning began to arc between them, outlining just how massive this dragon truly was. The dragon itself didn't make a sound as it hurtled downward, but the lightning snapped off it in loud *cracks*, burning the air around it.

It was coming straight for me.

I took a step back. And then another. But I couldn't run. I couldn't make myself look away.

Right before the dragon would have crashed into the earth, it spread its wings, catching an updraft that slowed its descent. The ground shook beneath my feet as it landed, its lightning claws digging into the forest floor and—

No. Not the forest.

Sand.

The trees were gone. The grass was gone. Beneath my feet lay red sand, heavy and thick. Sand dunes rose as high as mountains all around me. I was in a valley of sorts, alone with David's Dragon. There was a lone tree, bone-white and stunted, growing off to my left. The moon caused its shadow to stretch long across the desert floor, the branches reaching out like spindly fingers.

Then the dragon spoke.

"Sorceress," it said.

And that wasn't right. I wasn't a woman, I wasn't a—

"Dragon," I said in response, but it wasn't my own voice.

It was one only recently made known to me.

I wasn't Sam of Wilds.

I was Vadoma Tshilaba.

No. No, no no*nonono*—

"Why have you summoned me?" I asked, my accent thick on my tongue.

"I have felt it," the dragon rumbled. "Deep within the heart of this world. The blight. The cancer. It festers. He will come and consume everything he touches."

"Who?" I asked, and my voice trembled. Like I was *scared.*

"The dark one." The dragon crouched down until its chin almost rested on the ground. The sand swirled as its nostrils flared. "The burning man. A plague of locusts. Once he betrayed those that loved him more than life itself. He was exorcised from this world, trapped in a realm of shadows, as they could not find the strength within to end his life, even at the cost of their own souls. But a door will be cracked open, and he'll crawl from the depths to devour everything he sees."

"Why do I hear this?" I asked, my heart heavy in my chest. "Why have you chosen me?"

The star dragon shifted, raising its head toward the night sky above. I looked up, following its gaze. The stars were moving, dancing in the dark. They rushed toward each other, molding until they made the shape of a man and a woman. The man had his arm wrapped around the woman's shoulders.

His other hand was resting on her swollen belly, and they were *smiling*, they were *smiling*, and it was made of starlight, and I (*Sam* and *Vadoma* and *others?*) felt my throat thicken at the sight.

"A child will be born," the dragon said. "He will be yours by blood, birthed by those you have banished. He will be kind and brave. And foolish. Headstrong. His heart will be lightning-struck and marked as if scarred. There will be goodness in him, and a power unlike the world has ever seen." The man and woman made of stars suddenly exploded, flashing brightly. The dragon sighed as he looked back down at me. "If only he can control it. There will be temptation. The path to the light is always shadowed by the dark. But for none more so than him. It will whisper to him. And he must resist."

My hands were shaking. "My grandson?" I whispered.

"Yes," the star dragon said. "When the time comes, he will call upon my brethren five. He will allow their voices to be heard. The white. The fire. The two-snow." The dragon wrinkled its nose in disgust. "The… Kevin."

"The… Kevin?" I repeated.

The star dragon sighed, wings drooping. "It's best if you don't ask too many questions on that one."

"O… kay?"

"Trust me when I say it wasn't my idea to include him. Fate's a strange thing with a sense of humor most can't understand."

"But—"

The dragon reared back, wings spread wide. "The boy must be protected until the time comes when all will be revealed. He must gather my brethren five at his side. Then and only then will he be capable of fighting back the darkness."

"And who is this darkness?" I asked.

The dragon said, "One who is known."

I sighed. "Specifics?"

The star dragon shrugged. "It's a prophecy. It's *supposed* to be vague."

I frowned. "I do not like you. I do not like most magical creatures."

"Trust me. You weren't my first choice either. There was this nice man in a village to the north, but he accidentally turned himself into a ghoul and now spends his time eating rotting flesh. I could have gone to your daughter, but the magic in your blood skipped a generation. So here I am."

"I'm your last choice."

"Precisely."

"Useless," I said. "Just like the rest of your kin."

"Oh, so you've met many dragons, have you?"

"I don't need to have met many to know you're useless."

The dragon rolled its eyes. "I've done my job. I'm going back into the sky now. Try not to let the world die or anything. Oh, and find Morgan of Shadows. He'll watch over the boy until the time is right."

"Morgan of Shadows," I repeated.

"He'll know," the dragon said simply. "He's expecting this, even if he doesn't know it yet." And then with a great flap of its wings, it rose back into the sky. The lightning exploded, and the stars hurtled into the dark until they'd resumed their rightful place.

I took in a great gasping breath and—

I was back in the Dark Woods.

"What the fuck," I whispered, running my hands up and down myself. I was in my own body again, which was good, because I couldn't imagine spending the rest of my life as an elderly gypsy woman. I was in control again. I was—

Everything around me was charred black. The forest. The trees. The ground. Embers floated in front of me, burning orange, bright and hot. Every breath felt like I was choking, a vise grip around my throat. My eyes stung from the smoke and ash. I turned and—

I stood outside the gates of Meridian City.

It was on fire.

All of it. I could hear the screams of the boys and girls who worked the streets as their flesh was seared from their bones. There was a bright flash, and something exploded just inside the walls of the city. A tall guard tower began to lean dangerously until it tipped over, the stones breaking apart as it collapsed. A large plume of smoke erupted into the air and I ran for the gate and it was *surrounded* by Darks. They chanted words in the ancient tongue, saying *fie* and *clo* and *wei*, and there was fire and ice and wind, and it *tore* through the gates.

"Stop it!" I shouted at them, and they all turned to me—

I stood outside the City of Lockes.

It'd been leveled.

Only remnants stood, broken and stark against the bloodred sky.

I said, "This isn't real."

I said, "This can't be real."

I said, "*This can't be real.*"

"Oh," a voice said from behind me. "But it is. Or it will be."

I whirled around.

There stood a man. Hidden in shadow. I couldn't make out his features, as the air around him seemed to be blurred and distorted. He was as tall as me, shoulders broad and waist tapered, but beyond that, the only thing I could make out was the smile on his face, genial and inviting.

He made my skin crawl.

"Who are you?" I took a defensive stance, digging my feet into the earth.

"Who am I?" he echoed. "I've asked this question of myself for longer than even you could know. I am a wizard. I am a lover. I am a brother. I am *existing*." He took a step toward me. "This isn't real," he said, looking around, taking in the destruction behind me. I didn't dare turn. "I dream. Now. I'm dreaming. I know this because I've done it for so long. How have you called me here?" Another step forward. The shadows trailed along behind him, clinging to him. There were whispers in them too soft for me to understand, though I swore I heard my name. There was a *pull* toward him, something that hooked itself in my chest, wanting me to step forward, to find out all he knew. I pushed it away. It was harder than it should have been.

"I didn't," I said. "I don't even know you."

"Perhaps," the man said. "But you feel it, don't you?"

"No."

"Lies," he said. "We're connected, you and I. We dance. What is your name?"

I said nothing.

"I can see you," he said. "Barely. You're a boy. But you're hidden by the light. It's so bright. Tell me, why do you burn so brightly?"

"Why are you hidden in shadows?"

He laughed. "Of course that's how it is. A bit hackneyed, don't you think? A boy. Their futile hope. Me. Their inevitable future. The light and the dark. I mean, could you *possibly* get any more cliché?"

"Seems pretty on point to me," I said, and there was gold and green all around me, stronger than it'd been in a very long time. It reminded me of the time on the dirt road outside of the village of the corn. The Darks and their lightning flowing through me as it electrified my heart. I swore the hairs on my arms were standing on end.

"This isn't about heroes and villains," the dark man said. "No matter what your narrow little view thinks it to be. It's never going to be as black and white as that. No, I'm firmly planted in the gray. Moralistically, I could go either way, I suppose. It just depends upon how much you've pissed me off on any given day."

"Gods," I groaned, unable to help myself. "You're just like everyone else, aren't you?"

"How's that now?"

"You *monologue*. Like the rest of them. Gods, I am so *sick* of you people, it's ridiculous."

"What do you mean by *you* people?"

I rolled my eyes. "You. The Darks. Every fucking bad guy that's ever had so much as a *thought* come into their heads. You're all the same. If anything's clichéd here, it's you."

"Ah." The man sounded amused. "There's a difference between them and me."

"Really. And what would that be?"

The smile twisted into something dark and wicked. "When I make promises, I keep them. You see, I know who you are, Sam of Wilds. I know your story. I know the choices you've made. The people who love you. The people who despise you. I know your life and how you came to be. The boy from the slums, brought up because of the inherent magic within you. Why, it's a story for the ages. Who *wouldn't* want to be a part of it? To have it. To hold it. To destroy it. I promise you this, Sam. Stand in my way and I will take it *all* from you. I am coming, and there is *nothing* you can do to stop me."

He moved then, quicker than anyone I'd ever seen before. One moment, he was still ten feet away, and the next, he was crashing toward me, the shadows whipping around him in black tentacles as if they were a conscious being. Before I could move, before I could even *think*, his hand covered my face and *pushed*. But it wasn't physical. It was *cerebral*, and I felt him in my mind, crawling through everything, filtering through memories, discarding them left and right as he pushed *further*. There was some kind of loop connecting us, and the images I got in return were quick and painful. There was fire and blood. Death and destruction. I heard him scream from a realm of shadows where he was dragged into the dark again and again. They tore into him, manipulating his magic, twisting it darker than it'd ever been before.

Eventually, he began to like it.

Then he found him. Found *Ryan*. The idea of him. The memories. My feelings. All about Ryan. And he *latched* on to it, *took* it in his hand, and said, "Cornerstones. Of course it always comes back to cornerstones. And so young, you are, having already found yours. You're just a child. And so is he. I know his face now. He will be the first, I think."

And I said, "No. You can't have him, *you can't have him*—"

His grip tightened on my face. He leaned forward, his cheek brushing against mine. The shadows that surrounded him crawled along my skin. His lips were near my ear when he whispered, "He is your heart. And I will rip it still beating from your chest."

And then he was gone.

I gasped, whirling around.

The City of Lockes burned.

The dark man was gone.

But I wasn't alone.

Vadoma. Or an approximation of her. She was younger here, even more so than she'd been in the desert with the star dragon. She was vibrant and beautiful, looking so much like my mother that it knocked the breath from my chest. But where my mother's eyes were warm and kind, Vadoma's were hardened like steel. It was disconcerting, seeing that difference.

"Why are you doing this to me?" I asked her, voice shaking. "Who *are* you?"

"Your grandmother," she said, looking at the remains of the City of Lockes. "A gypsy. I have lived a long, long life, Sam. Longer than you could possibly imagine. I have seen things come to fruition that were shown to me in the shadows. There have been times the shadows have lied, that the light between the screaming stars showed a path that was eventually averted by a thousand possible choices. But this... *this*, Sam. All paths end in this. Unless you accept your destiny."

"I don't *have* a—"

"You *do*," she said. "For the dark man will not stop until he's seen this world burned beneath his feet. Haven't you ever wondered *why* you were given the magic you have? Why, out of everyone in the *world*, the gods chose you as they did?"

"No," I said. "Because I learned not to question the gifts I've been given. Because any day they could be taken away."

"*Dilo*," she said. "You foolish man. Life is about questions."

"Life is about *living*," I said.

"Which you will not do," she said, trapping me neatly. "Unless you accept your fate and face what is coming. You don't ask the questions you should because you're scared of the answers you will get. He has touched you. Can you feel it?"

I could. The warm heat of his hand on my skin. "Who is he?"

She shook her head. "I know not. Much is hidden from me. You heard the star dragon."

"Of course it's hidden," I said, irrationally angry. "Because that's the way it works. Is that all it is? Smoke and mirrors? Is he even *real*? Or is this just some twisted game to you, allowing you to fuck with my mind? I don't have *time* for this."

I turned to go somewhere, *anywhere* that wasn't near her. I'd only made it seven steps when she spoke again. And though her words were few, nothing else she could have said would have scared me more.

"He will die, Sam. The one you love."

I stopped, heart racing. The City of Lockes had been devastated by *something*. And she… she was playing this *game*.

I didn't want to say anything else to her. But of course I did.

"Who?" Though in my secret heart, I knew.

"I have seen it." And she sounded desperate now. "No matter what happens."

I turned slowly. "Are you threatening him?"

"No," she said, and in that, I thought she was being honest. "I have no need. Especially if it's the truth I see."

"You're lying."

"Not about this."

"You're *lying*."

"Your eyes are not open, Sam of Wilds."

I took a step toward her and—

I was in the throne room.

It still stood, the walls and ceiling intact.

On either side of me were the people of Verania, their heads bowed in supplication. They wept, the women wiping their eyes, the men blowing their noses. Even the knights along the walls had tears in their eyes.

And I stood in the middle, walking down the main aisle, the red carpet leading to the dais soft under my feet.

But instead of the King's throne on the dais, there was something else.

I said, "No."

And took a step.

And then another. And another.

The people of Verania stared at me with scorn as I passed, as if what awaited me had been my doing. I ignored them as best I could, wanting to prove Vadoma to be a liar. This wasn't possible; it wasn't anything she said it would be. This was all a dream, a trick of the mind, no matter what Randall and Morgan believed. She had tricked them somehow, but she wouldn't get to me. I swore she wouldn't.

The King stood on the dais, head bowed. Justin was next to him. Gary and Tiggy. Kevin was nowhere to be seen. My parents. Randall. Morgan, my mentor, the man I trusted maybe even more than the knight who'd taken my lightning-struck heart in his hands to make it his own. Morgan, who had such *sadness* on his face, such *despair*.

"Morgan?" I said as I got closer, voice breaking. "Please. *Please*."

And he looked away.

On the dais sat a large rectangular stone. Atop this stone lay a knight in full armor, sword clasped between his hands. His eyes were closed. His skin was pale. His lips looked almost clear. He was as beautiful in death as he was in life. My knight.

"No," I choked out, trembling hands reaching to touch, to wash away this nightmare. "This isn't real. *This isn't real*."

"It will be," Vadoma said, and for the first time, she sounded regretful. "The paths I have seen. They lead to this, Sam. You think him your cornerstone, and he will die."

"I won't allow it," I said, running a finger over his eyebrows. He was cool to the touch. "I won't let it happen."

"Death awaits us all," she said, not unkindly. "For some, sooner. How did you think this would end? You heard the dark man. He has promised to take from you. And he will. Some paths more than others. Yet in every single one I have followed, every single thread I have plucked, this is the one thing that cannot be avoided. Even if you defeat the dark."

My eyes burned. "I don't understand. How can Ryan still be taken from me if I destroy this darkness?"

"Randall," she said. "Morgan."

I looked up at them. They were already watching me passively, but they didn't speak.

"They outlived their cornerstones," she said. "As all wizards do."

"What?" I whispered.

The scene changed. The King was gone. My parents were gone. Randall was gone. Gary, Kevin, and Tiggy were there, looking almost as they did now, though they were a little thicker. Justin was there, and even though he'd aged into an old man, I still knew him. He was slim and still had his strength, but the lines around his eyes and mouth were pronounced. There were dark spots on the back of his hands. His hair was mostly white, thinning and held in place by the crown atop his head.

Morgan was there too but looked as if only twenty years had passed, not a lifetime.

Ryan, though.

Ryan had fallen to the ravages of time as Justin had. He was bone-thin, and his beautiful hair was gone. His skin was wrinkled and his hands gnarled as they held the sword to his chest. His armor didn't fit like it had when he was young, much larger than he was now. He looked almost like a child playing dress-up, skin pale in death.

And I caught my reflection in the shine of the armor.

I looked almost the same.

"No," I said. "No. No."

"It's inevitable," Vadoma said. "The passing. You are a wizard, Sam. Your life… is not your own. The magic in you. It will prolong your years until most everyone you love has passed through the veil and ascended to the beyond. Randall is almost seven centuries old. Morgan almost three. Their cornerstones. They… learned from them what they could. They loved them deep in their hearts. And then the time came in which they had to say goodbye. Because cornerstones are just a beginning, Sam. They build you toward becoming what you're supposed to be. And then you have to let them go. And when they don't have magic in their veins, when they're *ordinary*, you will lose them sooner."

I couldn't speak. I couldn't speak because I couldn't think of a single word to say. How this had never crossed my mind, I didn't know. It should have. The moment my magic said *finally* when Ryan stood at my side, I should have known. The moment Morgan even *told* me about cornerstones for the first time, I should have asked. How Randall had been able to say goodbye to Myrin. How Morgan had been able to say goodbye to Anya. I never knew the extent of their relationship with each other, but someone who meant that much to you, someone your magic recognized as a means of completion, their passing could not have been anything but devastating. But I'd never even thought of it, so wrapped up in having Ryan at my side, that I didn't think of the repercussions. Gary and Tiggy and Kevin were magic. They still lived and would most likely live beyond even the oldest of wizards. My parents weren't there because they were dead. The King was dead. Randall was most likely dead.

And Ryan? Ryan had died of old age. After a life lived.

"But…," Vadoma said, sounding regretful.

"But what?" I asked roughly, wiping my eyes. "You tell me a man is coming. That a star dragon predicted my birth and told you that I would face a rising darkness. That even *if* I defeat the dark man, even *if* I gather the dragons and *somehow* am able to stop the darkness, that in *all* possible endings, Ryan dies? But. *What.*"

"It is the price of the power you wield."

"Then maybe I don't *want* this godsdamned power!" I shouted at her. "Maybe I don't *want* any of this!" My voice echoed around the silent throne room.

"It's not about you, *chava*," she said. "It's about the greater good. There are more forces at work here, forces that care not about the love you think you carry for the Knight Commander."

"I don't *think*. I *know*."

"Do you?"

"You said *but*."

"I did. But I don't know if you'll hear me." She sounded regretful.

And I fell right into her hands. "I'm listening."

"Because you'll do anything for him."

"Yes."

"You care for him."

"Yes."

"Do you treasure him?"

"Yes."

"You would lay down your life for him."

"Yes." And then I knew what was coming, because we'd done this dance before.

"Would you let him go if it was for the greater good? If it meant he could live a life free from the pain of an early death? Free from the trappings and attachment that come with those that aren't purely mortal?"

And I hesitated. Of course I would. Because I was a wizard, and maybe I was more powerful than anyone else in the world, but I was still human. I was still covetous. Jealous. Prideful. What was mine was mine, and I wanted nothing else to touch it.

Vadoma came to stand before me, reaching up to cup my face. "You will lose him," she said quietly. "One day. Either by the hands of your enemies or by the passage of time. You will watch him fall when a sword pierces his flesh. Or when magic stops his heart. Or, and maybe the worst of all, you will watch him age while you do not. You will see the end coming and won't be able to do anything to stop it. The moment you chose to love him was the moment you chose to watch him die."

"No," I said hoarsely. "I refuse to believe it. I *refuse*."

She dropped her hands. "And that is your right, naïve though it may be, *chava*. But I speak only in truth. Morgan and Randall have hidden so many things from you, least of all this. But I can offer you something more. An... alternative. Something that may have your Knight Commander live to see another day."

"What?" I asked, hating the way hope bloomed in my chest.

"Ruv."

I stilled. "What about him?"

"He is the Wolf. The magic in him is latent, but it is there. His life, while not as long as yours, will be extended. It is the gypsy way. Your mother forsook it when she chose that... that *man* over her own people. She is my daughter, and I will love her until the end of my days and beyond, but I cannot follow her path. I can bring you home, Sam. Where you belong. With your family. Continue as you are and everything you love will crumble before you. At least with our people, you have a chance."

And, okay. You know what?

I'd had enough.

Fuck this bitch.

I narrowed my eyes at her. "You thought it'd be that easy, didn't you?"

She cocked her head. "That easy?"

"You thought I was what... young? Stupid? Naïve, I think you said." I took a step toward her. She stood her ground. "I have seen things in this life that defy logic. I have stretched the boundaries of my magic more than you can possibly imagine. I have *done* things in the name of the people I love and would do so again without regret. And even if the dark man comes for me, even *if* he tries to take from me, I will have my family at my side fighting with me, *for* me, every step of the way. And there is nothing you or Ruv or your *people* can say that would change my mind. Ryan Foxheart is my gods-damned cornerstone. I won't let anything happen to him. You say you've seen the paths I will walk? Fuck you. Because I'm about to blaze my own fucking path, and you won't even see me coming."

"Insolence," she breathed as the throne room began to crack around us. The runes on my skin began to itch and burn, but I didn't look away from her. "You would risk everything?"

"For them? For him?" I didn't even have to think about it. "Yes. Because they would do the same for me. We are better together than we ever will be apart. We are *bound* to each other. And nothing, *nothing*, will change that. Not you. Not the Dark. Not anything."

The roof cracked overhead as she said, "It would seem I have underestimated you."

I snorted. "No shit. Maybe next time, don't come in here pimping a half-naked guy when I already have someone's junk to play with. Not cool, Grandma. Not fucking cool."

She nodded. "I see that now," she said slowly, and her skin began to sag and wrinkle as she aged right in front of me. The walls were shaking. "I wish there could be another way."

"There doesn't need to be," I said, attempting a rakish grin that I didn't quite feel. "In case you didn't know, I'm Sam of Wilds. I can take whatever's coming our way."

"I hope you remember that," she said. "When the time comes."

The roof caved in and I—

CHAPTER 10
The We-Hate-Sam-A-Lots

I OPENED MY EYES.

Only to find myself lying on the ground, squinting up toward the sky. And since everyone I know couldn't be normal, I had Mom, Dad, Tiggy, Gary, the King, Justin, Randall, Morgan, Kevin, and Ryan all staring down at me with the same weird look on their faces.

"You're all a bunch of creepy-ass motherfuckers," I said. "Sorry, Mom."

"Your little towel thing fell off," Gary said. "During your stoned dream quest vision gypsy thing."

Gods, I felt like shit. Like we'd spent the night drinking apple wine and I didn't understand the meaning of the word *moderation*. "Oh?"

"Yeah." Gary nodded solemnly. "Your bits and bobs were just flopping all over the place."

"That sounds about right." I scrubbed my hand over my face. "So of course you all are staring down at me now."

"I just had to make sure your testicles were all right," Kevin rumbled. "Because I care."

I groaned as I pushed myself up, trying to breathe past the shooting pain in my head. The runes on my skin were dead, the magic depleted, but they still itched. I saw someone had had the decency to cover me up. Probably Ryan, as he tended to get uncomfortable if anyone else saw me naked. ("It's *weird*, Sam, you don't just *forget* to put on pants!" Uh, yeah, smartass, sometimes I did.) Ryan knelt beside me, running a hand up my back, a worried look on his face.

"I'm okay," I said, giving him a weak smile.

"Really," he said in that tone that meant *bullshit*.

"Well, reasonably okay. As okay as one can be when one has seen the destruction of Verania, a star dragon that predicted my birth, and a bad guy who denied he monologued, but then monologued anyway about how he was going to destroy me. Oh, and he might have been covered in shadows and then tried to mind suck me a little bit. Or something. I don't even know. I feel slightly vomity right now."

They all stared at me some more.

"Freaking weirdos," I mumbled, "with your staring and your faces."

Randall groaned. "Nothing is ever easy with you, is it?"

I glared up at him, squinting against the afternoon sun. "Oh yes, because it's *my* fault I got whammied by my grandma."

"Phrasing," Dad said, reaching down to grab my hand and pull me to my feet. I felt dizzy as I stood. Ryan had an arm firmly wrapped around my waist, supporting my weight against him as my knees felt like jelly.

"What did she do to you?" Ryan muttered in my ear, and for a moment, I had a flash of him both young and old, skin sallow, eyes closed, clutching his sword in his hands.

"Showed me her version of the truth," I said through gritted teeth. "Where is she?"

Mom tossed a glare over her shoulder before stepping aside. "She blew that powder in your face. And you started convulsing." She was angry. More so than I'd seen in a long time. "Then her eyes rolled back in her head and she collapsed when you did. You were both out for almost twenty minutes."

"We couldn't get her to let go of your hand," Dad said. "Not without hurting either one of you."

"I wanted to break her wrist," Mom said. "But your father wouldn't let me."

"So bloodthirsty," I said in awe.

"I wasn't trying to stop you," Dad said. "I was trying to get Ryan to give me his sword so I could chop off her hand."

"Such violence," I whispered. "Those are my *parents*."

"So we just tried to pry you apart, but it didn't work very well," Mom said.

I shook my head. "She needed it. To maintain connection. She was there too. She…. I was her. And she showed me things." I looked up, vision clearing slightly.

Vadoma was sitting on the ground, head in her hands, muttering something to Ruv, who crouched down next to her. Her tone was quick and clipped, but I couldn't make out anything she was saying, if she was even speaking Veranian. Ruv glanced back at us, gaze finding me almost instantly. His expression was blank, but it was enough to cause Ryan to harrumph and pull me tighter against him. I didn't complain because I was sure I was going to be awkwardly clingy toward him for a while yet while I parsed through what Vadoma had shown me.

"Is she all right?" I asked Ruv.

He hesitated, eyes searching mine, as if trying to gauge my sincerity. He must have found me worthy, because he said, "She'll be fine. It's draining on her to perform that level of magic. She is not a wizard like you. You draw from the earth. She draws from her blood."

"Have you seen what she showed me?"

He shook his head. "It was not for my eyes. It was meant for you."

"But she thinks you're a part of it," I said, and Ryan tensed beside me. "She thinks that you will be my cornerstone."

He shrugged, looking younger than he had before, more vulnerable. "We don't know what fate has in store for us. The paths are many, Sam of Wilds. Ours could converge."

"There is no path for you with him," Ryan said. "I'm sorry that you were misled, but you cannot have what doesn't belong to you."

"And does he belong to you, Knight Commander?" Ruv said, cocking his head like a bird. "Because in all our conversations, you've spoken of him like an object and not a man. Someone of his strength and caliber cannot be possessed like you seem so fond of doing."

"Oh, girl," Gary breathed. "Shit's about to get for real right now."

"My money on Knight Delicious Face," Tiggy said.

"You don't have any money, kitten," Gary said. "Remember? We were cruelly forced to invest it because Morgan said otherwise we'd be frivolous and buy things like brooms and scarves, which, in all fairness, is completely true."

"Aw." Tiggy crossed his arms over his chest and pouted. "I never get anything."

"Ask them if they'll get naked and cover themselves in oil before they fight," Kevin hissed. "It makes it more erotic—I mean, it makes it hard. Er. Harder to fight. Therefore making it even. And erotic."

"There's going to be no naked oil wrestling," I snapped. "And if there is, it's only going to be between Ryan and me. Ryan, hand me my trousers. I'd rather not be naked when I'm talking about you and me being naked."

Ryan sighed but did as I asked.

"Do you ever get the feeling like we know too much about our son?" Mom asked Dad.

"All the time," Dad replied. "We should also consider the oil wrestling for ourselves. You know. For reasons."

"Perhaps now is not the time for this discussion?" Morgan said, looking like he was about as done with today as I was. "Surely we can talk about getting oiled up back at the castle."

"Gross," I said, buttoning up my trousers. "I don't want to ever think about you oiled up."

"I really wish you'd stop saying oiled up," Randall said. "Why, back in *my* day, we wouldn't even *need—*"

"Nope," I said. "Nope, nope, nope. Not even gonna listen to that. Ryan! Babe! Stop glaring at Ruv and abscond with me to the castle so I can forget about all of this." Which, frankly, I knew was going to be impossible.

"There will be no absconding until we have a discussion," Morgan said. "This isn't something you can just ignore, Sam."

I snorted, feeling irrationally angry. "Oh, I'm well aware of that. Especially when the star dragon mentioned you specifically by name."

Both Randall and Morgan startled at that. "Come again?" Randall asked.

"The star dragon," I repeated slowly, as if they were both daft, "told Vadoma. To find *you*. And she did. And then *you* found me. And now, apparently, I'm supposed to gather the five dragons of Verania to take on some gigantic douchebag. Oh, Kevin, by the way. Good job. You're one of the five the star dragon mentioned. Don't let that go to your head." Which, honestly, I knew was already too late even as the words left my mouth.

"*Me?*" Kevin said, rearing up and sitting on his back legs. "The star dragon talked about *me*? A dragon made of stars came down from the heavens and started spouting prophecies about *me*?"

Gods, I really needed to learn to keep my mouth shut. "It's not just about *you—*"

"Why, this is so unex*pected*," he continued, ignoring me completely. "I mean, I always assumed I was destined for greatness, given that people make religions out of me and leave me human sacrifices that I won't eat because I respect all nature *like a good dragon should*. Aside from sheep, of course, because fuck those guys. Seriously. Floofy little cotton rats. That's all they are. I don't know *why* you humans insist on gathering them in flocks as you do, especially since it's so much more fun to chase after them and hear them scream."

"This is all your fault, you know," Gary said to me.

"I know," I muttered. "Also, shut up."

"But a *star dragon* came down from the night sky and said that *I*, Kevin, the fearsome Beast from the East would be the one to unite Verania under a banner of my epicness. It truly falls on my broad and muscular shoulders to save the kingdom and those I love from the clutches of tyranny."

"How much longer is this going to go on?" Ruv asked.

"Three hours," Tiggy said. "No. Wait. Seven days."

"If we're lucky," the King said.

"I was kidnapped by him for weeks," Justin said. "We're not that lucky."

"And after I have vanquished the evil back to the darkness from whence it came, there will be *parades* in my honor. People will come out and *cheer* for me. They'll say, 'Oh my gods, it's Kevin! He's so *handsome* and vascular, and I bet his penis is at least two feet long.' And then there will be so much *pie…*"

"Couldn't have kept that one to yourself for a little bit longer?" Ryan asked me.

"You know how my filter works."

"By that you mean not at all."

"You know me so well."

"…there will be songs sung in my honor, songs with verses extolling all my virtues." And since everything about my life was ridiculous, he actually started singing. "Kevin is the greatest thing! He deserves a gold ring! We should crown him and make him king! Let's listen to him siiiiiiing."

"You are all *dili*," a voice snapped suddenly. "Crazy."

We turned toward it.

Vadoma stood, eyes ablaze, hands curled into fists at her sides. There was an unmistakable aura of power emanating off her—not quite magic, but close. The air felt thick, and if she had been a Dark wizard, I would have assumed she was about to attack.

"Mark my words," she said, eyes on me. "You will sing *brigaki djilia* by the time this is over. The songs of sorrow. The *mulo* will come for you, Sam of Wilds. The spirits of the dead will haunt you when this is said and done. You will live only to die alone with just the memories of your failings to usher you through the veil."

"Yeah," Kevin said. "You seem like you'd be fun at parties."

"I like parties," Tiggy said.

"Vadoma," Morgan said. "I have given you leeway in this. I have bitten my tongue as you've done nothing but waggle yours. No longer. I frankly must insist that you back off before there are complications."

"There will be no backing off," she scoffed. "You are a wizard, but you are still a man. The stars have spoken for the gods, and Sam must answer to them. You can't hide him away any longer, Morgan. He is no longer a child. He's not yours."

"And he's not yours either," Mom snapped, taking a step forward. "After all this time, *daj*, you have no right to come here and make demands of him. We raised him. Myself. Joshua. Gary. Tiggy. *And* Morgan, who has done more for him than anyone else. You know nothing about him."

"I know his fears," Vadoma said. "I know his hopes. I have seen into the heart of him. I also know the lies he's been told. The secrets kept from him."

"I think it's time for you to take a step back," the King said. "Regardless of what your beliefs are, regardless of who you are and are not related to here, surely you can agree that I am still your King. And as your King, I am ordering you to shut your mouth."

"That might have given me an erection," Gary said to Tiggy.

"Power kink," Tiggy said.

"Like you wouldn't even believe," Gary agreed.

I expected Vadoma to defy even the King, but she didn't. I didn't think it mattered. The damage had already been done. It probably didn't help that I had to choke back my magic as best I could, because I *wanted* to launch it at her, wanted to call upon the earth to wrap her in stone, call upon the skies to rain lightning down upon her. Something, *anything* to get rid of that look on Ryan's face.

"Is that true?" Ryan asked quietly.

"I don't know," I admitted. "I'm learning that there's a lot I haven't been told."

"Oooh, someone's in trouble," Gary whispered.

"Is it me?" Tiggy asked. "I in trouble?"

"No, kitten. It's not you. You're too wonderful and could never do anything wrong and everyone loves you."

"Tiggy smash?"

"Possibly. I'll have to get back to you on that."

Tiggy glared at just about everyone after that, as if they were all capable of needing a smashing.

"Maybe Morgan or Randall can fill in the blanks," I said. "Since they're obviously so knowledgeable on the subject."

Randall and Morgan didn't react. They were good. They were very good.

But right before I was about to be better (and undoubtedly make them break and wail in pain at the power of my appropriately demoralizing comments), Dad said, "Huh. I don't think I've ever seen Pete run that fast unless there was gravy involved."

Which didn't really make much sense in the current conversation.

We all turned, and sure enough, you would have thought we were all made of gravy with how fast Pete was hauling ass toward us. It was a sight to see, those thick tree trunk legs hefting up and down, his sloping gut falling side to side.

"Well, that can't possibly be good," I said.

"He's going to give himself a heart attack," Justin said, crossing his arms. "Shouldn't he just retire already?"

"In his own time," the King said to his son. "He's just worried about getting bored."

"What is it?" Ryan asked me.

"I don't know," I said. "But there's got to be a reason."

It didn't take long for him to reach us. His face was bright red and slick with sweat. He took in great gasping breaths as he bent over, hands on his knees.

"There, there." Tiggy patted him roughly on the back. "There's no gravy here, tiny Pete."

"I don't... only run... for gravy," Pete gasped out.

"Mostly," the King said. "It's one of the things I love about you."

Pete glared at him, but it only lasted a second. His gaze darted around until it settled on me, as I feared it would. Whatever had caused him to rush out here had to do with me. As if today couldn't get any worse.

"Whatever it is, I didn't do it," I said, trying to be as preemptive as possible.

At least five people snorted at that. Which was okay, because that meant there were five fewer people I had to buy birthday presents for. Those assholes.

"There's... a gathering," Pete said. "In front of the castle gates."

"A gathering," the King repeated. "And what type of gathering had you running like you were on fire?"

Pete winced. "A protest."

Justin frowned. "A protest? What in the name of the gods could they be protesting? No new legislation has been announced, and the Crown's latest poll numbers have been higher than they have in years."

"Yes, um. See? About that." Pete swallowed. "They're not protesting the Crown."

"Out with it," Morgan said. "We don't have time for—"

"Sam," Pete blurted. "They're protesting Sam."

Everyone turned slowly to stare at me.

"Uh," I said. "What?"

"Oh snap," Gary said. "Does this latest twist signal the end of our adorable yet whiny hero? Will we finally get to the point of this prophecy? Will Vadoma finally tell me where she gets her hair done, because girl, I want to avoid that place like the plague? And will the most handsome unicorn in all the land get laid?"

"Yes," Kevin said. "Yes, he will."

"Find out coming up next on... *Castle Lockes*. Annnnd... we're clear. Hold up. Who are these bitches that think they can protest my babycakes? I will bring the *pain* down upon some motherfuckers, don't think I won't! Kevin! Hold me back. Hold me back!"

Kevin reached down and did just that.

"Godsdammit," I muttered.

I HAD DONE MANY STUPID THINGS in my life.

That was an indisputable fact.

(Even if I could say most times that I was coerced by my companions.)

I could own up to my mistakes. If I did something wrong, I could admit to it. And then I'd try and fix it to the best of my ability. Sometimes I could. Sometimes I made things worse. But my heart was always in the right place, and I never tried to let anyone else take the blame for something I did.

Not when it counted.

But for the life of me, I could not understand why dozens of people would be marching in a circle in front of Castle Lockes, all wearing coarse-looking shirts that had my face drawn on them with a bright red X slashed through it, carrying signs that said such fun things as: *SAM OF WILDS IS A HORRIBLE PERSON!* and *SAM OF WILDS PUNCHES BABIES* and *SAM TRIED TO TAKE MY VIRGINITY AGAINST MY WILL.*

"You tried to take *what*?" Ryan asked.

"I didn't!" I sputtered. "I don't even know who that is!"

And I really didn't. I didn't recognize any of them marching in the circle, shouting, "*Hey, hey, ho, ho, Sam of Wilds has got to go! Hey, hey, hi, hi, we would like to see him die!*"

"Well that's just rude," Mom said.

"And maybe a little uncalled-for," Dad said with a frown. "Unless he did punch babies and we didn't know about it. If that's the case, then I should be marching with them."

"I didn't punch any babies!"

"I can vouch for that," Gary said. "I have never seen Sam punch a baby."

"*Thank* you, Gary," I said.

"But," Gary said, "I'm not with him all the time, so for all I know, he's a secret serial baby puncher and I'm protecting a madman who commits unthinkable crimes."

"I will put my foot up your ass," I growled at him.

Gary's eyes went wide as he pranced beautifully behind Tiggy. "Everyone, watch out! His baby-punching rage is forthcoming. Hide your children! Keep them safe!"

"This is the greatest day ever," Justin said, looking rather pleased at the situation. I knew that, as my best friend, he would totally defend me, but as the Prince of Verania, he had to listen to his people and they came first. So of course he looked happy about this. He had to front, even though it was probably tearing him up on the inside.

There was a crowd starting to gather around the protesters, people whispering to each other, pointing at us. Though I suppose we weren't very inconspicuous, seeing as we had a thirty-foot dragon standing behind us, wings folded at the sides so he didn't scrape against the brick of the buildings that lined the streets. It probably didn't help either that I was shirtless, my skin still covered in Vadoma's runes, which were now smeared and flaking, my hair sticking up every which way. I probably looked like I'd just come from a sacrificial orgy where I'd punched at least seven babies and taken four virginities to sate my carnal cravings.

Ryan squeezed my arm and went to the outskirts of the crowd, saying something that I couldn't hear over the din of the protesters.

"Fuck my life," I muttered.

"Indeed," Randall said. "I concur. Fuck your life, because this is getting ridiculous."

I couldn't even disagree with him. That was the sad part.

"I thought everyone loved Sam," Kevin said. "Isn't it supposed to be one of the biggest complaints about him? That he can charm even the blackest hearts until they are tripping all over him?"

"Yes," Gary said. "That and the fact that he never shuts up, is immature, and makes everything a joke that usually revolves around sex. Okay, I just realized that describes me, and since *I'm* amazing, Sam must be too. Sam. Yoo-hoo! *Sam.*"

"What, Gary," I said through gritted teeth.

"You're *amazing.*"

"Thank you, Gary."

"You're welcome. Gosh, I feel good. Don't you all feel good and in love with Sam again?"

"*Hey, hey, ha, ha! Let's go punch Sam in the jaw!*"

"Oh," Gary said. "That was unfortunate timing."

"*Hey, hey, he, he! Shoot an arrow into his knee!*"

"They're so violent," Gary said. "Gives me the tingles in my nether regions."

"*Hey, hey, hu, hu! Let's go kick him in the tooth!*"

"That didn't even rhyme," Gary said. "But at least they've run out of vowels now."

"*Hey, hey, har, har, put his heart into a jar!*"

"Apparently they don't need just vowels," Gary said.

Ryan came back, clutching a piece of parchment, brow furrowed in that way he sometimes got when he wanted to kill something or someone but couldn't find the thing or person he wanted to kill. I called it his murder eyebrows. I thought it was adorable. He didn't think it was funny that I equated his eyebrows with death.

(But it was.)

"I'll find you something or someone to kill," I said, because I loved him so. "Like a deer or an assassin. I know you need to feel the sweet release of stabbing something with your sword."

He scowled at me. "Stuff like that is probably the reason these people are afraid of you."

"*Afraid* of him?" Gary said, shocked. "Who in their right mind would be afraid of a skinny little twink like him? He weighs like four pounds."

"Hey!" I barked. "I'm not a twink! And I've been working out! I have abs. Okay, maybe just one."

We all stared at my bare stomach. Not much going on there.

"Fine," I said with a scowl. "But I'm not a twink."

Gary rolled his eyes. "Yeah, okay. Sure you're not."

"Little twinky Sam," Tiggy said. "Mens in your yard because of milk-shakes."

"I don't even want to know what that means," Ryan said. "Like most of the things you guys talk about. But you should probably take a look at this."

He handed the parchment over to me, and I felt everyone else crowd around me, trying to read over my shoulder. I was annoyed for a second, but it fell away as soon as I saw the words printed on the page in large, blocky letters.

ATTENTION! ATTENTION! ATTENTION!
SAM OF WILDS IS THE SCOURGE OF VERANIA!
FOR TOO LONG, HE HAS BEEN GIVEN FREE REIN!
HE HAS ACTED WITHOUT REGARD TO HIS FELLOW VERA-NIANS!
AREN'T YOU TIRED OF PAYING FOR SAM'S MISTAKES?

THE CRIMES OF SAM OF WILDS:
—GOT THE PRINCE KIDNAPPED
—CAUSED UNTOLD AMOUNT OF DAMAGE TO THRONE ROOM
—HAS BEADY LITTLE EYES THAT ARE CONNIVING
—A HOME-WRECKER WHO DESTROYS HAPPY AND LOVING RELATIONSHIPS
—PROBABLY CURSES PEOPLE TO DO HIS BIDDING
—HAS DONE OTHER THINGS THAT ARE ILLEGAL
—IS FRIENDS WITH A UNICORN IN AN INTERSPECIES RELA-TIONSHIP WITH A DRAGON
—WHICH IS GROSS
—SUBJECTS THE MAGNIFICENT PRINCE JUSTIN TO HIS STU-PIDITY

SAM OF WILDS CAME FROM THE SLUMS!
HE WAS NOT QUALIFIED TO BE THE KING'S WIZARD!
WAS HE EVEN BORN IN VERANIA?
SHOW US HIS BIRTH CERTIFICATE!
WE THE PEOPLE DEMAND IT!
IF YOU HATE SAM OF WILDS AS MUCH AS WE DO, THEN IT'S TIME TO FIGHT BACK!
PICK UP YOUR SIGNS!
TELL THE CROWN WE WON'T STAND FOR SAM OF WILDS!
THE PEOPLE OF VERANIA SAY NO!
JOIN US AND HELP US RID VERANIA OF THIS SCUM!

PAID FOR BY THE WHSAL FOR A SAM-FREE VERANIA

"*What?*" I yelped. "None of this is even remotely true!"

"To be fair," Justin said, "You do subject me to your stupidity, you did get me kidnapped, broke up my sort-of-real relationship, and I am magnificent."

"Gross?" Gary said, outraged. "*Gross?* I'll have you know that my love for Kevin is a beautiful thing! Sure, some of the things we do can be classified as *gross*, but that's between me and my future baby daddy!"

"Consent truly is important if you plan on being in a BDSM-style relationship," Kevin agreed. "And our children will be glorious. Much better than our practice child, Sam, who I think we can all agree is an unmitigated failure."

"And the Darks did come after you in the throne room," Randall said.

"And you did ask me when you were twelve if there was a way to curse that boy from the kitchen so he could bring you more cookies," Morgan said.

"Your eyes are tiny," Tiggy said. "Tiny Eyes. Capitalized. It true now."

"And I suppose you are from the slums," Mom said.

"Which might have made people trying to be the apprentice to Morgan of Shadows slightly angry," Dad agreed. "Given that you were plucked from obscurity and handed this job that they all wanted and had been working for all their lives and that you did nothing for."

"And you do illegal things all the time," Ryan said. "Even though I tell you not to. Because they're illegal."

I glared at all of them.

"And this is your family," Vadoma said. "Saying such things. For shame. You come home with Vadoma. I show you what it means to have a family."

"Okay, first things first," I said. "Fuck all of you. Second, Vadoma, I swear to the gods, if you are behind *any* of this, you're going to see a side of me you haven't seen before."

She grinned. It wasn't a very nice-looking thing. "I didn't do this. This is something you did all on your own."

Yeah, she could fall off a cliff and I'd be okay with it. Especially if at the bottom of said cliff, there was a bunch of hungry kelpies who would stomp her face until it was a bloody mess.

"What the hell is the WHSAL?" I muttered irritably.

"You don't want to know," Ryan said. "You really, really don't want to know."

And before I could find a way to respond to *that*, the chanting behind us stopped. I turned back around, thinking maybe this was over. I had other things to worry about. I didn't have time for stupid people.

But it wasn't over. Because of course it wasn't.

The crowd had quieted because they were focused on a single individual.

A girl who now stood up on a wooden box in front of everyone, a bright purple megaphone in her hands. She wore an expensive white dress with little blue ribbons at the waist and on her shoulders. Her hair fell in flawless blonde ringlets. Her makeup was expertly applied. Her eyes were wide and bright. She made the perfect picture of innocence. A beautiful girl on a bright sunny morning, shimmery in her pretty dress and her bubble-gum pink lipstick and nail polish.

And I *knew* she was behind all of this.

It seemed just like her. She was trying to exact her revenge. And I'd fallen right into the palm of her hand. She couldn't have planned this any better had she tried.

"That motherfucking *bitch*," I yelled without thinking. "I'm going to kick her fucking *ass*, oh my gods, I don't *care* if she's a minor or a girl, she's *dead*. You hear me! *Dead*."

Which, of course, echoed across the plaza that had fallen deathly silent now that she had their attention. *Bitch, bitch, bitch*, echoed up one side of the plaza. *Dead, dead, dead*, came down the other.

My most mortal of enemies smiled the long, slow smile of the victorious. Seventeen years old and she was already so inherently evil that any other evil parties in her vicinity paled by comparison. It didn't help that she had the countenance of an angel. That did a lot to hide the fact that her soul was the rotting, bloated carcass of a fish lying out in the sun for six days.

Gods, how I hated her.

And I really hated the fact that I apparently had just yelled at her in front of at least a hundred people. Not the best idea I'd ever had. Which probably described most of my ideas.

"And that, ladies and gentlemen," Lady Tina DeSilva said, staring straight at me, "is indicative of the *true* nature of Sam of Wilds."

"That wasn't very nice at all!" someone in the audience cried.

Many others murmured their consent, shooting me looks of such disappointment that I almost felt *guilty* about it. Guilty about saying something to *Lady Tina*, of all people.

"No," Lady Tina said. "It wasn't. But that's Sam of Wilds for you in exactly five words: not very nice at all. Perfect, don't you think?"

The crowd agreed quite vocally.

"Oh my gods," Gary whispered. "She's like an evil queen. I want to *be* her when I grow up and use my powers of persuasion for nefarious purposes."

"You know," Mom said, "if I didn't know any better, I would think this is them pulling each other's pigtails."

"Except our son is gay," Dad said.

"And Lady Tina is an asshole," Mom said so fiercely that I couldn't help but love her just a little bit more.

"You are here," Lady Tina said, snarling into her megaphone, "because you are *tired* of seeing Sam of Wilds walk all over the good people of Verania. You are *tired* of hearing about his exploits where he puts our knights in danger or gets members of the royal family taken. You are *tired* of villains of every shape, size, and color coming to *our* city just because they have a bone to pick with Sam of Wilds. How many times has your day-to-day life been *ruined* because Sam picked a fight with the wrong people? How many times are we supposed to bend over and *take* it, just because Sam of Wilds has somehow fooled your King into believing he is an actual human being instead of the excrement left behind by a pack of sick dogs? How many times are we *forced* to listen to how perfect Sam is, how wonderful Sam is, how *godsdamned special Sam is*, just because he enchanted the King's Wizard with his slippery ways?"

"She's purpling her prose all over me," Gary breathed. "She is a master and I am but a pawn in her love game."

"I do *not* get slippery with Morgan," I said, quite loudly. "And I *am* an actual human being. Oh my gods, why are you even *listening* to her? Pete! Do something!"

Pete winced as one of the Castle Guards came over and whispered in his ear. "Sorry, Sam," he said after patting the knight on the shoulder. "Looks like she applied for all the proper permits. She has the right to protest, as long as it remains peaceful."

"But she's protesting *me*."

"And she's allowed," Pete said, sounding apologetic.

"Okay," I said. "Fine." I turned toward the King. "Your Majesty, I never ask you for anything."

"You really don't," the King said, sounding amused. "It's one of the most annoying things about you."

"Good," I said. "I'm glad we agree. And we'll come back to the part where you called me annoying at a later date, don't think we won't. I need a favor."

"Anything within reason," the King said.

"I need you to behead a teenage girl for me."

"Hmm. The reason?"

"I hate her."

"Would it be the same teenage girl that's saying disparaging things about you currently?"

"Coincidentally? Yes."

"Sorry, Sam," the King said, and I couldn't be too mad at him because he did sound honestly regretful that he couldn't agree to behead a teenage girl. "I'm going to have to deny your request. But feel free to ask me for anything else."

"I want to hang the painting I did of you in the throne room."

"The one where I have three breasts and am a monster destroying Meridian City?"

"Yes."

The King turned to Pete. "Has she done anything we can behead her for? Did she maybe sign the permit request on the wrong line? File it too late? *Anything?*"

Pete shook his head. "Also, public executions are illegal."

"Fine," the King said to me. "We can hang the painting in the throne room."

It made me feel a little bit better that everyone would be able to appreciate my art.

But Tina was still going. "And since *when* do we allow people from the *slums* to hold such high office as the apprentice to the King's Wizard? No matter what they want you to believe, no matter what they try and tell you, make no mistake. Sam of Wilds *looks* like he's from the slums, but how can we be sure of that? Is it too much to ask that he show us his birth certificate so that everyone can see who he truly is? Especially since he *does* have the King's ear."

"Godsdamned birthers," I muttered.

"We love you, Lady Tina!" a woman screamed in the audience. Some others began to cheer, and Lady Tina closed her eyes, as if she was letting the applause wash over her. I thought it would be the perfect moment for a meteor to fall from the sky and squash her flat. Alas, none fell, and I was disappointed that the gods didn't see fit to smite her where she stood.

"And I love you," Lady Tina breathed into the megaphone. "So, so much. For having the *courage* to stand here today, in the face of what appears to be overwhelming odds. To show that *no*, Sam of Wilds is not universally beloved, as he would have you believe. *No*, we won't go quietly into the night, letting him walk all over us with his horrible fashion sense, his strange-looking teeth, his obvious lack of any culture *whatsoever*. Do we even *need* to discuss the fact that he came in with his stupid face *and destroyed the most wonderful thing in the world known as Rystin? No one likes HaveHeart, you sanctimonious piece of filth. It's against nature and disgusting and I hate you so much for it.*"

The audience didn't cheer much at that. In fact, most of them looked confused.

Lady Tina coughed. "I mean, he's costing the great people of Verania their sense of security?"

The crowd clapped slowly. "Yaaaaay?" someone asked.

"Maybe I should go out there and protest," Justin said. "She was pretty much right about most of that."

"Best friends don't protest against each other," I reminded him. "It's against the bro-code."

"Bro-code," Justin said, like the very words made him ill.

"And *that* is another thing!" Lady Tina cried. "Just *look at them*. A unicorn and a *dragon*. Why, that goes against the very face of the gods! Everyone knows that interspecies relationships are *wrong*. And they just *sit* there, *forcing* us to watch it, like we want to even *see* something like that. If there's one thing that I know, it's that when I'm staring at someone to judge them, they should *not* be allowed to shove their *filth* down my throat!"

"Wow," Gary said. "She's a few cookies short of a bake sale."

"Our love is not wrong," Kevin said. "Everyone knows that there is *magic* in what we have. Why, our romance will be sung about for *ages*. The Beast from the East and his one true semimonogamous love, the beautiful unicorn."

"Hmm," Gary said. "I can't help but notice that you gave yourself top billing there."

"Well, yes," Kevin said. "I don't know if you heard, but a star dragon said that I'm one of the, if not the most important, parts of a millennia-old prophecy."

"Riiiiight," Gary said. "But I still don't think that makes your name before mine."

"Dear," Kevin said, a little curl of smoke coming out of his right nostril. "You're embarrassing me in front of all these people. Maybe we can discuss this later?"

"Oh, *really?*" Gary said, eyes narrowing. "I'm sorry I'm such an *embarrassment* to you."

"Um, guys?" I said. "Maybe now is not the—"

"Fine," Kevin said, rolling his eyes. "If it's *that* big of a deal to you, then you can be first."

"Oh no," Gary said mockingly. "I wouldn't even *dream* of wanting to take something away from you that is so important and that you obviously deserve. You know. Because of all your accomplishments. After all, I'm not the one that speaks for disabled magical creatures everywhere."

"How are you disabled?" Kevin asked.

"I don't have my *horn!*" Gary shouted at him.

"I don't think you speak for anyone but yourself," I said, only to have him glare at me. "Right, mouth shut. I am so not involved."

"Can't you see?" Kevin said, clutching a clawed hand to his chest. "You're letting them tear us apart!"

"No," Gary said, voice breaking, eyes glittering with tears. "You're doing that well enough just on your own."

"Gary sad?" Tiggy said, breath hitching in his chest.

"Oh no," I whispered.

"I am so *sad!*" Gary wailed. "My dragon lover thinks his name should be first!"

"I sad too!" Tiggy yelled, gathering Gary up in his arms and rocking him back and forth. "Sam! Be sad with us!"

"Godsdammit," I muttered, taking a step toward them.

"What are you doing?" Ryan asked, grabbing me by the arm. "We have to deal with this."

"Bro-code," I said. "Bros before hoes. Sorry, babe."

"I am *not* a ho."

I patted him on the hand. Poor guy. Denial was a terrible thing.

Before I could get to Tiggy and Gary to hug it out, Kevin stopped me, leaning down until his large head was eye level with me. "I hope you know that I'll still be there for you, champ," he said gruffly. "Even if your mother and me are no longer together. Weekends, okay? And I don't want you to worry if I get a new... friend. You'll always be my number-one brave little sexy guy, okay?"

"Still not used to that at all," I said.

"None of us are," he said, tongue slithering out and brushing on my fingers.

"Oh, gross," I muttered.

"Sam!" Gary cried. "Get over here and love me!"

"Sam!" Tiggy yelled. "We need love!"

And really, what else could I have done in the face of that? Nothing, I tell you.

I went. And just as soon as I got within grabbing distance, Tiggy's large hand wrapped around my arm and jerked me into his chest, holding me tight. Gary was crying prettily against him, these precious little sniffs coming out his nose in periwinkle sparks that did little to Tiggy's thick overshirt. "Sam," Gary said wetly. "Is this what heartbreak feels like? Like I've left on nipple clamps for so long that I'm numb to everything only to have them taken off and slapped, sending pain shooting through my body like lava burning my insides?"

"That's actually surprisingly accurate," I said, reaching out to run my fingers through his mane.

"See what you've done?" Kevin yelled at the crowd. "Your hatred just tore the love of my life from my arms. How dare you, ladies and gentlemen. How *dare you*."

The crowd murmured amongst themselves, taking a step back.

"What is happening?" Vadoma asked. "What is all this?"

"Par for the course," Randall said. "This is actually quite tame for them. Unfortunately."

"Nothing has been lit on fire yet," Morgan said. "So I count this one as a win."

"Pretty Gary," Tiggy murmured. "There, there. There, there."

"That bastard," Gary said. "How could he end this on something as trivial as not giving me top billing when I obviously deserve it? I want to murder him and leave his bones out in the sun to dry—you know what, time out." His eyes dried immediately, and he lifted his head from Tiggy's chest.

"Can we all agree to not talk shit about my ex? Especially since he's part of Sam's destiny. It'll just make things awkward in the long run."

"Agreed," Tiggy said.

"I also agree," I said. "I'd like to add an addendum. Can we never refer to me having a destiny ever again? Because that's really lame and I hate it."

"Struck down," Gary said. "Because you do."

"Strike it, motherfuckers," Tiggy said.

"Godsdammit," I said.

"Good," Gary said. "So we're in agreement. Rule number one thousand, two hundred, and twenty-seven of the Sam/Gary/Tiggy friendship has been ratified. No talking shit about Kevin because of Sam's magical super destiny. Except for me, a little, because I've been the one spurned."

"Aye," Tiggy and I said, while I also added, "You bitch," because of the principle of the matter.

"Good," Gary said. "Okay, time in." Tears burst from his eyes so bright and shiny that they almost looked like diamonds. "I am going to be alone for*ever*," he wailed into Tiggy's chest.

"I never leave you," Tiggy promised.

"Oh, my heart," Kevin said, putting his clawed hands over his eyes. "What bright pain is this, taking my breath from me? O, tremble, sweet nothing, because that is what I have inside me now that my heart has been shattered: nothing. I have *nothing*."

"*This* is what you want for the future of Verania?" Lady Tina demanded into her megaphone. "This is what you want for *your* future? These— these bumbling *idiots* are going to be what represents us as a country? What if the Darks come back? What if some group outside of Verania comes back? You think anyone will take us seriously? You think the Prince, the future *King* of Verania, will have any control over his own court with *these* ridiculous cretins getting in the way with their shenanigans? We need to banish them from Verania, then build a wall around the *entire country* so none of them could ever get back in!"

"A scathing and completely on point representation of the state of the court of Verania," Vadoma said. "I like this girl."

"Do you think the King would execute my grandma if I asked?" I said to Gary and Tiggy. "I mean, I get he said no to Lady Tina, but come *on*. Vadoma is so executable."

"I could make it look like an accident," Gary said. "I've done it four times before. Accidentally."

"Tiggy smash her," Tiggy said, squeezing us tighter.

"No," I sighed. "I don't want you guys to murder anyone. Lady Tina will probably just find some way to use it against us."

"I'm glad you think that murder is bad because of how someone can use it against you," Ryan said. "But if you three are done, I'd like to point out that the crowd is starting to get a little angry."

"What?" I said, pulling away from Tiggy.

And holy shit, was he right.

For everyone in the crowd had turned to face us. Lady Tina still stood on the box, the wind blowing through her hair and ruffling her dress, the sunlight falling perfectly on her shoulders. They weren't looking at her, but I was, and I could see the evil smirk she had on her face. The crowd around her had varying expressions, from disgust to disdain to outright derision. They were a mixture of middle- and upper-class. I didn't see anyone from the slums, but rarely did they come up near the castle unless they were summoned. It was two different worlds, no matter what the King tried to do about it. There were rich people and there were poor people, and as much as we wanted to change it, it couldn't happen overnight.

"Sweet molasses," I whispered. "She's *billowing*."

And how unfair was *that*?

"And that is why today," Lady Tina announced, "I'm announcing the official We-Hate-Sam-A-Lot Castle Lockes Chapter's new initiative. The petition to have Sam of Wilds removed as the apprentice to the King's Wizard and banished from Verania. With enough participants, we can present it to the Good King in hopes that he will take our concerns seriously. I hope I can count on your support. And if you sign, you will get an official We-Hate-Sam-A-Lot pin that you can wear to proudly display your contempt for what is obviously a mistake that must be course corrected. I also brought muffins." She grinned at me. "They're blueberry. And *delicious*."

TWO DAYS LATER, THE *CITY OF Lockes Gazette* published an editorial with the headline *IS SAM OF WILDS TOO WILD FOR LOCKES?* They proceeded to eviscerate me over every one of my perceived failures, including the alleged murder of Lartin the Dark Leaf.

At the very end, it was noted that a petition started by one Lady Tina DeSilva had garnered almost five thousand signatures. "We're very pleased," she was quoted as saying. "But not surprised. After all, Sam of Wilds can only flirt his way out of so many disasters, can he not? It's time he's held responsible for his actions. Long live Rys—I mean, peace be with you."

CHAPTER 11
Decisions Made

SO THINGS KIND OF WENT TO shit a little bit after that. Gary and Kevin weren't speaking to each other. I wasn't speaking to Randall and Morgan. No one was speaking to Vadoma. Ryan was speaking to Ruv, but it was usually in grunts and groans as he tried to do something he considered manlier than whatever it was that Ruv was doing. ("Who eats soup with a *spoon*? I drink it directly from the bowl! Like a *man*.") Justin would just glare at me in that best-friend way he did, the King would squeeze my shoulder and tell me everything was going to be fine, but even I could see that he was worried. Mom and Dad were walking on eggshells around me, and I didn't know how to make them stop.

And on top of all of that, all I could really focus on was what the star dragon had told Vadoma, what the dark man in shadows had told me, and the fact that I had never even considered that one day, Ryan would die and I would remain here, trapped in a body that wouldn't age as normal given the magic that coursed through my veins.

All in all, not the best week I'd ever had.

And I didn't know what to do about it.

I lay beside Ryan in the dark, his hand clutched in mine as he whispered in my ear. He said, "We'll figure it out, okay? I promise you we'll figure it out. You're not going to lose me. Not now. Not ever."

We both knew that no one could make promises like that, but I let him make them anyway.

"How do we even know she's telling the truth?" I asked him.

"Could she be making this up?"

I shrugged. "Anything is possible."

"Do *you* think she is?"

And I hesitated, which was answer enough.

He sighed and leaned over to kiss my bare shoulder. "You know I'll follow you in whatever you decide."

And I knew that. Of course I did. The thought scared the hell out of me. Because I couldn't get the image out of my head of him as a young man, or him as an old man, in death upon that cold slab of stone, eyes closed, heart stopped, sword atop his chest.

And if I was a little rougher that night when we fucked, he didn't say a single thing about it.

"YOU CAN'T IGNORE US FOREVER," MORGAN said when we were next in the labs. "Honestly, Sam. It's getting ridiculous."

I ignored him, focusing instead on my Grimoire. It was my job as a wizard's apprentice, after all. And there had to be some secret, something I hadn't yet thought of so that Ryan and I would never have to be apart. Romantic, yes, and ultimately foolish, but I wanted to explore every avenue I could.

"He's behaving like a child," Randall said from his chair in front of the fire. "I don't know why we thought he'd be mature about this. There's enough evidence to the contrary."

I had to grind my teeth together to choke back any response while writing.

"Not helping," Morgan said.

"And you're coddling again," Randall said, grunting as he massaged his knee. "I've told you time after time that you handle the boy with kid gloves. Maybe it's time the gloves come off and he be given a proper spanking."

Which... okay. That was an image I really didn't need in my head.

"It's a lot to take in for anyone," Morgan said. "To find out you have some prophecy hanging over your head."

Yeah, and that maybe everyone in this room aside from myself knew about it.

Randall snorted. "Back in *my* day, we didn't let things like *prophecies* knock us on our asses. We actually *listened* to what they were about and faced them head-on rather than mope around like a little bitch."

I was going to turn so many things of his into penises.

"And I suppose there's the feeling that he thinks we lied to him," Morgan said. "Like *I* lied to him."

Bingo.

"Of course he would think that," Randall said. "Because he's selfish. He doesn't think of anyone but himself. He can't possibly see anything as being for the greater good. Can you imagine having to tell an eleven-year-old boy that one day, he'll be facing a potentially insurmountable obstacle? Even now, I don't think he has the faculties to grasp the extent of it. And it's not *lying*, per se. It was more of an omission of the truth."

"I suppose you're right," Morgan said with a sigh. "I couldn't have actually told a child that his grandmother he'd never met had told me of his birth beforehand and that he would be responsible for a great many things."

"Why, that way would just lay madness," Randall said wryly. "Could you imagine the ego involved in hearing such a thing? Granted, he obviously didn't need that to have an ego. Maybe that Lady Tina had a point. Sam might just need to be knocked down a few——"

"She did *not* have a point, oh my gods," I exclaimed shrilly. "Are you *insane*? She was created for nothing but the sole purpose of waging war against me, and I will see her vanquished on the battlefield with her blood squelching between my fingers, *mark my words*."

Randall and Morgan gaped at me.

"I went to a very dark place," I said. "I admit that freely. And I don't feel sorry about it at all."

"Told you it would work," Randall said to Morgan. "Just had to get him riled up is all. He's so predictable."

"You *manipulated* me!"

"Gods, maybe I liked it better when he *wasn't* talking," Randall said. "It all has to do with the volume. It's either nothing or too much. There's no in between with him."

"You can't hide from this, Sam," Morgan said lightly. "I know you want to, I know that your first instinct is to try and ignore it until it all goes away, but you can't do that now."

"How do you know that?" I asked, refusing to look up from my Grimoire. "Maybe I'm just——"

"I know you," Morgan said. "As well as anyone does. I have watched you grow up from a little boy to the man you are today. I have seen your successes. I have witnessed your failures. So, yes. I know you. And I know how you think, Sam. And I know your first instinct is to push this away."

He had me there, and all of us in the room knew it. I didn't know what kind of relationship Morgan and Randall had when it was just the two of them, if it'd been any different when Randall had been Morgan's mentor, however long ago that'd been. I didn't know why I hadn't worked up the courage to ask about them yet, not sure if the bond between a mentor and his charge was meant to be private. I didn't tell Gary or Tiggy or Ryan everything that Morgan and I talked about, and they didn't ask. They knew a wizard was meant to have his secrets and so far hadn't yet put me in a place where I had to lie to them. Lying was different than withholding the truth, or at least that's what I told myself. I hadn't told anyone what the Great White had said the first time Vadoma had whammied me. I hadn't told anyone everything that had happened the second time, either.

I really needed to stop getting whammied by my grandma.

And Dad was right. That phrasing was terrible.

"Okay," I said begrudgingly. "Maybe there was a small chance I was considering trying to ignore the whole... *destiny* thing until it went away. But that doesn't mean that we still can't do that, right? If we all collectively agreed that it doesn't exist, then no big deal. We'll forget it ever happened and go on with our lives like nothing changed. Maybe start a bowling league. I don't know."

"Until this dark man comes," Randall said.

I glared at him, because of *course* he'd have to bring that part up. "So you believe her now? What happened to her fortune-telling being a scam?"

He shrugged as if he couldn't care less. "You believed it. The moment you came to in the field, you believed. Whatever you saw, whatever she showed you, it scared the hell out of you. That's enough to make me believe that being cautious is better than being dismissive. You can't hide your head in the sand without expecting your ass to get burned."

I didn't want to admit that he had a point, so I said nothing.

"We need to be prudent about this, Sam," Morgan said. "If there is any truth to the matter."

"And you don't think that it's just Vadoma having ulterior motives?" I asked. "She obviously made plans for me with Ruv that Ryan disrupted. How do we know this isn't all just a ploy to bring me back to the homestead? I would make a terrible gypsy. I hate bracelets, and I don't like the desert."

"Anything is possible," Morgan said slowly. "Which is why we have to tread carefully here. If there *is* any validity to what she's saying, we need to be prepared."

"Then who is this dark man?" I asked.

And they hesitated.

They didn't want me to see it. I almost *didn't* see it. It was a split-second thing, a darting glance shared between the two of them that anyone else would have missed. But I knew them. I knew *Morgan*. I had spent years by his side, studying under him and studying *him*. I knew when he would withhold the truth, for the most part. I knew that he tried not to lie to me, even if he felt it was for my own good. Secrets between a wizard and his charge were far and few between, and never if it meant one or the other would be in danger.

So I knew when he opened his mouth to respond that whatever came out would be a lie.

"We can't be sure," Morgan said. "He could be some nameless Dark rising through the ranks, as we've said."

"Or an outsider who has somehow taken control," Randall said.

"An outsider," I repeated. "You think an outsider will gather the Darks and they would willingly follow."

They looked relieved at the thought that I had swallowed it hook, line, and sinker. I was almost insulted at how naïve they thought me to be. "We need to explore every possibility," Randall said. And then he frowned. "Isn't there still a Dark or two in the dungeon that haven't been sent out to the prisons yet?"

"Wan," Morgan said thoughtfully. "Wan the Dark Hunter. He's still here. Interrogating him didn't get much information after the attack on Castle Lockes. He was to be transported at the end of the year. I suppose another attempt could be made. To find out what he knows."

"I suppose I could—"

"No," I said. "I don't think you will."

They paused.

"What was that, boy?" Randall asked, cocking an eyebrow.

"You've tried already," I said. "Nothing came from it. Maybe it's better to go into it with a fresh pair of eyes."

"Really," Randall said. "And just who do you suggest we use as a fresh pair of eyes?"

"WAN, IS IT?" GARY ASKED. "WAN the Dark Hunter?"

"Yes," Wan said, sitting back in his chair, shackles rustling on his arms and legs.

"Can I just call you Wan?"

"I suppose."

"Good. Can I get you anything? A cup of water? A hot towel?"

"Really," Randall said. "This was your plan."

"Admittedly, it might have sounded better in my head," I said.

We stood outside the interrogation room, watching through an enchanted window where we could see in but the occupants of the room couldn't see out. Wan the Dark Hunter, handsome fellow that he was, was chained to a thick wooden chair, a small table separating him and his interrogators.

And what fearsome interrogators they were! Even *I* was suitably impressed, and everyone knew it took a lot to impress me. Tiggy stood near the back of the room, slightly hunched over so his head didn't hit the ceiling, massive arms crossed over his considerable chest. He was frowning, and even though I knew it meant he was concentrating on the task at hand, to most everyone else, it looked as if he was contemplating the best way to proceed with a murderous rampage.

Gary, for his part, had decided that the best interrogating ensemble included having his hooves painted a deep purple, with matching streaks through his mane. His eyelashes looked impossibly long, fluttering in a lovely manner every time he blinked. He had a black scarf tied around his neck, black eyeliner under his eyes, and black silk woven through his tail. "I'm a Gothic princess," he'd whispered to me as we'd made our way down to the dungeon. "He'll cave in seconds. And it's also my look of mourning for my relationship with your step-dragon-father. That bastard. I hope he's suffering."

I hadn't even bothered to respond to any of that. I'd learned a long time ago that it's best never to question a unicorn, given that it usually ended in sparkles or threats of Gore City *up in here.*

Wan didn't look intimidated. If anything, he was coolly amused, sitting back in the chair, legs spread out in front of him in a cocky fashion. I wondered if Gary was going to murder him before the day was out. Anything seemed possible.

"Are you comfortable?" Gary asked, voice sticky sweet. "A blanket, perhaps."

"I'm good," Wan said, reaching up to stroke the goatee on his face like a smarmy villain. Given that he *was* a smarmy villain, I wasn't surprised. I still hadn't forgiven him for interrupting Ryan's confession of eternal love to my face and soul on the day the Darks had attempted foolishly to attack Castle Lockes. I had advocated to have him tarred and feathered, but then Ryan had given me this really great fingerblast and I forgot all about it.

Until now.

"His skin should be melted from his bones," I grumbled to no one in particular.

"Oh boy," Ryan said, standing at my side, shoulders brushing mine. "Here we go again. Do I need to do that one thing?"

"He's talking about sexing me up," I said to Randall and Morgan. "In case you didn't know."

A dungeon guard behind us started choking.

"We know," Morgan said. "Everyone knows."

"Good," I said. I leaned over and kissed Ryan on the cheek. "Thanks, but I'll have to take a rain check. On the sexing. Because we're trying to be serious right now. Not everything is about butt play, babe."

He was blushing. I wanted to devour him whole. "You didn't have to say it like that," he muttered, glancing back at the guard.

I rolled my eyes. "Like your underlings don't know that you get laid on the reg. They probably tell stories about how you finally were able to land all of this."

"It's good to know his ego's still intact after the protest," Randall said.

Yes. That. I was going to have to deal with that. Sooner rather than later. I wondered if it was too gauche to call Tina out for a duel. Did people still duel over things? I'd never been invited to one, so I didn't know. That made me a little sad. Because maybe people hadn't invited me to duels because they didn't *like* me, just like Tina said. Fine. Whatever. I'd have my *own* duel and not invite them either! Perfectly mature response.

"What we were talking about again?" I asked. "I was too busy thinking of ways to murder—I mean, feed homeless kittens."

Morgan and Randall sighed in unison.

"So, Wan," Gary said. "Do you know why we're here?"

Wan shrugged. "Not exactly."

Gary nodded sympathetically. "Of course. How could you? Having been locked up all this time."

"Ask him if he poops in buckets," I muttered, even though Gary couldn't hear me.

"Am I being transferred?" Wan asked.

"Am I being *transferred*," Gary said, pacing in front of the table. "That's what you're asking me."

"Yes?"

"Was that a question? Because it sounded like a question."

"I don't know?"

"You. Don't. Know." Gary stopped pacing. "What *do* you know?"

"What?" Wan asked, sounding confused. "Listen, I don't—"

"No," Gary snarled suddenly, stomping his hoof on the floor. "*You* listen."

"Eep," Wan squeaked.

"I'm a loose cannon," Gary said, baring his teeth. "Everyone down at the precinct says so. Loose Cannon Goth Princess Gary they call me."

"Oh no," I moaned. "He's role-playing again. Whose idea *was* this?"

"Yours," Randall said. Like an asshole.

"Loose Cannon Goth—" Wan started.

"Did I *say* you could call me that?" Gary roared, spittle flying from his lips. "My husband just left me because he couldn't handle being the spouse of a cop. Do you think I have *any* fucks left to give?"

"No!" Wan said shrilly. "No fucks!"

"You're godsdamned right I don't," Gary said. "And if you think *I'm* bad, you just wait until my partner gets ahold of you."

Tiggy let out a low rumble.

"You remember him, don't you?" Gary whispered as he leaned forward, his face inches from Wan's. "He's the one that made sure Lartin was spread evenly along the cave wall."

Wan's eyes were wide.

"Spread him like butter," Tiggy agreed. "Bloody, bloody butter."

"So badass," I whispered fervently to Ryan. "I *know* them."

"I know you do," Ryan said, patting me on the shoulder.

"Do you want to be Tiggy's bloody butter?" Gary asked.

"No!" Wan said, looking like he was starting to cower.

"Then you'll tell me what I want to know?"

"Yes!"

"Good," Gary said. "I only have one question for you. And you're gonna be my good boy and answer it, aren't you."

"Such a good boy!"

"I know you are. You ready?"

"Yes," Wan whimpered.

Gary leaned forward and whispered, "Who is the dark man in shadows?"

"You don't know what you're asking," Wan said, and he was visibly trembling. I'd never seen him like that before. Not even at the battle in the throne room. He'd struck me as fearless, or so close that it didn't matter if he wasn't.

"I do," Gary said, lip curling. "Tell me."

Wan shook his head. "I've never met him. I've never even *seen* him. But I heard the stories, okay? There's nothing you can do to stop it. The fact that you already know of his existence means it's already begun. You won't be able to—"

I felt it first. Out of all the magic—the half-giant and the unicorn, the two powerful wizards, the inherent magic in Ryan as he was the cornerstone—I felt it first. It was just a brush along my skin, like a caress, fingers trailing along my arm.

The hairs on the back of my neck stood on end.

I frowned. "That's—"

Wan sat straight up, the fear leaving him as if it'd never been there at all. He looked loose, relaxed. He had a small smile on his face. He drummed his fingers along the tabletop as if he were playing a song on a piano. He shook his head and sighed. "You would think," he said, voice deeper than I'd ever heard it before, "you wouldn't send a horse to do a man's job."

Gary's eyes narrowed as he cocked his head. "Excuse me?"

Tiggy took a step forward, growling low in his throat.

Wan's smile widened. "I heard about how it happened, you know. When they took it from you. Your horn. The way you screamed. It was like cutting through bone, wasn't it? To feel a part of you taken away in such a violent manner. Well. No one can blame you for screaming, could they?"

Gary took a step back, rear bumping into Tiggy, who put a hand on his flank.

"Of course not," Wan said. He rocked his neck side to side, like he was stretching out the kinks. "To have such a precious thing torn from you the way that it was. You screamed. For days, didn't you? And when you stopped screaming, when it was over, you felt severed from everything else. Because unicorns are pure magic. Their whole beings are light. But if you snuff out that light, if you take away the concentration of their magic, what's left besides a common horse?" He smiled widely before turning to look directly at me, even though he shouldn't have been able to see through the enchantment. His gaze flickered over to Ryan before it settled on me again. "Isn't that right, Sam? Take away the concentration of their magic, and what is left?"

"That's not Wan," I breathed.

"What?" Ryan said. "What do you mean that's not Wan? He can't see us. He can't do *anything*. The room is *warded* against Dark magic—"

Morgan was already moving toward the door when Wan raised his hand toward it, chains rattling around his wrist. There was a bright flash in the room, and I *felt* it, the hook in the center of my chest, tugging. It was sickly and weak and *wrong*, but it was there. And for a moment, I almost took a step forward, wanting to follow it, wanting to feel that *badwrong* bittersweet pain, like pressing my tongue against a loose tooth.

Even as the light began to fade, the imprints still dancing along my vision, I felt the wards shatter as if they were paper-thin and had been created by an amateur. One moment they were healthy and strong, and the next, they were in pieces that stabbed along the green and gold, made up of a sickly yellow that felt like infection. I grunted at the force of it, more shock than pain. Ryan's hand was on my shoulder, and he was saying my name in my ear.

Randall was next to me, standing tall, and I felt his magic *curling* around me and mine. It was different than I'd ever felt from him before. Normally Randall's magic was used on me to prove a point, to teach me a lesson of some sort. The last time I'd felt it had been in the training fields when we'd come back to the castle after rescuing Justin. Then he'd been testing a theory on cornerstones without my knowledge, shocking me full of lightning he brought down from the sky. It was of the offense variety, an attack on me.

This was different. This was warm, and it meshed with my magic more than I thought we ever could. Mine felt young and vibrant, a little out of control. His was strong and ancient, moving with a measured grace. I was a cacophony. He was a symphony, and he pushed his magic over mine, wrapping it wholly, muting it so it felt like it barely thrummed under my skin.

"Gary," I managed to say as soon as I'd caught my breath. "Tiggy."

"He's blocked us from getting into the room," Morgan said from the door. "I've never felt anything like this before. It's more than it should be."

"I can't get in," Randall said, brow furrowed. "It's not—"

"Of course you can't," Wan said, and I pulled myself upright at the sound of his voice. Because I *knew* it now, skirting along the edges of hazy memory.

"It's him," I said. "It's *him*."

Ryan drew his sword, little though it would do. "Wan's the dark man in shadows?"

"No," I said, taking a step toward the glass. "He's a vessel. He's been taken over."

Tiggy was backed into the corner of the room, as far away from Wan as he could get. Gary was shoved behind him. Gary wasn't playing the damsel in distress, however, and it was taking Tiggy all he could to keep Gary from launching himself at Wan, his glitter rage pouring out around him, eyes blazing.

Wan paid them no mind. He looked down at his wrists, frowning at the manacles. He jiggled his legs, hearing the chains rattle against the floor. "Interesting," he said with a sigh. "I'd heard much about the Dark Hunter. It seems that my expectations were set far too high. That's... disappointing."

In one fluid movement, he jerked the chains up, and I *felt* them snap, not by force of strength, but by that sweet *badwrong* pull of his magic that was kept in shades of black and gray and magenta. There was the whisper-roar of his magic, but his mouth stayed shut, not a single word falling from his lips, either in Veranian or the ancient tongue. Morgan could do that. Randall could do that. No one else should have been able to do that, as there were no wizards as old as they.

But for some reason, I could too, though it came in fits and starts.

And now him. This man.

Which meant his power was not a lie.

He stood. The chair scraped loudly along the stone floor.

"Let me at him!" Gary yelled. "I'll rip his dick off and shove it down his throat so he can tell *everyone* he fucked his own mouth!"

Tiggy, of course, didn't let Gary go, but kept a level, cool gaze on Wan.

Wan didn't pay them any mind.

He turned toward the enchanted glass, that unnerving gaze on me again. I thought about taking a step toward him, but Ryan's grip on my shoulder tightened, and Randall hadn't moved from my side. Morgan stood near the door, but he was no longer trying to get inside. And though I only glanced at him for a second, what I saw on his face was something I'd never seen on Morgan of Shadows.

Fear.

Morgan was afraid.

"I can feel you," Wan said. "Your strength. The power that rolls through you. Tell me, Sam of Wilds, have they made you promises? Has Randall whispered in your ear little secrets about how you'll be a great wizard one day? Has Morgan put his arm around your shoulders and held you close, telling you that you don't have to be afraid? Sam. Sam, Sam, Sam." So quick that I could barely see it happening, he raised his hand and slammed his palm into the glass. It vibrated but did not break. "They're *lying*."

"Who are you?" I asked.

Wan smiled at me, wide and toothy. "I'm the inevitable. The gods don't deal in partiality, Sam. Did you know that? For every force that fights for good, there is an opposite that pushes against it. And Sam, I am going to *push*."

The glass began to crack.

The first was small, minute, the break following along Wan's middle finger. Then came a second and a third, and then I could *hear* the glass beginning to break apart.

And before I could think, before I could even come to the decision, I'd already moved forward, standing directly in front of him, the enchanted glass the only thing separating us. Morgan said, "Sam, *don't*!" but I couldn't listen to him. I couldn't take the chance. I slapped my hand up to the glass, lining it up perfectly with his. There was no other thought in my head but keeping his attention on me and not on my family in the corner behind him, my family shouting out behind me.

Up close now, I could see the differences. I didn't know if Wan was gone completely or if he was trapped in his own body, screaming to be freed. The skin on his face bulged as if it were trying to make a new shape, shifting and collapsing. His eyes were bright, brighter than Wan's had ever been. Wan had been a villain, but in the end, he'd been harmless.

This was not a harmless man.

I felt the cracks spreading under my fingertips, and there was green and gold and blue and it was *bursting* within me, more than I'd ever felt it before. He was pushing, so I did the only thing I could.

I pushed *back*.

His eyes widened briefly. The smile on his face fell. "I see," he said. "It's strong. More than I expected. You are more than I expected. Oh, this is going to be *fun*."

"You won't touch them," I said through gritted teeth. "I won't let you."

"Ah, sentimentality," he said, and the smile came back in full force. It was disconcerting, being this close to it. "I was like that. Until it was taken from me. And once divested from the chains that bound me, I was freer than I'd ever been before. Sam, I am the contradiction. The gods cannot play favorites. I have seen the star dragon. He has shown me the way to bring Verania to its knees. You have a destiny of dragons, but my destiny is *you*. For I am your contrary, Sam of Wilds. You will stand against me as all tragic heroes do, with your people at your back and mine tilting their faces toward me in benediction. And I will use that to take everything from you. I can promise you that. Then and only then—after everyone you have loved is lost—will I end you. Your cornerstone will be the first. And you will be the last."

"Monologuing," I growled. "You're fucking *monologuing*. Just like the rest of them. You're no different than anyone else that's come before you. You think you're the first person to threaten me? To threaten my family? You're not. And I've beaten them. Every single one of them. And I will beat you."

"And that's where you're wrong," he said, leaning forward until his forehead pressed against the glass. "Because there has never been anything like me before. Isn't that right, little brother?"

I didn't understand. I didn't understand because I wasn't his brother. I never *had* a brother. It would have—

"There has never been anyone like you before," a voice said behind me, despondent and weary. "That much is true. It was the very reason we had to do what we did to stop you to begin with."

My control slipped, just the barest amounts.

Because *what*.

It couldn't be—

"Morgan?" I whispered.

Wan—or the thing *in* Wan—chuckled, looking rather gleeful. "Surprised, aren't you? Of course you are. Because he wouldn't have told you a single thing about me. His dark secret. His greatest pain after the death of his beloved Anya. Would you like to hear another?"

"Don't do this," Randall said. His voice was rough and pained, something I'd never heard from him before. "If there was ever anything good inside of you, please don't do this."

But the man on the other side of the glass ignored him. "They have kept much from you, Sam of Wilds. All in the name of the *guilt* that wracks through them. Do you think they dream of me at night when they close their eyes? Do they see my face, twisted in betrayal, when they look upon you? You see, I loved them. The both of them. My brother, Morgan. My heart, Randall. But it wasn't enough. *I* wasn't enough. Even if *I* was the only family Morgan had left. Even if *I* was Randall's cornerstone. *I still wasn't enough.*"

I felt like I could barely breathe.

He smiled terribly at me. "You know who I am, Sam."

And there, in the deepest parts of my memories, a name rose through the storm in my head. A name that had always been hidden in shadows the rare times it had ever been mentioned. "No." I shook my head, feeling the glass *bending* under my hand. "It's not possible."

"Say it," he said, teeth bared. "*Say my name.*"

And gods help me, I did.

"*Myrin,*" I whispered.

His face softened, just a little. "Good. That's real good, Sam. You're more than I had hoped you would be. I believe this will be an honorable death for you in the end. But it needn't come to that. I will give you this one chance, Sam. Now, here. Surrender yourself to me. Stand by my side. Forsake all others. I will never lie to you like they have. I will teach you the secrets of magic that they wouldn't dare touch. Learn the truth of the magic that flows within your blood. Why a cornerstone will never be anything more than a hindrance. Together we can bend the world to its breaking point. Stand with me, Sam, or prepare to lose everything you hold dear."

I didn't know what to think. Everything was swirling in my head. The anger. The fear. The truth of the man standing in front of me. For it *was* the truth. Randall and Morgan hadn't denied a single word of it. And that's what stuck with me the most. That the man in front of me, this man who, before today, was nothing but myth and legend, had laid more truth at my feet than Morgan and Randall ever had.

Gods, how I was angry. I was so angry. I couldn't even *breathe*—

"Sam," another voice said. An arm wrapped around my waist. A broad chest pressed against my back. His cheek scraped against mine as he hooked his chin over my shoulder. There was green and gold everywhere. And it was for him. It was *because* of him. "Sam," Ryan Foxheart said again. "I know you're scared. I am too. There's nothing we can do about that now. But I'm with you. Right here. Right now. And I will never leave your side. Do you hear me? I will *never leave your side.*"

There was my truth. That was what I could believe in. And in Tiggy protecting Gary at all costs. And Gary still struggling to get to me, eyes wide, begging Tiggy to let him go so he could *cut a godsdamned motherfucker.*

Everything I did was for them.

I screamed as I shoved everything I could against the glass. It rippled around my fingers as if it were liquid, the gold and green sparking off around my hands. There was a resistance, and it was heavy when it tried to push back, but it was *nothing*. He was *nothing*, and in the split second before the glass shattered, I saw the look of surprise cross Myrin's face. Then it was gone when the enchanted glass exploded around us, large chunks trapped up in the roiling magic, swirling around us. For the briefest of moments, my hand touched his, and there was the *badwrong* pull between us when our magic mingled, intensified beyond anything it'd been before. I could feel it in him, the blood in his veins, how similar it was to Morgan. It was *familiar*, but off in a way that sent a spike of pain through my head. Morgan's magic had always felt like home. Myrin's felt like a fire coming to burn that home to the ground.

And then the glass stopped around us, suspended in air, spinning slowly, glittering in the light from the torches on the walls. Ryan was a long line of heat pressed up against me, his fingers digging into my side where his arm was still wrapped around me. Tiggy had turned to face Gary, shielding him from the glass and magic. I saw reflections of Randall and Morgan in the spinning glass, their images fractured and distorted. Both were pale and shocked, looking older than I'd ever seen them before.

But I didn't have time for them. Not now.

"This," Myrin breathed, "will be a good fight."

He chuckled.

And then took a step back. Another. And then another, hand still raised, his magic still a wall against mine, poking and digging, looking for weakness.

A bead of sweat dripped down my forehead, stinging my eye.

My arm trembled.

Ryan's breath was hot on my neck.

I knew it was going to happen the moment before it did. Myrin winked at me, an obscene and twisted flirtatious gesture, before he found the weakness he was looking for. The glass floating around us snapped into place as he closed his raised hand into a fist, the wicked sharp edges pointed directly at us. The only thing I thought of was *Ryan*, and as Myrin's magic began to vibrate around us, calling upon the glass to skewer us into the wall, I dropped to my knees, pulling Ryan down with me, slamming my hand against the stone floor. The air sizzled around us as lightning began to arc from my fingertips, rolling up my arm to my shoulder and into my chest. It wrapped itself around my heart, and I *pushed*. Electricity flew up all around us, snapping bright white and blue as it vaporized the glass and cracked the floor underneath my hand. Randall and Morgan were knocked off their feet by the shock wave. Tiggy staggered forward with a grunt, head hitting the wall as he hunched farther over Gary.

Myrin was knocked back against the far wall of the interrogation room, grunting as his head rapped against stone.

Ryan held on, even as he shook against the electricity coursing through the both of us.

I tried to call it back, I tried to pull it back in, but it was so much, it was *too much*—

"*Sam*," Ryan whispered harshly in my ear. "*Sam*. It's *done*."

I gasped and closed my hand into a fist on the floor, the cracked stone scraping against my knuckles.

I felt the lightning leave my heart as quickly as it'd come, blood rushing in my ears, vision swimming.

It was quiet in the aftermath.

I raised my head slowly.

Myrin, in his Wan suit, smiled at me.

"Soon," he said. "I'll see you real soon."

And then he snapped his head viciously to the right. There was the wet crack of bone.

Wan the Dark Hunter slumped against the wall, legs skittering on the floor.

It only lasted a few seconds. It felt like hours.

And then it stopped.

Wan's eyes were open and glassy.

His chest did not rise.

"Mother*fucker*," Gary yelled. "That godsdamned dirty fighting *ass* bitch. He called me a horse! He's dead! He's so fucking dead, he don't even *know* how dead he is!"

"So dead," Tiggy agreed. "Punch him in his brain."

Randall groaned as he pulled himself up off the floor.

Morgan sat on his knees looking down at his hands.

I stood, regretting when Ryan's arm fell away from me.

"You okay?" I asked as I turned toward him. He didn't seem any worse for wear, no visible signs of injury, though he groaned when he reached down to pick his sword up from the floor.

"Fine," he muttered. "Though I could have done without the whole up-close-and-personal-with-the-lightning thing."

"Would you say it was... shockingly close?"

"Oh my gods. Did you just—"

"We don't have time for your jokes," I said dismissively. "We have plans to make. Gary! Tiggy! Stop lazing about. Get up and get moving!"

"Fuck you, Sam," Gary said. "I have been *traumatized*, okay? You don't even know what I've been through. I am *emotional*, and I would like a cup of hot chocolate and to have someone rub my hooves and tell me I'm pretty."

"We don't have time for that now," I said, heading toward the door, knowing the others would follow. "We've got work to do."

"You're pretty," Tiggy told Gary.

"*Thank* you, kitten. It's high time someone recognizes that."

"Sam," Randall said, his voice a whipcrack of warning.

I stopped but didn't turn around. I couldn't. Not now. Not after every-thing. I felt Morgan's gaze on me, and as much as I wanted to go to him, to have him make everything better, to take all of this away, I couldn't. I didn't know what I was feeling toward him right then, but it wasn't anything char-itable.

"Sam," he said quietly. "What are you going to do?"

When I spoke, my voice was strong, more so than I expected it to be. "I've got a douchebag monologuing villain whose ass I need to kick, a king-dom to save, and a godsdamned destiny of dragons to face. You can sure as shit bet I'm going to do everything I have to."

I didn't look back as I left the interrogation room. Tiggy, Gary, and Ryan followed me without hesitation.

Randall and Morgan did not.

II
THE DESERT DRAGON

CHAPTER 12
The Will of the Gods

THE SUN BLAZED ABOVE AS THE shadows of five travelers stretched along the worn path between mountainous red sand dunes that rose around them. The wind was fierce and unforgiving, blowing particles of sand that would scrape against any exposed skin. The land was desolate, no plant life able to withstand the extreme conditions. It was—

"Holy fuck," Gary groaned loudly. "It's hot as motherfucking *balls*."

That was more succinct than my internal narration. Because it *was* as hot as motherfucking balls. And when one is as hot as motherfucking balls, one tends to be uncomfortable and grouchy. "You didn't need to come along," I reminded him. "In fact, I told you that you didn't. You insisted. I believe the wording you used was *Sam, don't be a dippy cunt. Of course I'm coming with you. You need me.*"

"Why was your voice all high and whiny?" Gary asked. "I don't sound anything like that."

"Some," Tiggy said, trudging forward, leaving large footprints in the sand behind him. He was barefoot, and I'd thought the sand would be too hot for his feet, but it hadn't bothered him at all, the lucky bastard. I wished I could be a half-giant.

"Some?" Gary asked. "Tiggy, say it isn't *so*."

"Okay," Tiggy said. "But I don't lie."

"Insolence," Gary said. "You should carry me."

"Your tummy sweats," Tiggy said with a grimace. "That's gross."

"*You're* gross," Gary muttered.

"Sam," Kevin rumbled above us, wings spread to try and block the worst of the sand and wind. "Would you please tell Gary that his stomach *does* sweat, and while I don't find it disgusting, some other people might, and therefore he shouldn't try forcing others to do what he wants?"

"I'm not going to do—"

"And *Sam*," Gary said. "Would you please tell Kevin that not every-one wants to hear him talk with his mouth and his words, and therefore he should shut up?"

"Yeah, I don't think I—"

"*Or*," Kevin said, "you could tell Gary that maybe he should just *calm the fuck down* because *some of us* are sick of his shit?"

"I don't know why you put me—"

"You tell Kevin that he wasn't even *invited* on this adventure," Gary hissed.

"Invited?" Kevin snapped. "Uh, excuse me, *sweetheart*. I don't know if you've heard, but this whole adventure is *about* me. I'm someone's *desti-ny*, after all. You know what *your* destiny is? Never getting to have a piece of this fine ass ever again. So suck it."

"Oh *nooo*," Gary mocked. "Whatever shall I do? How will I possibly survive not getting something that I've already had a million times over *like everyone else in Verania*."

"Hey! I have a sexually adventurous spirit! You *know* I am a lover of many, many things. You *liked* it before you decided to put your head up your ass!"

"People grow up," Gary said loftily. "Things they wanted when they were far, far younger don't satisfy them like they used to. I am today's mature and modern unicorn. I don't take your shit for anything. My body, my rights. You don't own *any* of this."

And this had been going on since we'd left the castle.

Three weeks ago.

To say I was ready to choke a bitch would be an understatement.

"They still in love?" Tiggy muttered as Gary and Kevin continued to snipe back and forth.

I rolled my eyes. "Disgustingly so."

"Bet you broom they get back together by time we get to Freeze Your Ass Off?"

"Nah," I said. "It'll take them until at least the Dark Woods."

"Four brooms."

"Tiggy, that's still not how you barter when you—"

"Seven brooms!"

I sighed.

We shook on it.

"Sucker," Tiggy said.

"Hey!"

He went back to listening as Gary and Kevin volleyed insults back and forth.

"You know," Ryan said, voice slightly muffled from the cloth he had wrapped around his head and mouth, "you could probably just use magic to keep their mouths shut, right?"

"Probably," I said. "But you would just pop a boner, and I think it'd be uncomfortable to walk with that. And, as a side note, penises are so weird. They broadcast far too much and in such awkward ways. Oh look, an attractive *something*. Let's have all my blood rush to this one appendage and make it stick out during church."

"During… church?"

"I was thirteen," I mumbled. "The priest was hot. Whatever."

"I don't always pop boners when you do magic," he said. "And gods, I am never saying *pop boners* ever again. It's all your fault I talk like that to begin with now."

"Really?" I said, bringing my hand up, palm toward the sky. "My magic does nothing for you?" I barely had to concentrate before a smidge of sand was floating above my hand, forming a sphere that circled slowly. It caused the barest of tugs around my head and heart, and I knew that Ryan was probably feeling it too, given his propensity these days to be almost an extension of my magic.

"Ungh," he said, eyes glazing over slightly. He licked his lips, eyes darting from my hand down to my crotch.

"You're so easy," I said, letting my hand drop and the sand fall away. "It's one of the things I love about you."

"The first minute we get to ourselves," he muttered, "I'm going to suck your brain out through your dick and make you come on my face."

I tripped, falling face-first into the sand and rolling down a little dune.

Gods, I hated the desert.

*"A*RE YOU SURE ABOUT THIS?" M*OM asked, watching as I rolled an extra pair of trousers before shoving them into my pack. "She's getting what she wants now. Sam, she's my mother and I love her, but you shouldn't trust her."*

I shook my head. "I don't. And I won't. This isn't about her. Not anymore."

She reached over and touched my arm, causing me to pause. "Then what is this about?"

I couldn't look her in the eye, because if I did, I knew I'd spill everything to her, every single fear that I had: that I couldn't trust Morgan, that I couldn't trust Randall, that I was so angry at them for keeping this from me, that I was worried that I was going to fail. That I wasn't going to be enough. That I was making all the wrong decisions. That I should be listening with my head instead of my heart.

"It's about doing what's right," I said instead. "It's about doing what

I have to."

She sighed. "I'm going to tell you something, and I want you to listen to me. All right?"

"Yeah."

"Gypsy magic is mostly farce. It's guesswork and fraud. Manipulation. For the most part, that's all it will ever be. There are times when something else pokes through, something beyond the veil. Vadoma can do those things. I can't explain it, but I can't explain your magic either. You can do things that I can never even dream of. But the only thing that matters to me is that you're making the choice you are, not because of what others want, but because it's what you *believe in. Prophecies, no matter who they come from, no matter what they say, are never written in stone. You can change the future, Sam. No matter what anyone else says, nothing is set in stone. You are your own destiny."*

I looked up at her then. Her eyes were wet, but she had that fierce set to her jaw she sometimes did when she was readying herself for an argument. I didn't think I'd ever seen her look more beautiful.

"I love you," I told her, because I couldn't not.

She laughed. "Oh, I know. And I you, more than all the stars in the sky."

Two days later.

"Are we there yet?"

"No, Gary."

"Oh." Then, "How about now?"

"No, Gary."

"Hey, Sam."

"Yes, Gary."

"Did you know that unicorns aren't meant to survive in harsh conditions?"

"One can only hope, Gary," I said.

"Rude. Hey, Sam."

"*Yes*, Gary."

"Do you think I'll ever find love again?"

"I don't—"

"Oh, *here* we go again. You know what, Gary? I was *trying* to have some bonding with my *son*, seeing as you already claimed him for the holidays. *Again*. And now you're trying to make it all about *you*."

"Maybe we should just—"

"About *me*? *About me*? I'll *show* you making it about me, you overgrown sex reptile whose muscles I don't give the smallest of shits about! Just because you're going to have to move into that postdivorce depressing *singles* apartment when we get back, doesn't mean you get to act like an asshat!"

"For fuck's sake."

"Hey! I *like* that apartment! It's a bachelor pad, and I am going to live my *life* now that I'm not held back by the ball and chain of spousal tyranny! You know how many bitches I'm going to have? *So many bitches.*"

"Good! I hope your *dick* rots off!"

And then they were off again.

DAD AND I WALKED IN MOM'S *garden, making our way to the secret part toward the back that only a few seemed to know about. We hadn't said much between the two of us, but it helped just having him at my side.*

Finally, he said, "This is some fucked-up shit."

I couldn't help it; I laughed. "Yeah. It is."

"Star dragons and prophecies and shadow men. Never thought I'd see the day."

I felt a little pang at that. "I'm sorry," I said, because it seemed like the right thing to do.

He looked startled at that. "What on earth could you be sorry for?"

I shrugged, unable to look my father in the eye. "For... all of this. If... I don't know. If I hadn't been magic, if I'd just been normal like everyone else, we wouldn't be here right now. You and Mom wouldn't have to worry, and I could just... be. It's heavy. Dad. This weight. This responsibility. Sometimes I wish I didn't have this. That I didn't—"

He slapped me upside the back of the head.

"Ow." I glared at him.

"Yes, well," he said. "You deserved that, talking nonsense like you are. You're gonna listen to me. You got that, boy?"

"Yessir."

"There is much in my life I wish I could change. That I wish I could do over again. But if there is one thing I'm sure of, it's that I wouldn't change a godsdamned second, not a second, of the time I've had with you since you were born. You are the greatest thing that has ever been mine, and I know your mother agrees. We are as proud of you as we have ever been. The only thing you need to do is come home in one piece. You do that and we won't have a problem. You get me?"

I hugged the fuck out of him. He laughed wetly in my ear. We didn't move away from each other for a long time.

Three days after that.

"WHAT IS IT?" RYAN ASKED AS we stood on top of a sand dune. In the distance, shimmering in the sun as if it were a mirage, was a large stone complex, rising out of the middle of the desert. There were towers spread out around the outside of it, rising above the large wall that surrounded the buildings.

"It's Mantok," I said, voice low, even though it didn't matter. Gary and Tiggy knew where we were.

"The prison in the desert," Ryan said. "I've never seen it before. It's in the middle of nowhere."

"It's meant to be. It houses the worst of the worst. The murderers. The rapists. Those that deal in dark magic." I took a breath and let it out slowly to try and rein in the rage that ran through me. "Those that would keep magical creatures in cages and parade them around Verania in a carnival."

Ryan tensed beside me. "Fuck," he said. "The one that had Gary and Tiggy before you met them? What was his name?"

"Koklanaris."

"He's in there?"

"Yes. We should go before I do something I'll regret."

So we went, Kevin and Gary and Tiggy waiting for us at the bottom of the sand dune. Tiggy was trembling. Gary wouldn't look anyone in the eye, kicking at the sand with his right front hoof, nostrils flaring.

And if that night, Tiggy gathered Gary and me in his arms to keep us close, no one said anything to the contrary. Gary woke me up in the middle of the night, whimpering in some dream I couldn't chase away. I was going to reach over and run my hand over his snout to try and calm him, but the tip of a scaly tail was already there doing just that. Kevin was pretending to be asleep, but he didn't fool me.

I lay awake for a long time that night, watching the stars.

"WHY DO YOU DO THIS?" THE King asked as I stood before him and the Prince in the throne room. They were seated, and I was at the bottom of the dais, more formal than we normally were. Justin was sitting as if uninterested, but I could see the stiffness in his shoulders. "Why do you think I would ask this of you?"

I watched him closely, trying to find the right words to say. "Am I yours?" I finally asked.

"Yes," he said without hesitation. "You are mine."

"An extension of the Crown."

"And my family."

Justin didn't scowl at that.

I felt a little flustered at the King's pronouncement, even if it warmed me to the core. "Then you know why I have to do this. I am an extension of the Crown. I act in your stead. You trust me to make the decisions I have to in order to keep you safe." I glanced at Justin. "You and the Prince."

"Morgan told me," the King said. "About what happened."

I said nothing.

"Are you running away?" he asked lightly.

I was. A little. "No," I said. "Or at least that's not the main reason."

"But it is a reason. That, and I believe it to be coupled with the protests that took place in the streets."

I shrugged, because he wasn't wrong. "Even if it hadn't happened the way it did, even if he wasn't who he is, I would still believe now. That he can do what he says he will. And I can't let that happen."

"Because you love Verania. Regardless of what it thinks about you."

"No," I said. "Because I love you."

The King took in a great shuddering breath as he shook his head. "Do you want to know what I thought when I first saw you? I thought, here is this boy, loud and bright, and I believe he will change the world. I just didn't expect you to change mine too. I am proud to know you and call you my own. Please, stop this formality. Come here and hug me."

I did. Because I loved my King very much.

Later, after the King was gone with a kiss to my forehead, Justin and I remained. We didn't say anything for a long time.

Surprisingly, he spoke first. "I didn't feel the same way when you first came."

I snorted. "I know."

"I didn't like you. In fact, I hated you. I still do sometimes."

"I know that too."

"You have to come back."

I looked up, startled, only to find Justin looking more vulnerable, more determined than I'd ever seen him before. "What?"

"You have to come back. You have to be safe and come back and be my Wizard. I could do this without you. I know I could. I am smart. And I can be kind. Sometimes. My father has taught me well. I've learned a lot in the past year. I can do this without you. But I don't want to. The King of Verania needs his Wizard. It's how it's always been. So come back, and in one piece, or I swear to the gods, I am going to put you in the dungeon where you'll poop in buckets for the rest of your days. Do you hear me?"

KEVIN AND RYAN WERE SCOUTING AHEAD while Gary, Tiggy, and I hung back. I held my summoning stone in my hand, running my thumb over it. It'd remained dark since we'd left the castle four weeks before. No one had called me. I hadn't called anyone either. I didn't want to, afraid of what I would say that I couldn't ever take back. And I thought if I had to hear

Morgan's voice right now, I would have.

"So," Gary said.

"So," Tiggy said.

I sighed. "Say whatever it is you have planned."

"Planned?" Tiggy asked, feigning surprise. "No plan. Tiggy no got time for plans."

"Damn right," Gary said. "We don't need no plans. Everything we do is executed perfectly and without complaint and/or death."

They were idiots. "I heard you practicing whatever you were going to say to me last night."

"Told you," Tiggy said to Gary.

Gary glared at me. "Spying, are we? How uncouth."

"You do it to me all the time."

"I do *not*."

"Gary, one time you had your face pressed flat against a window watching Ryan and I have sex."

"I wasn't *spying*. I heard you making this awful banshee wailing noise and had somehow convinced myself that you were either passing a gallstone the size of a lemur, or you were getting murdered by an *actual* lemur. I was coming to *save* you."

"And instead of saving me, you were being a creeper instead."

"It's not *my* fault Knight Delicious Face was choking on your dick. Honestly, Sam. I could see it bulging in his *throat*."

"Good job," Tiggy said, patting my shoulder.

I glared at both of them.

"Fine." Gary rolled his eyes. "Maybe we talked about this behind your back and then practiced what we were going to say. But it's only because we love you, in case you hadn't noticed."

"A lot," Tiggy added. "This much." He held his arms out as wide as they could go.

"Damn you," I said with a sniff. "You make me have feelings when I'm trying to be annoyed. It's your face. It does things to me."

"I got good face," Tiggy said. And he was certainly right about that.

"I'll start," Gary said. "Randall and Morgan are both idiots. Vadoma can't be trusted. Ruv is hot, and if you were single, I'd tell you to stick your dick in his butt, but you have Ryan, and he's your cornerstone, and you love him and his asshole."

"Preach," Tiggy said. "Also, people be cray-cray."

"Exactly," Gary said. "People be cray-cray. This whole *prophecy* thing, which, do we even need to discuss why Tiggy and I weren't mentioned? We're not *sidekicks*."

"Nope," Tiggy said. "Tiggy no sidekick."

"You're *my* sidekick," Gary said.

"Oh. Right. Okay."

"Anyway," Gary said. "This whole prophecy thing. Maybe it's made up. Maybe it's not. Maybe a star dragon *did* come out of the sky and tell your crazy grandma that you were going to be born and do some shit, or whatever it said."

"Save the world from falling into darkness?" I said, trying not to be amused but failing miserably.

"Right," Gary said dismissively. "Saving the world and stuff. Maybe it's true and maybe it isn't. But you know what *is* true?"

"What?"

He looked right at me, eyes impossibly wide and glistening. "You'll always have us by your side," he whispered.

And no, *no* I would not break—

He fluttered his eyelashes.

"Damn you!" I cried at him, breath hitching in my chest. "Why must you *do* that to me?"

"I'm *sorry*!" he wailed. "We just need you to know you *mean* something to us!"

"Yeah," Tiggy said, great globular tears on his cheeks. "Mean something and stuff."

"You're so manipulative! The *both* of you."

"Yes, well," Gary said, suddenly dry-eyed. "It's necessary for the next part."

I groaned as I put my face in my hands. "I don't even want to know, do I?"

"Knight Delicious Face," Tiggy said.

I groaned even louder.

"We thought...," Gary started before trailing off. And there was something in his voice that made me think he was being serious now. "We thought you already knew."

I dropped my hands. "About what?" But I knew where this was going, and I didn't like it one bit.

"Mortality," Tiggy said. "Everyone's mortal. Some more than others."

"Can we not do this now?" I asked gruffly. "We don't have time to—"

"Sam," Gary said. "You need to talk about this."

"I don't," I retorted. "I don't need to think about it at all. Because nothing is going to happen to him. Not now. Not ever."

"Sam," Gary said. "That's not how this works. You know that. Maybe nothing happens to him from the man in shadows. We'll all be there together, and we'll do our best to protect him, even if that's going to piss him off. But what happens later?"

"Don't."

"He's going to age, Sam. And you won't. Your magic won't let you.

Not like a normal human."

"I said *don't*."

"It part of you," Tiggy said. "Inside. It big. Felt it first day."

"We both did," Gary said. "It's connected to you. It's what you're made of. Sam, I'm magic because of what I am, even if I don't have my horn anymore. Tiggy's magic because his blood is *literally* made of the stuff. You? You're more than both of us combined."

"Maybe I don't want to *be* magic, then!"

The sound of my voice rolled down the dunes in front of us.

In the distance, Kevin and Ryan turned around.

Gary and Tiggy were staring at me in shock.

"Did you ever think that?" I said to them, voice lowered. "Everything I am, every part of me, this *magic*, has been manipulated, guided. Vadoma knew about me. Randall knew about me. *Morgan* knew about me. What part of me is *actually* me if they all had a hand in it? Why would I want any part of something that will take me away from him, or him from me?"

"Without it," Gary said quietly, "you wouldn't have been with him—"

"You don't know that," I said. "You *can't* know that. Life is supposed to be about random chances. About choices. I randomly found the both of you. I got to *choose* the both of you."

"And you got to choose him," Gary said slowly. "Even if Vadoma had other plans for you."

"I'm not going to let anything happen to him," I said. "I will stop this, whatever it is. And then I'll figure out the rest. I'd rather be with him without my magic than be with him and have it. Some things are important. Other things are more important."

"And what of the kingdom?" Gary asked. "Isn't that the most important of all?"

I didn't respond, which was an answer in and of itself.

I didn't miss the look exchanged between them.

But I was good at ignoring things until I had to.

It was easier that way.

"YOU'LL TRAVEL TO THE DESERT, THEN?" Vadoma asked, a glint in her eyes that I didn't like one bit. We stood alone in the throne room per my request, though I was sure everyone was trying to eavesdrop through the Great Doors. They were nosy fuckers like that.

"I will," I said.

"Hmm," she said. "It seems as if we could have come to this agreement days ago."

"And yet here we are."

"Here we are," she agreed. "We shall leave immediately. Time, I

fear, is of the essence."

I barely restrained the eye roll. "It's waited a couple of decades. I'm sure it can wait a little bit longer."

"For?"

I shook my head. "I don't trust you."

"So you've said. But no matter how you feel on the matter, you are still my blood."

"Well, we all can't be perfect."

"Your tone," she said. "I have no use for it."

"Of that I don't give two shits. I'm going to tell you how this is going to go."

"Oh? Please. Enlighten me."

I ignored that. "You will take Ruv and leave tomorrow to travel back to the desert. We will follow by the end of the week."

"I don't see why we wouldn't just travel together when—"

"You'll be on horseback, yes?"

"Yes."

"Gary will kill you, because that's racist."

"How is that racist—*"*

"It doesn't matter. We'll be on foot."

"That'll take weeks," *she said.*

"Probably," I said. "But that's the way it's going to be. Think of it this way. It'll give you time to get to the desert before us, and you can plan further ways to try and use me."

"This is not about being used," she said.

"Isn't it?" I asked, daring her to be contrary. "Because that's exactly what it sounds like to me. You're here to use *me."*

She watched me for a moment, her dark eyes assessing. "I knew not of the dark man in shadows, aside from what was shown to me. His identity has always been a mystery. The secret kept from you about him was not my doing. Do not direct your anger at me for something I did not do. And if you let it fester, if you let it boil, it will spill over until it consumes you, chava. *Anger in your heart will lead only to misfortune and misery."*

I snorted. "Fortune-telling again?"

"Personal experience," she said, and that shut me up right quick. "I agree to your terms, as long as you do not dally. It may have taken this long for us to arrive at the point we have, but there are many parts in motion right now, Sam of Wilds. You are a cog in a machine that will shred you to pieces if you do not keep up."

She left me alone in the throne room.

I SAT ON THE TOP OF a large sand dune, the sky above bright with stars. The others lay asleep near the fire below, the thin line of smoke rising up into the air. The stars seemed to be bigger out here, away from all the light and noise of the cities. And I thought maybe there were more of them, more than I'd ever seen before.

I hadn't wished upon them in a very long time.

I hadn't needed to.

But now?

Now I didn't know what to do. I didn't know if the path I was taking was the right one. I didn't know if I'd made the right choices. I didn't know if I could trust the people that I had thought could always be trusted.

"Shit," I said to the stars.

They blinked back at me, ever watchful and silent.

"I'm a little lost," I told them. "Maybe more than I think I am. I don't…. I knew my place. I knew what was expected of me. Do this, Sam. Learn this, Sam. I'm going to monologue at your face after I've captured you for some stupid reason, Sam. There was good. And there was evil. And nothing in between. I am a good guy. I know I am. And I try to do what's right. Always. Even if it hurts." I sighed. "Why does this all feel so wrong, then?"

The stars didn't respond, of course. They never really did, at least not that I could hear.

I found David's Dragon, the cluster of stars to the north. I watched it for a long time. It didn't move as it had for Vadoma, if it ever did at all. I didn't know if what I'd seen was even real.

But still.

I said, "I'll do this. For you. But you have to do something in return for me."

A breeze blew across my face, warm even in the cool night.

It was probably nothing.

I said, "Make me mortal. When all is said and done. I will protect my King, this one and the next. I will protect my kingdom. I will do all that you ask, but I want a mortal life for my happy ending. This is my wish."

"Sam."

I squawked quite loudly and fell over, sure the star dragon was right behind me and was going to eat my brains and—

"Godsdammit," I growled as I looked up at Ryan standing above me. "Don't *do* that! You can't sneak up on me because I make weird noises!"

He cocked an eyebrow at me. "As opposed to any of the other times you make weird noises?"

"You think you're funny, but you're not funny."

"Kind of funny."

"Kind of stupid. With your face."

He held a hand out toward me, and I allowed myself to be pulled back up to a sitting position. I glared at him until he moved behind me, sinking down and pulling me between his legs until I lay against his chest, his chin near my shoulder.

"Is that better?" he asked quietly.

"No. You jerk." It was a billion times better.

"Good," he said, because he could see right through me. "What were you saying?"

"Huh?"

"You were talking when I was coming up here. What were you saying?"

I stiffened, and I knew he could feel it. "Wizarding… things?"

He chuckled near my ear. "Really. You don't sound too sure about it."

"I'm sure," I insisted. "You don't even know how sure I am."

"Sam."

"I hate it when you use that tone of voice."

"Nah. You love it. Like you love everything else about me."

"Wow. You really are sure of yourself."

"Yeah, I guess I am."

And if I laid my head back on his shoulder and relaxed into him, well. That was just between the two of us.

He waited for me, like I knew he would, giving me time to parse through everything. We hadn't yet talked about this, and I didn't know how much I wanted to. He, like the others both with us and back at the castle, knew the extent of what I'd seen. I couldn't justify keeping it from them, like Morgan and Randall had kept things from me. I was a lot of things. But I wasn't a hypocrite. Mostly.

Finally, I said, "I can't lose you."

"You won't."

"I could."

"Everyone dies, Sam."

"Some sooner than others."

"I'm not going anywhere," he said lightly. He kissed the skin behind my ear. "You know that. We're together, okay? All of us. We can do this. *You* can do this. I know you can. I believe in you."

"Sap," I muttered, even though I thought I was blushing.

"Yeah," he agreed. "Probably. Just don't tell anyone, huh?"

"I think pretty much everyone knows."

"There goes my street cred."

"You never *had* any street cred," I said and then shrieked with laughter as he knocked me over while tickling my sides. He came to rest atop me, hands on either side of my head, face hidden in shadow as he was backlit by a sea of stars. I don't think I'd ever seen him look more handsome than he did at that moment, sand-swept and smiling like he didn't have a care in the world.

I kissed him as hard as I could.

For as long as I could.

I didn't think he realized I'd never answered his question about what I'd been saying as he approached. If anything, I was good at distracting.

And besides. Everyone knows you can't tell others what you wish upon the stars for.

It won't come true if you do.

"So YOU'RE LEAVING," GARY SAID, COCKING his head at me. "To the desert. To the mountains. To the Dark Woods. To find these dragons."

"Yes," I said slowly.

"And you think we're going to stay here," Kevin said.

"Ye-es?" I said.

"Sweet Sam," Tiggy said.

"Lovely Tiggy."

"You an idiot."

"Hey!"

"Well you are," Gary said. "Did you really think we're just going to sit here and let you go off on an adventure without us? Sam. Are you fucking high?"

"No," I said. "Not since that one time."

"Do I even want to know?" Ryan asked.

"Sam eat forest mushrooms," Tiggy said. "That he found in forest."

"Of course he did," Ryan said.

"Way to generalize, Tiggy," I said. "You know it was part of the ritual I needed to perform in order to escape the clutches of my captors who were convinced they could sacrifice me to an evil sprite in the Dark Woods."

"Of course they did," Ryan said.

"Riiiiight," Gary said. "Which is why when Tiggy and I rescued you, you were sitting on the back of one of the bandits, singing about how you could taste colors and that the grass was alive and whispering grassy secrets."

"Of course you—"

"Ryan! Not helping!"

"I took drugs once," Kevin said. "At this orgy I went to. Crazy, crazy night. Long story short, it wasn't actually drugs, and I'd somehow crushed and snorted sixteen sugar cubes and then eaten a lot of centaur ass—"

"Excuse me," Gary trilled. "I could have sworn we were trying to stay on topic."

"We never stay on topic," Tiggy said, sounding confused.

"Well, yes," Gary said. "But we don't need to hear anything Kevin *might say."*

"Oh, here we go." Kevin rolled his eyes. "One moment we're happy and jolly, and the next, oh look! Gary *has an issue with* something. *Shocker."*

"I have issues? *Oh, do we even* need *to go over the veritable* laundry *list that is the psychotic psychosis of the dragon named—"*

"You're not coming with me," I said.

"Yes, we are," they all said at the same time.

And that was that.

"HOLY BALLS," GARY SAID AS WE crested the sand dune.

"That's… not what I expected," Kevin said.

"No more sand," Tiggy said, sounding giddy.

"Is that…?" Ryan started, eyes wide as he took in what lay before us.

Rising out of an oasis in the middle of the desert, surrounded by a forest of palm trees, was a city built upon a desert lake that shimmered in the heat of the sun. It looked cool and inviting, but I couldn't help but feel unease at the sight of it. I knew what waited for us there. I knew what waited just beyond the city in a cave that led underneath the desert.

"Mashallaha," I said. "The gypsy city."

"What does it mean?" Ryan asked. "The name."

"As the gods will," I said, trying not to focus on *that* part at all. "Come on. The sooner we get this done, the sooner we can go home."

"DON'T FORGET YOUR GRIMOIRE," A VOICE said behind me. I cursed under my breath, sure I'd come into the labs undetected. Which, in all honesty, was probably my first mistake. Undoubtedly, he had the entire castle warded so he knew who was where at any given time. He'd told me once that of course that was ridiculous, being such an invasion of privacy, but I wasn't feeling very charitable toward Morgan of Shadows right then.

"Wouldn't dream of it," I said airily, wanting to get out of there as soon as possible. Mean and petty, sure, but I was more than a little annoyed.

I took my Grimoire down from its place next to his on the shelf. My fingers brushed against the binding on his book, and I felt his magic jolt through me, sweet and familiar. I realized he'd never told me what his Grimoire was bound with, telling me I'd know when the time was right. I wondered what else he'd kept from me. What other secrets he had. Where was Myrin's Grimoire? Had he even had one?

I pushed the thoughts away. There was still much I had to do and a short time with which to do it. I shoved my Grimoire into my pack and hoisted it on my shoulder. I turned and gave him a nod, trying to keep the surprise off my face to see him by himself, no Randall in sight.

Morgan himself had a carefully blank expression, betraying nothing. I'd seen him with the same look when dealing with unruly heads of state, knowing his countenance didn't give away just how much of a dumbass he thought they were. Whether or not he was thinking the same thing about me, I didn't care. I needed to leave. I was angry at him. Very angry. It was deeply unsettling, because I'd never been that way with him before.

I forced myself to meet his gaze before heading for the door. Part of me screamed to turn around, to get everything off my chest, to never say goodbye without actually saying *goodbye, but I didn't. I reached the door. It felt like I was vibrating. I put my hand on the knob. I turned it. The lock clicked and—*

"He wasn't always bad," Morgan said quietly. "My brother."

I stopped. Tried to breathe through it.

"He was... smart. Strong willed. Vibrant. A sense of humor like you wouldn't believe. Everyone was charmed by him. He wasn't afraid to step on people if it meant getting what he wanted, but he would always make sure to apologize for doing so. And the difference between him and others is that he would be sincere *about it. If he did you wrong, he was genuinely sorry about it."*

I let go of the door but didn't turn around.

"He was older than me," Morgan continued. "By centuries. Our parents were... difficult, to say the least. More obsessed with furthering their magic than caring about their sons. They regretted us, I think. Or, rather, they were indifferent toward us. I don't believe they meant for Myrin to happen. They certainly didn't mean for me to happen, but sometimes, fate and magic have minds of their own, and when they intertwine, the results can be... unexpected."

"How is he Randall's cornerstone?" I asked begrudgingly. I didn't want to acknowledge any of it, but that question had been bugging me almost as much as why Morgan had kept what he did from me and what had happened to Myrin in the first place.

"Randall's... different."

"No shit."

"Like you're different."

I whirled around at that. "Are you comparing me to him?" I suppose it could have been a compliment to anyone else, but it was Randall. *This was not a compliment to me.*

He shrugged, face still blank. "It's not an off comparison. A wizard builds, Sam. That's what magic is. That's what the cornerstone is for. But even before you can build, you must design. You can't just start putting the blocks together without a coherent plan to do so. The results could be.... Well. That's what the Darks are. People who will not invest the time needed to follow the true path of magic. They are impatient. Cut corners. They burn out parts of their hearts and soul just to have a taste of magic on their tongue."

"I don't see what that has to do with Randall. Or me."

He drummed his fingers along the countertop. "Of course you don't. Because you don't see the big picture. You think of here. Of now. Not decades down the road."

"Maybe because parts of it have been hidden from me," I snapped.

And there it was, the barest of flinches, the smallest of cracks in the mask. I knew he wasn't indifferent to all this. I knew that. Morgan loved me, maybe more than anyone else in the world. That wasn't in question.

But he had lied. He had withheld the truth from me. I'd trusted him, and maybe part of me still did. I trusted him to protect the King and Justin. I trusted him to protect my parents. And Tiggy and Gary and Ryan. I trusted him to protect me. But everything else?

I didn't know anymore.

"There are reasons, Sam," he said. "For everything. Even if you're angry at me now, and even if you don't understand, there are reasons for everything I do."

"You didn't choose me," I said. "I always thought you had. But you didn't. I was forced upon you by some crazy lady from the desert. That's all this ever was. And to make it worse, you left us to wallow in the slums. You could have come for us earlier. You didn't. Do you know how many times my parents went hungry just so I could be fed? How many times I heard my mother crying at night because she thought she had failed me?"

The mask cracked further. He took a step toward me, made an aborted motion to reach out for me. Instead, his hand fell to his side and curled into a fist. "I was wrong," he said. "And for that, I'm sorry. I didn't know what to do. Randall was... adamant. That we let your life unfold as naturally as possible before needing to intervene. He thought it would build your character, that it would make you a better person. And while I don't disagree, I believe you should have been given more. And it is my fault that didn't happen. I should have fought harder. I am imperfect, Sam. No matter what you may have thought about me before. I am to blame as much as Randall is. If not more."

"Why? Why did he think that? Why would Randall put me through that?"

"Myrin," Morgan said. "Randall thought mistakes made in the past could be avoided in the future. He designed his magic, Sam. For centuries. More than anyone else has ever done before. And when it was time to find his cornerstone, he didn't have to look very far."

"What does that have to do with me?"

"You're like him in that you're different. But where he created design after design after design, your magic was already within you. What you did that day in the alley so very long ago should have been impossible. The design of your magic was at levels far beyond what I or Myrin or even Randall ever had. Which is why finding your cornerstone when you did, at an age so

young, was the right path meant for you. It was the only path meant for you. It wasn't just fate, Sam. It was necessary."

"And if I hadn't found him?" I asked, jaw tense. "If I hadn't found Ryan? Would you have pawned me off on Ruv when Vadoma came for me?"

He hesitated. "I would have laid out your options."

I snorted. "It's a good thing that I made my own choices, then."

"Yes, Sam. It is."

"I'm so angry, Morgan."

"I know."

"At Randall. At you. At Vadoma. This is my *life that you all meddled in."*

"I know."

"Do you?" I spat at him.

He looked older than I'd ever seen him before. "Every choice I've made, whether good or bad, has always been with your best interest in mind. Yes, I knew of you before. Yes, I could have done more. Yes, this impossible situation feels like our hand was forced. But Sam, I chose to love you as I do because of who you are, not who you were supposed to be. I love you because you mean the world to me. You have always been the joy that is in my heart."

"Godsdammit," I said, wiping my eyes. "That is so unfair. You manipulative bastard. Hitting me right in the feels."

There was a small smile on his face. "Is it working?"

"Maybe. I'm still mad."

"I know."

"I'm going to hug you, though."

I thought maybe his shoulders sagged a little in relief at that, but he put on a good front. "Must we?"

"We must," I said, shuffling forward. And I didn't even have it in me to chide him when his arms came up around me and held me tightly, his beard tickling my cheek. It was a good hug, but I didn't let it last very long. I had a point to prove, after all.

I pulled away, and he let me go. I took a step back, shouldering the pack again. I wanted to leave, to put some distance between us so I could clear my head, but I needed more.

"Myrin," I said.

Morgan looked away. "We couldn't save him. Not when he started walking a path we could not follow. Not I, his brother, nor Randall, his love, could drag him away from the dark. There was a king, long before the Good King, that was driven mad by Myrin's counsel. Randall brought the king back by the sheer force of his will, and together, we banished Myrin to a realm of shadows because we could not bear to end his life. We begged him. We pleaded with him. But he was already lost to the dark. And nothing we could do would have brought him back. We failed him, Sam. And I will have to live with that for the rest of my life."

"Did you know it was him?" I asked. "When Vadoma came to you about the dark man in shadows?"

"No," Morgan said. "Or at least I'd hoped. I've spent the decades making sure the seals remained in place between this world and the shadow world. I didn't even feel them crack."

"Then how did he come back?"

"That is the mystery, Sam."

I set the pack on the countertop and sighed. This was already more complicated than I had hoped it would be. "You have to tell me," I said. "Everything. Because if this is true, if the star dragon was right, then Myrin will come for me. And I will do everything I can to stop your brother."

And so he did. He spoke in a monotone, flat and expressionless. By the time he'd finished, his voice was hoarse and my heart hurt. For him. For Randall. And for what it was I was being called on to do. And I was trembling, because the story he'd told, the things that had been done, shook me to my very core. Before I left, I took his face in my hands and kissed his forehead as he gripped my arms.

He said, "Be safe, Sam of Wilds. The world depends upon it. As do I, because I need you so."

I nodded and left him standing in the labs with nothing but the memories of loss and betrayal.

And I didn't look back.

CHAPTER 13
The Gypsy City

As we approached Mashallaha, the picture became clearer as to what waited for us. I had never ventured this far west, knowing I was considered banished given that I was my mother's son. And the desert really didn't appeal to me. All that sand getting into my crevices was not my idea of a good time.

I knew of Mashallaha, as I knew of every major city in Verania. I'd heard the stories, seen the drawings, but nothing prepared me for the first sight of it.

It *was* in the middle of the oasis, the buildings and homes and shops built atop the lake that was fed from some underground source. Mashallaha was mostly wood, the city resting on thick pillars that were embedded into the lakebed below. Everything was connected by wooden planks and pathways above the water, with narrow channels built for speedier travel by long, thin canoes. It looked like paradise with its brightly colored flags and lights on strings that stretched between all the dwellings.

The rich would often come to Mashallaha on vacation, as it was as exotic as anything got in Verania. Most of Mashallaha's economy was built around tourism, with lavish and rustic hotels and gypsy customs that seemed mysterious and bizarre to the more refined city-folk. Traveling to Mashallaha was harsh and arduous but supposedly made worth it when you were lying on a bed padded with palm fronds, feeling the room rock gently around with the waves below, staring up through an open panel at the stars above.

I didn't have time for shit like that.

The last time I tried to take a vacation was six months ago with Ryan. We'd been halfway to Meridian City when we were attacked by a group of audacious trolls who were convinced that Ryan was somehow their queen,

something I had yet to let him live down. Needless to say, it'd ended up with
him wearing a crown of flowers while I was tied to a tree, too busy laughing
my ass off to try and save either of us. Eventually they'd let us go, but only
after Ryan had promised to return on a regular basis as their figurehead. He'd
been back twice so far. Gary was seriously jealous over it.

But other than that, between wizarding and some really spectacular
butt sex, I didn't have time for long getaways. The fact that we were here now
was because our hand had been forced. Even with the beauty of Mashallaha, I
wanted to spend as little time here as I could before moving on. It would take
us a good six weeks to reach Castle Freeze Your Ass Off after dealing with
the desert dragon, and I wanted to get there sooner rather than later so I could
give Randall a piece of my mind face to face.

"Oh, thank the gods," Gary moaned as we got closer. "This has been
hell on my thighs. I am going to find the most bronze cabana boy I can and
make him massage my flanks while feeding me little pieces of frozen fruit."

"And I shall find an even *bronzer* cabana boy and show him the wonders of a forked tongue," Kevin said, holding his head up high. "You know
what they say. You haven't been porked until you've been forked."

"No one says that," I said. "Literally no one at all."

"I heard it before," Tiggy said. "From Gary."

"Tiggy!" Gary shrieked. "I would *never*. I have a bit more self-respect
than *that*."

"Pfft," Kevin said, a little tendril of smoke curling from his nostrils.
"That's not what you said when you were sitting on my dick."

"You'd think I'd be used to hearing things like that." Ryan grimaced.
"You'd be wrong."

"Sam," Gary said. "Would you please tell Kevin that I am *much* class-
ier than—"

"Nope," I said. "Nope, nope, nope. Stop it. Just stop it. I'm tired. I hate
the sun. I have sand on the skin between my balls and my asshole. I am going
to a city run by my grandmother, who I believe is sketchy and nefarious. I
have to face a dragon who could eat me alive. All I want to do is lay on a
bed, not move for hours, and I cannot do that if I have to sit here and *listen
to your shit*."

"Oh *snap*," Tiggy said. "Sam go rawr."

"Can I be honest right now?" Gary asked. "That turned me on a little
bit. Like, at least half a chub." He fluttered his eyelashes at me. "You want
to go get a drink later? Maybe after, if you're lucky, you can finally find out
what it means to taste the rainbow."

"Oh my gods," I gagged. "Everything hurts. Everything *hurts*."

"I'm coming after your man," Gary told Ryan. "You best watch your
back. When Gary sets his eyes on something, Gary gets what he wants."

"Yeah," Ryan said. "You know what? I'm not too worried about that
this time around."

"Because you've already accepted the inevitable?"

"Sure," Ryan said, rubbing a hand on my back in a slow circle. "Let's go with that."

"I'm bigger than he is," Kevin grumbled. "And I mean *everywhere*."

"Hey!" I snapped. "It's not about the size, but what you do with it. Trust me, Gary's not even gonna remember your name by the time I get done plowing him like a—*holy gods, what am I even saying?*"

"Maybe a little worried." Ryan frowned.

"Someone's getting a piece of wizard tonight!" Gary crowed gleefully.

"I want some wizard too," Tiggy said with a pout.

"We can share," Gary told him.

"Over my dead body," Ryan said. "You do realize I have a sword, right? I will motherfuc—"

"No cussing!" I admonished him. "You're a godsdamned knight, for fuck's sake. Act like one!"

"—mothercracking *stab* you if you try and get up in his business."

Get up in his business, Gary mouthed to Tiggy, looking bewildered. Tiggy just shrugged. I felt a little tingly myself.

And of course, since we were distracted by Gary and his threats of spraying me in primary colors, we didn't see the guards standing at the gates to Mashallaha until one of them coughed.

We all turned to glare at them.

They took a step back, eyes wide, muttering to each other in the gypsy tongue. I was hit with a little pang at the thought of my mother, how much it sounded like her. She would have grown up in this place, and left it all behind to be with my father in the slums. She gave up a life in paradise to be with the one she loved. Gods, that was romantic as all hell.

"Sorry," I said, putting on my most winsome smile. "We were… distracted."

"Distracted by my dick," Gary muttered.

I elbowed him in the throat, ignoring the way he started choking like a drama queen. "We have come from the City of Lockes," I said. "I am—"

"We know who you are," the guard on the right said.

"We know why you've come," the guard on the left said, and it was only then that I realized they were twins, with beautiful dark skin, black hair pulled back tightly in a bun. They wore thin pants cinched at the ankles and brightly colored open vests with nothing underneath, showing off lean muscle on hairless torsos covered in tattoos. They carried spears in their hands, but they weren't pointed at us. Their dark eyes were trained on me.

"She is expecting you," Right said.

"We are all expecting you," Left said.

They bowed in unison.

"Creepy," Gary singsonged under his breath. "Do you think they make out at all? I'd be down with that."

"That's... good," I said to the twins, a little taken aback. "I am glad you're—"

They stood back up, ignoring me completely, looking up at Kevin instead. "Lord Dragon," Left said. "It is an honor to be standing in your glorious presence."

Everyone but Kevin groaned.

"No," I said. "You can't say that to him. You don't know what you'll *unleash*—"

"*Lord* Dragon, you say?" Kevin said, cocking his head. "*Lord* Dragon. Well now. *This* is certainly... expected. It has been far too long since I have been addressed as such."

Left and Right turned to glare at me.

"What?" I asked. "*I* didn't do anything. He's not a *lord*—"

"Don't listen to the plebian," Kevin said, affecting an air of superiority. Like an asshole. "He shan't know what he spaketh of. Thou shalt listen to me: Lord Dragon. The Beast from the East. Thy and they may calleth me his majestic majesty, King of all dragons.... Kevin."

"That's a terrible name," I whispered to Gary.

"He's a terrible dragon," Gary whispered back.

"I like it," Tiggy said. "Lord Tiggy, King of Brooms and Happy. Capitalized."

"It must be true now," Ryan said. "Because that's how that works. I know this because I'm a part of the group and fit in and belong."

"He tries so hard," Gary said fondly. "Too bad he fails more often than not."

"I do *not*!"

"Yes, your majestic majesty, king of all dragons, Kevin," Left said. "A most wonderful title. It... rolls right off the tongue."

"Yes," Kevin said, "it does. Things often roll right off my tongue. Like words. And bodily fluids from twins—"

"And that's probably something we shouldn't be talking about," I said quickly. "Because certainly a *lord* of your status wouldn't be so crass in front of *people we don't even know.*"

Left and Right glared at me again.

"What?" I asked, confused.

"Interrupting a dragon is a terrible thing to do," Left said.

"When a dragon speaks, his words are pearls of wisdom that must be collected," Right said.

"Have you ever heard a dragon speak?" I asked.

"No," they said.

"Wow. Then I am super sorry for raining on *that* parade, because—"

"I have pearls of wisdom," Kevin interrupted.

"Really," I said, dubious. "You do. *You*."

"Yes. I have them all the time!"

"Then by all means. Let's hear one right now."

Right and Left looked like they were about to swoon.

"Fine," Kevin said. He sat back on his haunches and cleared his throat. "Everything shiny leadeth to distraction. Distractions leadeth to sin. Giveth the Lord Dragon your shinies and I shall relieve you of your sins. So spaketh the Lord Dragon, as handsome as he is benevolent."

"Ooh," Left and Right said.

I face-palmed.

This was the worst adventure ever.

IT TURNED OUT THAT PRETTY MUCH everyone was enamored by the sight of Kevin, openly staring at him in awe as he walked through the city, the pathways creaking dangerously underneath his weight. They were indifferent toward Tiggy, much to his delight, and dismissive of Gary, much to his righteous anger.

But toward Ryan and me?

You would have thought we'd come to rob their women and pillage their men with the looks we were getting. For every person that squealed at the sight of the dragon, there was another person who looked like they were getting ready to junk-punch Ryan or me, or possibly even both of us at the same time. It wasn't something I was used to, this open hostility. While by no means universally beloved, I thought at least I had the will of the people at my back. And certainly, the dashing and immaculate Ryan Foxheart did, no matter where he went. Aside from that display by my archnemesis Lady Tina DeSilva and the protesters, we usually were respected, for the most part.

Except, apparently, in Mashallaha.

It wasn't until we'd gotten halfway through the city and I'd seen a man physically hold back a woman before she threw a clay vase at my head that I had to ask.

"So," I said to Left. "How are you?"

"Fine," he said, rather stiffly.

"That's good. I like your... spear. It's very sharp."

"Thank you. I made it myself."

"That's nice. I'm so glad we talked about this. Question."

"If you must."

"I must. I don't know if you've noticed, but there seems to be a large amount of people here that seem to want to chop off my legs and shove them up my ass."

That didn't even seem to faze him in the slightest. "Vivid," Left said. "And accurate."

"Uh-huh. Any—any specific reason for that, you think?"

He turned to glare at me again. "Surely you jest."

"I'm not jesting," I said. "I barely jest at all."

"He jests all the time," Gary said. "They call him Jester behind his back."

"Don't listen to him," I said. "He's a little sun drunk right now. Unicorns get like that and then stupidity falls from their mouths. He doesn't know what he's saying and should probably *shut up.*"

"Yikes," Gary said. "Someone needs food or a good dicking. I know which one *I'm* always down for—"

"Anyway," I said loudly. "What's the deal here? What's going on? What's the haps? Am I going to be murdered?"

"No," Left said, sounding exasperated. "Of course not."

"Oh good. Because I don't want to be murdered." It was probably in the top five things I didn't want to have happen to me. Maybe even the top three.

"The Knight Commander might be, though."

"That's fine, as long as it's not me—wait, what?" I stopped walking. Ryan crashed into the back of me. "What's this about Ryan getting murdered?"

"I'm getting what now?" Ryan asked, eyebrows almost disappearing into his hairline.

"Murdered," Tiggy whispered loudly before he started cackling like a maniac.

"Oh," Ryan said. "That's... not good. I would rather stay alive, thanks." He gave his most winning smile to Left and Right. My underwear almost fell off, but the guards didn't appear to be swayed at all. The smile faded slightly. I wanted to rim his butt to make him feel better, but now was not the time or place. For some reason, our powers of persuasion seemed to be dwindling. That was not a good sign. Especially in a foreign city surrounded by strangers.

"And why do they want to do that?" I asked slowly, inching my way in front of Ryan, even though he was scowling at me for it.

"Because of you," Left said, as if it were obvious.

"Because of who you chose," Right said, as if we were idiots.

"HaveHeart," they both said at the same time, sounding disgusted.

"Everyone knows that HaveWolf is better," Left said.

"HaveWolf is where the magic is," Right said.

"What," Ryan said flatly.

"HaveHeart for life, motherfuckers," Tiggy said, frowning deeply.

What the hell were they— "Ohhh," I said. "*I* get it. That's clever. Ruv is Vadoma's *Wolf.* And they think we should be together in a sexy way, if you know what I mean. Like, touching penises and stuff. So, HaveWolf. Wow, that sure sounds erotically charged and—"

Ryan's face did something complicated.

"—and absolutely ridiculous, of course, because I don't *need* to have any other name because I've already got my man right here. Who I love. With my heart. All of it, for true."

Nice save, if I did say so myself. Which I did.

Ryan didn't seem to think so, given that he scowled harder.

"Be that as it may," Left said. "You'll find that people here aren't as... welcoming."

"Given that the Wolf is a wonderful man with many fine qualities that you should probably inspect a little closer," Right said.

"In fact, we would be willing to set that up for you, if you'd like," Left said.

"And the Knight Commander could take his rest."

"Or go out into the desert for an extended period of time."

"By himself."

"For days. Or maybe forever."

"Subtle, aren't they?" Ryan asked, crossing his arms over his chest.

"A little," I said. "Maybe conniving too."

"I think I'm good here," Ryan said to the twins. "In fact, I don't know that I feel the need to let Sam out of my sight our entire visit."

"So controlling," Left said. "Troubling."

"So demanding," Right said. "Concerning."

"Babe," I said. "I'm my own man. I got this." I leaned over to kiss him on the cheek. Instead, I hissed in his ear, "Don't ever leave me because I'm pretty sure they're cannibals and will eat your flesh."

He started coughing quite loudly.

"You okay?" I asked him, pulling away, eyes wide and innocent.

He nodded, waving at me dismissively while bent over slightly, the poor dear.

"Left, Right," I said. "Because those are the names I've given you since I can't be bothered to learn your real ones. I'm going to set something straight right now."

"Please," Gary said. "You've never done anything straight in your life."

"Zing," Tiggy said, hoof/fist-bumping Gary.

I ignored them because they were stupid. "I love Ryan. He is my cornerstone. That's not going to change, no matter what anyone says or does. And if any harm comes to him while we're here, I will place blame on Mashallaha and will bring the full might of the Crown upon you."

They stared blankly at me.

"Also, I'll have Kevin burn this place to the ground. Kevin! Give them a demonstration of the power you wield!"

I grinned at them as their eyes widened, waiting for Kevin to rear up and blow a monstrous plume of fire into the air to show them what happened when they fucked with Sam of Wilds. Maybe he would even roar a little and shake the foundation of Mashallaha beneath our feet.

Of course, nothing happened.

"Kevin," I said without looking away from the twins. "Anytime now."

"Um," Ryan said. "He's... busy?"

I looked behind me.

Kevin was lying on his stomach, tail flicking back and forth rapidly as he accepted bright and shiny treasures from gypsies who were lining up ahead of him. "Oh yes," he purred. "I do like this muchly. Your Lord Dragon is pleased and will continue to bestow a bounty upon you and your household. Next, please. Oh, what's this? Is that *real* gold? My word, you get *extra* bounty upon your house. I just... wait a minute. This isn't *real*. My gods, this is *fake gold*. It's not even *fake gold*. It's... it's a tin can you painted *yellow*? You *dare* to try and defy your Lord Dragon? I have half a mind to eat your toes even though I am a vegetarian! Bah, be gone with you, waste of human space! So spaketh Lord Dragon!"

"Godsdammit," I muttered. "That hardly ever works."

"Maybe you should learn to be more intimidating on your own," Gary said.

"Ooh," Tiggy said. "Sam scary like butterflies scary."

I frowned. "But butterflies aren't scary."

"Tiggy wins," Tiggy said sagely.

"It probably doesn't help that you're diluted, either," Left said, and that brought the conversation around me to a screeching halt.

"Diluted," I repeated.

Right looked at me with faint disdain. "Your blood. It's been tainted."

"Oh no he didn't," Gary breathed.

"Oh yes he did," Tiggy said, growling low in his throat.

"I'm going to not make any assumptions here," I said slowly. "Because I want to be clear on what you mean."

Left was confused, like he couldn't sense the simmering anger. "Your father, of course. The northern people, pale as the snow. It has lightened your skin and diluted your blood. Your magic would be so much more if you were pure and from the gypsy clan. You are too... white."

"Tiggy," Gary snarled. "Hold me back. Hold me back!"

Tiggy grabbed on to him tightly.

Gary began to struggle. "Let me at him, you overgrown assface! Tiggy, let me at 'em!"

And I... well. I didn't know what to say to that. I didn't know that I'd ever been discriminated against for the color of my skin. Yes, I wasn't as dark as the people in the gypsy city, and yes, my father was white, but it wasn't a problem in the City of Lockes. Or Meridian City. Or anywhere else

I'd traveled in Verania.

But before I did something rash and accidentally exploded them where they stood, I thought maybe it didn't actually have to do with me, per se. Yes, they were talking *about* me, but it—

"My father is a good man," I said, voice as even as possible. "My mother is a great woman."

And there it was. The matching looks of derision. It wasn't so much that I was lighter in skin than they were, but more the prejudice over the fact that my mother had chosen to leave the clan rather than forsake her love. They saw me as tainted not because of my father, but because of my mother's choice.

You know what?

Fuck these guys.

I ignored the crowd that had started to gather around us, people whispering to each other, eyeing us warily. They were inconsequential at the moment. If they pressed forward any farther, then we'd have a problem. But right now, they were on the periphery.

Ryan had his hand on his sword, still sheathed at his side. He sounded like he was barely in control of his fury when he spoke. "I am the Knight Commander of the Castle Guard, serving under Good King Anthony and the Grand Prince of Verania. But if you say something like that again to Sam, I will cut your mothercracking heads off."

"And then I will bathe in your blood and put unicorn curses on your *children*!" Gary shrieked.

"So badass," I whispered reverently.

Kevin had ambled his way back over, the wooden platforms creaking under his weight. "Hear me, O people of Malapala."

"It's Mashallaha," I told him.

"Mashamasha."

"Mashallaha."

"Macarena."

"Kevin, just threaten them already!"

"Right, right. Ahem. *Ahem*. Hear me, people of Mash Potatoes…"

"Oh my gods."

"…I am a benevolent Lord Dragon, but I can also kick some major ass if called upon to do so. You may bask in my presence—in fact, I encourage you to do so because I am *glorious*—but if there is one wrong move made toward Sam of Wilds, I will burn the flesh from your bones."

The crowd took a step back.

"Damn right," Kevin growled. "I have motherfucking *spaketh*. Now give me your shiny shit and get out of my sight, you racist dickbags."

I don't think I'd ever seen so much gold thrown in my direction before in my life. I felt like a high-class stripper.

LEFT AND RIGHT DIDN'T HAVE MUCH else to say as they led us farther into the city. The people still stared as we passed, but they kept their mouths shut and averted their eyes anytime Kevin or Gary glared at them. Tiggy kept right at my heels and snarled at everything, like he was daring anyone to even look at me wrong. Ryan walked at my side, hand gripped in mine. I could almost pretend that everything was fine, that everything was *normal*, but when had any part of my life ever been normal?

That was slightly distressing.

We were in what had to be the middle of Mashallaha, the water below us crystal clear, the walkways shaded by palm trees, when Left and Right slowed to a stop. Ahead of us was what appeared to be four large carriages stacked atop each other. All the wheels were gone, and they looked to have been repurposed as a residence instead of part of a caravan. The carriages were stacked purposefully at odd angles, the middle jutting out to the left, the top facing toward the right. A wooden staircase wrapped around the outside of the dwelling, with a landing at each carriage house. Wind chimes hung over the bottom doorway, loud and obnoxious in the breeze. The door to the lowest carriage was a bright yellow, strange symbols carved into the wood.

It was loud and gaudy and over the top.

I loved it.

"Uh-oh," Gary said.

"What?" Ryan asked.

"Sam has that look on his face."

"What look?"

"We should live here," I said, ignoring the both of them. "Make this exact same house back at Castle Lockes and live in it forever."

"The crazy-eyed look he gets when he sees something kitschy and needs to own it," Gary sighed. "I blame his fairy drag mother. Mama always said Sam had an inner drag queen, just waiting to burst free. You should have seen him the day he discovered how to make his own feather boas. Those poor, poor ducks."

"Sam," Ryan said, touching me on the shoulder. "We're not going to live in a replica of this house ever."

I gave him a wounded look. My bottom lip trembled. "But... I've been dreaming of this for the last forty seconds."

"Don't you give me that look," Ryan warned me. "I swear to the gods, it's not going to work this time."

"It gonna work this time," Tiggy whispered to Gary.

"It always does, kitten. We've taught him well."

"We'll talk about it later," Ryan said, foolishly trying to hold on to his convictions. He should have known better by now. I would never let this go.

"Yeah, good luck with that," Gary said. "Guarantee you'll be living in your own gypsy palace a week after we get back."

"Two weeks," I said. "At most."

"Can we focus on the whole saving-the-world thing first?" Ryan asked. "Because I feel like that should be our priority."

"Gods," I muttered. "You're such a knight sometimes."

"And just what the hell is *that* supposed to mean?"

"Such a knight," Tiggy said. "Calm your tits, Knight Delicious Face."

Before we could go any further (and knowing us, this conversation would have probably gone on for at least another hour), the yellow door opened, and out stepped Ruv, the Wolf of Bari Lavuta.

"Does he *always* have to be shirtless?" Ryan asked. "Does he own shirts? I can give him one of mine. Probably would be too big on him. Because *I'm* bigger than he is. So my shirts would be too."

"It's embarrassing to witness, isn't it?" Gary said to Tiggy.

"No self-awareness," Tiggy agreed.

"Sam," Ruv said, a small smile on his face. "Welcome home. I hope the journey was an uneventful one. Mashallaha is honored to have you here."

"I have bunions," Gary said. "On my hooves. It was *not* uneventful. If anything, it was an *event*. I demand retribution because of—welcome *home*? Oh, no. No, no, no. I'm onto you, exotic twink. Don't think that I'm not."

"This isn't my home," I said. "But we appreciate the greeting nonetheless. Mashallaha is very beautiful. I can see why you would be proud of your city. But it is not my own." I could be diplomatic when the situation called for it. Morgan had made sure of that. But I was already on edge in being here, unsure of what else could be waiting for us.

"The people have been less than welcoming," Ryan said. "Insinuations about Sam's parentage, the lack of a proper honor guard. Is this how Mashallaha greets the King's Wizard?"

"Apprentice," Gary coughed. "Still an apprentice."

The smile on Ruv's face didn't shrink. If anything, it widened, just a little. "Forgive us, Knight Commander," he said, bowing the barest amount. "Vadoma doesn't stand on ceremony as they do in Lockes. And as far as the people are concerned, I assure you, they are merely curious about Mashallaha's long-lost son."

"The guards said he was diluted," Ryan spat. "That the gypsies thought him weak because he was lighter in color than they were."

Ruv's eyes narrowed. He turned and barked out something in his native tongue, the words clipped and harsh. Left and Right snapped to attention, nodding furiously before brushing past us back the way we'd come. Kevin snapped his jaws after them, and they squeaked as they ran faster. The dragon winked at me before sitting back up and glaring at Ruv.

"My apologies," Ruv said, voice kind. "No one should ever be judged by the color of their skin."

"I never have been before," I said. "Until today. It was… eye-opening."

"Some are stuck in old ways." Ruv stepped forward until he was right in front of me. We were the same height, and his eyes were dark and deep. He reached up, rested a hand on my bicep, and squeezed it gently. "But not all of us think that way. And I assure you, your grandmother does not."

I chuckled bitterly. "Right, because she showed kindness to my father."

"Tradition." Ruv shrugged. "Our culture is steeped in it, even if we don't understand much of it anymore. Such is the way of things. Come, you must be weary. Vadoma will meet with you now." He glanced over my shoulder, the quickest of things, before looking back at me. "Alone, if it pleases you. She would have time with her grandson, one on one. The others will be fed and shown to their rooms."

"Not gonna happen," Ryan said, taking a step forward, knocking Ruv's hand off my arm. "We don't know you, we don't know this place. You're not separating us at any point."

And that... well. I got what he was saying. I knew what he was trying to do. And I also knew that Ryan Foxheart's protective streak was a mile wide. I appreciated it, because I loved him. I knew what he'd lost in his life, and that he thought he didn't have much to call his own. But sometimes it almost pushed too far, like he thought I wasn't capable of handling myself. Like I knew Randall thought. And Morgan sometimes did, even though he'd deny it. And lumping Ryan in with those two was probably not my best choice at the moment, given that Randall and Morgan were on my shit list.

"Give us a moment?" I asked Ruv sweetly. "Gotta have a quick word with my babe."

Ruv bowed his head in response.

I gripped Ryan by the arm and started dragging him away from the others.

"Uh-oh," Gary said. "He's gone and done it now."

"Sam don't need no mens?" Tiggy asked as he started to unload the packs from Gary's back.

"He is a strong and independent twink who don't need no mens," Gary agreed.

"I am *not* a twink," I growled over my shoulder.

"Little bit," Kevin said. "Okay, a lot."

Ryan looked like he had geared himself up for a fight by the time we were out of earshot. So I said, "I love you," and he melted a little, like I knew he would. "But I also don't need you protecting me all the time."

"It's not *all* the time," he said, sounding chagrined. "It's just a lot of the times."

It would have been irritating if it wasn't so godsdamned adorable. "You won't always be there, Ryan."

That was probably the wrong thing to say. The expression on his face hardened. "I told you that I would, Sam. Nothing's going to break us apart."

"No," I said, shaking my head. "I didn't mean like—look. There are going to be times when you aren't around that I'll need to take care of myself. And if you hadn't noticed, there were twenty years before you where I did *just* that. I don't need you coming to my rescue all the time. I need you to trust me enough to know that I can handle things on my own."

"I *do* trust you. You know that."

Gods, I was such a sucker for earnestness. And no one could do earnest like the Knight Commander. "I know you do."

"But we're also a team," he said. "And sometimes I think *you* forget that. You're not alone. It's not just the Sam, Gary, and Tiggy show anymore. There are more of us here now, things *mean* more, and yet you still choose to be reckless."

Ouch. That... hurt. Probably more than it should have. "I'm not *reckless*," I said stiffly.

He sighed. "Of course that's what you took from that."

"What else was there to take? Enlighten me."

His face did that thing again where he was frustrated. "I just.... Sam, with all of this. This prophecy. This... your grandmother, the star dragon, all the *other* dragons." He hesitated. Then, "Myrin. I mean, have you thought all of this through? What the repercussions are? What this could mean for you? For us? For Verania? Or are you running away half-cocked like you always do?"

"Half-*cocked*? What the hell? And I'm not *running*. From *anything*."

"You ran from Morgan and Randall," he said, and I couldn't help but bristle at that. Only because he was right. "And don't tell me you didn't. We both know what happened. We both know the only reason we're here right now is because you're angry. I don't blame you for that. I don't know that I'd be any different. But that's why—"

"Wrong," I said coolly. "We're here right now because apparently something or someone saw fit to make sure I get screwed no matter what I want for myself. That if it's not one thing, it's another. I'm here because there is a man coming who could take away everything I love. I'm *here* to make sure that doesn't happen. And if I have to take the word of a fucking crazy old lady that I've never met before who claims I have a destiny written in the stars, then I will. Everything I thought I knew, everything about who I'm supposed to be has been a lie. This is the *last* thing I can do to regain control. And by gods, I'm going to do it."

"Really," he said, taking a step back and shaking his head. "Everything has been a lie. That's how you see it. So I suppose Gary and Tiggy wouldn't die for you. That your parents don't worship the ground you walk on. That the King of Verania doesn't think you're one of the greatest things he's ever known. That two of the most powerful wizards in the *world* don't bend over backwards to keep you safe." He laughed, but it was a harsh sound. "That I don't love you with everything I am. Because why would that be true?"

"Ryan—"

"You should go to Vadoma," he said, looking over my shoulder. "Alone. Like you wanted. She doesn't seem like the type who's okay with waiting. But that's okay. Since you can handle yourself and all."

He brushed past me without another word.

And I didn't even try and stop him.

CHAPTER 14
The King of Sorrow

"I've asked Ruv to join us," Vadoma Tshilaba said. "I feel it prudent to have his input. He is well-versed in the desert dragon."

I nodded but didn't speak. We sat in a darkened room, the windows covered in thick curtains, only a sliver of sunlight slipping through. The room felt warm, humid, and it wasn't helped by the numerous flickering candles she had lit in all corners. We were in the very topmost carriage, having walked up the staircase that wrapped around the outside until we reached a bloodred door. The room itself was smaller than I expected it to be, stuffed to the gills with books and trinkets and skulls of animals I didn't recognize. I could make out a large ornate desk on the other side near a block of windows, the top littered with sage and rosemary and thyme, all of which added to the heavy stagnant perfume that hung around us. There was a stone fireplace, the charred remains of *something* inside, blackened and cracked.

Vadoma sat across from me in a high-back purple chair. Strings of beads hung off the sides, her feet barely scraping the floor. Her hair was pulled back in a brightly colored scarf. The dress she wore was made up of reds and greens and blues. She had a white shawl wrapped around her shoulders, the fringes of which lay on her arms and lap.

Ruv stood next to her, wearing the sheerest of fabrics for trousers. He was backlit by that sliver of light, and I swore I could see right through them. Not that I was looking. Because I wasn't.

"If you insist," I said.

"Your travels were safe?"

"If you're asking if I was attacked by Morgan's brother, then no. If you're asking me if Randall's cornerstone appeared out of nowhere, then no."

"You're angry," she said.

I laughed. "Lady, you don't know me."

"Perhaps. But I do know my daughter. And I knew her when she was your age or thereabouts. She had the same look on her face. The same fire in her eyes. That is how I know."

That startled me, but I tried not to let it show. "It doesn't matter."

"Doesn't it?"

"I'm not here to be analyzed."

"And why do you think I'm analyzing you?"

"Gee," I said wryly. "Where would I have gotten an idea like that."

She chuckled. It was a soft, husky sound. "I like you," she admitted. "I didn't expect that. You have a... reputation."

"Do I?"

She shrugged. "People talk about you, Sam of Wilds. Your name is known throughout Verania."

"And what is said about me?"

"That everyone loves you. Most speak of you almost reverently, as if you are something to be cherished."

I squinted at her. "You were going around asking people if they loved me? That's weird. You're weird."

She scoffed. "I didn't need to ask about *love*. It was clear in their adoration. You and that... that *unicorn*. Why you feel the need to associate with such a blasphemous creature, I'll never understand."

"Because he's my best friend," I said. "And he gets me. And he'll kill or maim anyone who tries to hurt me. So. That's why. Oh. And Tiggy too. Except he's more into smashing things. Like faces."

"I'm not threatened."

"Oh. Wow. You should be, I think. At least a little bit. As a side note, the only reason you should feel threatened is if there *is* a reason to be threatened."

I didn't miss the way Ruv quirked a smile at that, like he found me funny but was trying not to show it. Hell, if that meant I had half the room on my side, I wasn't going to argue with that. I winked at him obnoxiously. Stupid Ryan Foxheart. Of *course* I could handle myself.

Ruv winked back at me. Maybe licked his lips a little.

I probably couldn't handle myself at all.

"Anyway," I said quickly, trying to push through the discomfort. "I'm glad you like me. I think. That'll make this... whatever this is, easier. I probably won't send you an All Hallowed Day card or anything like that, but at least I can tell people I met my grandmother. Yaaaay."

"You often talk without saying anything at all," she said.

I nodded. "Yes, ma'am. That's sort of my thing."

"Does that get you anywhere?"

"I'm here, aren't I?"

"I never knew the name of the man in shadows. Do you believe me?"

I cocked my head at her. "You like changing the subject whenever the mood strikes, don't you? That's annoying."

She said nothing.

Okay, then. "Does it matter if I believe you or not?"

"There needs to be trust between us, Sam, if this is to work."

I smiled at her. "Then the world is probably going to end. Such is life."

She sighed. "You do not take this seriously."

"It's a defense mechanism. You'll get used to it. Or you won't, because we probably won't be around long enough for that. Either I get the dragon and leave you behind, or we all die. Either way, it won't be long."

"I didn't know it was the Myrin of old," she said as if I hadn't spoken at all, which, honestly, Mom must have told her was the easiest way to deal with me. Damn her. "Though I probably should have. Given the star dragon's insistence that Morgan of Shadows be involved."

"Man in shadows, Morgan of Shadows, yeah, I would think that would have crossed someone's mind a time or two." And from what Morgan had told me, he'd pushed it as far from his mind as he possibly could. "Would you have done anything differently?"

She hesitated, which was answer enough. "Do you know how old I am?" she asked instead.

"No."

"I'm old, Sam. Much older than I appear. Not Randall's age, no, not even Morgan's, but enough to remember the stories. Why do you think it is that Myrin is mentioned only in passing? Why do you think it is that you can barely find his name mentioned at all?"

"Because Morgan—"

She arched an eyebrow at me.

"Because *Randall* erased him as much as he could," I corrected. "Because he couldn't bear the thought of the man he loved having done the things he did. So he erased him as much as he could from history, having banished him with the help of Myrin's brother, Morgan. Morgan, who was Randall's protégé."

"The *burn* that must have run through them at the betrayal," Vadoma said. "The pain they would have felt. For family, for a *cornerstone*, to turn as he did."

I said nothing.

"I do not need a cornerstone," Vadoma said, looking down at her hands. "I am not like you. I cannot create something real out of nothing. I can make you *see*, but that is the limit. I am not a wizard. I am not a witch. I am an old woman with an ability I never asked for, who has seen things she never asked to see. And yet, there is *magic* in me. And it has slowed down time. I have seen people come and go. Villages rise and fall. I have seen the weakness of kings. One, in particular."

"The King of Sorrow."

"Yes. I see someone's been talking."

I shrugged, not caring to answer.

"It was said that Randall pulled him out of his madness by the sheer force of his will alone. Tell me, Sam. Do you know why the King went mad in the first place?"

"No." Which, I probably should have, given I was going to be the next King's Wizard, but if there was one thing I hated more than anything else in the world, it was going through a thousand years of Veranian politics. It was the bane of my existence.

"The loss of love," Vadoma said. She rubbed a bony finger over the bangles on her right wrist. "The King's wife and daughter were killed. Burned to death in a fire. He lost himself to his grief. Randall pulled him back from the brink. But not with his will. No. He did it because he too understood loss. Pain. Suffering. That is not something that leaves you. Do you know that?"

"No," I said slowly. Because I didn't, fortunately enough. My parents were still alive. My friends were safe. The King and Prince I'd sworn to protect were guarded. Randall and Morgan were still around, even if I was pissed off at them. I'd never known loss. Not like she described. I didn't want to.

Then she did it again, and I wondered if she was trying to catch me off guard. "And the Great White. He said nothing to you? Tell Vadoma."

"No," I said without wavering. "He said nothing. For all I know, it was just a dream."

She laughed, dry and rusty. "*Chava*. That was not a dream. I made you *see*."

"You can *see* hallucinations," I said. "That doesn't mean they're real."

"That mouth of yours," she said with a frown. "I blame the unicorn."

"He is pretty sassy," I agreed.

"And you will not banish him?"

I snorted. "Not hardly. And if I tried, he'd probably just laugh at me, call me a bitch, and then sit on me for a little while until I apologized. Just how he is."

"Impertinent creature," she said. "I knew a unicorn once. Backstabber. Literally. He stabbed people in the back."

"Did those people deserve it?"

She waved a hand at me dismissively. "Not the point. Consider getting rid of him. For your grandmother's sake."

"Yeah," I said. "I don't think I'm going to do that."

"This is the family I was given," Vadoma said to Ruv. "Now you see why the gods mock me."

Ruv was amused. "I think Sam has a point here."

"Do you?" she said, arching an eyebrow.

"Unicorns are fiercely loyal creatures. And this one has bonded with

Sam and the half-giant. He would do anything to save them."

"He would," I said, smiling at Ruv. At least one of them got it. Ruv, of course, smiled back at me, those dark eyes on me unnervingly. I wondered what he thought when he saw me, what he'd probably been told about me for years. Vadoma had probably built me up in his head somehow, a boy with a destiny of dragons and that Ruv would one day be the anchor for his magic. I thought maybe he was disappointed with what he'd seen in me and—

Those were not thoughts I needed to have. That way lay madness and would be exactly what Vadoma wanted. In fact, I thought maybe all of this was exactly what Vadoma wanted. Divide and conquer. It had taken less than a day upon her arrival in Castle Lockes to weave disharmony and chaos into my carefully constructed life. I'd gotten my happily ever after, and now look where I was: in a hot and dusty room so very far away from home with people I didn't trust, all the while I wasn't speaking to my mentor nor *his* mentor, Kevin and Gary were getting divorced (or something, I didn't even want to know), Ryan was being an asshat who I wanted to kick in the shins, but then also suck his cock. That left Tiggy. Sweet, wonderful, reliable Tiggy. I would seek him out as soon as I left here.

"Ruv," Vadoma said, sounding pleased about *something*. "Perhaps you can show my grandson here Mashallaha. Alone. Just the two of you. By yourselves."

And there went subtlety right out the window. "Maybe we could—"

"It would be my honor," Ruv said, bowing low.

"There isn't *time*—"

"Nonsense," Vadoma said. "You are our guest. Ruv will show you Mashallaha. Tonight, we have a feast in your honor. Tomorrow, you will go to the dragon. And we'll see what we see."

"I really must insist that we—" I tried again.

"I'm an old lady," Vadoma said. "I'm tired now. I must rest. Leave me."

And I was ushered out by Ruv before I could even say another word.

OUTSIDE THE STACKED CARRIAGES, I BLINKED against the harsh sunlight, my eyes having gotten used to the darkened room. It took me a moment to realize that Ruv had his hand on my arm still, and I pulled out of his grip as gently as I could. He didn't react.

"There are many wonderful things about Mashallaha," he said. "The greatest wonders in all of Verania."

"I'm sure there are," I said. "And your city is very beautiful. But we've been traveling a great distance and—"

"Your mother grew up not that far from here. Did you know that?"

Well, no. I hadn't. And while there was an itch under my skin to go find Ryan, to make sure he and the others were okay, I couldn't pass up the opportunity to see where she'd come from. Because regardless of what had brought us here or why she'd left to begin with, this was my history. And I was immersed in it for the first time. Granted, this place and its people hadn't made the best first impression, what with the racism and the general sense of coercion for me being here at all, but still....

"She did?" I asked.

Ruv smiled at me. "I didn't know her, obviously, as she was gone before I ever came to be. But I've heard the stories. People speak of her with much love and respect."

I frowned. "I thought they weren't allowed to speak of her at all. Isn't that the point of being shunned?"

"She followed her heart," Ruv said. "And while tradition is important, there is something romantic about it that sparks the imagination. And here you are now, returning to where she left. It's like a circle has been completed."

In a weird way, it was. This place didn't feel like home—it would never feel like home, I was sure of that—but there was something about it. Something that felt familiar. And it wouldn't take long, right? The others probably wouldn't even notice I'd been gone by the time we'd get back. And to think about what I could tell Mom I'd seen when I got back to Lockes....

So I said, "Yeah. Sure. Okay. Lead the way."

And the Wolf's smile widened.

MASHALLAHA WASN'T BIG, CERTAINLY NOT COMPARED with Lockes or Meridian City, or even compared to the Port. But it was bustling in a way the others weren't. Lockes always carried with it the divide between the classes, the rich and the middle and the slums. In Meridian City, the heart that beat within it was diseased and corrupted, and it was every man (or woman) for themselves.

Mashallaha was different in that there was a *thrum* to it, an order to everything everyone did. There didn't seem to be any disparity in wealth, no sense of desperation or deviousness. There were no nobles. There were no working whores on the street corners. Oh sure, people hawked their wares, shouting in bright, colorful voices—that was something similar, something I thought was universal in almost every market. But it was the *way* the people went about it. There didn't seem to be any slick solicitation, no shifty-eyed *I'll make you the best deal I can.* People came, people bought what they needed, and they left.

It was... different.

It didn't mean it was better, though.

Because I could see the curiosity on their faces, the barely disguised looks in my direction before the gazes turned away and the whispers began. It made sense, really, because while there wasn't a specific division in say, the affluence of the people around me, there *was* a major difference between those *from* Mashallaha and those that weren't. Those that *were* from Mashallaha were dark skinned and dark haired, dressed for the desert. Most were barefoot in loose clothing made of thin, sheer material. Both men and women wore colorful scarves around their heads to protect them from the sun above.

Then there were the tourists, the light-skinned people who wore clothing perhaps not best suited for the desert, sweat on their faces as the women cooled themselves with large ornate gypsy-made fans, the men wiping away excess moisture with small embroidered gypsy-made kerchiefs.

And then there was me. Stuck somewhere in the middle. I was not as light skinned as the tourists. I was not as dark as the gypsies. I was somewhere in between. That coupled with the fact that my grandmother was the leader of most of the people around me no doubt added to whatever mystique they thought I had, for better or worse.

It was uncomfortable, that feeling.

I was used to being stared at these days.

But not to the point of where I knew I was being judged for something I really had no control over.

As if he could read my mind, Ruv said, "They don't hate you. Not really."

"That's not as assuring as you think it is," I muttered as we made our way through the crowd.

He shrugged. "They just don't understand, I suppose."

"Understand what?"

"You. Your heritage. The choices made. You are not your mother, but you come from her. She left the *roma*. Or, more formally, the *vitsa*. The clan."

"She left because she loved."

"And some think she should have loved her people more."

"Really," I said. "Because that doesn't seem fair."

"Why?"

"Because it shouldn't be either or. You shouldn't have to give up one for the other."

"But life is choices," Ruv said. "And what is love but a choice? You love your unicorn. And your half-giant. What if the choice came between them or your parents? Who would you choose?"

"Easy," I said, curling my lip. "I would fight the person forcing me to make a choice."

"Violence." Ruv shook his head. "It's not always the answer."

"No, but it sure feels good to kick a villain's ass."

"And Ryan?"

"What about him?" I asked, tone flat.

"If it came down to saving his life—"

"I would fight the person forcing me to make a choice," I repeated.

Ruv grinned at me. "You care for him."

As if there was any doubt. Ryan was a pain in my ass, and I in his (literally), but I wouldn't change a godsdamned thing about it. Except for him being a jerk right now. And the fact that I was probably also being a jerk.

"Ah," Ruv said. "How fortunate."

"I don't get you," I admitted.

"You don't know me," he said, leading us away from the market. The noise of the crowd behind us gave way to the creaking of the walkway under our feet, the lap of the water beneath the city. The buildings that rose around us cast the path in shadow. It was cooler here.

"And I'm not going to. Not like Vadoma wants."

"What Vadoma wants is to help the world survive."

I snorted. Because that sounded terrible. "She also wants you and me to get funky."

He laughed brightly. Even I could admit it was a nice sound. "Yes. There is that. Funky." The word sounded strange from him, like he was tasting it for the first time. "She spoke of you. Often."

"She doesn't know me."

"Perhaps not. But her blood is in your veins."

"You all keep saying that. But blood isn't everything. It doesn't define us."

"No?"

"No," I said. "Because Tiggy and Gary and Kevin aren't my blood, but they're mine. The same with Ryan. And the King and the Prince."

"And Randall and Morgan? Even after their secrets?"

"Yes," I said. "Because even if I'm angry with them, even if I don't agree with the choices they made, I could never cast them away. Because they're my family. And that bond will always mean more than blood."

His smile seemed more genuine then. Softer, somehow. "You are a strange man, Sam of Wilds. I like that about you."

"Thanks? I think."

"It's refreshing."

"I can't tell if you're hitting on me or not," I said. "Because most times when that happens, people are usually more blatant about it."

"Does that happen a lot?"

"Sometimes. Usually by people who want to kill me."

"Why?"

"Don't really know. Just a thing that happens. They threaten, I smile, they flirt aggressively, something blows up or someone gets kicked in the face, and then there's a lot of screaming and running involved."

"That's... not surprising, actually. From what I've heard about you."

"And what else have you heard?" I asked, curious.

"You really have no idea what the people say about you?"

"Not really. I don't... care? Mostly. I mean, if it's bad, yeah, then maybe I want to know so I can do something about it."

"Like those people in Lockes. Marching and shouting."

I rolled my eyes. "Oh no. That's just Lady Tina DeSilva. She's my archnemesis."

"The little girl? In the dress?"

"Hey! She might be little, but you'll *never* meet a blacker heart. She is *festering* with a diabolical mind that seeks to do nothing but cause me pain and misery. She lives for nothing more than to destroy me. And one day, I shall *strike her down* with the force of the *gods*—why are you laughing at me?"

He wiped his eyes. "I've never seen someone get so worked up over a teenage *girl* before." He continued to laugh and leaned over to brush his shoulder against mine.

"Yes, well, she is—"

"Isn't *this* awkwardly cozy?"

"Fuck me sideways," I muttered before turning around to see Gary and Tiggy standing behind us, Tiggy with his arms over his chest and Gary cocking a perfectly sculpted eyebrow at me. Which—

"When in the hell did you get eyebrows?" I demanded. "Unicorns don't *have* eyebrows. How did you—are those *painted* on?"

"Of course they are," Gary said, switching between arching the left eyebrow and the right. "I needed them for this exact moment to look suspicious when interrupting your lovers' tryst. Now tell me, Sam. How sweet does the betrayal taste? I mean, I assume it's sweet because of the gypsy diet."

"Oh my gods," I said, putting my face in my hands.

"Ah *ha*," Gary crowed. "Exactly what I would expect a guilty *trollop* to say! Tiggy, Sam has broken the sanctity of his marriage."

"Sam," Tiggy said, and I didn't know that I'd ever heard my name said with more disappointment in my life. I actually felt guilty for something that hadn't even happened.

"Okay, one, I'm not *married…*"

"Oh, so now we have excuses, ladies and gentlemen! Next you're going to tell me that you didn't even do anything wrong!"

"…and *two*, I wasn't even *doing anything wro*—godsdammit."

"Uh-huh," Gary said, arching both his fake eyebrows at the same time, looking like he was surprised, but also like he was plotting to take over the world. "Spoken like a *true* adulteress. For *shame*, Sam. You have Knight McBottoms Like a Champ waiting for you, but after one lovers' spat, you find solace in the arms of an exotic *stranger* while on holiday in a strange land. It's so sordid, I'm almost impressed. Hell, I *am* impressed."

"No." Tiggy frowned deeper.

"Sweet molasses," I said weakly. "Okay, look. All Ruv was trying to show me—"

"Oh, it's *Ruv* now, is it?"

"Yes, Gary. That's his *name*."

"Oh. Right. Continue on."

"He was trying to show me where Mom grew up. That's it."

"Really," Gary said dubiously. "Then why did Vadoma tell us that you were indisposed at the moment because you were having some alone time with Ruv?"

"She what," I said flatly.

"She said you doin' stuff," Tiggy said, uncrossing his arms and cracking his knuckles, all while glaring murderously at Ruv.

"Exactly," Gary said. "*Stuff*. Why, if Kevin hadn't been there to hold Ryan back, I'm positive Ruv's head would be lopped off by now. You're lucky my ex-husband is so thoughtful. And muscular. Gods, he's so muscular, the way he was able to hold back Knight Delicious Face as if he were *nothing*. Mmm. Did I ever tell you about the time Kevin put his—"

"Yes, Gary."

"Are you sure? It was when he ate my—"

"Yes, Gary."

"Ah, well. No matter. The past is the past, and the love we shared has flickered out like a candle in the wind. Apparently like *your* love, given that you're here all slutty-cozy with a man whose penis you are *not* familiar with... at least not yet."

"Did you know about this?" I asked Ruv.

He shrugged. "I cannot control what the *phuro* says. She does have a mind of her own, you know."

"Not after I'm done with her," I muttered. "Gary, you go back and tell the others there is *nothing going on*. Tiggy, you can stay with us."

"Right," Gary said. "Because I only saw you rubbing your shoulder with *his* shoulder, which *everyone* knows in a romantic comedy is a sign of affection that leads toward a dick being shoved down someone's throat."

"Oh my fucking gods," I said, gaping at him. "What the hell have you been *reading*? You know what? I don't even want to know. Obviously it's something that has no literary merit whatsoever and should be burned. Tiggy, you go back and tell Ryan that I'm just seeing my mom's old home. Gary, you stay here so I can keep your freaking mouth shut."

Tiggy brought two fingers to his eyes, then pointed them at Ruv. "I see you, tiny human."

"Eep," Ruv said, but managed to cover it up well enough.

"Don't you worry, kitten," Gary said. "I won't let our Sam here be swayed by gypsy dick. Not even if I have to throw myself on it and sacrifice my butthole so that Sam remains faithful."

"I wish I could tell you they're not normally like this," I said to Ruv. "But that would be a lie."

He laughed. "They care about you very much."

"Too much. Way, way too much."

"House, then back," Tiggy said to me. "Or I come after you."

"I'm not going to—"

"You don't want that."

"No, sir," I said quickly. "Sorry, sir. Yes, sir."

Tiggy waited a beat more before grunting. He reached up and ran a hand down Gary's mane. "Pretty Gary," he murmured. Then he glared at Ruv before whirling on his heels and walking back toward the market.

"I do love that half-giant," Gary said fondly, watching Tiggy go. Once Tiggy had disappeared, Gary turned his head slowly, right eyebrow cocked so high that I thought he was going to strain some muscles in his face. "Now. Where were we?" He obnoxiously pushed his way between Ruv and me, almost knocking me on my ass but not appearing apologetic in the slightest. "There," he said. "That's better. Don't you think? After all, Ruv, I would hate to see what you would look like with a sword through your chest. Or maybe I wouldn't. I haven't decided yet."

"Are your friends always this violent?" Ruv asked me.

I didn't even have to think about it. "Always. So are my mom and dad. And the King. And the Prince. And Randall and Morgan."

"We tend to maim when Sam is involved," Gary agreed. "Hop to it. I'd like to get back before sunset, as there is a feast being thrown in my honor."

"I don't actually think it's in your honor—"

"You really want to go there right now, Sam? Because we can go there right now if you want."

I didn't want to go there.

IT WASN'T MUCH. THE HOUSE WHERE my mother had lived. Not like where Vadoma lived now. It was set off a narrow walkway, the planks beneath our feet a bit more rickety than those on the main thoroughfares. But it was late afternoon, and the sun was in the west, and the light fell in a perfect line between the buildings until it hit a bed of flowers, colored in reds and greens and oranges and golds. And even though she hadn't been here for over two decades, I knew this was where she'd come from. This was her touch. It felt almost sacred.

"They were hers," Ruv said beside me in a quiet voice. "Or so Vadoma says. Her flowers. She loved them, apparently."

"She loves them still."

"Does she? That's… well. I know you don't trust me. And I know you don't trust Vadoma. And that's your right. But before Vadoma was the *phuro*, she was a mother. And she loved her daughter. Her hands were tied by tradition far older than she could ever be. Older than you or I will ever live. She had to uphold that tradition."

"She didn't, though." I looked at the small house with the faded siding.

It wasn't ostentatious. It looked like a home, nicer than anything we'd had in the slums. And she'd given that up for my father. "She didn't have to force my mother away."

"She comes here," Ruv said. "And tends to the flowers. Every week, she is on her hands and knees caring for them. I asked her once why she had let her own flowers die after her daughter left, but not these. Why she wanted the reminder in front of her face, so brightly colored, of how she banished her own daughter."

"What did she say?"

"She said it was where she felt closest to her. That even though she was gone, even though she was far away, there was still a piece of her here. And she was going to hold on to that piece with all her might."

"Is that supposed to make things better?" Gary asked.

Ruv shrugged. "No. I don't think it is. But regardless of what else she may be, regardless of what secrets she has kept, she is a mother too. That's not something that will change. And I think, in the end, we all hold on to whatever we can, even if it's just a memory."

I watched the sunlight on the flowers for a long time.

We were nearly back at Vadoma's when I stopped Ruv with a hand on his shoulder. "Gary, can you give us a minute?"

Gary's nostrils flared. "You gonna suck his balls?"

I sighed. "No, Gary. I'm not going to suck his balls."

"Are you going to suck his—"

"Oh my gods, *Gary*, I'm not going to suck his *anything*."

"Just making sure. You have one minute. If you're not done in that minute, I will describe in excruciating detail that one time my hoof got stuck in Kevin's asshole. You understand me?"

I gagged. "Why do you *say* such things?"

"Because I love you more than life itself. One minute. Ruv, try anything and I'll eat your liver. Don't think that I won't."

Gary whirled away in a cloud of glitter and violent rage.

"How does he do that?"

"Look so beautiful and scary all at the same time?"

"Yes."

"He's a unicorn. It's a species trait."

"You've met other unicorns?"

"Um. No? But his parents are swingers and he has a brother named Terry that he doesn't really talk to, so I just imagine they're all like that."

"Terry and Gary."

"Right? Isn't it terrible?"

"And his parents are what?"

"Oh, they travel around and have group sex."

Ruv's eyes bulged.

"Yeah," I said. "I don't ask too many questions because it's easier that way. Also, can we hurry this up, because Gary *will* tell me about his foot in Kevin's asshole, and I've already had to listen to them scream my name while they were fucking, and I'm traumatized as it is."

"Sure," Ruv said, looking dazed and disgusted all at the same time. Like a champ.

"I know what Vadoma wants," I said. "And I understand what you've been told. But, man. I gotta tell you. You seem nice. You're hot. You've got that whole mysterious thing going for you. And you seem pretty bendy."

"Thank you," he said, sounding rather pleased.

"Sure. No problem. But, dude, I love Ryan Foxheart. Like, I can't even begin to tell you how much. Well, okay. Maybe I can. I used to disguise myself and go to Ryan Foxheart Fan Club meetings with teenage girls. One time, we talked about his biceps for six hours. I'm not even joking."

Ruv took a step back. "What."

"Right? Oh, man. It gets so much worse. I've inserted things into my anus while thinking about him before we were together."

"Like sex toys?"

"Not all the time," I said.

"Wow," Ruv said faintly.

"It's something I'll have to live with for the rest of my days," I said. "And him, too, if I'm being honest. I know what Vadoma wants. What she thinks. And I don't know how she knew you'd be... that. For me. Like he is. I know you've been waiting. And I know promises were made. But I don't love you. I won't love you. I love him, and I always will."

He watched me closely. "What about when his skin starts to wrinkle? When his hair turns gray? When he ages beyond you while you stay as you are? Can you say you'll love him then?"

"If it comes to it, yes," I said. "But I aim to make sure that doesn't happen. Either he'll go with me or I'll go with him, it doesn't matter. I'm a godsdamned wizard. One of the most powerful there has ever been, if Morgan and Randall are to be believed. I'll figure it out."

"You truly believe that."

"I do. Because once upon a time, he told me that he looked upon the stars and wished for nothing more than me. And that's not something I can ever let go."

He nodded and took a step back, putting a respectful distance between us. "I can respect your choice," he said. "Even if there was never really a choice at all."

I nodded. "Thank you. That's a relief, man. And I'm sure there's a great dude or chick out there for you, you know? Hey! Justin's single! How do you feel about royalty?"

He smiled at me. "Why don't we just work on surviving first?"

"It's been longer than a minute!" I heard Gary shriek behind us. "So, there I was, not even *thinking* about how my hoof was about to go into a dragon's asshole when *suddenly*—"

Fuck my life.

CHAPTER 15
That One Time Kevin Was Possessed

THE FEAST VADOMA THREW IN OUR honor was held in a massive square in the middle of Mashallaha, strings of large paper lanterns stretching out above us. The night air was warm, and the palm trees swayed. People were laughing and shouting, well into their cups by the time I arrived.

I hadn't seen Ryan when I'd gotten back to Vadoma's. He wasn't in the room that we'd been given for the duration of our stay, though our bags were placed at the foot of the bed. Tiggy had said he'd gone off with Kevin to check out the rest of the city. I knew he'd made it seem like he was sightsee-ing, but as was ingrained in him as a knight, he was most likely running the perimeter, fanning out in circles around Vadoma's, memorizing every path in and out in case we needed to escape. Strangely enough, that happened to us quite a lot, so I didn't blame him for doing it.

But I also knew he was avoiding me. Or rather, letting me avoid him. We were assholes like that.

There had been clothes left for me on the foot of the bed. They were soft and brightly colored, the material thinner than what I was used to. The dark green vest had a hood attached, which Gary made me pull up and over my head. "It'll make you look more mysterious like a wizard should be," he'd said. "And not like you're some seventeen-year-old apprentice twink."

"I'm not a godsdamned *twink*—"

"Isn't it funny how the louder you get, the less I listen to you? I won-der why that is."

The trousers sat low on my hips, held up by a black sash tied around my waist.

"It's a good thing you manscape," Gary said approvingly. "Don't need no man bush trying to crawl out the waistband and scaring the locals."

I looked at my reflection in the mirror. "I look like I work at a brothel in Meridian City."

"Yes, how about that. Tiggy! Hold him still just like we planned!"

"Wait, what? Tiggy, don't you fucking—"

Tiggy came up behind me and wrapped his arms around me, then fell back until he sat on the bed. The frame groaned at the weight but didn't collapse. My arms were trapped at my sides, and my legs were held between his. And it was about that time that I noticed Gary carried a makeup brush between his teeth, a determined look on his face.

"I will curse the *both of you*," I snarled at him. "I'm not a girl. I don't *need makeup*."

"Boys can wear makeup," Tiggy said. "Not just for women. That a social construct."

I tilted my head back to gape at him.

He shrugged and leaned down to kiss my forehead.

"You are the wisest half-giant I have ever known," I said reverently.

He was pleased at this, even if he was the *only* half-giant I had ever known. He was still pretty fucking wise.

"Fine," I said, looking back at Gary. "But I expect to look like a *high-class* working girl, not one of those that looks like they work the docks at the Port. You hear me?"

Gary rolled his eyes before descending upon me.

"Okay," I said when they'd let me up again so I could look in the mirror. "*I* would totally pay to have sex with me, oh my gods. Why don't I wear this *all the time*? I look epic!"

And I did. He'd used the eye shadow sparingly, just enough to create a smoky look around my eyes, almost like I was wearing a mask. Coupled with the hood over my head, the vest opened against my chest, I looked like I could fight crime *and* get nailed by businessmen, all in the same day. It was *glorious*.

"Ryan's gonna get such a boner over me," I breathed. And maybe then we could stop fighting and fuck around.

"Ugh," Gary said. "There are just some things you don't want to hear from your older sister."

"I am not your fucking older sister, you asswipe. You have *decades* on me. And not to mention that I have to hear about *your* shit all the godsdamned time!"

"Well, yes," he said, arching his evil eyebrow at me. "But I'm the unicorn equivalent of a princess. There's a difference."

And I really couldn't argue with that.

And so there I was, looking like an expensive whore, standing in the center square of the desert city, the stars shining down on me, a unicorn with painted-on eyebrows to my right and a half-giant on my left.

Needless to say, we entered that feast like fucking badasses.

Well. Mostly. People *did* stop and stare at us, so I figured we must have been at least a *little* mysterious. It probably helped that the gods decided to bless me right at that moment and send a breeze to wash over me, causing my vest and trousers to billow slightly.

"Why are you walking like you're in slow motion?" Gary hissed at me.

"Because it fucking looks cool," I hissed back.

"You look like you're having a stroke!"

"No, I don't! I look like I run through the city at night, taking out bad guys while having sex with high-powered executives during the day for tons of money."

"That's... huh. Okay. I don't even know what to say to that."

"Right. Just go with it."

"Okay, I can work with this."

And then he tossed his mane back, eyelashes fluttering, the air beginning to shimmer around him in green and blue sparkles. He snorted heavily, more sparks shooting from his nose.

"Oooh," the crowd said.

"You need to strut more," Gary whispered to me.

"I know how to strut!"

"That not strutting," Tiggy said. "This strutting." And then he proceeded to strut far better than a being his size ever had any right to. His hips rolled, and he looked like he was made up of large piles of bitchy sass.

"Ahhh," the crowd said.

"I taught him how to do that," Gary said fondly.

"I want the crowd to make noises at me," I said. "Move, it's my turn." I shoved my way past Gary, ready to be appreciated and—

"I don't know that you could be any more ridiculous than you are right now," a voice said near my ear, which, of course, caused me to squeak, trip over my own feet, and fall face-first onto the ground.

There was silence. Then someone in the crowd shouted, "Thank the gods he's the chosen one! I know *I* sure feel safe now!"

I rolled over onto my back and glared up at Ryan Foxheart, who stood above me, hands on his hips, head cocked as he peered down at me. "Okay, I take that back," he said. "You *could* look more ridiculous. I'm impressed."

I scowled at him but accepted his hand when he reached down for me. I momentarily forgot that we were fighting when I saw he was similarly dressed as I was, but *his* vest was stretched much tighter across his frame, and he had chest hair that I wanted to just bury my face in.

"I want to paddleboat your boobs," I told him, staring at his pecs.

He sighed. "So you've told me before. And so you've *done* before, even though I threatened to never let you touch me again."

"It was totally worth it," I said. "You've get a nice rack. Good job with that whole… thing."

"You objectifying me, Sam of Wilds?"

I leered at him as the music began to pick up around us again. "Is it working?"

He grimaced. "It was until you made *that* face. How many times have I told you can't make that face around other people? They'll think you're coming to take their children away."

"Sam's sexy face is scary," Tiggy said to Gary. "Run! It scary Sam!"

"He tries so hard," Gary said. "Too hard, really."

"I'm not objectifying you," I said, even though I totally was. "I respect your autonomy and your right to not have me paddleboat your boobs."

He snorted. "Bullshit you do."

Now that we'd gotten that out of the way, I glared at him. "I'm still mad at you."

"I can tell. I'm still upset with you, if it makes you feel any better."

It really didn't. I deflated slightly. "We need to talk."

"We do."

And he agreed to that way too easily. "But not like the breakup we need to talk," I said quickly. "But the *we've got to talk* that means open communication and words and then some really awesome makeup sex. Right?"

He rolled his eyes, but his hand found his way to the back of my neck, squeezing as he pulled me close. My bare chest pressed against his as he leaned in and laid a filthy kiss upon my lips, more tongue than was probably warranted. Not that I was complaining.

"Yes, Sam," he said, murmuring against me. "That kind of talk." He kissed me again, slow and sweet.

I sagged against him slightly in relief. "Good. I'm sorry I acted like a douchebag. I love your face. I've also got a boner right now that I really don't know what to do with, seeing as how we're in public."

He chuckled. "And I'm sorry I acted like an ass. I love you too. Also, I can feel your boner."

"I love love," Tiggy sighed behind us.

"Gods, they're just sickening," Gary muttered. "I hate it when people act like that."

"Seriously," Kevin rumbled. "I'm so glad we're broken up now so I don't have to be a part of a loving couple anymore. I don't know what I was thinking."

"Me too," Gary said. "It's so much better like this."

"Right," Kevin said. "Even if it's our boy in love that we have to watch."

"Even if," Gary said wistfully.

"Maybe they should just rub each other a little bit," Kevin suggested. "You know? I mean, they're already *there*, they might as well, right? Just do it, right? Just start *rubbing*—"

"And the erection's gone," I said, stepping away from Ryan. "That's much better."

Ryan did this complicated motion with his eyebrows. "I don't know if that's *better*."

Gods, he looked awesome when he pouted.

And I was about to tell him as much when a cheer went up over the crowd, rolling through it like a wave. We were stuck somewhere in the middle of it, and I couldn't help but notice the people of Mashallaha had formed a circle around us, but keeping their distance. I didn't know if it was fear of us or dismay at the sight of us that kept them as they were. I didn't know that it mattered. These were the people of Verania, *my* people for all intents and purposes, yet I'd never felt so far from home before in my life. It was good that I had Ryan next to me. Tiggy and Gary and Kevin at my back. I thought maybe I could do this without them. I just didn't want to.

But the people weren't focused on us. They were cheering for Vadoma.

She stood on a raised wooden platform, the eyes of her people all on her. She looked beautiful under the lights, younger than she actually was. I wondered just how old she was and who my mother's father had been, as my mother had never known. Or so she said. But regardless of what I thought of Vadoma, I could see my mother in her. I could see myself in her. It unsettled me more than I cared to admit.

Ruv, the Wolf, stood at her side.

"Oh," I said to Ryan in a low voice. "That reminds me. Ruv won't be trying to get up in my business anymore. He knows you're my one and only."

"Or so he says," Ryan muttered. "For all we know, it's part of his diabolical plot to get in your good graces and then *bam*! His legs are over your shoulders and you won't even know how you got there."

"Nah," I said. "It's only your legs over my shoulders that I care about."

Gary sniffed. "That was really sweet."

Ryan thought so too, but since he was a man, he had to cover it up by scowling at me. Which was okay, because I knew.

The noise of the crowd around us crescendoed until it was nearly earsplitting. But the moment Vadoma raised her hands toward them, palms down, they quieted as if they hadn't been screaming at all.

Except for Tiggy.

"*GWAAAA*aaahh...," he said before looking around at everyone staring at him. "Oh. No more yelling?" He nodded. "No more yelling."

"People of Mashallaha," Vadoma said, voice ringing out over the crowd. "Honored guests. Tonight, I bring to you tidings of great joy."

Her people cheered again.

"More yelling!" Tiggy yelled.

"Why is she speaking in Veranian?" Ryan muttered in my ear. "Most everyone here is a gypsy."

He had a point. "Maybe it's for our benefit?"

"Does she seem like the type to do anything for our benefit?" Ryan asked, which, fair point. But he hadn't seen the flowers that still stood where my mother had been raised. Maybe that was all bullshit designed to sell me on the idea of the gypsy clan, but I thought not.

So I said, "I don't know," and it was the truth.

"Many of you have heard that I traveled far from Mashallaha," she said. "Out of the Luri Desert and into the green lands. The Dark Woods stand as they always have, swallowing the heart of Verania in gnarled roots that dig deep into the earth."

"Couldn't she have just said there was a big fat forest in the middle of everything?" Gary muttered.

"This fancier," Tiggy said, looking enthralled, as if he'd never stood inside the damn Dark Woods a day in his life.

"I entered the City of Lockes," she said, "and stood before our King. I told him of the power of sight, of what was shown to me as having been written in the stars. I warned the King to take heed of my words. That there are only shadows when darkness begins to cover the light."

"Ooh," Gary said. "I get it now. That sounded ominous and scary and wicked cool."

"You don't have to give commentary for everything," I reminded him.

He looked scandalized. "Of *course* I do. That's how you know we're having fun."

No one paid us any mind. They were all under the spell of my grandmother. She reminded me briefly of a woman who had fed her followers corn mixed with truth serum, and I shuddered at the thought. I hadn't been able to look at corn since without feeling the need to blurt out secrets. It was a terrible affliction.

"And the King bestowed upon me a great gift," Vadoma said. "My grandson. The wizard Sam of Wilds, who is here to save Verania."

Everyone turned slowly to stare at me, even as Gary coughed, "Apprentice," as loudly as he could.

I gave everyone two thumbs-up like the cool cat that I was. "Heyyy," I said. "What is up, y'all?"

"So awkward," Gary whispered to Tiggy.

No one gave me a thumbs-up back. Apparently Mashallaha was completely inhabited by people who didn't know cool even if it jerked off on their face. Good to know.

"And I'm not a gift," I added quickly, just because it needed to be said. And because I always had the incessant urge to fill the silence. "Think of me as being on loan. Or not even that, because I'm not a thing. I'm a person. I came here because my grandma bad-touched me in the hallway and made me have visions of stuff."

"You might want to stop talking now," Ryan said through gritted teeth.

"Yep," I said. "Good idea. Back to you, Grandma!"

The silence was deafening. But then, the silence usually was when it pertained to me. I was used to it.

Vadoma didn't look affected. She was very good. "The star dragon has spoken! He has used me as his vessel to spread the word of the man in shadows that threatens our very existence. We must take his words of warning as truth. If we do not, we risk being swallowed into the dark, along with the rest of Verania."

"Not that that's going to happen," I spoke up, because fuck her for trying to instill fear in people. "Because I'm going to gather the dragons of Verania and kick some motherfucking villain ass. You'll see. I got this." I grinned rakishly at them. "I'm Sam of Wilds."

"And how do you plan on gathering the dragons?" a voice called out.

The entire crowd turned to face me again.

I grinned less rakishly. "Um. What?"

"The dragons. How do you plan on gathering the dragons? You *do* have a plan, right?"

"Oh," I said. "Well. Um. You see. It's not that simple. But it's not that complicated either! I swear. I mean, I already got one after all. See?" I pointed my thumb over my shoulder at Kevin.

They all looked up at him.

Kevin preened. He tapped his chest with a fist and cleared his throat. "Hello, my dutiful subjects. I am the Lord Dragon, here to taketh your shinies and your virginities—"

"Exactly," I said loudly, stopping that before it could start again. "So. One down, four to go, right? And I got *him* with no troubles, so how hard can it be?"

"Sam," Kevin hissed at me. "You're making me sound as if I was *easy*."

"You sort of were," Gary said. "I just had to flutter my eyes at you and you were gone."

"This is pretty much true," Kevin said. "But! I am my *own* dragon now, single and ready to mingle! Maybe I'll find some nice young thing here to take back to my keep. I've done it before. And this time, there won't be any pesky wizard telling me I can't take my hoard with me! How about it? Is there a fit gypsy man with abs who would like to punch my junk?"

"All of your hoard was moved into the castle," I reminded him. "Because you wouldn't stop bitching about it. You literally go in and lay on it almost every day. And then you come out and *tell* everyone about it. For *hours. Oh, look at me, my name's Kevin, I like to go lay on rubies and books and other shit*."

"I have brooms," Tiggy told the crowd. "Kevin give me brooms. I keep them because they're mine."

"And I fought the dragon bravely," Ryan said. He started to pose, miming that he had a sword, taking a defensive stance. "The fierce and mighty creature roared and breathed fire, but I rode in on my trusty steed to save my true love…"

"*Who you callin' a steed, you pasty-ass motherfucker?*" Gary snarled at him.

"…sword drawn and at the ready. The battle was long and arduous, but soon I had vanquished the dragon so Sam could gather him as part of his quest to save Verania," Ryan finished with a flourish, winking like an asshole at the crowd.

I snorted. "That's not what happened at all. In fact, I didn't even *need* to be saved. I was doing just *fine*. And I wasn't even gathering dragons then. He just sort of followed us home. Besides, you just stood there and poked Kevin with your sword."

"*Yeah*, you did," Kevin said, forked tongue slithering out and running along his teeth. "You want to poke me again, Knight Commander? Once you go dragon, all the rest is lag—"

"I have a push broom," Tiggy said. "And a whisk broom." He paused, brow furrowing. "And a dust broom…."

"Call me a steed again," Gary said, pressing his face against Ryan's cheek as he crowded against him. "One more time. I *dare* you."

"Meep," Ryan said.

"And that's how I plan on getting the dragons of Verania," I said in conclusion, feeling really good about this whole thing.

However, the only sound we received in response were crickets. Actual crickets. I didn't know they had any in the desert. Talk about bad timing.

Then, "Are you sure you got the right person?" someone called out from the crowd. "Because I don't know if you got the right person. I mean, he has a dragon and all, but. You know. Are you sure?"

I was moderately offended.

Vadoma was glaring at us.

Ruv's lips were twitching, like he was holding back a laugh.

"Hey," Gary snapped at them, looking away from Ryan, who sighed in relief that the unicorn's ire had been focused on someone else. "Sam is pretty good sometimes at what he does occasionally!"

Pretty good sometimes, I mouthed to no one in particular.

"Yeah," Tiggy said. "Sam so cool. I love him and he my friend and Tiggy smash if you hurt him."

"*And*," Kevin said, "in case you hadn't noticed, I can actually *talk* when he's around. Before, everything was all *rawr snort grr*. And if he goes too far away, it happens again. Also? I happen to be a motherfucking *dragon*. You know? From the motherfucking *prophecy*? And maybe Sam didn't *gather* me intentionally, but you can bet that I'll follow him anywhere." He looked down at me and winked. "And I mean *anywhere*."

"Gross," I said. "And thank you."

"Kevin's right," Ryan growled. "He's the motherfucking dragon from the motherfu—"

"A*hem*," I coughed.

"Oh, come on," he said, looking pained. "You can't make me do that in front of everyone."

"Ryan."

"*Sam.*"

"Are you, or are you not, a Knight of Verania."

He scuffed his foot against the wood. "I am."

"And are there, or are there not, impressionable young children here who might one day want to grow up to be just like their hero Knight Commander Ryan Foxheart?"

He sighed. "There are."

"Then watch your motherfucking language, okay?"

"Gods."

"You may continue your defense of me. It was very sweet. I love you."

"Whatever."

"Anytime now."

"Well maybe I don't want to do it now."

I leaned over, cupping my hand over his ear. "I'll rim you until you cry if you do."

He shuddered as he bit his bottom lip. "Yeah?"

"Fuck yeah."

"He's a mothercracking *dragon*," Ryan snapped. "From the mother-cracking *prophecy*. And I'm the Knight Commander to the Castle Guard and here on order of the King, who I speak for. So when I say Sam's the right person, *yes*, he's the right godsdarn person." He folded his arms across his chest and glared, as if daring *anyone* to contradict him.

I wanted to mount him in front of everyone.

But that needed to wait.

I had a job to do.

I took a step forward.

The crowd around me took a step back.

Inwardly, I shrieked gleefully that I was intimidating.

Outwardly, I was a stone-cold killer.

"You can question me," I said. "I don't blame you for that. You don't know me. Not like others do. And maybe I've made mistakes in the past. I'm not perfect. But if any of you can say differently about yourselves, then by all means, go ahead. If any of you are willing to step forward and go to the desert dragon, then do it now before I've had enough of you wasting my time."

A murmur went through the crowd, but no one spoke against me. I could see the ire on some of their faces, and the fear, but there was awe there too. I was young, and most likely foolish, but I was sure news of our exploits had reached the desert. Couple that with whatever Vadoma had told her people about me—especially as the grandson of the *phuro*—I thought that maybe I could strike a chord with them. I was still only an apprentice. I was still only twenty-one years old. But I could do things that no one else could do. And even though I was sure all the stories spoken about me weren't true, it would hopefully add to whatever legend of me they'd built in their heads. Morgan had taught me it was better to have people fear you a little than be indifferent toward you. I had never really understood what he'd meant until that moment.

"He is strong," Vadoma announced, eyes on me. Her people turned to look back at her. "Rough around the edges, but strong. Listen to Vadoma. We have waited for this moment, for the blood of the gypsies to pulse around the heart of Verania. Be proud, because he is one of us, and he will rise against the Dark."

There was her angle. And it was smart one. Gypsies weren't looked down upon, not in the way people from the slums were. But they certainly weren't revered. It was more out of sight, out of mind. And when they *were* thought upon, it was with a disdain for mystics and fortune-tellers, something of which I'd been guilty of myself. But by relating me to them and my position in Verania, it would help them align themselves with me. The will of the people was the strongest thing one could have.

And then she opened her mouth and ruined everything.

"It will also help us in the long run that Ruv, the Wolf of Bari Lavuta, is his cornerstone. The one who will help Sam of Wilds build his magic so that he may defeat this man in shadows." The smile she gave was beatific and grandmotherly, as if she didn't have a care in the world.

The crowd gasped dramatically.

"Bitch say *whaaaa?*" Gary exclaimed as his eyes narrowed, glitter beginning to sprinkle from his body. "Is Gary gonna have to cut someone up in here?"

"Ah hells nah," Tiggy said, cracking his knuckles.

"What the fudge?" Ryan growled. "What the heck did she just say?"

I almost had a mind to compliment him on the restraint of his language, but I was a little too shell-shocked to even formulate a proper response. I glanced at Ruv, but his expression was blank. I didn't know him well enough to see through it, to figure out if he'd known this was coming. If he did, then he'd certainly played me for a fool. If he didn't, then he was just as much a pawn in this as I was, and Vadoma was an asshole for doing that to the both of us.

I took a step forward, meaning to give her a piece of my mind, to make sure *everyone* within hearing distance knew who my true cornerstone was when Kevin spoke behind me and everything else just stopped.

"Sam," he said in a voice I'd never heard before. It was dreamy and soft and filled with such *wonder* that it clenched at my heart. I didn't know why. "*Sam,*" he said again.

I turned to look up at him.

And took a step back.

For the dragon Kevin stood above me, wings spread, the tips scraping against buildings on either side. Little tendrils of smoke curled up from his nostrils, and I could *feel* the heat from the fires that burned inside of him. It struck me as odd that this was probably the most I'd ever seen him actually *look* like a dragon since the first time he'd crawled over that hill, chasing after sheep before he'd knocked me through an equipment shed and kidnapped Justin. I knew him now, knew what made him tick, knew how his mind worked, crazy though it was. Kevin wasn't *just* a dragon. He was my friend.

But this wasn't my friend. Not now. Now he was a beast, far larger than anything I'd faced in the past.

His eyes were glowing like starlight. They'd never been that color before. They'd never *glowed* before. That probably wasn't a very good sign.

"Kevin?" Gary asked, sounding unsure. "Are you okay?"

"He has awoken," Kevin said, eyes flashing like a storm in summer. He never looked away from me. I could see his tail twitching dangerously behind him. "My brother. Deep in the earth. He *wakes*. I can feel him. In my head. In my blood. It vibrates. Sam of Wilds, he is calling for me. He is calling for *you*. He's—oh gods. I can *feel* the—"

"Look!" someone in the crowd shouted, and whatever it was caused the others to mutter quietly in their native tongue, words dropping like music notes, spoken almost in veneration, like they were praying.

"Holy shit," Gary said.

I didn't take my eyes off Kevin. "What is it?"

"David's Dragon," Ryan said, sounding awed. "It's so *bright*."

I took a chance.

I looked away from the dragon toward the heavens.

A chill ran down my spine.

For it seemed all the other stars in the sky had faded into almost nothing, consumed by the light of David's Dragon. The constellation was so vivid, so *real*, that it knocked the breath from my chest. I'd never seen it like that before.

"The star dragon!" Vadoma crowed. "The gods have shown you how it *shines*."

"Well fuck me silly," Gary said. "This is some mystic hoodoo shit. I don't deal in mystic hoodoo shit. I am a godsdamned unicorn. I am glitter and sunshine and motherfucking good feelings. Those stars better stay in the sky or I'm gonna get my rainbow on all up in this bitch."

"Motherfucking rainbows," Tiggy echoed.

I tore my gaze away from the stars and looked back toward Kevin. I didn't flinch when Ryan found my hand, squeezing my fingers tightly.

"The desert dragon," I said slowly, unsure of who I was talking to. I hoped Kevin was still in there somewhere, but I couldn't be sure. Because the color of his eyes matched David's Dragon above. I didn't know if I was speaking to my friend or a god.

"He of the fire," the dragon said. "Buried in the sand. He has felt your presence here, Sam of Wilds. His soul is bound to yours as one of the five. But he will fight it until he deems you worthy."

You are not ready, a memory whispered in my mind.

"Am I worthy?" I asked. "Or will this all be for nothing?"

The dragon's eyes narrowed. "That is not for me to decide. I have seen all possible paths, Sam of Wilds. I know of all possible endings for you. I do not choose sides."

That made me angry. "So you're nothing but a messenger. Fat lot of good that does me."

The people of Mashallaha moaned around us.

"Um, Sam?" Gary hissed. "Let's not try and piss off the really large dragon who seems to be possessed by a constellation. If you don't mind."

"The stars do not pass judgment, little one," the dragon said as it took a rumbling step forward. He lowered his head until his face was only a few feet from my own. I felt his breath blowing against me, furnace hot and moist. "They stand and observe."

"So you'll watch and do nothing. The gods will watch and do nothing. What if the darkness comes? What if we're consumed by it?"

"Then you weren't meant to live at all," the dragon said as if it were that simple.

"He spoke to me."

The dragon said nothing.

"Did you know that? You must have. If you can see all paths. All possible outcomes. Myrin."

"Myrin," the dragon said. "The man in shadows."

"Him," I agreed. "He told me that you've shown him the same. That anything we've seen, he's seen as well."

"It's the light," he said. "And the dark. Two sides. Opposites. The balance must be maintained."

"But he can't get to the dragons," I said. "Can he?"

And the star dragon hesitated. Then sighed. "Well shit," he muttered, his voice suddenly less ominous. He still *sounded* like Kevin, but *just* off enough for me to know that it wasn't our dragon. "You weren't supposed to figure that out yet."

I blinked at him. "What."

"I think you're being scolded by some stars that have possessed my ex-husband," Gary whispered.

"That's... not a sentence I ever expected to hear you say."

"Yeah. You know, even for us, this is really weird."

"I don't even know why I ask questions anymore."

"Hey, guys?" Ryan said. "Maybe save the banter for later. You know. When we're not about to be eaten."

"Stars don't eat food," the dragon said. "We're stars." It looked at me like Ryan was *my* fault. "Is he for real?"

"Um, I think so?"

"Right. Good job landing that one."

"Hey!"

"Anyway," the dragon said. Suddenly it leaned forward again, eyes glowing the brightest they'd been. "Get thee to the desert dragon. Test your will against his. The world is in your hands."

Its shining eyes began to fade as the dragon reared back. "Wait a minute!" I shouted, taking a step forward. "You can't just come in here all mysterious and then try and *leave*. Who *does* that? You want to know who does that? *Assholes* do that!"

It raised its head toward the sky and opened its mouth. At first nothing happened, and then David's Dragon pulsed, and lightning shot from the open maw. It arced upward, splitting across the sky in a blinding flash.

Then it was over.

I opened my eyes, aftershocks dancing across my vision.

"Whoa," Kevin said. He blinked and shook his head. "I felt *every-thing*. The power. The *strength*. And I can *hear the desert dragon now*. Do you know what this means? My body is a godsdamned *vessel to the gods*. Bow before meh, hoomanz. Dis is yer god spakin. I thou commandeth you to do whatever I say for all time! Eth!"

"Well, fuck," I said succinctly.

CHAPTER 16
Sam Go Boom

IT WAS EARLY MORNING. THE OTHERS still slept, though they'd be waking soon as we had a walk ahead of us. I slipped out of the room, leaving Ryan asleep in our bed. He'd be sore when he woke up, given how hard I'd fucked him against the wall the night before. He'd been almost gagging for it, anxious to get to the makeup sex so we could put the fight behind us. His eyes had gone glassy when I'd pushed him to his knees and come all over his neck and chest. We felt better after, the both of us. Like we were on the same page again. That no matter what Vadoma had said, no matter what she'd announced to everyone else, he knew his place with me. And I'd whispered those words in his ear while I fucked him, telling him there was no one else, that there would *be* no one else, because he was mine and I was his.

He slept deeply.

I didn't.

The morning air was cool. Light was beginning to dawn in the east. Desert birds called out from the trees quietly. There was barely any movement in Mashallaha as I left Vadoma's and walked along the pathways, trying to find a hidden corner to have some privacy. I passed few others, and either they ignored me or eyed me warily as they hurried away. It didn't matter. I didn't care what they thought of me, not anymore. The color of my skin wasn't good enough. I wasn't going to do anything with Ruv. I'd gone against what their *phuro* had decreed. They were not pleased with me. They doubted me. I didn't have anything to prove to them, but they'd see. When all was said and done.

Not that it mattered. I had other things on my mind.

I found a wooden path that led to a dock overlooking the lake. The water was clear, reflecting the fading night sky above. I sat on the edge of the dock, legs hanging over. My toes trailed along the surface, ripples expanding in steady beats.

I sighed and pulled the summoning crystal from my pocket. For the briefest of moments, I considered chucking it into the lake but knew I'd regret it at some point. Instead, I cupped it in my hands and thought of *Morgan, Morgan, Morgan.* There was a tug in my head, like a hook in my brain, and it *pulled.* A small light burst deep in the crystal like a shooting star.

Then, a single word.

"Sam."

And it was said with such *relief* that I had to blink the burn away. Not because of anything remotely close to anger, but because I felt the same. Relieved. Relieved to hear my mentor's voice, even if it was just the one word. We'd been apart for longer periods of time. But we'd never gone this long without talking.

I was still mad at him. But for now, it was in the background.

"Hey," I said roughly.

"It's early."

"Yeah, sorry."

"No, it's okay," Morgan said. "I wasn't asleep."

"Why?"

He chuckled dryly. "I guess you can say I've got a lot on my mind."

"Yeah. No, I get that."

"How are you?"

"Um. Okay? I think. Vadoma announced in front of everyone that Ruv's my cornerstone. So. You know. There's that."

"Is she still alive?"

I snorted.

"I'm actually being serious," he said.

I gaped at the crystal. "I wouldn't *murder* her for that."

I could hear the smile in his voice. "I wasn't talking about *you.*"

"Ryan didn't kill her."

"Did he want to?"

"Yeah, but I boned him so he wouldn't go after his sword."

Morgan sighed. "Of course you did."

"Sharing is caring, Morgan. Not that you would know anything about that." I winced as soon as the words came out. "Dammit. I'm sorry. That's not what—"

"I deserve that," he said. "Probably."

"Maybe."

"Why now?"

"What?"

"Why are you calling me now?"

"Oh. Um. The star dragon sort of possessed Kevin last night? And said stuff? And now we're going after the desert dragon today and I don't know what's going to happen and I just... I just—"

"I'm glad to hear your voice too."

I deflated. "Yeah?"

"Yes, Sam. Always."

"I'm still angry with you," I said. "Really, really angry. And it's probably going to take a long time for me to get over it."

"But you will." It wasn't a question.

"But I will." Because I would.

"Good. You'll do fine."

"But what if I don't? Morgan, I don't even know what I'm *doing*. I'm going in blind to face a dragon I've never seen before and to what...? *Gather* it somehow? What does that even mean?"

"You've done it once before," he reminded me.

"And if you'll recall, I got knocked through a building for it!"

He scoffed. "I thought it was just a shed?"

"Semantics," I growled at him.

"I'm afraid I don't know what to tell you, Sam. We've never been in this position before because there has never been anyone quite like you."

"Stupid prophecies," I grumbled. "Why do they always have to be so vague?"

"Because you've been through so many prophecies before."

"Har, har."

"Sam."

"What?"

"You know I believe in you, right?"

"Ugh. Really? That's so lame." I kicked at the water. "Yeah?"

"More than anyone else," he said softly. "Because I know your heart, Sam of Wilds. I've seen the way it beats, how it's been lightning-struck. And I know you're angry with me, and you have every right to be, but one thing I need you to know above all else. I would have found you, prophecy or not, because you and I are tied. Always."

"You're a jerk," I said with a sniff. "I'm going to give you such a hug when I get back."

"Only you can make an act of affection sound like a threat."

"It's part of my charm."

"You're scared. It's why you called."

"Yeah," I said, looking at the light in the horizon. "I'm scared."

"You'll do fine."

"I know. I just needed to hear it. But if...."

"If?"

"If I'm *not* fine, will you... will you tell Mom and Dad I love them?"

He was quiet for a moment. Then, "Yes, Sam. I will. But you'll be able to tell them yourself soon enough."

"Okay. Um. Anything?" *About Myrin* was what I couldn't say.

"No," Morgan said. "Nothing."

And I didn't believe him.

"RUV KNOWS THE WAY," VADOMA SAID as we stood outside Mashallaha later that morning. The sun was at our backs, as we would be traveling farther into the desert. "He will guide you. Keep you safe. Take you to the desert dragon."

"Yeah," Ryan said. "Except I think I'll do just fine keeping Sam safe." I shot him a look that had him fumbling. "Or we'll keep each other safe, that works too, which is exactly what I meant in the first place."

"You could just stay here," Vadoma suggested. "I don't see the need for why a knight would have to go any farther. You stay here with Vadoma. I bake you cookies. You like cookies? Yes. You like cookies." She glanced balefully at Gary. "You should also stay. But no cookies for you. You get hay from the barn. Because you're an animal."

"Hate you too, bitch," Gary muttered under his breath.

"In fact, Ruv will guide Sam with the dragon," Vadoma said. "And nothing more will happen, of course. Like coupling or gazing into each other's eyes and realizing that they are meant to be." She started swaying, covering her eyes with a gnarled hand. "Oooh, I am having a vision! A dire, dire vision. It says that you should listen to Vadoma! I am the *drabarni*, the seer. You will perish if you leave! Oooh."

"Wow," I said. "You're just... terrible. Like... awful, man. What the hell. How are we even related?"

She dropped her hand and glared at me.

I shrugged. "Pretty much true. Not even sorry, dude."

"Sam not go without us," Tiggy said. "If I stay here, Tiggy smash everything."

"He will too," I said. "You ever hear of Lartin the Dark Leaf? Oh man. May he rest in pieces."

"You mean rest in peace," Ruv said.

I shook my head slowly. "No. I don't. He was in literal pieces by the time Tiggy was done with him."

Tiggy growled just to prove my point. It was awesome when Vadoma and Ruv both flinched.

"I, too, don't want to stay here any longer," Gary said to Vadoma, flipping his mane. "You dress immaculately, but everything else about you makes me wish I had my horn back so I could stab your face. No offense. Actually, I take that back. All the offense. Heaps of offense. Just all of it over your beady little eyes."

"And everyone knows I *have* to go," Kevin said. "Since this is essentially all about me. I mean, raise your hand if *you've* been possessed by a star dragon lately." He raised his claws and looked around. "No? Anyone else? Oh, well, would you look at *that*. Just me! Kevin! The Beast from the East! Do you know how much gold I'm going to get for this? I anticipate a lot. Just so you all know."

"Maybe Ruv should stay here," Ryan said. "We don't actually need him. Just point us in the right direction. I don't know if you know this, but I have a sword. It's been said by many people that I look like I know what I'm doing. It's kind of my thing. Dashing and immaculate, they call me. It was even in the papers."

"Yeah, babe, you tell them." Sometimes Ryan looked stupid with his sword. Most men did. But I didn't say anything when he was trying to be intimidating like the rest of us.

Vadoma shook her head. "You'll need him. For the sand mermaids."

I blinked at her. "I'm sorry. We'll need him for the what, now?"

She turned and started walking back toward Mashallaha. "Don't die," she called over her shoulder. "I'm sure it would be very sad."

"We'll need him for the *what, now*?" I shouted after her.

But since she sucked, she didn't even acknowledge me.

"Shall we?" Ruv asked, cool and calm as ever.

"I hate this place so fucking much," I muttered.

A FEW DAYS LATER, I WAS ready to murder everyone.

"I spy with my little eye something that is sand!"

"Is it sand?"

"It *is*. Tiggy, dear, you are so *good* at this game. Sam, yoo-hoo, *Sam*. Did you hear that? Tiggy is so *good* at this game."

"I heard you, Gary," I said, pulling the hood tighter around my face. "We all heard you. We've been hearing you for the last two hours."

"Well, if you've been listening, one would think you would have tried to guess by now, wouldn't you? Bah. You don't know how to play travel games, you big sore loser. Go brood with your broody face somewhere else. Tiggy! Let's go again. I spy with my little eye, something that is... sand dunes."

"Is it... sand dunes?"

"Oh my gods," I said.

"Is he ever going to figure it out?" Ryan asked, trudging along beside me.

"If he hasn't by now, I'm not holding my breath about it. Maybe we'll get lucky and find a cliff and then he'll fall off that cliff and I'll never have to hear him again."

Ryan bumped his shoulder against mine. It was sweaty and gross and pretty awesome. "You'd be devastated."

"Not hardly."

"A little devastated."

"Barely."

"You got a plan?"

"For?"

He rolled his eyes. "The whole dragon thing."

"Ah. That. Sure I've got a plan."

"Good," he said, sounding relieved. "You had me worried there for a little bit."

"My plan is to wing it."

Ryan sighed. "Godsdammit."

"Watch your mouth, Knight Commander."

"Or what?"

"Or I'll have to spank it with my dick."

He tripped and almost fell. It was glorious.

I laughed at him. He blushed and muttered vague threats in my direction.

We walked on.

Kevin and Ruv were ahead of us, the dragon's tail dragging behind him and leaving long grooves for us to walk on. Ruv had a small wooden board attached to the pack on his back with black hinges on the top and bottom. There was a thick cloth folded against the sides. I hadn't asked what it was for, but I was curious about it. I didn't know if it was some kind of weapon we could use against the desert dragon or some form of protection from whatever the hell sand mermaids were.

I probably should drill him for information while I had the chance.

"Keep an eye on the idiots," I muttered to Ryan. "I gotta go talk to Ruv."

"You act like they'll wander off if we look away," Ryan said, squinting against the sun. "Wait. As soon as I said it, I realized they *would* wander off if we looked away. Got it. Oh, and one more thing." He grabbed me by the back of the neck and pulled me in, kissing me, hard and filthy. His tongue was against mine, and I felt his teeth scrape on my lips. He rolled his hips once, twice, and then pushed me away. I blinked slowly at him. He grinned that smug grin that I hated and adored. "That's better."

"Guh," I said.

"Exactly. Go get 'em, champ." He smacked my ass hard and then turned toward Gary and Tiggy. "Gary! I am going to explain this game to you *one more time....*"

Have you ever tried to walk through a desert with half a hard-on in

00000000000000000000 0000000000 00000000 00000000000 00

your pants?

It sucks.

"Stupid sexy knights," I muttered as I hurried to catch up with Kevin and Ruv, adjusting myself in the process. "With their stupid sexy everything."

"Who's sexy now?" Kevin asked, looking back at me, eyes narrowing as he saw me randomly groping myself. "Are you checking me out again, Sam? From the back, even. See something you like, sailor? Do you want to dock your ship into my port?"

"Whyyyy," I moaned, trying to get *that* image out of my head. "Do you *have* to do that?"

"Yes," Kevin said. "Obviously."

"Whatever. I need to have a chat with our good friend Ruv here."

"Do I need to make myself scarce?" Kevin asked, but he sounded like that was the last thing he wanted to do. It was good to know he didn't trust Ruv either.

"Actually, I think you should stay. Because this probably concerns you too."

"Ah," Kevin said. "The whole thing where I'm the chosen one and will save the world and be given much treasure as a thank-you. Got it."

I sighed. "Sure. Why not."

"You are an odd mix," Ruv said, sounding amused.

"How's that now?"

"You. The dragon. The unicorn and the giant. The knight. The gods must have a sense of humor if they have put the fate of the world on your shoulders."

"I don't know if you're complimenting us or insulting us," I said slowly. "If it's an insult, fuck you. If not, thanks, that's a very nice thing to say."

His smile widened. "She didn't expect you to be as you are."

"Vadoma?"

"Yes. And I think it threw her off."

"She thought I was going to fall in line and do whatever she said."

"You're here, aren't you?"

And that—dammit. "It wasn't her."

He arched an eyebrow at me.

"It wasn't *just* her," I amended. "It was... everything else."

"What she showed you," he said.

"Yeah, I guess." And a thought struck me again, one that I'd let stew in the back of my mind. "Of course, she could have just showed me what she wanted me to see. Magic is manipulation, after all."

"Perhaps," Ruv said. "After all, she would want the most powerful wizard in an age doing her bidding, don't you think?"

"That doesn't really make me feel any better."

"I didn't know it was supposed to."

I frowned at him. "The whole enigmatic thing you've got going on? Stop it. It's annoying, and I don't give two shits about it."

He laughed. "Comes with being the Wolf to the *phuro*."

"Being groomed doesn't mean you get to act like a mysterious dick."

There was a flash of something on his face that told me I was treading on dangerous ground. "I wasn't *groomed*," he said tightly. "I was chosen because of who I am. I didn't need to change to fit others' opinions of me. I'm not you, Sam."

Ouch. And maybe deserved. But still. "No. You're not me. And I'm not you."

He shrugged. "I noticed."

"The sexual tension just *drips* between the two of you," Kevin breathed. "This is like my own private erotic show. I don't have any money, but will you take requests? And if so, what are your hard limits? How do you feel about object insertion?"

"Against," I said at the same time that Ruv said, "Depends on the object."

I gaped at him.

Kevin purred. "I *like* the desert."

"How did we even get here?" I asked. "And why do I always end up asking myself that?" I shook my head. "Stop distracting me. I am here for a very specific reason."

"And what would that be?" Ruv asked.

"The dragon. Vadoma said you were an expert in it."

He hesitated. Barely, but it was there. "Expert might be... a misnomer."

"Really," I said. "Shocking."

"I don't know that *anyone* could be considered an expert in dragons. We can't exactly talk to them."

"Hi," I said, pointing up at Kevin. "Remember me? I can talk to dragons. And because of me, they can talk to everyone else. What does it look like?"

"Serpentine," he said. "Long and thin. The scales are hardened and the color of fire. The wings on its back are small, but they're useful when it dives from the air and into the sand, burrowing deep into the earth below. It has razor-sharp spikes that line its back that can flex if attacked from above. It does not have legs, but it moves quickly, especially on top of the sands. Its given name is Jekhipe. It means 'oneness.' Because it is one with the desert."

I paled as I swallowed thickly. "So. What you just described sounds like a gigantic flying snake."

"Exactly."

"I don't like gigantic flying snakes. Or, really, any snakes at all."

"Ah. Well. Hopefully, you'll get over that shortly. I've always heard that to conquer a fear, you have to immerse yourself in it."

"That sounds like a terrible idea," I said. "Why would anyone do that?"

"Because they choose to. You, on the other hand, do not have a choice."

Godsdammit. "When was the last time you saw it?"

Ruv's brow furrowed. "Saw... it? What do you mean?"

That didn't sound good. "When did you last lay eyes on it?"

"Oh! I understand now. The answer is never. I've never seen it."

I stopped walking. "What."

Ruv looked back at me, confused. "No one has seen the dragon in many, many years."

"Then how do you know what it looks like?"

"Drawings," he said, as if I were stupid.

"Drawings," I repeated. "And how do you know where it is?"

He laughed. "Everyone in the desert knows where the dragon sleeps. You'll see as soon as we get there."

"That... sounds worrying."

"A little."

"You do realize this doesn't make you an expert on the dragon. In fact, you're the furthest thing from an expert there is."

"*I* didn't call me an expert."

"Vadoma did," I pointed out.

He shrugged. "She is the *phuro*. She can say what she pleases."

"Do you think he'll like me?" Kevin asked. "Jekhipe. Which, honestly. What a terrible name."

I looked up at him to find him looking nervously off in the distance. "Why wouldn't he?"

"*You* didn't like me when we first met."

"You were trying to kill me."

"Or fuck you."

"Or fuck me, yes. I remember. I won't ever *not* remember that, thank you. But I got over it, right? You're my buddy now. You know that."

"And you're my sexy son," Kevin said, grinning around a mouthful of sharp teeth. But then the smile faded. "I've never met another dragon before." He looked away, wings drooping a little. "I just don't want to disappoint anyone, you know? What if I'm not good enough?"

"Pick me up," I demanded.

He stared at me for a moment, but complied. He was gentle as his claws curled around me, bringing me up until I was level with his face, feet dangling into the air below.

"Closer," I said.

He did.

"Closer."

He did, going a little cross-eyed as he continued to focus on me.

I punched him in the nose.

"*Ow!*" he roared, jerking me back. "What the fuck!"

"You don't *get* to talk bad about yourself!" I snapped. "You're good enough! You know what, you're *better* than good enough. So I don't want to ever hear you talk like that about yourself again, you hear me?"

He growled at me, exhaling hot smoke that caused me to cough. "You didn't have to *hit* me!"

"Oh, fuck off. You probably didn't even feel that. Me, on the other hand. My *fist* hurts like a motherfucker. Why is everything about you so hard?"

"Yeah it is," he said. "You want to see how hard I can—"

"Stop it."

He pouted. "You said it, not me."

"You didn't have to rise to the godsdamned bait, you—"

"I *always* rise, I'll have you know—"

"Kevin!"

"Sam!"

"What are they doing?" I heard Ruv ask below.

"It's better not to ask," Gary replied. "This is how we do. Just roll with it, honeybunch. It'll make things easier."

"Don't hate the player," Tiggy said. "Hate the game."

"*I* still don't even understand it sometimes," Ryan said.

"You listen to me, okay?" I said, taking Kevin's face in my hands as best I could. There was a contented rumble in his chest as I put my chin on top of his nose so he could see me properly. "You are good enough. And if any other dragon, or any other person, says you're not, they're wrong and they'll have to deal with me, okay?"

"You are my favorite human," Kevin said quietly. "In case you didn't know."

"I'm everyone's favorite human. I'm used to it by now."

He tilted his head away and laughed. As much as we antagonized each other, I really did love that sound. A laughing dragon was a happy dragon, and I wanted nothing more than for him to be happy, especially since he and Gary were broken up. It wouldn't last, I knew. Eventually they'd pull their heads out of their asses and then go back to putting their heads up each other's asses, or whatever sexual perversions they got up to. But while it did, I needed to make sure he was okay, just as much as I did Gary. I thought maybe I'd forgotten that.

He was smiling that weird reptilian smile when he leaned forward again and said, "Cheeky little bugger. I ought to spank that pert little ass of yours until it's… it's… huh."

I squinted at him. "Did you really just lose your train of thought while thinking about my ass? Gods, you're so weird. I don't know why you can't just—"

He reached up with his other hand and used a single claw, pressing it gently against my chin, turning my head west.

At first, I didn't see it.

It looked like only sand, stretching on without end.

But then there was a flash of light in the distance, shimmering in the heat waves. There was *something* there, a smudge against the horizon where the flash had come from.

"What is it?" I asked quietly, even though I knew. "You can see better than I can."

"Ruins," Kevin said. "It looks like ruins."

IT SAT IN THE MIDDLE OF a valley of sorts, a tumbling pile of black stone. There was the outline of a structure there, something that had long since collapsed. There were archways and pillars, almost as if it'd been a castle of sorts. I dug back in my memory as far as I could go to see if I could remember any mention of a castle this far out in the Luri Desert, but I came up empty.

The sand dune we came upon was smaller compared to the rest around the ruins, the grade shallow as it dipped down. A large flat length of sand stretched out ahead of the ruins, something we'd have to cross if we had any hopes of reaching the crumbling rock. From where we stood, I could see a large dome in the middle of the ruins, cracked and decayed. The side of the dome facing us had collapsed, leaving an entrance that was hidden in shadow. I thought it was a good possibility that the search for the dragon would start there. I tried not to think about the idea of a gigantic lizard snake burrowing in tunnels underneath our feet.

Ruv had been leading the way, but he'd stopped before we stepped out onto the flat sand ahead of us. He was tense, shoulders squared, looking out across the expanse. I didn't know *what* he was looking for, but I didn't see anything myself, aside from the fact that he was hesitating when we were *so close* to reaching our target. Why he was trying to delay the inevitable, I had no idea.

"We don't have *time* for this," I growled, attempting to push past him.

His arm shot up against my chest, holding me back. "You *don't* want to do that," he said. "Trust me."

I scoffed. "You know I don't. We have a job to do, though I'm still not quite sure how to do it. And since you aren't exactly in the know either, *expert*, I think you should let me go."

"And if you don't take your hand off of him," Ryan said, gripping the handle of the sword at his side, "I can remove it for you."

Ruv muttered something in his native tongue that I was sure was not a compliment before pulling his pack off his back. He dropped the wooden contraption into the sand, the cloth around it fluttering. He reached into the pack and pulled out three spherical stones, all smooth and bone-white. He was still grumbling to himself as he fitted the pack back around him and held out one stone to Ryan, one to me, and kept the other one for himself. "You throw left," he told Ryan. "Sam, right. I will throw down the middle. As hard as you can."

I could admit to being curious, which is probably why I didn't argue. Ryan glanced at me, and I shrugged. Ruv knew something we didn't, and I was willing to give him the benefit of the doubt. For now.

I threw my stone. It landed a good distance away, but instead of a puff of sand when it landed, the sand itself *rippled*, as if I'd thrown it into water.

"Um," Gary said. "What just happened?"

"Bad feeling," Tiggy said. "Baaaaaad feeling."

Ryan threw his. It went farther, of course, and he looked a little pleased at the fact, given that he would always be a little bit of a douchebag, gods love him. It impacted with the same curious effect, rippling outward.

Ruv went last, throwing his stone down the middle. His went the far-thest. Ryan looked grumpy at that. But instead of rippling, his landed with a hard *thunk*, as if just under the sand was something solid.

I blinked. "Okay, what the hell?"

"Something smells weird," Kevin said, nostrils flaring. "Almost like… rotted fish."

Ryan drew his sword. "This can't possibly be good."

"Watch the outer stones," Ruv said.

We did.

It only took a minute more.

The ripples died. Little granules of sand got caught in a small updraft, dancing along the surface.

And then—

"Nope," Gary said. "Fuck no. Fuck this whole thing. Fuck you. Fuck them. Fuck this place. Gary out."

But he didn't even try to leave, transfixed by the same thing all the rest of us were. Because out of the sand where I'd thrown Ruv's stone rose five claws attached to five fingers, which led to a hand whose palm was white as a fish's belly but whose skin was mottled green around the back, like wet moss growing on trees. The hand, of course, led to a thick forearm that had to be as wide as I was. Whatever the hell was under the sand was big, bigger than it had any right to be. The arm bent over, veins jutting out as the sharp claws closed around the stone before sinking back underneath the surface, the sand moving like waves.

On the other side, the same thing happened with a slightly smaller arm. No one spoke until it too had disappeared in the sand.

"Huh," I said. "All those in favor of turning around and running away, say *aye*."

"Aye," Gary said.

"Aye," Tiggy said.

"Aye," Kevin said.

"Guys, we can't," Ryan said, because he was righteous and brave and so, so stupid. "We have a job to do."

"Okay, then," Gary said. "You go out there first."

"Well, let's not be too hasty," Ryan said quickly, taking a step back. "We should at least talk about it before anyone does anything."

"Sand mermaids," I said to Ruv, who was still looking out at the sands. "That's what Vadoma called them, didn't she?"

"Yes."

"And obviously she left out the part where they were large scary monsters."

"Have you seen real mermaids before?"

I nodded. "Once. It involved lesbian pirates who tied me to the front of their ship to use my magic to get to the mermaid treasure."

"Oh, *right*," Gary said. "I *remember* that. What was that song they sang again?"

"If you use your fingers to scissor," Tiggy sang, "you best put your mouth up and kiss her."

"Gods, I had that in my head for *days*," I said. "And also, I was sufficiently scarred because mermaids are terrifying creatures."

"The sand mermaids are even worse," Ruv said. "Or so I've heard. Twice the size of traditional mermaids. Four rows of teeth—needle sharp. They have little pockets in the back of their throats like a water skin. It holds poison that paralyzes the prey. They like it when you're alive when they start to eat you. Something about the blood tasting different than off a rotting carcass."

"Well shit on my chest and call me kinky," Gary said. "Let me guess. There's no other way to yonder rockopolis aside from straight through this little sand ocean."

"You're into scat play?" Kevin said. "That is *not* something I would have expected."

"What?" Gary said. "Gross. Of course not. Don't be stupid. It's a common expression."

"No one says that," I told him. "Absolutely no one."

"And besides," Gary said, ignoring me completely, "it's not like you know *everything* about me."

"Bullshit," Kevin said. "I knew you inside and out. And in again. And then *out* again—"

"For fuck's sake," I muttered. I glanced back at Ruv. "The middle stone. There's a path?"

He nodded. "Any deviation from it will... be less than ideal."

"How the hell did you figure that out?"

"Trial and error."

If *that* wasn't chilling, I didn't know what was. "How many died?"

"Figuring out the path? Sixteen. The sand mermaids were... quite vicious."

"Why doesn't Kevin just fly us across?" Ryan asked. "He's got wings. One at a time, and we wouldn't even have to worry about them."

"Hey! I'm not some kind of *pack* mule—"

"The vibrations from the wings," Ruv said. "They'll move across the surface of the sand. The creatures can sense them. And they can jump out of the sand higher than one would think. Kevin will have to stay here. Tiggy and Gary too. We must move with lightness under our feet."

"Did he just call me *fat*?" Gary said, sounding outraged. "Bitch, I ain't *fat*. I am motherfucking *jolly*—"

"And you know the path?" I asked, looking out at the sand. Tiggy had been spot-on. I had a bad feeling about this.

Ruv nodded.

"Shit," I said. "This isn't going to go well, is it?"

"Sam," Gary said. "You can't possibly be considering listening to him. We can't *trust* him."

"Gary's right," Kevin said. "There has to be another way. Can't I just roar like the manly dragon I am and call him out?"

"And risk the sand mermaids?" Ruv said.

"Everything risks sand mermaids," Tiggy said.

"He's got a point," Ryan said. "We have Sam's magic. He can just, you know. Do his finger-zappy thing and turn them to stone or something."

"My finger-zappy thing," I repeated. "Gosh, babe. Way to make me sound so awesome."

He flushed. "You know...." He glanced at the others and flushed deeper before continuing. "You *know* what I meant. And you know how I feel about the... finger. Zappy thing."

"Damn right I do." I leered at him.

"Ryan gets a boner when Sam does magic," Gary told Ruv. "It's sweet. And really fucking awful for the rest of us."

"How lovely for him," Ruv said wryly. "And magic wouldn't be the best idea. They're drawn to it. Like bugs to firelight. It calls to them. It's why they stay here, around the dragon."

"So what you're saying is that I'm effectively neutered," I said. "This... isn't going to go very well, is it?"

Ryan scowled. "What happens when we get over to the island or whatever it is? Will the dragon wake? What then?"

"It's why I'm here," Ruv said. "I'm the distraction."

"*What*?" That wasn't what I expected to hear. "Vadoma sent you here to be the *bait*?"

"Oh no," Ryan said. "That's so sad. Gods, I really hope nothing happens to you."

"I forget how bitchy Knight Delicious Face can be sometimes," Gary whispered to Tiggy. "Makes me want to lick his face."

"We lick him later," Tiggy said.

"Oooh," Gary said. "Deal."

"I could get in on that," Kevin agreed. "Have him spread out like some big ol' knight buffet and just gorge ourselves—"

"Let's stop right there before it goes any further," I said. "Because it will. It always does. And Ryan, stop looking so godsdamned smug. It's disturbing and you haven't earned the right."

He scowled at me.

I turned back to Ruv. "I can't in good conscience let you be *bait*. And even if I wanted to, it's not something the King would allow. I am here as an extension of the Crown."

"Sam," Ruv said, reaching out and squeezing my arm. "Your concern for me is sweet…"

"It's really not," Ryan muttered.

"…and I know you don't trust me, but I know what I'm doing. I've gotten to the… *island* before."

I frowned at that. "But you've never seen the dragon?"

"It wasn't meant for me to see," he said simply. He looked at Gary, Tiggy, and Kevin. "I will help them. I promise. But you must promise me that unless it's absolutely necessary, you stay back."

Gary glanced at me. I nodded. He narrowed his eyes as he looked back at Ruv. "If anything happens to them," he said coldly, "I will hold you personally responsible. All jokes aside, I will make sure you never leave this place."

"Ditto," Tiggy said, cracking his knuckles menacingly.

"Double ditto," Kevin growled. "There won't be enough of you left to bury by the time we're finished. I once ate a woman who threatened them, and I'm a vegetarian. That should show you how serious I am."

Ruv swallowed thickly, and that made me feel a little bit better to know he could be intimidated just like anyone else. "Understood."

"Don't die," Gary said to me. "But if you do, I get all of your stuff."

"I want some stuff," Tiggy said.

"How touching," I muttered. "Okay, so how are we going to do this?"

Ruv picked up the wooden contraption and fixed it to his pack again. "One step at a time."

WHEN ONE IS CROSSING A SEA of sand with gigantic monsters circling sight unseen underneath, one tends to get slightly nervous. Couple that with the fact that one's best friends are waiting behind, offering such pearls of wisdom as "Don't look down!" and "If they start to eat you, poke them in the eyes or something!" it tends to make the situation a little tense.

"Would you guys shut *up*?" I growled.

"*Some*one's moody," Gary muttered. "And you guys have only moved like five feet. This is taking *forever*."

He was right. It *was* taking forever. Ruv was in the lead, with me behind him and Ryan bringing up the rear. Both of them were crowding me slightly, causing Kevin to make some crack about wanting to be stuck in *that* sexy sammitch. If I thought I could get away with it, I would have demanded the sand mermaids kick his ass.

But it was slow going, and the island looked as far away as it did when we first stepped out onto the pathway. It hit me with that first step that there *had* to be some measure of trust in Ruv, but not because *I* was willing to follow him out (I'd always been a bit stupid), but because I was allowing *Ryan* out on the sand. Granted, Ryan would never have let me go alone, but still; I trusted Ruv enough that he knew what he was doing.

I didn't know what to do with that.

And it certainly didn't help that I could feel my magic as I always could, wrapping around me and Ryan, almost like it was a sentient thing. It *knew* him, because I did, because of what he was to me. But it also pulled toward Ruv. Nowhere near as much, of course. Ryan and I had been through too much together for that to ever happen. But it *was* there, a possibility. But it was a door that I firmly held shut with all my might. Ruv said he understood. I might have trusted him to have our backs, but I didn't trust him about the cornerstone business. I doubted I ever would.

So there we were, far from home in the middle of the Luri Desert, the sun burning down on us, shuffling through the sand, trying to keep as quiet as possible. Ruv was looking ahead, seeing some path that neither Ryan nor I could see. Ryan still had his sword drawn behind me, and I knew he was keeping an eye out for any sign of movement in the sand.

Me?

Well. That was another story.

Because between the pull of my magic toward Ryan and Ruv, there was something else. Something more. I felt it the moment we stepped out onto the sands. It whispered to me, low words that I couldn't quite make out, like a breeze across my mind. It was warm and familiar and *old*. Gods, it felt old.

And it was pulling me forward.

I felt it in my head.

I felt it in my bones.

And I wanted nothing more than to find it.

We shuffled our way forward. For the most part, the path was straight. There were times when we veered slightly right or left, and how Ruv knew to do that, I didn't know. Either he'd walked this path many times before or the so-called *trial and error* had been ingrained into him. Either way, I was thankful for it.

It wasn't until we were halfway to the island that things went to shit.

Because it was *pulling* me more now.

And I could see where it was pulling me to.

Through the ruins, through the remains of what had once obviously been a castle of old, stood the dome, crumbling and cracked. There was a large stone archway at the bottom. I didn't know what it'd been, what purpose it'd served, but it was where we needed to go. I was sure of it. We needed to—

I took a lurching step forward.

I bumped into Ruv.

He glanced back at me, a questioning look on his face. "What's—" His eyes widened. "Uh, Sam?"

"Yeah?" I said, distracted. We needed to hurry. I knew that much. Something was happening on the island, and I needed to get there.

"Do your eyes normally glow red?"

That got my attention. "What?"

"Your eyes are glowing red."

"Sam?" Ryan asked, sounding concerned. "Sam, look at me."

I did, and his rough hands came up to cup my face. Everything was awash in colors, shifting brighter than it'd been before, seen through a haze. The magic was *leaking* out of me, and the only other time I had to compare it to was that day years before with the bird in the forest. That had been unintentional. This was too.

"Sam," Ryan snapped, as if he'd been saying my name repeatedly.

"I can feel it," I said, voice slightly slurred. "Ryan, I can *feel it.*"

"Did this happen before?" Ruv asked him. "With the other dragon?"

"No," Ryan said, thumbs rubbing over my cheeks. "It wasn't like this."

"Then why is it happening now?"

"I don't know."

"Figure it out," Ruv said. "If this keeps going, we might as well just jump in the sand."

"You worry about getting us there," Ryan snapped. "I'll take care of Sam." He looked back at me. "What is it?"

"It's...." I frowned. "I think it's in my head. The dragon. It's waking. I think it knows we're here."

"Shit," Ryan breathed.

"I gotta get to it," I said, trying to pull away. "Let me go. Ryan, you gotta let me *go.*"

"Never. You hear me? *Never.* Sam, I am *never* letting you go. We do this together, you get me?"

I did, and it was enough to push through the haze of magic. It was slightly startling in its clarity, and for a brief moment, I could see sharper than I ever had before. I blinked. "Ryan?"

"Hey," he said. "There you are."

"We have to hurry."

"I know. But you need to breathe. Sam, your magic is everywhere. Even I can feel it, and you know what that means."

It meant that any magical creature would be able to feel it too.

Say a unicorn. Or a half-giant.

A dragon.

Or a sand mermaid.

I was probably broadcasting like a godsdamned beacon.

I tried to pull it back as much as I could.

With Ryan there, it should have worked. He was my cornerstone. Even if I doubted everything else in the world, I would be certain about that. Ryan Foxheart was my cornerstone.

And I knew that every cornerstone worked differently for every wizard. I knew it was a private thing, a magical thing between two people, a bond unlike any other. He made me stronger. Better. We were building my magic into something that had never been seen before, if Randall and Morgan were to be believed.

So it should have worked.

It had in the past.

Any time I'd felt slightly out of control. Anytime we'd fought villains or faced danger, there was always a sense of control. He *was* my control.

So it should have worked.

And for a moment, it did.

I felt the magic dull.

The red in my eyes must have faded, because he smiled at me. "There you are," he said. "I knew we could—"

Then:

Wizard, a voice said, low and growly. *Feel you. Hear you. Smell you.*

Everything came surging back. My spine snapped ramrod straight, mouth falling open as I shuddered against it.

"Shit," Ryan said. "It's not—"

"Ryan," I gritted out. "Watch... your motherfucking... *language.*"

"Oh my gods," he said. "You *dick.* How could you even think of *that* right—"

"Uh-oh," Ruv said.

"What uh-oh?" Ryan said. "Why *uh-oh?*"

"We have company."

"Uh-oh," Ryan said weakly.

I had enough of my faculties left about me to know that wasn't good. I looked where Ruv was pointing and almost wished I hadn't.

Because off to the right, crawling slowly along the surface of the sea of sand, was a sand mermaid.

"Sweet molasses," I managed to say.

When one thinks of mermaids, one thinks of fairy tales, of beautiful creatures with long flowing hair, ethereal skin, a fantasy built around seduction. The mermaids that had captured me in the ocean were just that, humanoid beings that sang their prey to them. Some could even be good, though, and had alliances with the King just like other magical creatures of Verania did.

This was not those creatures.

This mermaid had only the vaguest of human attributes upon its countenance. There was a nose, yes, flattened with slits running down the middle. And eyes too, deep black pools that glittered in the sunlight. But the gaping maw that was its mouth was most certainly *not* human. It was almost perfectly circular in shape, with rows upon rows of sharpened teeth wrapping around the interior. Its skin was green that faded into black, looking fetid and tight, like it'd died decades before and then been baked by the sun. Its arms were long and thick, the claws on the hands it used to *pull* itself toward us bigger than I thought they were, curved into wicked hooks that looked as if they were made for eviscerating. It was obviously female, breasts hanging down into the sand. The lower half of its body was fishlike, with iridescent scales that caught the sunlight and cast reflections onto the surface of the sand. The tail at the bottom had fins that curved off outwardly.

But what stuck out at me the most aside from the sheer horror of it, the *size* of this thing crawling toward me, were the seashells that looked as if they were *embedded* into its skin, shells that were green and gold and red and white and *jutted* out from its face and neck and shoulders.

"Sam!" Gary called.

"Yes, Gary."

"Now would probably be a good time to run."

"Thank you, Gary."

"Also, Sam?"

"Yes, Gary."

"There's another one crawling up on the other side."

"Godsdammit," I said as we whirled around, because sure enough, another horror was crawling up and out of the sand, moving toward us as if it had all the time in the world. "I am going to have such fucking nightmares after this."

"Maybe we should—" I heard Kevin start.

"*No*," I shouted at them. "You *stay* back there, you hear me? Don't. Not until—"

Wizard, the voice sang, from the heart of the ruins or in my mind, I didn't know. *Come to me.*

"Fuck," I said, bending over and clutching my head. I felt Ryan put a hand on my back, anchoring me with his presence. "It's *calling me*. We have to—"

"Here's what's going to happen," Ruv said, sounding far calmer than he should have been. "I'm going to draw them away. And you're going to get to the island as quickly as possible. Don't stop. Don't look back. The path curves left, then right, then left one more time. Ryan, do you see that large stone? Looks like a tree."

"Yeah. I see it."

"That's where the path ends. Get him there."

"What are you going to do?" Ryan asked, sounding dubious. "You can't go out onto the sand. They'll pull you under."

I looked up as Ruv said, "Not if they can't catch me." There was a glint in his eyes that I didn't like, but before I could say anything about it, he pulled the wooden contraption off his back and threw it out onto the sand to the right, off the path. It landed but didn't sink. And as soon as it hit the sand, it *popped* open, the wooden slats snapping on the metal hinges, until it was a long, thin board, curved up along the edges. A wooden pole shot up in the middle, the cloth tied to either end. The wind blowing over the surface of the sand sea caught the cloth, and it billowed out, like a sail. The board began to slide along the sand.

"Holy shit," I said. "Are you going to *ride* that?"

The Wolf of Bari Lavuta winked at me, a cheeky grin on his face. "Told you I knew what I was doing." And then he took a few steps back, bounced on his heels once, twice. He took four running steps forward and jumped, then landed on top of the board. It caught his weight and sank the slightest amount into the sand before it bounced back up and skittered along the surface. The sail flapped, and the momentum of his jump caused the board to pick up speed, away from us and toward the sand mermaid. Ruv bent his knees and jutted his hips, turning the board to the left.

"That's not something you see every day," I said.

"I bet *I* could do that if I wanted to," Ryan said, though he too sounded impressed.

"Over here!" Ruv yelled. "Come and get me!"

The sand mermaid let out an unholy roar, something that caused my bones to ache. Its tail snapped back and forth, and for a moment, I thought it was going to reach out and pull him right off the board, but he moved at the last second, directing himself toward the large sand dune that surrounded one side of the valley we were in. It began to chase after him, sand shooting up around it as it dove under the surface.

"Crap," Ryan said. "Where'd the other one go?"

He was right. It was gone too. The sand rippled, but there was no sight of it.

"It went back under," Kevin called out. "When the other one did. Maybe you guys should consider *moving your asses*?"

"Don't be salty," Gary said. "But he's right. *Move your fucking asses*."

I took a step toward the island and stumbled as there was another blast of *something* from the island, my head spinning with so many colors that it felt like I was *choking* on them. I pitched forward and thought, *Oh fuck oh fuckohfuckoh*fuck, but a strong hand wrapped around my arm and pulled me back right before I fell off the path. Ryan pulled my back to his chest, wrapping an arm around me.

"That was close," he breathed in my ear. "Don't suppose you'd consider letting me carry you?"

I turned my head to glare at him. "Are you out of your *mind*? I'm not some damsel in distress that you need—"

"Right," he said. "Because right now you'd choose to be difficult. And notice how I am not bringing up the whole damsel thing, even though you technically just swooned right in front of me."

"That's such crap, and you know it—"

"Are you guys *really* doing this right now?" Gary bellowed. "Oh my gods, you idiots, *run*!"

"Move, Sam!" Tiggy yelled. "Don't get eaten! I would cry!"

"You heard him," I said. "I would feel guilty for the rest of my life if I died. We should probably avoid that if possible."

"Fine," Ryan said. He let me go but trailed his hand down until he caught mine, holding tight. "I lead. You follow. Got it?"

I opened my mouth to argue but closed it just as quick. I'd give him shit for it later. We didn't have time for me to be an asshole right now. Especially since it was probably better that he take the lead, given that I was still feeling the pull of whatever waited for us on the island. "You're so cute when you get all huffy," I said instead.

And there was the eye roll I was looking for, even as he blushed. "Shut up. I do not."

"Totally do."

"I really fucking hate you guys right now," Gary said. "Just so you know."

"Let's go," Ryan said, looking toward the ruins.

Left, Ruv had said. Then right. Then left.

We had this.

Ryan pulled me forward, sword still gripped in his other hand at the ready. Each step he took was deliberate, kicking up the sand, making sure we kept to the path hidden underneath. I followed him closely, trying to keep an eye out around him.

Ruv had started to drift up the incline of the sand dune that wrapped around the ruins. The sand mermaid following him leapt out of the sea, hooked claws reaching, but Ruv swerved at the last moment, and the creature flew into the sand dune, disappearing with the last flick of its tail. Remarkably, I could hear Ruv's laughter, like he was having the time of his life.

I didn't see the other one, though. And it made me nervous. I tried not to think about what would happen if there were more than two. That probably wouldn't bode well.

Ryan paused briefly, hand tightening around mine as his feet found the first ledge. We began to move left and—

Wizard. Wizard. I feel you. Are you worthy? Are you ready?

I gritted my teeth against it, forcing myself to remain upright as Ryan led the way. It was urging me on, calling me to it, and I didn't want to fight it. I wanted to sing back to it that I was coming, that I heard it too—

"*Watch out!*" Gary screamed behind us.

The path under our feet shook.

We turned slowly.

Behind us, only a short distance away, sat the other sand mermaid, on the path, tail flicking back and forth.

"Oh, we are so boned," I said weakly.

"Run," Ryan whispered in my ear.

And we did.

I had trusted Ruv to lead us on the path, trusting that he knew where to go.

Ryan didn't know where to go.

And I trusted him more than anything.

We ran.

The mermaid snarled behind us, and I didn't have to look back to know it was coming after us. I hoped that the others were being smart and staying where they were supposed to. They weren't going to—

A shadow passed overhead.

I looked up.

Because *of course they weren't fucking smart.*

"Incoming, motherfuckers!" Gary screamed. "Tiggy, fuck that shit up!"

"*GWAAAAHHH!*" Tiggy bellowed as Kevin flew right above us, Gary clutched in one set of talons, Tiggy in another. I watched as Kevin released Tiggy, the half-giant shouting that ridiculous cry he thought meant the sound of war. He hurtled toward us as Kevin and Gary continued on, heading toward the ruins.

"Oh, fuck me sideways," I squeaked as a nine-foot half-giant fell toward us.

Ryan jerked my hand, pulling me forward as we ran *under* Tiggy.

The sand mermaid roared behind us, sounding like it was *right there*—

I shot a look over my shoulder in time to see Tiggy land on *top* of the mermaid, squashing it against the hidden stone path. A great plume of sand burst up around them, swallowing them both, but not before I saw the mermaid's face twist in pain as it screamed.

But even as I thought to cheer Tiggy for kicking ass and taking names,

I heard the stone beneath our feet begin to shift and crack.

Which was not a good sound to hear when we were still far from the island.

Ryan didn't try to pull me away from Tiggy, which was the only reason I held on to his hand still. The sand settled around Tiggy and the mermaid, enough so that I could see the creature's arm skittering around, trying to find purchase as the crack of stone got louder. Tiggy was trying to hold down the mermaid, but the thing was strong, and it looked like the half-giant was in danger of getting bucked off.

"Tiggy, it's going to break!" I cried at him. "You need to *run!*"

Tiggy looked at me, a determined look on his face. "No, Sam. You run. Get to dragon. Tiggy *smash.*"

My eyes widened. "No! No smash! You'll fall in the sand."

The mermaid shrieked and bucked up again, and Tiggy almost went over and into the sand.

"Fuck this," I snarled. I began to pull my magic toward me, drawing it from the dry desert air, the earth, the sky, the few clouds there were, the rays of the sun, *anything* so that I could get to kill this bastard of a thing and—

And of course Ryan felt it, of course he knew what I was doing, because he pulled me back against him. "You can't," he muttered in my ear. "We don't know if there are more of these things or what the dragon will do."

"If you fucking think I'm just going to *leave* him—"

"Kevin's coming back," he said. "We gotta move. Kevin will help him."

"He *can't.* You heard what Ruv said. The *vibrations—*"

"I'm pretty sure we're past vibrations now—"

"Then just let me do this!" I jerked out of Ryan's grasp and was about to fucking *bring* it when Ryan cried out behind me. I whirled around in time to see *another* mermaid rising out of the sand, a clawed hand wrapped around his ankle. He'd fallen on his ass and was being *pulled* toward its mouth, the needle-sharp teeth so close to his boot. He was reaching for his sword, which had gotten knocked out of his hand.

"Ryan!" I ran toward him, scooping up the sword as I went by, tossing it handle first, the blade slicing shallowly into my palm, wetting the metal with my blood. Ryan caught the sword and, with a yell, turned and shoved it into the mermaid's mouth and down its throat. The mermaid's eyes bulged as the blade pierced its insides, and I was almost to him, I was almost—

It flailed back, hand still gripping Ryan's ankle. Ryan was lifted up and *over* the mermaid, slamming back down on the other side of it.

Out in the sea of sand.

The mermaid began to sink. Ryan's sword still stuck out of its mouth.

And it still held on to him.

His eyes were wide as he began to dip below the surface.

"No," he said hoarsely. "Don't you do it. Sam, *don't you do it.*"

"Sam!" a voice cried out behind me.

And somehow I was able to turn away from Ryan in time to see Tiggy knocked into the sand as well, thrown off the back of the mermaid. It instantly flipped itself back into the sand and dove beneath the surface.

Tiggy began to sink immediately, his weight pulling him down. He thrashed and kicked and fought, but it was no use.

"Sam," Ryan said, and I turned back toward him, heart in my throat. The sand was up to his armpits. "Get to the dragon." He was scared, I could see that, *gods* how I could see that, but he was trying to keep himself calm for my sake. "You gotta get to the dragon."

Everything was slowing down around me. Too much was happening at once. Ruv was too far away, on the other side of the island, the same mermaid still chasing after him, but now a second one too, both tails whipping back and forth as they surged after him.

Kevin had set Gary down on solid land and looked to be coming back, but he wouldn't make it in time. Not for either of them.

Blood pounded in my ears.

Everything was brighter than it had ever been. Sharper.

I breathed in deeply as Tiggy slipped below the surface of the sand, raising his hand and wiggling his fingers at me, a little wave goodbye.

Ryan said, "I love you, Sam. I always have."

And then he was gone too.

And I just—

"No," I said. "No, no, no."

I stood slowly.

Once upon a time I went into the Dark Woods to find something unexpected, as tasked by Morgan of Shadows. In those woods I found a hornless unicorn and a half-giant. I saved them from an evil man, and every day since then, they saved me from myself.

Once upon a time I saw a boy who'd come to the castle. I was told he was from the army. That he was to be a knight in the Castle Guard. I'd never seen such a beautiful boy before, and that day, I gave my heart away, even though I thought I'd never get his in return.

They weren't going to be taken from me. Not now.

Not ever.

Wizard, the waking dragon whispered to me. *What will you do?*

Everything, I said in return.

There is an old tongue spoken by wizards. It is in these words that magic forms in those that have it in their blood. The spells and incantations and words of power that bring the magic surging forward, from out of the blood and into the real world. It draws from everything around us. It draws from everything in us.

Only a few didn't need those words.

Morgan.

Randall.

They had centuries of experience to draw upon. They were *one* with the old tongue, the language of magic. They didn't need the words aloud because they'd built it up inside of them. Their cornerstones had given them the foundation to become something stronger than the world had ever seen. They formed their words in their heads and hearts, and the thoughts alone brought the magic into the world.

I was like them, in that respect.

I didn't need those words either.

But there was a difference.

Sometimes, I didn't even need the *thought*.

So when I pulled myself to my full height, there was no clear plan in my head. There was only the thought that someone had taken from me, had taken Tiggy, my friend. Had taken Ryan, my cornerstone.

And it was enough.

The sand began to swirl at my feet. First it was just a small corona, whipping itself around me as if caught by a moderate wind.

But it grew.

Clouds began to form in the sky above us, and as I turned my face upward, I felt what little moisture there was being *sucked* out of the air. The clouds were black and gray, and they *trembled* and they *shook* even as the thunder began to roll.

The corona was bigger now.

Much bigger.

The path was made clear beneath my feet, an old, worn stone thing that had been rubbed smooth by the moving sand.

And it grew bigger still.

Lightning arced in the clouds above. I wasn't ready for it yet.

And it didn't matter that I hadn't done this before. That I'd never used this much magic before. None of it mattered. The only thing I could think of was Tiggy. And Ryan. And getting them back.

The corona had given way to a tornado.

The sky was dark now, almost like night had fallen, though it was still midday.

There were others, I knew. Other people I cared for. But they were safe. They would let me do this.

And then I raised the entire sea of sand.

It shot up around me on either side of the stone path, rising high up toward the storm above.

And I could see them then. Through the sand.

The mermaids.

There were *dozens* of them.

Later I was told that only seconds passed when Ryan and Tiggy were pulled under the sand. That everything that happened and everything that followed was only *seconds*.

But it felt like ages when I stood there under a desert storm, an ocean of sand on either side of me.

And when I brought the lightning down, when it sparked down from the sky toward me, there was only one thought in my head.

You won't take them from me.

The lightning struck me, entering through my head, snapping across my brain, down the back of my neck until it settled in my chest, wrapping itself around my heart. It was mine, and it'd always been *there*, but this was the first time I'd actually called it to myself, however unconsciously. Three times I'd been lightning-struck: once by Dark wizards on a dusty road on the way to a dragon's keep, once by the wizard Randall in an attempt to make a point, and now.

It was warm. It was electric. It felt *alive*.

And every time a mermaid was swept toward me, the lightning would arc out of me, out of my hands, out of my chest, my eyes and mouth and throat and heart. It snapped into the sandstorm, electrifying the sand and solidifying it as the lightning traveled through it. It smashed into the heads and chests and tails of the mermaids.

Lightning had a curious effect on sand. I'd seen it once on a beach near the Port after a great storm had rolled through the coast. There were several strikes along the beach, each leaving scorched holes in the sand. When they dug around the holes, there were glass-lined hollow tubes that branched off into the ground. Petrified lightning, Morgan had said it was called.

And that was what I created now.

The mermaids screeched and rocked their heads back as they were electrocuted, clawed fingers flexed and stiff at their sides, eyes open, their gaping maws pointing up into the sandstorm around them. The swirling sand fused into their skin, hardening until it cracked into place. Electricity poured from their mouths, colliding with the sand, lining their insides with solid crystal that grew out of them in ominous shapes.

And it was as this storm raged around me, as it froze these creatures into glass, that I searched for my loves. I pushed through the sand, the lightning so hot at points that it didn't solidify so much as it vaporized the sand away from me. There was electricity at my feet, and with every step I took, the sand became solid and supported my weight, creating a staircase through the roiling sea.

One of the mermaids caught some kind of draft and hurtled toward me, claws reaching to tear my throat out, but the moment before it touched me, the moment before hooks sank into soft skin, I *pushed* toward it, and it exploded in a bright flash.

I found Tiggy first, caught in the storm. He was spinning in a slow circle with the remains of several mermaids floating by, the pieces of them reflecting the lightning as it swirled around him. He reached out, a look of awe on his face as he pushed one of the pieces, watching it twist in place, electricity crawling along the surface, little sparks trailing where he had pressed against it.

His great brow furrowed when he saw me. He cocked his head. "Sam?"

I nodded, unable to speak, unable to do anything but find them, keep them safe, keep anything from hurting them.

"You do this?" he asked.

I nodded again.

He smiled at me as thunder rolled above. "Sam magic is strong magic," he said, reaching a hand out for me. He trusted me completely. He knew I could never hurt him.

I put my hand in his and we went away, away, away.

There weren't as many of them now. The mermaids. Most had been frozen or shattered. But now, instead of coming for us, they tried to get away. A brief thought pierced through the haze of magic, like sunlight through clouds, that I should let them go, that I should leave them be, but then the clouds took away that sunlit thought, and they too went the way of their sisters.

We found Ryan cocooned in a swirl of sand and pieces of glass, like some enchanted prince from a story of old. His eyes were closed, sword hanging loosely in his hand, which rose in front of his face. Another sunlit moment pierced the magic, and I remembered the vision my grandmother had shown me, of my beloved resting upon a stone dais, sword lying atop him, handle on his chest, blade pointed toward his feet. This moment burned, and I was filled with such an overwhelming sense of grief that I thought I would shatter from it. I would blow away, the petrified pieces of me caught in the swirling storm. I was lightning-struck, yes, but I too could break so easily.

I said, "Ryan."

My voice broke.

He opened his eyes.

And the sunlight went away again. I reached for him, and he reached for me, and the moment our hands touched, the moment his fingers met mine, I felt a great and terrible rage that something like this could be taken from me, that they had *tried* to take this from me. I knew, deep down, there was a price to pay for the magic used, but all I could think about was tearing everything apart until there was nothing left but my family.

I walked through the storm.

They drifted after me.

They spoke, I heard their voices, but I didn't hear what they said.

I was too entrenched in magic, too far underneath whatever the storm had done to me. It wasn't until we stood upon the stone path again that I felt Ryan tugging against me. I tried to pull away, trying to find more of them, trying to get rid of them while I still had the chance, but he wouldn't let me.

And since I could never hurt him, I went. He wrapped his arms around me, holding me close. I tucked my face against his neck and held on for dear life. A moment later, I felt Tiggy gather us both against his chest, rumbling in a deep and soothing fashion, hand against the back of my head.

And then Ryan Foxheart tilted his head, his lips near my ear, and said, "Sam. Oh, Sam. It's okay to let go now. It's okay to let go."

And I cried out against the skin of his neck, my magic *exploding* out of me. I put everything into that cry I could, the last weeks, the revelations, the sense of loss, the secrets kept, the anger I felt. The fact that I'd almost lost Tiggy and Ryan. Everything.

Lightning struck. Thunder cracked.

A moment later, everything fell quiet.

And a moment after that, I felt the sun on my skin again, burning bright and hot.

I took in a breath. And then another. And another.

"Wow," Tiggy breathed, still holding us close. "So *high*."

"Sam," Ryan murmured. "You okay?"

But before I could speak, I was *pulled* again.

Wizard, the dragon spoke. *Wizard. Wizard.*

For now it was truly awake.

I opened my eyes.

I blinked against the sunlight.

It took a moment for my vision to clear as Ryan pulled away enough to be able to look at me. His face was the first thing I saw, slightly out of focus, edges blurred. I blinked it away and everything cleared.

"You with me?" he asked, hands on my arms.

"What happened?" I croaked out.

"Sam go boom," Tiggy said. "Bright and shiny boom."

I looked up at him. "I did what?"

"Boom," Tiggy said softly, nodding his head toward the sea of sand that—

No longer existed.

Where there'd once been an ocean of sand filled with creatures that hid underneath the surface was now just empty air.

"What the fuck?" I said.

We stood on the stone path that had, for the most part, remained intact. But on either side of us now was a cavern whose bottom was so far below where we stood, I couldn't see it. The sand was gone. The mermaids were gone as if they'd never existed at all. The path behind us was broken where Tiggy had fallen from Kevin's grasp. The path ahead twisted just like Ruv said it would before it ended against the island, the ruins of the castle sitting atop a large rock pillar that stretched into the cavern below. Kevin and Gary stood at the edge of the island, watching us, waiting. They both looked tense, like they were getting ready to rush over to us at any moment.

"Where's Ruv?" I asked, slightly panicked. He'd been surfing along on that—

"There," Ryan said, pointing off to the other side of the cavern. Ruv stood on a sand dune, looking down into the empty space before him, scratching the back of his head. He must have felt us watching him because he looked up and waved.

"Sam go boom," Tiggy said softly, waving back at him.

"Sam go boom," I echoed faintly.

CHAPTER 17
Snake Dragon Monster Thing

I<small>T WAS SLOW-GOING TO REACH THE</small> island, given that my legs felt weak and I was exhausted. I scowled at Ryan as he tried to hold me up, but Tiggy wouldn't hear any of it, and picked me up and threw me over his shoulder, grunting, "Sack of Potatoes Sam. Capitalized, motherfucker."

It didn't stop me from grumbling about it. When one is being held against his will by a half-giant, one must grumble. I was sure that was Veranian law.

Ryan trailed after us, and since I was cranky, I thought it best to give him a piece of my mind.

"You," I said. "You are in so much trouble, you don't even know."

"Am I now." It wasn't even said as a question, the bastard.

"Yes, you are." I scowled at him to show just how serious I was. He didn't seem to be affected in the slightest. I lowered my voice in a mocking approximation. "*Go after the dragon, Sam. Leave me here to die, Sam. Look at me, I'm a godsdamned martyr!*"

"I don't think that's quite how it went."

"It might as well have! And Tiggy, don't think I've forgotten about you! You're gonna get yours, you can bet on *that*, yes, *sir*. You think you can just *wave goodbye* at me and *not* get into trouble? Oh, you are *sorely* mistaken, my friend. You're in deep shit too!"

Tiggy patted my butt and said, "Okay, Sam."

"Stop placating me!"

"Pretty Sam. Pretty, loud, boomy Sam."

I pointed my finger at Ryan, craning my neck to look back up at him. "So much trouble."

"What's he screeching about now?" I heard Gary ask.

"Martyrs!" I yelled. "I'm surrounded by martyrs!"

"Oh boy," Gary said. "He's getting loud. That's never a good sign."

"Put me down!"

Tiggy did just that, but apparently I wasn't as recovered as I would have liked. As I stumbled forward, Gary was there to stop my momentum, my hands going around his neck, his mane soft under my fingers. My legs were shaking, and I sagged against Gary, letting him take my weight for a little bit.

"Kevin," I heard Ryan say. "Can you go grab Ruv? I don't think he can make it over."

"On it, boss man."

"Don't call me that."

"Sure thing, boss man."

"Godsdammit. Just... get him."

"Leaving now, boss man."

"You okay, kitten?" Gary asked, rubbing his cheek against mine. "That was... impressive."

"I'm fine," I muttered. "I don't... I don't know what happened."

"You put on a very powerful display," Gary said softly. "Something I don't think I've ever seen before."

"Great," I sighed. "Because that's just what we need right now. Me getting more out of control."

I felt Gary shake his head. "Don't think we can call it that, Sam."

"Maybe. Whatever it was, I'm sorry it took too long. I know you don't like to worry."

Gary pulled back so he could look at me. "Took long?"

I tested my legs, bending slightly at the knees. They still felt a little soft, but it was getting better. My strength was slowly returning, which was a good sign. "Yeah, I don't even know how long I was stuck in that storm. Felt like ages before I found Tiggy and Ryan."

Gary opened his mouth and then snapped it closed again.

"What?"

"Sam," he said slowly, like he was choosing his words carefully. "It only lasted seconds."

And that sent a chill down my spine. "What?"

Gary glanced at Tiggy and Ryan before looking back at me. "Ryan and Tiggy went under. Kevin and I were about to come after you and them when you just... exploded. Sam, I could *taste* the magic in the air. One minute you were standing and the sun was shining, and the next, there was a thunderstorm overhead and the sand just *rose* around you. We could barely see you on the path. Before we could even shout for you, you were struck by lightning and then you were moving."

"Moving," I said. "I don't—"

"To put it bluntly, kitten? You were surrounded by a gigantic ball of lightning and were moving almost faster than the eye could see. One moment you were on the walkway, and the next, you were electrifying everything. It was so bright, we had to look away. When I could see again, the sand, the mermaids... everything was gone."

"Huh," I said. "That's... something."

Gary leaned in until his face was pressed against mine. "You want to know how it happened?" he asked, breathing heavily. "Because I can tell you."

I was going cross-eyed trying to look at him. "Why did it happen?"

He panted against my face. "Because of *love*."

I groaned and pushed his face away. "You shut your fat mouth."

He was laughing, but it had a hysterical edge to it. "Sam, I'm not even joking. You thought Tiggy and Ryan were in trouble, and you literally *destroyed a sea of sand* to get to them."

"Hey! They *were* in trouble! They were the ones stupid enough to get themselves sucked under!"

"I love you too," Tiggy said. "You my favorite wizard."

"Damn right I'm your favorite wizard," I muttered. "Too bad you're both on my shit list right now."

Ryan wrapped his arm around my shoulders, pulling me to him and kissing the side of my head. "You love me," he said into my hair.

"You can go fuck yourself."

"You love me."

"Less and less every second."

"You love me." He kissed me again.

I clung to him, just a little bit. "You can't do that," I said in a low voice. "You can't do that to me again."

He turned me until he could cup my face in his hands, forcing me to meet his gaze. I wanted to look away, but I couldn't. "You came for me," he said. "Even though I told you to go."

"You have stupid ideas."

"Oh gods," Gary moaned from somewhere behind me. "They're going to start getting sappy. Tiggy, kill me now."

"No," Tiggy said. "Tiggy loves you. No killing."

"You adorable, wonderful giant. How I cherish you."

"You came for me," Ryan said again. "Just like I would come for you."

"I never said *I* was smart either."

He leaned in and kissed me sweetly, lips lingering. I wanted to deepen it, make it more than it was, but I knew it would be tinged with desperation. I still felt frantic, the image of him slipping under the sand burned into my mind.

"They're so fucking cute it's terrible," Gary said. "Tiggy, will I find love that makes other people want to vomit and punch me in the spleen?"

"You did."

"Why, I have no idea of what you speak!"

"You an idiot," Tiggy said succinctly.

"Don't do that to me again," I murmured against his lips. "I swear to the gods, if you die, I will resurrect you just to kill you myself."

I felt him smile against me. "Deal. And stop worrying about the magic."

I pulled away. "I'm not *worried*."

"Sam."

"Okay, fine. Maybe a little worried. But you saw what I did. Ryan, no one should be able to do that. *Randall* can't even do that."

Ryan shrugged. "He's already said you're more powerful than he is. He just thinks you're unfocused."

"Being unfocused with that level of power will get someone killed," I said.

"It's a good thing you have me, then."

"Oh my gods. Of course you would make this about your ego. You dickbag."

He rolled his eyes. "You're the most powerful wizard in an age. I'm your cornerstone. Therefore I'm the most powerful cornerstone in an age. It's my destiny, after all."

I wiggled my fingers at him. "I will curse your tongue so it falls out of your mouth."

"Ungh," he said, eyes glazing over.

"Heart boner definitely gone," Gary muttered behind us. "Their sex games are so weird."

"I don't like sex games," Tiggy said. "I like puzzles."

"Gaah, I love your face. Tell me I'm beautiful."

"You're beautiful."

"I know."

There was a flap of wings, and a large shadow passed overhead. Dust and sand kicked up around us as Kevin lowered himself back onto the island, holding Ruv in his claws. He let Ruv drop down before he landed, folding his wings against his sides.

Ruv was wide-eyed as he stared at me. "They said you were powerful." He shook his head. "They have no idea, do they?"

"I don't think anyone does," I said honestly. "It's still a work in progress."

"A work in—Sam. I have *never* seen that kind of magic before."

"Oh. Well. You're... welcome?"

"How can you *do* that?"

"The power of positivity?"

"He doesn't know," Gary said. "Isn't that fun? You meet him, you think, oh, there's a cute little twink with a perky butt, and the next, *wham!* He's exploded your liver and turned your blood into burning oil."

"I'm not a twink!"

"Notice how he didn't deny the other stuff," Gary whispered to Ruv. "Think about that the next time you let Vadoma call you his cornerstone and you don't try to correct her."

"Eep," Ruv squeaked.

"Yesss," Gary hissed. "Your fear gives me strength."

"Well," Ryan said, clapping his hands. "As fun as threats against Ruv are, we should probably move forward before something else happens."

I stared at him in horror. "Why would you *say* that? Now something else is going to happen because you *jinxed* us!"

"Sam," he said with a sigh. "Something always happens when you're involved."

"That's not even—okay. Yes. That's pretty much true. I have nothing."

"Sam, before we go, if I may."

"Yes, Kevin."

"I know your mother and I have ended our relationship."

"I changed my mind. Stop."

"And I know I've been a distant stepfather at best."

"Oh my gods."

"But son? That whole lightning thing? That was *hot*. I would just *destroy* you if you'd let me."

"Oh my gods."

"Remember when I used to hate your magic because wizards suck?"

"I wish that was still the case."

"Well now I *like* it, and I *hope* wizards suck."

"Why aren't you defending my honor?" I asked Ryan, poking him in the chest.

He shrugged. "I don't disagree with what he's saying."

"Useless. All of you. Since Ryan jinxed us, we should get moving before we get eaten or—"

From farther into the island came the deafening roar of an unmistakably large creature. It echoed through the cavern around the island until it finally faded.

"—or the dragon wakes up and knows we're here," I finished weakly. "Because holy fuck, it's awake and knows we're here."

We all turned toward the dome, expecting to see it slithering toward us, teeth bared, ready to eat our legs and patellas, but there was nothing there.

But I could *feel* it. It wasn't whispering to me in my head anymore, at least not in words. There was just that hook in my brain, jerking me forward, and all I could think was *now, now, now*.

"Well shit," Gary said. "Sam's got glowing eyes again. That will never not be freaky."

"Kevin?" I asked without looking away from the dome. "Can you feel it?"

"Yes," Kevin said, sounding dreamy. "He's in there."

"He?"

"Yes."

"Can you talk to him?"

"No. It's not.... I can just *feel* him. He's awake. He's waiting for us. He's waiting for you."

"Eh, maybe we should think about this," Ryan said. "Since anytime we've rushed headfirst into anything without thinking it through, it's never really worked out in our favor."

"You rescued the Prince and landed the wizard without thinking it through," Gary pointed out. "In fact, I don't know that you *ever* think things through."

He glared at Gary. "*I* think things through all the time. It's not my fault I'm surrounded by all of you people."

Gary narrowed his eyes. "And just what do you mean by *you people?*"

I ignored them. "Anything else we should know about Jekhipe before we go?"

Ruv was watching me with a look on his face that I couldn't quite place. I didn't know if my eyes were still doing their weirdness, but I thought they probably were. I didn't think he was scared, but... wary? Cautious, probably. My little display had probably thrown him for a loop. I didn't know if that was a good or a bad thing. Or what'd he'd say to Vadoma when we returned to Mashallaha.

"Just that he's dangerous," Ruv said finally. "A trickster. You cannot underestimate him."

I rolled my eyes. "I don't underestimate anything."

"Um," Gary said. "You do it all the time."

"No one asked you, Gary!"

"Okay, you need to point those freaky eyes at someone else, Miss Thang. I don't need your creepy hoodoo business all up in my shit."

"I think they're hot," Ryan whispered to me.

"I know," I said. "But you're really weird, so."

"It's not *weird.*"

"What they whispering about?" Tiggy asked Gary.

"Probably something disgusting," Gary said. "Remember when Sam was a virgin? I miss those days."

"His precious flower," Tiggy said mournfully.

"Team Sam, move out!" I announced.

Which, of course, everyone protested, because they were lame and wouldn't know a good team name if it punched them in the throat.

THE RUINS WERE IN FAR WORSE condition than they'd appeared from far away. Everything that still stood—the parapets, the battlements, the towers—looked to be on the verge of collapse. Great piles of stones littered the whole of the island. Everything was smooth and bleached, worn down by blowing sand and sun. There were vague shapes in the broken statues—feet here, an arm there. There was a stone hand that held a dagger lying on the ground near the remains of an archway.

The ruins felt dead.

And haunted.

"What was this place?" I asked Ruv, even as the dragon whispered unintelligibly in my head. "I've never heard of a castle this far out."

Ruv stepped over a mound of stone. "The name of the castle has been lost in time. But the gypsy people call it *Prikasa*."

"What does that mean?"

He didn't even blink when he said, "Bad luck. A dark omen."

"Of course that's what it means," I said. "Because you guys suck."

He ignored me. "It's supposed to be older than Verania itself. There was a man, or so it is said, a fierce warrior, who ruled over many lands. He and his army worked their way east, laying siege to everything in sight, taking it for himself. He was blinded by greed and power and the need to own all he could see. By rights, he was very good at what he did. He built himself castles for every new territory he consumed. This was said to be one of them."

"What happened to him?"

"What happens to all men with great power," he said. "Someone wanted it more and killed him for it."

"I feel like you're trying to tell me something."

I didn't miss the faint smile. "You are so wise, Sam of Wilds."

"Now you're mocking me."

"I wouldn't dream of it."

"How are we going to get this dragon on our side?" Ryan asked. "Are we just going to walk up to it and say, 'Hey, dragon. Come be on Team Sam. It's great.'"

"Yes," I whispered reverently. "I *knew* Team Sam would be a thing."

"We're going to need to sell it better than that," Gary said, rolling his eyes. "Give him some incentive."

"Oh?" Kevin said. "And just what kind of incentive can *you* give? Is that how it's going to be? Move on from one dragon to the next? For shame. For *shame*."

"Well," Gary said. "Once you go dragon, all the rest is laggin'."

"Hey!" Kevin said, sufficiently outraged. "That's *my* saying! You can't weaponize it and use it to stab me in the heart!"

"They're so in love," Tiggy said to me. "Tiggy knows."

"We'll figure it out," I told Ryan. "You gotta trust me. I know what I'm doing."

He frowned. "I trust you, Sam. But you never know what you're doing."

Which. Okay. That was pretty much true. I tended to be more of a by-the-seat-of-my-trousers kind of planner. I figured that since I was still alive after all these years, I must be doing something right.

As we approached the dome, I could see it was bigger than I'd thought. There were large square sections cut out of it, openings that looked as if they had once held windows or a covering of some kind. The stone was cracked along the dome, and some pieces had collapsed, but it still stood and looked solid. Or at least I hoped it was, because I had a bad feeling that we were going to be heading inside.

"It was an aviary," Ruv said, coming to stand next to me as I stopped to look up. I had to blink against the sun shining along the curve of the dome.

"Those would have been some damn big birds," I said.

"The world is a mysterious place, Sam," Ruv said. "Before today, you never knew sand mermaids existed."

"And I was totally okay with that."

His grin was rather unsettling. "Just because you ignore it doesn't mean it will go away." He continued on toward the dome.

"Fucking gypsies," I muttered.

As we got closer, the whispering in my head got louder. It wasn't forming words anymore, only sound, like a low hum. It itched and rankled, but the hook only pulled harder. Ryan walked closely at my side, his hand brushing against mine. It grounded me, kept my head mostly clear.

"They're getting brighter," he said as we walked into the shadow of the dome. "Your eyes."

"It doesn't feel like I'm seeing anything differently," I said, though it felt like a lie. "They red?"

"Very."

"That's probably not a good sign."

"Probably."

The front of the dome had a large archway where I was sure had once been an entrance akin to the Great Doors into the throne room in Castle Lock-es. But those doors were long gone, either corroded or destroyed at some point in the past. Now it was just a cavernous opening, and it was eerily reminiscent of the mouths on the sand mermaids, sans teeth. That wasn't the image I wanted to have while walking into it.

But it wasn't completely dark inside. In fact, it was rather beautiful, with shafts of sunlight crisscrossing through the openings in the dome, illuminating large swaths of ground. And while it was magnificent, it wasn't what caught my attention.

No, what caught my attention was the life inside the dome.

For even though it was surrounded by a harsh and unforgiving environment, and even though it should have died a very long time ago, the interior of the dome was *teeming* with plant life. It was startling, seeing the bursts of colorful flora that bloomed within the dome. There were trees that looked almost as old as anything I'd ever seen in the Dark Woods. There were flowers of orange and violet and blue and ocher, much larger than the blossoms that grew in my mother's garden. I heard the loud chirp of birds, their calls and songs echoing in the dome.

It was, in a word, extraordinary.

I glanced at Ruv, who looked just as shocked. "I thought you said this *used* to be an aviary."

"It was," Ruv said, taking a stuttering step forward. "It was *dead*. There was nothing but sand and stone on the inside from what we could see."

"When was the last time you were here?"

"A year ago. Maybe a little more."

That... I didn't know what to do with that. "Those trees. They're older than that."

"He did this," Kevin said, sounding just as awed. "The dragon. When he woke. *He* did this."

"Godsdammit," I said. "I don't know *anything* about dragons."

"If it makes you feel any better," Kevin said, "apparently neither do I. Why can't I do anything like this? The only thing *I* can do is be amazing at everything I do."

"Most everything," Gary said. "And don't feel intimidated. I'm sure this new dragon is lacking *something*. I mean, it's obvious that all dragons have their flaws."

"You weren't complaining about my flaws when I had you on your *back*, you hussy."

"*Hussy*? I'll show you *hussy*, you gigantic—"

"Hey, Gary."

"Yes, Sam."

"Shut up."

"But he—"

"No."

"He started—"

"*No*."

Gary gaped at me. Then, "That made me tingle. I can see why Knight Delicious Face gets off on you being all *grr*."

"Nope," Ryan said. "Not even a part of this."

"You've never seen the interior?" I asked Ruv.

He shrugged. "As much as it can be seen when looking from the out-

side in. Remember, it was dead inside. Not like this. It was *Prikasa*. This is…
not. You can feel it, can't you? The dragon. The magic."

Yes. I could. And the closer we were, the more it pulled. It didn't *hurt*,
but it was borderline *pleasurepain*. I was all but ready to charge into the
dome, to immerse myself in it. I was able to hold back.

Barely.

"We shouldn't all go in," I said. "I don't know how easy it'll be to get
through the growth. It'll be… easier if it's only a couple of us. If we had to
run."

"I'm not letting you go in there without me," Ryan said. "So don't
even think about saying it."

"I wasn't," I assured him. "You. Me. Tiggy."

"Shouldn't I go in?" Kevin said. "I *am* a dragon, after all. You might
need me."

"How would you feel had another dragon tried to enter your keep?"
I asked.

"I would have torn him limb from limb!" Kevin snarled.

"Yeah, that's what I thought."

"I would have burnt him to a crisp!"

"And you really think it's a good idea to leave me out here?" Gary
asked, staring up at Kevin, who was working himself up in a right state. "Seriously? You bitch."

"He needs someone to keep him calm," I said.

"Who is this unnamed foe who dares to touch my hoard? Why, I
oughtta knock his *teeth* in! Does he know who he's *messing* with?"

"And that someone has to be me," Gary said flatly.

"I'm the Beast from the East! Lord Dragon to the gypsies! A god to
people who ate entirely too much corn to maintain a healthy diet!"

I shrugged. "Who better than you? You love him."

"I do *not*."

"Sheep *fear* me. They cry and scream and run whenever they see me
coming, and while I won't eat them, I *will* gobble up their delicious terror!"

I rolled my eyes. "Just do it, Gary."

"I will have my revenge, Sam," Gary hissed. "Mark my words. One
day when you least expect it, I will *have my revenge*."

And he totally would, too. Years could go by before he enacted whatever diabolical plot he concocted. Unicorns were assholes like that. "Just…
nothing with the face. Or my hair. I've got really good hair."

"Oh, I make no promises." Gary chuckled evilly.

I looked at Ruv. "Make sure they don't do anything stupid."

"And how am I supposed to do that?"

"I don't know! Gods, Ruv. Show some *initiative* for once in your life.
Sand mermaids, magical plans, it's like I'm doing *everything* here."

"Yikes," Ryan said. "That's not even what happened."

"You got yourself sucked under the sand by a monster," I said. "You're lucky I'm even inviting you to be on Team Sam at all. So shut it."

"Bitch," Gary coughed.

I ignored him. "Now, do what I told you to do, or I'm going to light someone here on fire, so help me gods."

Tiggy grinned smugly at Gary. "I get to go," he said. "Team Sam for the win."

"Fine," Gary said with a sniff. "We'll just have Team Gary out here, and everyone knows Team Gary is the *better* team. We get to have cool things like cupcakes and fascinating discussions about what people love best about me."

"Cupcakes?" Kevin asked, ears perking.

"*Not that kind of cupcake*," Gary hissed. "I'm trying to make a point."

"Thanks for this," Ruv grumbled. "Really. You should go before more things happen."

"Gods, what is *with* all of you and jinxing me? Team Sam, front and center!"

Tiggy snapped to attention, standing straight, legs together, arms at his sides, chin tilted up. Ryan drew his sword again and posed, because he was a douchebag and he couldn't not.

We were going to die horrible and painful deaths.

STEPPING INTO THE DOME WAS A surreal experience. The sandy ruins of the castle in the dry, scorching heat gave way to cool, dank air redolent with the strong perfume of flowers and the crisp scent of the trees, as if we'd walked through some kind of portal to a land far, far away from the desert. I thought maybe it was an illusory magic, that the dragon or whatever caused this was projecting, but if it was, it was the most convincing façade I'd ever seen. The grass and leaves were soft beneath my feet. The tree bark was rough against my hands. The flower petals were velvety, the pollen sticky on my fingertips. If it was a lie, it was good. But if it was real, it was extraordinary. The stories we heard as kids said that dragons were beings of pure magic, more so than any other creature in existence. That their blood was made of stars and had led to the Creation of Man. Man, so it was said, came from pieces of stardust. If dragons were made of stars, then it was thought we came from dragon's blood. I'd always listened with wide eyes as a child but fell into cynicism as a teenager, as children often did.

I'd never asked for Kevin's blood. I would never have done that to him, no matter how much it could have advanced my Grimoire. Others had tried, he'd told me in broad strokes. He'd been captured and hurt before managing to escape. It was where his distrust of wizards had come from. It'd taken me a long time to overcome that with him, and I'd never do anything to set us back.

But still. If this was real, if this dragon had awoken and created all that I could see in this interior, from the plants to the bees that flitted between the flowers to the birds that sang out from the trees, it was something beyond anything I'd ever dealt with before.

Kevin was a dragon. He had magic, we knew. We just didn't know how it would manifest. Kevin said it was because he didn't want to show us yet. I thought it was because he didn't know, and Morgan and Randall were convinced that he was too young.

But this dragon did.

"Smells like home," Tiggy said, brow furrowed.

"Like the castle? Or the woods?"

He shook his head. "Like before. Before you. Before Gary."

Ah. The ever-vague before. I exchanged a quick glance with Ryan, who looked startled. Tiggy didn't often speak of before Gary, and I thought it was because he didn't like to think of a time before Gary. From the bits and pieces we'd been able to put together, we thought it sounded like Tiggy had been cast out with his parents at some point for being a half-breed, however unjust that was. Usually, such discrimination was found to be appalling (though, with my experience in Mashallaha, it apparently was more prevalent than I thought), but the giants hailed from outside of Verania, beyond the mountains to the north. Tiggy couldn't remember much, but the last time we'd been within a week's journey of the land of the giants (after an ill-advised trip to the elven realm in which I only found out later Gary had been tied up and spanked by a centaur—don't ask, long story), he'd refused and made us travel south as quickly as our feet could carry us.

So the fact that he even *mentioned* a time before, much less unprovoked, was a big deal. I took in a great breath, trying to smell what my friend did, hoping for some understanding. It was different for me. All I smelled was the normal scent of a forest. Maybe it was tinged with the crisp burn of magic, but beyond that? It didn't seem different than anything else I'd scented before. "It smells good," I decided.

He nodded. "I like our home better. Smells like us. Like HaveHeart and Gary and Tiggy."

"Me too, dude. I like home better too."

"We gonna go home some day?"

"Yeah. Someday."

"After the dragons."

"Yeah. Soon. Won't be forever. Gotta get those dragons first, you know?"

He frowned. "Dragons are scary." He bared his teeth and snapped his jaw. "They bite. Kevin's not scary." He took in another deep breath. "This dragon doesn't feel scary."

I didn't know what to do with that, but I thought he was right. I could remember what it'd felt like, the first time Kevin had crested that hill, chasing after the sheep. I'd been scared shitless, but then a flying lizard the size of a house had been rushing toward us. But even though this dragon was supposed to be some kind of large snake (which, ugh), it didn't *feel* like we were in danger.

But I knew of poisons disguised in beauty. We couldn't lower our guard.

Added to the fact that there was still a low hum in my head and that I was pretty sure my eyes were at the very least flickering red, we couldn't risk anything.

"Yeah," I said. "But you smash if you need to."

"I always smash."

"You fell from the sky, dude. All badass and everything. Saved my life, you know?"

His chest puffed out as he preened. "I am badass. Tiggy so badass."

"Darn right, mothercracker," Ryan said, holding out his fist, which Tiggy bumped with pleasure. I liked that these were my people.

We moved farther into the dome. I glanced back and could see Kevin and Gary peering at us from the entrance. I waved back at them, and they acknowledged me before Gary leaned over to say something to Kevin I couldn't make out. I didn't see Ruv anywhere, but I knew Gary wouldn't let him get up to anything.

Without ever having been here before, I knew where I was going. Oh, I didn't know the layout of the forest in the desert. I didn't know the trees or the brush at my feet. But I knew where I was heading, where it was waiting for us. For how long we'd traveled, for how much was at stake, I felt woefully underprepared. All anyone knew of Jekhipe was apparently stories and drawings passed down. I didn't know how to claim it as one of mine.

The forest became denser, and I was reminded fleetingly of Vadoma's bad-touch, when she'd sent me... *somehow* into the Dark Woods and an audience with the Great White. There were beams of sunlight here, fat and warm, piercing through the thick canopy of the trees.

I needed a plan.

I could do this. I'd already done it once.

Sort of.

But hey, fuck it. It counted.

So I'd already done it once.

I could do it again.

"Why do you have that look on your face?" Ryan asked me suddenly.

"What look?" I asked.

"That scrunched-up, constipated look you get when you're planning something that I usually end up not liking because it's dangerous and or requires you—" He glanced at Tiggy before continuing in a low voice. "—sticking weird things in me because you think it'll be kinky."

Tiggy snorted, because of course he'd heard. He heard everything. But like a good giant, he let it go. Gary was such a bad influence.

"Well if I wasn't thinking of sticking something in you, I am *now*," I said. "Thanks for that. You couldn't keep your sexy words until we were out of here? We're on a *quest*, babe. We don't have time right now to get down."

"That's *not* what I said."

"Tiggy?"

"That's what he said."

Ryan glared at him. "We just fist-bumped. I thought we were cool!"

Tiggy squinted at him. "Just one time. Settle down, Knight Delicious Face."

"He got you there, dude," I said solemnly.

"I don't know why I put up with any of you. It's not like—" He broke off as he gave me a weird look.

"What?" I asked, looking down at myself. "Do I got something on me? Is it a fucking bug? I swear to the fucking gods, if it's a gigantic bug, I am going to burn this whole place to the *ground—*"

"Not a bug," Ryan said. "It's, ah. Your eyes. They're getting... brighter."

"Like all red and shit?"

"Yeah."

"Huh. Keep your hands to yourself. I know I'm irresistible to you right now, but now's not the time, Ryan."

"Bright, Sam," Tiggy said quietly. "Feel it?" He reached over and tapped my forehead. "Here?"

I nodded. "It's—I can't understand it. It's... like I'm underwater. I can hear *something*, but it's muted, you know?"

"Is it hurting you?" Ryan asked, jaw tensing.

I shook my head. "No. It's not. It's just... strong."

"You know where we're going, don't you?"

I didn't even try to lie. "Yeah. How'd you know?"

"You've been leading us very deliberately. Like you knew."

"It's pulling me."

"Are you sure this is a good idea?"

"What choice do we have?"

"There's always a choice, Sam. We could turn around right now. Walk away. Go back to Castle Lockes. We don't need to be here. We don't even know if Vadoma's telling the truth."

"But what if she is?" I scrubbed my hands over my face. "Look, I get what you're saying. I do. But Ryan, even if we think she's full of shit, *what if she's not*? I can't take that chance. Not now. Not since we're so close."

"I'm not scared."

"I know." Because he really was of the fearless sort.

"I'm worried."

"I know that too."

He jerked his head. "Keep on?"

"Keep on."

"Keep on," Tiggy agreed.

IT WAS IN THE CENTER OF the dome. I figured it would be. There was a circular opening at the top of the dome, and when the sun was at its peak, I was sure the light shone straight down inside. But it was past that already, for better or worse.

And I thought it was probably worse.

Because before us was a large circular hole dug into the earth and rock.

Like something big had burrowed down deep underground.

"That's a big motherfucking snake," I breathed. "This can't possibly be good. We can probably go home now."

Ryan and Tiggy crouched near the edge and peered into the hole. There wasn't enough light to see very far down, so it was impossible to tell just how deep it went. But I'd seen how large the cavern that surrounded the island was now that the sand was gone. The pillar had reached all the way to the bottom. For all I knew, there were multiple tunnels dug through. Which meant there could be other holes somewhere in the dome.

Ryan and Tiggy looked up at the wheezing groan that came out of me. I waved my hand at them, trying to get them to ignore me, but Ryan stared at me expectantly.

"What?" I said, trying not to sound irritated. I didn't think I succeeded.

"Do your thing," he said, standing up. "You know. Like, magic. Or something."

"Like magic or something," I repeated flatly.

He shrugged. "You gotta call the dragon up somehow, right?"

"Why do *I* have to call it up? *You* call it up if you want to see it so bad—wait. Right. Destiny of dragons and all that. My bad. Still hate that word, by the way."

"You okay?"

"Fine," I said. "Just fine. So what if you want me to call up a gigantic snake dragon monster thing whatever just to watch it slither around all un-naturally."

"Sam scared of snakes," Tiggy said helpfully. Like an asshole.

"I'm not *scared* of snakes," I said. "I would just like it if they never existed near me at all. Or anywhere ever. I don't think that's too much to ask."

"But it's not a snake," Ryan said. "It's a dragon."

"Thank you, Ryan. That was very helpful. I truly appreciate it."

He squinted at me. "Why didn't I know this about you? It's a little adorable. You're trembling."

I scowled at him. "Shut up. It's *not* adorable. I'm not *scared*."

"Okay, then," he said, bending over quickly and scooping up a chunk of rock. "Then you wouldn't mind if I dropped this down the hole just to see if we can get this thing up here."

He held out his arm over the opening, stone in hand.

And smirked.

"Ho, don't you do it!" I squeaked. And then coughed. "I mean, uh. We don't want to *hurt* it, Ryan. Gosh. That would just be mean, okay? I'll... I'll take care of it." I licked my lips.

"All right." He took a step back and nodded toward the hole. "Get to it."

"Yeah," I said. "I'll just... do. That."

I took a step toward the edge, already imagining the snake dragon monster thing that would come for me the moment I opened my mouth. It would probably be the largest thing in the world and would have really big fangs and spit poison in my mouth as it wrapped around me and slowly choked me, its tail rattling back and forth, its slit-eyes trained on me as it slowly drove me insane from fear. I'd probably end up shitting myself.

We took the worst trips.

I hated destinies with a passion.

I looked down into the hole. Cleared my throat. Opened my mouth and said, "Hey. Uh. Dragon."

Nothing happened.

"Um. So. Do you want to come up here or...?"

Silence.

"No? That's... uh. Cool. I'm totally cool with that. You do you, dude. That's the only way to be."

Ryan snorted from behind me.

I glared over my shoulder at him. "What?"

"Nothing," he said, holding up a hand to placate me. "I just wonder what the rest of Verania would think if they heard the guy that's supposed to save them trying to summon a dragon saying *you do you, dude*."

"Oh?" I snapped. "You've got a better idea, asshole?"

"Sam, I think *any* idea is a better idea. You could've started with Flora Bora Slam and it would've been a better idea."

"Hey! I only work with what I'm given, okay! Just because *you* wanted to drop a *rock* down the hole, doesn't mean you get to make fun of *my* idea. And I'll have you know, Flora Bora Slam is still considered to be one of the greatest nonspells *ever* created. They put that shit on shirts, Ryan. *They sell shirts with Flora Bora Slam on them.*"

"I'm in a calendar," Ryan said smugly. "It's always the most popular month."

"Well, *yeah*," I said. "You have epic nipples. I used to buy it every year and masturbate furiously to—I mean, I read it for the articles."

He frowned. "You read… the calendar for the articles?"

I nodded. "Exactly. Oh no. Look at the time. Maybe we should just come back tomorrow. Or never. Never is good also."

Ryan started forward. "I'll just drop this rock down and *then* we can go."

I gave a hoarse battle cry as I jumped on his back, trying to reach for the rock to stop him from calling up the gigantic snake of doom.

"Oh yes," he grunted, trying to hold the hand with the rock as far away from me as possible. "Because *that* was an appropriate response. Get off me, you weirdo!"

"Give me the damn rock, Foxheart!"

"Never!"

"We playing games?" Tiggy asked. "Jump on Knight Delicious Face?"

"What? No, *no* jumping on Knight Delicious—"

"Yes, Tiggy!" I cried. "Jump on him! Squash him flat!"

Tiggy crowed happily as he started running toward us.

Ryan and I stopped struggling. "This may have been a very bad idea," I breathed.

"We're so fucked," Ryan agreed.

"Watch your mouth, oh my gods, think of the *children* you ass—oomph!"

What happened next I would take full responsibility for, even if the argument could be made that we wouldn't have even been *in* this mess if I'd never been born, so blame could also rest mostly with my parents. Damn them and their libido.

Tiggy slammed into us.

Ryan and I were knocked off our feet.

We landed on the ground with a crash.

Ryan's hand struck the dirt.

The rock bounced out of his hand.

"Noooooo," I said, because everything felt like it was moving in slow motion. "Sommeonnnnne geeeeet theee rooooooooooock!"

But alas, it was no use.

We watched as the rock rolled toward the edge.

And it started tipping *toward the edge*—

But then it fell back onto solid ground.

It didn't go over.

We all breathed a sigh of relief. The gods were smiling down upon us! Oh joy, oh happy day, I could just *shit*, I was so happy—

Then Tiggy sneezed, the force of which sent the rock careening over the edge.

"Excuse me," Tiggy sniffed as he wiped his nose. "Pollen. Itchy."

The gods hated us.

And we all cringed as the rock seemed to bounce off *every part of the wall it could*. In the history of the world, I doubted there'd ever been a louder noise. It was as if the dome was literally crashing down around us while a thousand birds shrieked and a group of children played their instruments in a concert that parents have to attend and clap and pretend to love, but really are all regretting not practicing safe sex.

Add to the fact that the large hole was apparently all the way down to the center of the world, as it seemed to stretch on for a good few minutes. I winced with *every* crash and bang, sure that at any moment, a nightmare was going to crawl out of the hole and come for us. It probably didn't help that the hum in my head had all but ceased as soon as the rock began to make its way down. Which, you know.

Probably wasn't a good sign.

Eventually, the noise fell away.

We stayed quietly where we had fallen in a tangle of limbs, Ryan on the bottom, me lying on top of him, Tiggy above both of us, propped up on his hands so he didn't actually crush us under his considerable weight.

We barely breathed.

Nothing happened.

Tiggy lifted himself slowly.

I pushed myself up off Ryan.

Ryan stood, knees popping, brushing off the seat of his trousers.

I gave it one more moment.

Still nothing.

"Okay," I said, sure we were fine. "Maybe it's not even there. This was probably all for nothing. We should—"

The snake dragon monster thing roared, and then *that* was the loudest thing in the world.

"—run as fast as we possibly can," I squeaked.

And then the ground started to shake beneath our feet, the trees shuddering, the flowers swaying back and forth. The birds took to their wings, flying up and circling overhead.

Tiggy didn't even hesitate. He scooped up Ryan and me in his arms and took great bounding steps toward the front of the dome. My hands were on his shoulders as I stared behind us, tree limbs slapping against my back and neck as Tiggy grunted. Ryan was shouting something, but I was focused on the hole as it got farther and farther away. There was another roar that echoed through the dome, and Tiggy stumbled as the ground cracked beneath his feet. We pitched forward dangerously, and for a panicked second, I thought we'd go crashing down, but Tiggy caught himself at the last second, spinning out of the way to dodge a falling tree, clutching us tightly.

"Holy shit!" Ryan cried, and I couldn't even be bothered to tell him to think of the children, because *holy shit* was right. "We have to get out of here!"

"*Trying*," Tiggy growled. "Next time, *you* carry *me!*"

"Well try *harder!* You can't just—"

Everything fell away after that, like a veil had dropped over the world. The colors were softer, the sounds muted. Tiggy and Ryan continued to bicker, but it wasn't important. It was background noise. I could hear the breaths I took, the shift of the magic in the air. It was green and gold and red, and it was *everywhere*. It was in the trees, the flowers, the brush, *everything*. There was a concentration of it in this dome, and the hook in my brain gave a sickening *pull*, a wave of nausea rolling through me. We were going the wrong way. We were going the wrong way. *We were going the wrong—*

Wizard, it whispered, clear as day. *Wizard*.

I am coming.

"Oh no," I whispered.

The dragon burst from the hole in the floor of the dome in a crumbling, forgotten castle. It was thinner than I thought it'd be, but far longer. Its underbelly was white, the scales on its back and sides a fiery red that glittered in the beams of the sun, causing fractals of light to shoot off around the dome. It had no legs, and its wings were paper-thin, flapping almost like an insect's, quick and light. Its head was hooded like a snake's, with sharp white spikes jutting out down the sides toward its neck. The same spikes ran up its head toward its blunt snout. It was completely out of the hole when its head jerked toward us, black eyes blinking. Its mouth opened as it hissed, forked tongue flicking out between rows of teeth that ended with two gigantic fangs that unfurled from the top.

In other words, it was a fucking nightmare, and I wanted to be anywhere but where I was.

"Sweet molasses," I managed to say.

"And *further*more, you weigh like *eight times* more than I do. I couldn't even carry you if I—*holy gods that is a giant snake!*"

If we lived through this, I was going to give Ryan so much shit for the way he'd shrieked that.

Jekhipe curled in the air, bringing up its body underneath it, wings flapping furiously. The hood on its head flared out, the spikes rattling against each other as it shook. It opened its mouth again and *roared*, a sound that felt like it was vibrating into my bones.

"We're so fucking screwed," I whispered.

Jekhipe jerked forward, lightning quick, body hurtling toward us.

"*We're so fucking screwed!*" I screamed.

"Talk to it!" Ryan shouted at me.

"*You* talk to it!"

"I'm not a godsdamned wizard!"

"Maybe you should be!"

"It's your *destiny*, Sam!"

"You shut up about my destiny!"

Tiggy leapt over a fallen tree, skidding in the dirt and sand when he landed, turning to the right as he ducked under a thick low-hanging branch. The birds were screeching overhead, and Jekhipe was moving toward us, *exactly* like a godsdamned snake would, body curling and twisting behind it.

"There," Tiggy grunted. "*There.*"

I turned to look ahead of us and could see the entrance to the dome. Gary and Kevin were waiting for us, eyes wide, Gary stomping his feet as he yelled, "What the hell is going on!"

"Giant snake dragon monster thing!" I shouted back.

"Giant snake what to *what*?"

"Running would be good!"

Kevin didn't even hesitate. He grabbed Gary around his middle and hoisted him up even as Gary shrieked at him to put him down, what did Kevin think he was *doing*, did he think Gary could just be *manhandled* in such a way? Kevin ignored him and took a lumbering step back, trying to clear out of the entrance of the dome to give us room. I glanced back over Tiggy's shoulder, and Jekhipe was getting closer, tail twitching, tongue flicking out, tasting the air.

Wizard, wizard, wizard.

"Fuck you!" I bellowed back at it.

"Maybe it's not a good idea to anger the dragon with big teeth!" Ryan said, clutching his sword.

"You've got a better idea?"

"How was that even an *idea*? It's—"

"Hold on!" Tiggy yelled, and I felt him begin to crouch, the muscles in his legs coiling. I circled my arms around his neck, hanging on for dear life as Ryan did the same. One of Ryan's hands gripped my arm tightly and Jekhipe *was right there.*

Tiggy leapt toward the entrance of the dome.

One moment we were in a cool, dank forest.

The next, we burst into bright, harsh sunlight, the desert air burning around us.

It went from green to burnt gold in the space of a heartbeat, like we'd torn through one world and into another.

The momentum carried us past Kevin and Gary, who stood off to the side.

Jekhipe followed us into the sun. I didn't know why I'd thought it wouldn't be able to.

It was.

Its mouth opened wide, like its lower jaw was unhinged. The top fangs lowered again. The bony spikes along its hood rattled, and it was *right there—*

Kevin slammed a foot down as it went by him, driving its tail into the ground. Just as Jekhipe was about to snap its teeth around us, its eyes bulged and it said, "*Urk*," as it jerked back, slamming down in a cloud of dust and sand.

We landed hard on the ground, Tiggy squeezing us close as we rolled, trying to protect us from the impact as much as he could. I had sand in my nose and mouth and eyes, and the world was spinning around me, flashings of sky then ground then sky again. We came to a stop when Tiggy's back collided with a battlement that still stood. It swayed above us, and for a moment, I thought it was going to come falling down on top of us, but it held, only chunks of loose stone falling from the top and landing around us, kicking up a dirty plume into the air.

"That," I wheezed, "sucked balls."

"Understatement," Ryan groaned. "Remind me why we're doing this again."

"Fate of the known world."

"Oh. Right. Still don't know if it's worth it."

"Tiggy, all right?"

"Sand in my trousers," Tiggy said, sounding grumpy as he sat up, pulling us up with him. "Sand, Sam. In my *trousers*."

"Yeah, dude," I said, patting his arm. "That's terrible. Believe me, I know. I have sand everywhere too."

"Stupid snake dragon monster thing," Tiggy said.

Speaking of.

The dust was clearing by the time I stood. I shook myself out, trying to get as much sand off me as I could. I took a step forward as I brushed off my arms and—

A shadow fell over me.

Because apparently the day couldn't get any worse, Jekhipe rose above me. Its body was still mostly on the ground, muscular and agile, red scales bright in the sun. The lower third of its body was wrapped around Kevin, holding his arms against his chest, Gary tucked under his neck, trapped in its grip. Kevin was trying to snap down at it, but he couldn't reach. I thought for a moment he'd breathe fire at it, but it would run the risk of burning Gary, and I knew he wouldn't take that chance.

But Jekhipe wasn't focused on them.

It only had eyes for me.

And I was *furious*.

"That's it, then?" I growled up at it. "That's all you got. Come on, you bastard."

For a moment, I thought I saw its eyes widen slightly.

"Um, maybe not anger it, huh?" Ryan said. "That's probably not—"

It jerked its head toward the sound of his voice, hissing at him, tongue out and *tasting* Ryan's scent.

Which, no.

It squeezed Kevin and Gary tighter, causing Gary to cry out in pain.

Which.

No.

"Hey!" I shouted at it, taking a step back. "You look at me when I'm talking to you!"

It reared its head back as it turned to me.

"That's right," I said, taking another step back. "Thaaat's right. It's me you want. And I'm right here."

"Sam? What are you—"

"Don't move," I said, not taking my eyes off Jekhipe. "I got this. Tiggy, get him out of here when I say."

Ryan sounded furious. "And you get pissed at *me* for acting like a martyr?"

"Tiggy! Do you understand me?"

"Sam got a plan?" Tiggy asked, sounding worried.

"Yeah," I muttered. "Yeah, I got a plan."

That was a lie, but they didn't need to know that.

"Bullshit," Ryan said. "Tiggy, he's going to—"

Jekhipe coiled to strike.

"Tiggy, *now!*"

Three things happened at once:

Jekhipe struck, teeth flashing;

and,

Tiggy grabbed Ryan and bolted to the side, out of the way;

and,

I jumped in the other direction as Jekhipe snapped its fangs at me. I felt the heat of its mouth as it missed me by inches. It slammed into the precarious battlement face-first. The tower swayed dangerously and then it tipped, tipped, *tipped*—

And then collapsed on top of Jekhipe's head.

I scooted back as quickly as possible, trying to avoid falling stone. When it landed on Jekhipe, its body tensed and began to writhe. For a moment, I thought it was going to squeeze Kevin and Gary further, but it released them, causing them to sag toward the ground as Gary gasped sharply.

"Sam!"

I turned and looked toward the other end of the island, where the sea of sand had been before I'd destroyed it.

Ruv stood there, waving his arms over his head. "Sam, this way!"

I pushed myself up off the ground and started to run.

Jekhipe roared behind me as I heard it pull itself out of the collapsed battlement. I didn't look back, didn't stop to see if it was coming after me or how close it was. All I focused on was Ruv.

Wizard wizard wizard wizardwizardwizard—

My lungs burned with every step I took as I jumped over the ruins of the desert castle that lay spread out around me. Magic was curling itself against my skin, and I knew my eyes were flashing again. The ground shook beneath my feet as Jekhipe tore after me. I could do this, I could *make* this—

"Sam!" Ruv shouted. "Left, move *left*!"

I moved left.

Jekhipe's head came down on my right, jaws snapping closed around nothing, much closer than I thought it'd be. The eye on the left side of its head focused on me, still black, but there was a hint of a reptilian shape in the cornea.

I kept running.

I distinctly remembered the island being much shorter than it was right now. Fear and terror of being eaten by a snake dragon monster thing apparently caused me to misjudge distances, because one moment, Ruv looked like he was as far away as the City of Lockes, and the next, I was about to crash into him.

"Go!" I shouted at him. "Go! Go!"

He started moving, and by the time I caught up with him, was running full tilt.

"What's the plan?" he shouted at me, darting to the left when Jekhipe tried to snap at him.

"The *plan*? I thought *you* had a plan! You told me to start running toward you!"

"It was about to *eat* you!"

"It's about to eat me *now*!"

The stone path that led across the cavern lay ahead. We were quickly running out of land on which to run. And the path was broken halfway through, probably farther than we could jump, from where Tiggy had fallen from the sky on top of the mermaid.

We were so fucked.

Wizard, it hissed in my head.

And then—

"That thing!"

Ruv looked at me, face red as he panted. "What thing!"

"Your sailboard sand thing!"

He reached behind him and unhooked it from his pack.

I could do this.

"We get to the end, you go left. You *go left* and you throw that thing out as hard as you can."

"What are you going to do?"

I laughed, sounding crazed. "I'm going to jump."

His eyes bulged. "Are you fucking *crazy*?"

I grinned at him. "I'm Sam of Wilds."

We careened toward the edge of the island.

I heard Kevin roaring behind us somewhere, either in the sky or on land, I didn't know. He wouldn't get to us in time, regardless. I didn't know where Ryan and Tiggy were. I hoped they were safe.

And as I reached those final steps, I knew this was quite possibly the stupidest thing I'd ever done.

Ruv went left, just as I'd told him to. As he went, he curled the arm holding the wooden contraption against his chest, then flung it out in a flat arc. The hinges creaked as the board unfolded and the sail rose.

My feet caught the edge of the island, leg muscles coiling, and I pushed myself off into nothing.

It was a good jump. Really, ten out of ten. If I'd seen anyone else do it, I probably would have cheered and thought how cool it was.

But since it was me leaping above the cavern, I couldn't help but shriek quite loudly, because that shit was *insane*. I was going to have to have a talk with the others about allowing me to do such stupid things without thinking of the repercussions.

And it was then—flying through the air, trying to reach for Ruv's sailboard like I had any idea how to use it, a gigantic snake dragon monster thing beginning to flap its wings to lift off and take after me—that I had a very real thought about the state of my life.

The thought?

I might be a fucking idiot.

And there was green and gold as my hand wrapped around the pole that held up the sail. There was red and *yellowyellowyellow* as I pulled it toward me, putting my feet down on the wooden board as I felt the ominous tilt that signaled a descent.

Jekhipe snarled behind me.

And I *pushed*.

The magic that had been crawling along my skin burst outward in a brightly colored flash. It hit the sail, causing it to stretch out like it'd been hit with a gale force wind. Instead of falling, the board started to tilt back up, and it was going to be enough. I was going to make it to the other side. I was going to clear this motherfucking jump and it was going to be *awesome* and I—

I started to fall again.

"Fuck, fuck, fuckity fuck*fuckfuck*!"

My magic was going haywire, creating short, sharp bursts that hit the sail, causing me to jerk forward, but not enough to lift me up. I couldn't find the edges to grasp on to it, to hold it close, to force it to do what I wanted to do. I thought maybe it had to do with the burst of energy I'd used against the sand mermaids. Magic wasn't infinite. There wasn't an endless well within that I could draw from. Used long and hard enough, I felt drained, tired, weak.

Sort of like I was feeling right now.

As I started to plummet into the cavern.

I had three choices here:

I could get eaten by Jekhipe.

I could smash into the side of the cavern.

I could fall all the way to the bottom.

None of those sounded like a good way to go. In fact, they all sounded terrible.

And just as I was sure I was about cross the veil, there came the most idiotic and wonderful thing I'd ever heard in my life bellowing out above me.

"Duh da da daaaaaaaaaaaaa! Kevin's here to save the daaaaaaaaaay!"

I looked up.

Kevin was dive-bombing directly toward me.

Jekhipe curled in the air, eyes darting from me to Kevin, like it was trying to decide who to go after.

It decided on me.

So there I was, with a dragon the size of a large house with his wings tucked at his sides plunging toward me, and another dragon made of nightmares, jaws open, ready to force me down its considerable gullet, all while I was falling to my death in a cavern I'd made when I'd vaporized sand mermaids so they wouldn't eat my boyfriend and my half-giant.

Yeah. I know.

Fuck my life.

It happened quicker than I expected.

Kevin twisted himself until he could stretch a clawed hand toward me.

Jekhipe's tongue came out, and I could almost feel it on my skin.

Kevin pinched the pole holding up the sail between two claws, digging into the wood.

"You better hold on to something," he shouted gleefully.

"Oh no," I said.

His wings snapped open, catching an updraft.

Instead of falling, suddenly we were shooting *upward*, my gut immediately sinking to my feet as I fell flat on my stomach, stretching out along the board, holding on for dear life.

I looked down in time to see Jekhipe fly right under us with a snarl of outrage. If I were so inclined, I could have reached down and touched it since it was so close.

Kevin allowed the wind to fill the membranes of his wings, stretching them out and pulling us upward. He curled his arm, bringing me closer to his body.

"Who's a badass?" he crowed.

I vomited over the side of the board.

"Oh *gods*. Why do you always *do* that when we fly?"

"My bad," I said feebly, spitting out a gross *something*. "Maybe it has to do with the fact that I *almost died*."

"Yeah, and whose fault is that? By the way, I'm pretty sure your knight shit himself silly when you jumped. You might want to prepare yourself for an epic ass whooping when we get back. If you want to repay me for saving your life yet *again*, you could let me watch said ass whooping. He's got such big *hands*—"

Jekhipe roared again behind us.

"Godsdammit," I said, looking back. "Even *you* weren't this much of a pain in my ass."

"Yeah, only because you won't *let* me—"

"Not the time!"

"It's *never* the time!"

"Where are we going?"

"Back to the island."

And we were. Kevin had circled around and was flying lower and lower. "What! No! You can't bring that thing back to everyone else. Kevin, what the hell!"

"You stupid idiot," he said fondly. "We're in this together. And that's the way it's going to be."

And for once, I couldn't think of a single thing to say.

We landed quickly, Kevin coming in and hitting the ground running as he held me up and away so I wouldn't fall. He slid to a halt near the dome, kicking up the dust around us. I jumped off the board and could barely resist falling to my knees and kissing the sweet, sweet earth beneath my feet.

Instead I was manhandled into a hug by a pair of strong arms, a face mashed against my neck, breath heavy against my skin.

"I hate you so much right now," Ryan Foxheart said hoarsely. "You have no idea."

I hugged him back. "Would it help if I said sorry?"

He pulled back, a scowl on his face. "Sorry. You're *sorry*. You… you… *mothercracker*."

I grinned at him.

His nose wrinkled. "Why do you smell like vomit?"

"Annnnnd moment over," I said, stepping out of his arms.

"Did you vomit because your tummy got sick?" Gary asked sympathetically. "He's got a very sensitive tummy, in case you didn't know. Yes. Yes, you *do*."

"Shut up," I muttered. "We don't have time—"

The ground shook.

I turned.

Jekhipe slithered toward us, stopping a short distance away. It reared back. Its hood shook. Its teeth were bared.

Ryan stood to my right. Ruv was at my left. Gary stood behind me, head over my shoulder. Tiggy was next to him, pressing up against my back. Kevin towered over us, wings spread, snarling in anger.

"Oh my gods," I whispered reverently. "I bet we look so fucking *cool* right now. Shit! I gotta say something witty!"

"Sam," Ryan said, exasperated. He flourished his sword because he couldn't *not*. "We don't have *time*—"

"I got it!" I puffed out my chest and glared at Jekhipe. "I feel like playing dice, boys. I just need some *snake eyes*."

Everyone groaned.

"What! That was good!"

"Is it possible he's getting worse?" Gary asked. "Because it seems like he's getting worse."

"He so special," Tiggy cooed.

And then, because I wanted to get this godsdamned show on the road, I bent over, picked up a good-sized stone, and chucked it at the motherfucking snake dragon monster thing.

It was a good throw, if I do say so myself.

Especially since it hit Jekhipe right in the eye.

"Ha!" I crowed. "Take *that*, motherfucker!"

And Jekhipe said, "Ow! Why you gotta be so *mean* like that?"

I scoffed. "Because you *deserved*—wait. What."

CHAPTER 18

And That Was How I Met
a Teenage Emo Dragon

"You hit me in the eye," the snake dragon monster thing known as Jekhipe said.

"Wow," Kevin said. "I am *sorry* for him. If it makes you feel any better, he did the same thing to me when we met. I'm starting to think he has a thing for hitting dragons in the eye. Which is *rude*, by the way."

"I don't know why I'm so surprised you can talk," I said to Jekhipe. "Like, I heard you in my head and everything, but you're like... you know. *You*. What the fuck."

"Yeah," Ryan said. "What the—"

I glared at him.

"—heck?" he finished with a scowl on his face.

"Of *course* I can talk," Jekhipe said. "I've *been* talking to the wizard since I woke up." He frowned and then slumped to the ground, laying his chin in the dirt. His wings drooped at his sides, and the hood around his head sagged. "Then he had to go and be all mean to me." He blinked the eye I'd hit with a rock rapidly.

"Are you... are you *pouting*?" I asked, incredulous.

"I'm *allowed* to pout," Jekhipe said, sounding morose. "I'm in pain and everything is really lame right now, okay? Gods." His wings drooped farther.

"What the hell is going on?" I asked faintly.

"I think you hurt his feelings," Gary said, sounding amused.

"*I* did? He was trying to *eat* us!"

"*Excuse* you," Jekhipe said. "I was *not*."

"Then what the fuck was that whole coming-after-us thing!"

"I thought we were playing around."

"Is this real life?" I asked Ryan. "Or did you get me drunk again to try and have your way with me and this whole thing is a hallucination?"

"Yeah, because I need to get you drunk to do stuff to you," Ryan said dryly. "All I have to do is look at you and you're ready to go."

"Bullshit."

He smoldered at me.

"Sweet molasses," I whispered. "It's like you were dipped in sex and I need to *lick* it—"

"Ugh," Jekhipe groaned. "Gods, old people are so disgusting."

"Ha!" Tiggy said. "He called you old."

"Old?" I said, outraged. "I'm not *old*."

"Bitch," Gary said to me. "You gonna get wrinkles if you keep making that face."

"I've been drugged," I decided, because it was the only thing that made sense. "Somehow, I've been drugged, and this whole damn thing has been some weird side effect. I'm probably in the castle, in my bed, hallucinating my balls off."

"Let me handle this," Kevin said, pushing me out of the way as he stepped forward. "I obviously am trained in dealing with these exact situations."

"You've trained your dragon for this?" Ruv asked. "That's impressive."

"We haven't trained him to do anything," Ryan said. "He usually just does what he wants and we let him. Because he's bigger than us."

"Ah," Ruv said. "How emasculating for you."

Ryan frowned. "Are you insulting me?"

"Hello!" Kevin said, standing in front of Jekhipe, who was still moaning about getting hit in the face by old people. "I am the Lord Dragon, Kevin. The Beast from the East. As you can see, I, too, am a dragon. And as you can also probably see, I am far more masculine than everyone here. My virility is legendary. People worship me. I am in charge of this group that you see behind me. I also act as ambassador, rugged mascot, and sexual liaison."

"Literally none of that is true aside from his name," I said. "Absolutely none of it. Kevin, what the hell."

Kevin tossed me a glare over his shoulder. "Sam," he said through gritted teeth. "I'm trying to make a *connection* here, so if you could please stop *undermining my authority*." He turned back to the snake dragon. "Sorry about that. He gets a little... jealous when my attention is on others. He's very possessive of me, Sam is."

I groaned into my hands.

"It okay," Tiggy said, rubbing my back. "You learn to share. I teach you. Don't touch my stuff."

"You're so good at everything you do," Gary said, pressing his face against Tiggy's arm. "My big, sweet brute of a giant."

"Pretty Gary," Tiggy said, kissing him on the ear. "Prettiest unicorn ever."

"You *were* insulting me," Ryan said to Ruv. "Hey! I'm a man. I'm *all* man."

"How wonderful for you," Ruv said. "And obviously, because you feel the need to say it."

"We come in peace," Kevin said to Jekhipe. "And bringeth you tidings of great joy from the King of Verania, on whose behalf I speaketh on. He wisheth you a long and healthy life. Eth and thou."

"Urgh," Jekhipe groaned, curling in on himself. "I feel like my soul is getting turned inside out and it's filled with crows and lament."

I pushed my way past Kevin, giving him a good kick in the leg as I went by, though I knew he'd barely feel it. It made *me* feel slightly better, at least. I was cautious as I stood next to him, staring at Jekhipe, who was moaning about how the world didn't understand him, that all he wanted to do was crawl back into his hole and sit in the dark and be left alone, gods.

"Why the hell are you acting like a sullen teenager?" I demanded, trying not to get *too* close in case this was all a ruse and he was going to snap at me.

He opened a single dark eye to look at me. "Uh, *duh*. I *am* a teenager."

I said, "What."

"You don't even *listen* to me," he wailed, curling in on himself again. "Nobody ever understands me and my deep thoughts and feelings!"

"Um, Ruv?"

"Yes, Sam?"

"Is this the dragon from the drawings you've seen passed down by your people?"

"Yes, Sam."

"Okay. So. Just. Wait." I frowned. "I'm lost. Kevin?"

"Beats me," Kevin said. "We're not the same kind of dragon. Don't be racist, Sam. I don't say that all you humans look alike. That's mean."

"That's *not* what I was saying!"

"What's so hard to understand?" Jekhipe said. "I sleep for ninety-nine years, stay awake for one, and then go back to sleep. I'm not *that* old."

This was bad. This was very, very bad.

"Okay," I said. "Okay. So. How old are you?"

"One thousand four hundred years old," Jekhipe said, as if I was the most annoying thing in creation.

"And you're only awake for one year at a time."

"Yeah, that's what I said, gods."

"And you sleep the rest of the time."

"*Yes*. Why are you on my back about this?"

"So," I said slowly. "Technically, you are fourteen years old."

"Wow," Jekhipe said. "Look at you. Do you do any other tricks aside from math? Gods, why can't you all just leave me alone so I can contemplate the meaning of my existence and why we're all probably just some sort of cosmic accident put here to achieve nothing but endless suffering?"

And that was how I met a teenage emo dragon.

I SAT ON A ROCK, MY face in my hands, rocking back and forth and moaning. "Why. Why does this happen to me? Why? Whyyyy?"

"At least this continues to prove my point I made a long time ago," Ryan said from beside me. "You're the common denominator in all this. It feels good being right."

I peered through my fingers to glare at him.

"Not helping," he said hastily. "Right. I can see that. Look, if it makes you feel better, it's really not your fault."

"Thanks," I said, dropping my hands. "That does make me feel a little bit better."

"Good," Ryan said, smiling at me. "After all, it's not your fault the gods seem to have it out for you and throw every obstacle in your path that they can."

I put my face back in my hands again and said, "Whyyyy."

"I wonder what this means for the others?"

"What others?"

"The other dragons. If this one is… like this, what does that mean for the mountain dragons? Or the Great White?"

I almost told him that the Great White was already an asshole, but then remembered I hadn't said anything to anyone about the dragon's words to me in the vision. I thought maybe I should say something, but I didn't want anyone thinking I couldn't do this. Because I *could*. And I would prove to the Great White and the star dragon what I was capable of.

Of course, that meant dealing with Jekhipe. Which, you know, sucked.

Ryan took my hands away from my face and held them in his on his lap, digging his thumbs into the palms. It felt good, being this close to him right now. I felt like I was flying in a hundred different directions, and I think he knew that, knew I needed something grounding me. I was still tired from expending as much magic as I had, but my strength was returning, slowly but surely.

"We'll figure it out," he murmured. "You'll see. We always do."

"Yeah. One dragon at a time, you know? I'm sure the others will be a clusterfuck too, but no need to worry about that until we get there."

"You good now?" I heard Gary ask.

I looked up, squinting against the sunlight to see Gary and Tiggy standing over me.

"Define good."

"Better than you were?"

"Maybe."

"Good. So, Kevin and fake-Ryan are talking to the dragon, trying to get him to open up."

"Damn right he's a fake me," Ryan muttered.

"And how's that going for them?"

Tiggy shrugged and held up his hand, seesawing it back and forth. "Eh."

"Great. That's just great."

"We did get a couple of things out of him," Gary said. "One, he *did* feel you coming and could hear you like you could hear him."

"That's... good?"

"Two, he says he didn't want to eat you, because he thought you were just playing a game."

"A game."

"Yeah. Like tag. Or something."

The urge to rock back and forth was almost too much to resist. "Go on," I said through gritted teeth.

"Um. Okay. Also. Don't get mad."

"Because of course when someone says that, it obviously works every time."

"Someone is sassy today," Gary said. "Tiggy! Guess who's sassy to-day!"

Tiggy scrunched his face up. Then, "Sam?"

"You win!" Gary cried, prancing in place. "Guess what you win!"

Tiggy looked excited. "What do I win?"

"You get to tell Sam that one thing that might make him mad!"

Tiggy started clapping. "Yes! Yes! I win! That—" He frowned. "That not good."

"Might as well hit me with it now," I said. "I'm already knocked on my ass. What's one more thing in this desolate wasteland known as my life?"

"Yeah," Ryan said. "You and the new dragon are going to get along just fine."

"I'm not an emo teenager!"

He patted my hand.

"Okay," Tiggy said. "Sam not mad?"

"I'm not mad," I assured him.

"Sam stay not mad?"

"Depends."

"On?"

I narrowed my eyes at him. "If you say something I don't like."

Tiggy swallowed and wrung his hands together. "Okay. So. Dragon. We tell him. 'Bout destiny. And stuff." He glanced nervously at Gary, who nodded for him to continue. "And he said. Um. Fuck off?"

"Fuck off," I repeated.

"Yes. He said Sam fuck off. He not help."

"Oh my gods."

"Shh, Sam," Tiggy said, pushing a big finger against my face.

"Oh my gods."

"Shhh, shhh, shhh."

"Tiggy," Gary hissed. "His face is doing that twitching thing! Stop touching him before he bites you or takes away your soul!"

"Tiggy keep his soul," Tiggy said, taking a step back, bringing his hands up to cover his chest. "It mine."

"If that dragon wasn't large, scary, and could eat me," I snarled, "I would so kick its ass right now! Godsdamned Jekhipe!"

"Oh," Gary said. "That's one other thing? He doesn't like the name Jekhipe. Says that was the name the gypsies gave him."

"Of *course* he doesn't like it. Okay, you know what? I'll bite. What does he want to be called?"

Gary's lips twitched. "You need to remember that mentally, he's only fourteen years old. And has a lot of feelings. And says that we'll never understand his pain."

"I'm the denominator," I said to no one in particular. "That's just who I am. It's like all I get is the crazy. Everywhere I go."

Gary was rather gleeful when he said, "He says his name is Zero Ravyn Moonfire."

I hated everything.

JEKHI—EXCUSE ME, *ZERO RAVYN MOONFIRE*—told us in no uncertain terms that we were not allowed to stay in the dome come nightfall. "It's mine," he growled. "And you already took away my best friends, so I don't even want to *talk* to you right now!"

"Your best friends," I repeated, trying to get a handle on the situation.

"The mermaids!" Zero shouted at me. "You completely destroyed the *mermaids*!"

"They were your *friends*?"

"Yes! Sort of. Okay, not really, but they *understood* what it felt like to be an outcast with a face that no one could possibly love!"

"Oh," I said. "Come on. Your face isn't… that bad."

"Good job," Ryan said. "Really. I believed it."

Zero slithered toward me, the hood around his face expanding, spikes twitching.

"Eep," I said, taking a step back.

"See?" he wailed as he deflated. "I'm *hideous*."

"There, there," I said. "It's…. There, there."

"My gods, Sam," Gary said. "Are you actively *trying* to make things worse?"

"Hey!" I said. "It's not *my* fault I'm a handsome devil and don't know how to talk to children!"

"I'm not a *child*," Zero said. "I'm *fourteen years old*. I know *a lot* of stuff, okay? You're all just old and don't remember what it's like to be *my* age. You don't know what it's like to be me. You don't know my *life*."

"Zero?" Gary cooed. "Honeybunch. Listen to your aunt Gary, okay? *I* knew Sam when he was fourteen, and guess what? He went through the same thing you're going through. He was… well. Awkward is probably the nicest thing I can say. You ever see those birds with the tiny bodies and really long legs that do nothing but squawk all the time? Yeah, imagine that in human form. That was Sam."

"What?" I rolled my eyes. "No it wasn't. I was never *awkward*. Tiggy. Tell him."

Tiggy scratched the back of his neck.

I narrowed my eyes. "Tiggy. *Tell* him."

"Don't like lying," Tiggy said.

"But… you wouldn't be…. Tiggy. *Tiggy*. Of *course* I wasn't weird and awkward as a teenager. I skipped right over that whole thing and was amazing as I am today!"

"You're weird and awkward *now*," Kevin said.

"Hey!"

"So there's hope," Gary said to Zero. "You'll see. One day, when you're Sam's age, you'll blossom into the most handsome snake dragon monster thing that ever did live."

"But I don't *want* to wait until I'm forty-five!"

"Forty-*five*?" I shrieked. Then I coughed, slapped my hand against my chest a couple of times, and responded much more reasonably. "Forty-five? I'm not forty-five. That's ridiculous."

"Oh," Zero said. "Do we not round up anymore? It's been a while since I've been awake. I could be wrong."

I stepped forward, meaning to choke the life out of the gigantic dragon, but Ryan snagged me by the arm and was able to stop me before I could even get my hands on him, which was probably for the best, what with the destiny thing and all.

"Easy," he whispered in my ear. "You don't want to piss him off even more."

"He's pissing *me* off."

"Yeah, but you're the older one here. *Not* like that, don't give me that look. You know what I mean."

"I wasn't awkward as a teenager," I said.

"I knew you when you were a teenager," he reminded me. "Maybe a little awkward."

"You never even talked to me."

"I stared at you a lot." He shrugged.

"You creepy bastard. It wasn't bad, right?"

He grinned softly and leaned in to kiss me on the cheek, lips lingering. I saw Zero watching us, but when he saw he'd been caught, he quickly looked away. "Not bad," Ryan said. "I maybe even loved it a little."

"Sap," I muttered, but my heart was tripping all over itself, so maybe I was too. I cleared my throat and looked back at the others. "Look. It's getting late. It's been a long day. Kevin, can you fly back to the other side of the cavern and get our packs? We can stay inside the dome tonight and worry about everything—"

"Wow," Zero said. "Way to ask. Gods."

I closed my eyes and counted to five, taking a deep breath and letting it out slowly. "I'm sorry?"

"The dome is *mine*," Zero said. "That's where *I* live. You can't just go in there without asking."

I opened my eyes and forced a smile on my face. "Okay. That's fair. I'm sorry, Zero. Can we please stay in the dome tonight?"

"Thank you for asking," Zero said. "And no, you may not."

I blinked. "Excuse me?"

"What part of me saying it's *mine* did you not understand?"

I had to remind myself it was illegal to murder dragons.

"Maybe I should handle this," Kevin whispered to me, even though everyone could hear him. "After all, I'm also a dragon, in case you've forgotten."

"Fine. Just... do it."

"You make the best decisions when you agree with what I say," Kevin said.

I almost punched him in the eye.

Kevin turned toward the snake dragon. "Hey, buddy," he said, thumping his tail near Zero's. "Hey. What's going on? What's happening in that noggin of yours? Hmm? You can tell me. I'm like your older brother, you know? You can tell your big bro anything. You know that, right? Bros stick together, you know? You're my brother from another mother. You know?"

"What," I said.

Zero eyed me suspiciously before he rose up until he was right near Kevin's ear. He started whispering. Kevin nodded. "Uh-huh. Okay. Right. No, that's fair. You're right. He *does* look like—right. Wow. That's... uh-huh. No, I totally see your point. I wouldn't want him there either."

Kevin turned to glare at me. "You are a terrible person."

"What!"

"Zero reminded me of a very important point. You suck sometimes."

I glared at Zero, who didn't even seem chagrined. "Okay. Fine. I'll bite. What is it that I am supposed to have done now?"

"You have to be *invited* into a dragon's lair. You can't just *enter* anytime you want. You did the same to me!"

"I did *not*. If you'll recall, you *kidnapped* me and took me back to the keep because you were going to try and have your *way* with me."

"Everything tries to have sex with him," Ryan told Ruv with a sigh. "Dragons, Darks, you."

"I didn't try," Ruv said. "Believe me. You would have known if I had tried."

"No one would feel sad if I ran you through with my sword," Ryan muttered.

Ruv grinned.

"That's not how *I* remember it happening," Kevin said. "But I suppose your recollection would have been colored by the fact that you were awed by my masculinity. I'll allow it."

"Whatever," I said. "Fine. I don't even care anymore. I'm tired. I'm hungry. And I am sick of everyone's shit. We'll sleep out here. Under the *stars*, where I *like* it. And then tomorrow, we'll—I don't even know what we'll do. Fuck it. Fuck this whole day. Fuck you. Fuck everyone."

"He's cranky," Tiggy said.

"Yes, kitten," Gary said. "That's what happens when you find out that your destiny rests in the hands of a bunch of idiots and an amazing unicorn."

"Exactly," Tiggy said. Then he frowned. "Wait."

"I need to break something," I told Ryan.

"Why are you looking at me for that?" Ryan asked. "Don't break *me*."

That wasn't what I'd been thinking at all, but now it seemed like a good idea. I turned and stalked away before I could act on it. It seemed like the better thing to do.

"How did you all find each other?" Ruv asked us later that night. We sat around a fire, the sparks shooting up toward the night sky filled with what seemed like a million stars. I was actively avoiding looking up at them, though, sure I'd be cursing David's Dragon until it fell from the heavens and I had yet *another* mess to deal with. I didn't think I'd be wishing on the stars for a very long time to come.

"Sam stole me away from my keep," Kevin said.

"Sam stole Tiggy and me from the Dark Woods," Gary said.

"Sam stole my heart," Ryan said.

"I did *not* steal you from your keep. And Tiggy and Gary all but *followed* me home. And Ryan, I am going to fuck you until you're cross-eyed later. You don't even know."

"Ew," Gary said, nose wrinkling. "You kiss me with that mouth."

I snorted as I stoked the fire. "Like you have any room to talk."

"You talk about sex a lot," Ruv said, cocking his head. "I've noticed that."

"You get used to it," Ryan said.

"Why shouldn't we?" I said. "Everyone does it. Why does it need to be something no one talks about?"

"Merely an observation," Ruv said. "We are not so... free in Mashallaha. It was rather shocking to come to the City of Lockes. It was loud. Very different."

"Had you left the desert before that?" I asked, curious.

He shook his head. "No. That was the first time."

"I can't imagine having to stay in one place all the time," I said. "I would get too restless."

"But you're the King's Wizard," Ruv said with a frown.

"Apprentice," Gary coughed.

"I am. What about it?"

"Shouldn't you be staying in the castle at all times? As the Wolf of Bari Lavuta, my job is to be by the *phuro*'s side."

"You're not right now," Gary pointed out.

"Well... yes. But it is because I was ordered here. I do what the *phuro* commands. Is it not the same for you and your King? Or Morgan of Shadows?"

I laughed. "I guess. If they ask me to do something, I will usually do it. But they give me the freedom to do what I want. To make my own mistakes."

"There is no room for mistakes," Ruv said seriously. "Mistakes only lead to weakness."

"But if you don't make mistakes, how can you possibly learn anything?"

"By listening to your elders. They impart their knowledge and wisdom and you learn from them."

"How would this have worked?" I asked.

"What?"

"You and me. Vadoma must have been telling you for years about me. What she thought you were to me. What she thought we could be. What she wanted for you. For me. Without even taking what *I* would have wanted into consideration. How would it have worked had I agreed to it? To have you be my cornerstone?"

I knew everyone else was listening as intently as I was for the answer. This, out of everything, was probably something that I needed to be focusing on the least, but I was interested in knowing Vadoma's angle on all this. What her endgame was.

For a moment, I thought Ruv wasn't going to answer. Then, "You would have come to Mashallaha. Lived amongst your people. Learned your heritage. The ways of the gypsy. Vadoma would have been your teacher. She would have shown you the path home."

She was ballsy, I had to give her that. "Mashallaha is not my home," I said, trying to keep my voice even. "The gypsies are not my people. They looked down upon me as if I was lesser than them. They consider my blood diluted because of who my father is. And even if I could change their mind, why would I ever put myself in a position where I'd have to start something like that to begin with?"

"Really?" Ruv asked. "And I suppose the people of Lockes have shown you the same kindness? Just how many people in that crowd were... how did you put it? Looking down upon you. In Mashallaha, people are not trusting of outsiders, especially those with your power. But it's because they do not know you. And they are mired in tradition."

That... stung. More than I thought it would. Because he did have a point. I'd given my all to the people of Lockes. Or at least I thought I had. Sure, I'd made mistakes. I wasn't infallible. But there'd always been an undercurrent there, a low hum ever since I'd been pulled from the slums and placed at Morgan's side. There'd been an initial outcry, but it'd died down quickly thanks to Morgan and the King. But had it ever truly gone away? I knew I could charm my way out of most situations, but what good did that really do me in the long run?

I couldn't place all the blame on Lady Tina for the movement against me, even if I wanted to. She merely latched on to something that had apparently already been there. She'd just given voice to it.

She was still a bitch, though.

"I can't make everyone happy," I said slowly. "Even if I wish I could. It's not possible. No matter what you do, there is always going to be someone who doesn't like it. And I can't spend all my time trying to change their minds, even if I wanted to."

"And yet you still fight for them," Ruv said. "Otherwise you wouldn't be here. You may have put up a good front, but you're still here."

"Of course I'd still be here," I said. "Why wouldn't I be? People deserve to live how they choose, free and not governed by another's will. Because that's exactly what will happen if... the Darks get their way." I couldn't say his name. It was stuck on the tip of my tongue, but I couldn't force myself to say it. Not after what Morgan had told me about him before we'd left Castle Lockes. Not after... everything.

"You are a good person, Sam of Wilds," Ruv said. "Naïve, I think, but good. I believe you will do what Vadoma thinks you will do."

"Um, thanks?"

"Of course he will," Ryan said, sounding grumpy. "Sam is the best person I know."

"And he does what he says he's going to do," Gary said.

"And he makes *me* happy," Tiggy said. "And I love him."

"And he takes care of us," Kevin said.

I was a little choked up at that.

"Plus," Kevin added, "he's got a really great ass."

I couldn't help but laugh. There, under the stars. So far from home, I laughed. And out of the corner of my eye, I saw Zero in the shadows of the dome, listening to every word.

CHAPTER 19
The Magic of Zero Ravyn Moonfire

EVERYONE WAS ASLEEP EXCEPT FOR ME, Ryan's hand lying loosely on my waist, Tiggy sitting up against Kevin with Gary in his lap. Ruv was lying a little ways off from everyone, but that was okay. The embers in the fire still burned, a tendril of smoke rising up toward the night sky. The air was cool but not uncomfortable. I felt small here in the middle of nowhere. Overwhelmed by everything that had happened and everything that would come.

I looked over at Ryan, whose mouth was slack, soft little snores on each exhalation. His brow was furrowed, like he was concentrating on something difficult. I reached over and brushed a finger from his forehead down between his eyes to the tip of his nose, the lightest of touches. He relaxed under the touch, and I hoped that whatever dream he was in didn't hurt. I couldn't stand the idea of him being hurt.

I sighed and was about to close my eyes to try and force away the whirlwind of thoughts in my head when I saw a pulse of light coming from inside the dome. It was soft and low and it pulled on my magic, but not in the way I'd felt when we'd first come to the island. This was a caress, a question instead of a demand.

I carefully shifted away from Ryan, putting my small straw pillow in his arms so he had something to hold on to. He frowned in his sleep until I leaned down and kissed his forehead. At the press of my lips, he made this little hum deep in his throat that squeezed at my heart. Maybe I had lied a little to Ruv when I said I'd still be here for everyone even if they'd turned against me. Maybe I would. But I was mostly here for him. Because I refused to believe the future was written in stone.

The light pulsed again.

And the whispers in my head began again.

I rose and left my friends behind, moving toward the dome.

The closer I got, the more it pulled, but it remained gentle, even as the magic in the air thickened. I wondered if my eyes were red again, wondered how Zero was able to do what he did. Because I thought maybe the forest inside the dome was his doing, that he grew the trees and the grass and the flowers the moment he started to wake. That he made something beautiful out of a place of ruins.

He had to know I was coming. I knew he felt me as much as I felt him.

If I'd had any doubts remaining about this whole destiny thing, that was the moment I finally began to believe.

I hesitated, briefly, at the entrance to the dome.

But there was no reason I could think of to not continue on.

So I did.

There was the moment, that little pinprick in time, when I passed from the desert into the dome. Where the air changed, became damp and cool, the smells of a wild forest all around me. I didn't know how Zero did this, how it was possible for something so frightening to make something so beautiful, but I didn't know that it was my place to ask. I needed Zero. I knew that now. He fit somehow. Even if he was already a pain in my ass. The rest of them were as well, but I loved them fiercely. Surely I had room in my heart for another.

And it wasn't as if I had a choice in the matter.

(Which of course led to thoughts of the mated mountain dragons and the Great White, but I pushed that away—one day at a time. That's all I could do, because anything else would become too much.)

I found Zero coiled up toward the south side of the dome. He was awake, but he didn't turn his head toward me, even though I was making enough noise to make him aware of my approach, just to be safe. I maintained a careful distance, because even if I thought Zero wouldn't hurt me, he was still a large fucking snake dragon with big-ass fangs, and I didn't want to take the chance. Plus, he scared the shit out of me, though I was trying to keep that at bay as best I could.

The pulse was brighter now, that light I'd seen from outside the dome. And now I could see where it came from, my heart felt like it was stuck in my throat.

There were little balls of light, almost like they were fireflies (terrible, terrible things, those), flitting about in front of Zero. There were dozens of them, and they brushed along Zero's face, swirling around the spiked horns on the hood. The lights were of varying sizes, some as small as specks of dust, others as big as a coin. There wasn't anything ominous about them; in fact, the exact opposite was true. They felt warm and safe, like they wouldn't—*couldn't*—hurt him or me. Or anyone, really. I was sure of that, though I couldn't say how.

I also didn't know if they were sentient. It didn't seem like the right way to describe them. I thought maybe the lights were a *part* of Zero, his will or dragon magic manifested into something tangible. I thought the lights *were* Zero, like my magic was me.

And as I looked on, they began to move. The lights began to gather together, slipping off Zero and gathering on the forest floor in an open space where nothing had grown. The lights started to spin in a slow circle, a glowing corona that took my breath away. It reminded me of a long-ago day in the forest when I held a dead bird in my hand, telling myself that it wasn't fair, that nothing about it was fair.

I wondered if Zero was thinking the same thing.

His eyes were open, glittering in the dark, trained on the spinning lights.

I waited, wanting to see what they would do.

It happened only seconds later.

The lights began to rise off the ground, still moving at the same slow, deliberate pace. While the air above the corona remained empty, the air *below* it did not. As the lights rose higher and higher, they left behind the trunk of a tree, the roots fused into the earth. The lights began to expand the higher they rose, widening the circle in which they spun. The tip of a branch appeared once they were eye level, wide green leaves seemingly appearing out of nowhere.

And when it was finished, when the lights exploded outward silently and rained down around us, a large tree stood in front of us, healthy and full of life. It was as tall as any tree I'd seen in the Dark Woods. Without looking at Zero, I walked to the tree and put my hand on the trunk. The bark was rough against my skin. Rough and real.

None of this was an illusion. I was in awe of it. Of him.

A few of the lights fell on me, on my cheek and arm, and each light made a sweet sound in my head, like a musical note that echoed faintly.

I heard Zero shifting slightly behind me. "I like making pretty things," he said quietly. "It makes me feel safe."

"I can see that," I said. "You're very good at it."

"You don't have to say that," he said bitterly. "I know you don't mean it."

I looked back over my shoulder. He'd raised his head slightly off the ground, staring straight back at me. "I don't often say things I don't mean."

"But you do sometimes."

"Diplomacy calls for it."

"Is that what you are? Diplomatic?"

I gave him a small smile. "I don't think anyone would ever use that word to describe me. When it comes to diplomatic situations, my mentor usually asks that I remain quiet."

"Oh," Zero said. And then, in a flat voice as if he couldn't care less, "Who's your mentor?"

"Morgan of Shadows."

"I've heard of him."

"Have you?"

"Yes. He's been around for a couple of the years I've been awake."

"He's a good man."

"Is he? He's a wizard. Sometimes wizards aren't good people."

"I know. But sometimes they are."

"Are you a good person?"

"Most of the time," I said honestly. "I try, but it can be hard. Can I ask you a question?"

He tensed, like he'd been expecting this. I didn't know what he thought I was going to ask him. "I don't—"

"Do you do this every time you wake up?" I asked, waving my hand toward the rest of the dome. "Do you make all of this by yourself?"

Zero looked surprised at that, like he was expecting something else from me. Which, to be fair, I could have gone in a million different directions. He didn't know me, but then I didn't know him either. "Yeah," he said, sounding a little petulant. "I *can* make things, you know. I know I look scary, but I can—"

"It's beautiful," I said. "I don't know that I've ever seen anything like it before. It's impressive, Zero. You must be very strong."

If it were possible for snake dragon monster things to blush, I thought maybe he would have been right there. He averted his eyes and made this strange snuffling sound out his nose. His forked tongue flicked out, tasting the air, and I wondered if this was a way for him to know that I was telling the truth, if honesty had a weight to it that he could pick out amongst all the other notes in the air. I didn't think it likely, but I knew it would be better for him to hear nothing but the truth from me rather than find out he could catch me in a lie.

"Thanks," he finally said begrudgingly. "It's not that hard."

"How do you do it?"

"What?"

"How do you make everything?"

His eyes narrowed. "Why?"

I shrugged. "I'm curious. Magic, it… baffles me sometimes."

"But you're a wizard."

"Apprentice, but yes, I'm a wizard." Gary would be proud.

He sounded confused. "But then you do magic all the time. How can you do something without understanding it? That doesn't make any sense."

Too right, but that pretty much summed up my life: able to do things that didn't make any sense. "I don't think anyone understands my magic, least of all me. I'm what you might call a special case." I grimaced. "Yeah, that didn't sound like I wanted it to. I'm just… different."

"Why?" He looked less tense now. Not comfortable, exactly, but not as on guard as he'd been. He sounded younger too, and it was strange to think that he'd only been awake for thirteen full years before this, if he'd been telling the truth. And I thought maybe he was. Would I still be alive the next time he woke? Would I be alone, with everyone I loved nothing but dust and bones? Or would it all be gone?

"No one is quite sure how my magic works," I said. "I can do things other people can't. Sometimes, I do things that I'm not even trying to do."

"The mermaids," Zero said. "I… felt it. It was bright. And smelled like…. I came here to this place in my sixth year. I wanted to be alone, you know? The mermaids let me pass. I don't know why. It was like they didn't even care that I was there. I didn't question it. Then, that night, there was a terrible storm. It rolled over the desert, and everything flashed in the sky. I've never heard something like it before or since. I thought I was going to be blown away, that the gods were so angry they were going to bring fire down on the world. But it passed, eventually. You smelled like that storm. You felt like that storm. Like lightning."

"I'm sorry about the mermaids," I said quietly. "They were going to hurt my friends. I couldn't let that happen."

He rolled his eyes. "They were jerks. I didn't talk to them. I even ate one once."

I laughed, a little shocked. "You did what?"

Zero looked rather pleased with himself. "It tried to come in here," he said. "It wanted to hurt my plants. My trees. It wouldn't leave. So I ate it. It was… chewy." He deflated a little. "But I suppose they weren't any worse than I am. They were monsters, like me."

And that hurt. I barely knew this… this *thing* in front of me, and that still hurt to hear. Maybe it was because I knew what it felt like to be an outcast. Maybe I knew what it felt like to have people scared of me. I didn't know. But it hurt.

"They were nothing like you," I said quietly.

His head snapped, tail twitching dangerously. "*You* were scared of me. Just like you were scared of them. I *felt* it."

I nodded. "Yes. But then you're huge and you have really big teeth and you pointed them in my direction."

He grinned at me, or as much as he could. The top two fangs descended slowly, glistening in the dark. "These teefs?" he slurred between the fangs.

My throat clicked as I swallowed, fighting every instinct I had to take a step back away from him. "Yeah. Those teefs."

The fangs ascended again, and he cocked his head at me. "You're strange, even for a human."

"That's not the first time I've heard that."

"And how are you speaking to me? How did you all learn to talk like me? I've never had anyone be able to do that."

I scratched the back of my head. "Yeah, see? That's one of those things that we don't quite know. It's not us speaking like you. It's you speaking like us."

He looked offended. "I'm speaking *human*? That's *terrible*. You're all so... *chewy*."

"Thanks," I said dryly. "Really."

"Well, it's *true*. How is this even possible? Gods, I don't even want to open my mouth anymore."

"It's proximity," I said. "Something about me. We don't really know why. Dragons just suddenly seem to be able to speak like we do when I'm around. It's kind of my thing."

"Maybe you should just go away, then. I don't want to speak human."

"Sorry, dude. I don't know that I can do that. It's actually important, the reason I'm here."

He groaned and laid his head back on the ground, blinking at me slowly. "I just want to grow my plants and be left alone. It's why I came all the way out here, so I didn't have to see anyone."

"Where did you come from?"

"Far away," he said stubbornly.

Which gave me an idea, something Mama had taught me a long time ago. She'd even used it on Ryan once to find out what she wanted to know. It had been illuminating, to say the least. "That's interesting. I've come from far away too. Can I ask you some more questions? Just about your plants," I added before he could refuse.

"Sure," he said slowly.

"Cool. Which is your favorite?"

He nodded toward a large orange flower that blossomed to our left. "That one."

"What is it?"

"I don't know. I saw it once in—I saw it once."

"Why is it your favorite?"

"I like the color. It smells good."

"What does it smell like to you?"

"The wind."

I began to speak faster. "Do you like to fly?"

"Yes."

"Do you stay here every year?"

"Yes, I don't like to leave."

"How do you eat?"

"I store up the oxygen put out by my plants and trees. It helps me sleep."

"Have you ever met wizards before?"

"Yes, and I never wanted to see them again."

And then, "Did you know I was coming?"

Without giving himself time to think, he said, "Yeah, the star dragon told me."

My eyes widened.

"Mother*fucker*," Zero growled. "How did you *do* that? Mind control? Are you trying to take me over, wizard?"

"No," I said quickly. "No, no. It was just—the star dragon. Really?" I sighed. "Godsdammit. This is just getting more complicated as it goes."

"It's not *my* fault!"

"I didn't say it was. It's just… I didn't know about any of this until a few weeks ago. It just makes me wonder how everyone else knows more about me and my destiny than I do. It's annoying."

Zero scoffed. "You try minding your own business and then, out of nowhere, get told that someday, a wizard was going to come for you. That I would have to make a choice between doing what I wanted or doing what was right. And that what was *right* wasn't always going to be obvious."

"Yeah, I can actually relate to that. Except mine was my long-lost grandma who I'd never met before."

"Weak," Zero breathed.

"Dude," I agreed. "So weak. Mind if I sit down?"

Zero hesitated, but then said, "I don't care. You can do what you want. Wizards usually do. You're all terrible people. Really terrible people."

But I got the feeling that if he didn't want me there, I sure as shit wouldn't be there. I took a seat at the base of the tree he'd grown when I'd found him, my back against the trunk, facing him.

I waited until I could gather my words, wanting to say the right thing without sounding too rehearsed. It was important, maybe as important as anything I'd ever had to say before. I needed him, I knew, and I had to make him believe I needed him. *How* I needed him or *why*, I couldn't exactly say. But I did. My magic didn't exactly mesh with his, but it didn't either with Kevin right away. And it still didn't, not completely. But it wasn't the same. Gary had magic. Tiggy did as well to an extent, given he had giant's blood within him. It would never mix like mine did with Morgan's. We weren't the same. I was human. They were not. Magic was different to different species.

But I could *feel* him, like I could feel them, though nowhere near as strong. And I didn't think I could convince him to leave this place behind to give us time to bond like I'd done with the others. I thought it would be too much too soon. I didn't know how much time we had, so when I spoke, I wanted it to be the right thing to say.

"You said you knew Morgan of Shadows," I said finally. "Or knew of him."

"Yes."

"Do you know Randall?"

I didn't miss the way he twitched. "Yeah—yes. Um. He's scary."

That gave me pause. "Have you ever met him?"

He shook his head. "No, but the year after the star dragon came to me, I woke and heard whispers of a wizard unlike any that had ever existed before."

And that— "How old were you when the star dragon came?"

"Oh. Uh, I was… seven. Seven years old. Just a kid. I'm old enough now, if that's what you're thinking!"

I closed my eyes. "Seven hundred years ago, the star dragon came to you. About me."

"Yes? Why?"

Why. Why, indeed. Why had the star dragon prophesized me to Zero *seven hundred years ago*, well before I had been born, before Morgan, before Myrin, even before *Randall* had been born? And if that was the case, *why* couldn't Myrin have been stopped the first time around? What was it about *this time* that was different? Why now?

Why me?

"Did I break you?" Zero asked, stretching out toward me. He moved slowly, as if unsure, his hood tucked to the side of his head. He didn't look as fearsome now. Still snakelike, but he reminded me of Kevin in a way, and it'd been a long time since I'd been afraid of Kevin.

"No," I said, but it came out as a croak. "No. Just… surprising, is all. It's not what I expected to hear."

He didn't pull away, just rested his head on the ground, closer than he'd been before, eyes on me. If I stood, we'd probably be eye level, given how big he was. "It's the truth," he said. "Time is different for me."

"I can imagine. It must be difficult, jumping through the years like that."

It almost looked like he shrugged, but since he didn't have shoulders, I couldn't be sure. "I guess. It's hard to make friends that way, given that they'd probably all be dead by the time I woke up again." His eyes widened. "Not that I want friends or anything! I don't *need* friends. I don't even *want* friends. Friends are way lame."

"Sure," I said easily. "I totally get that. Friends are difficult, sometimes."

"Right?" he said. "And even if they *aren't*, they don't *live*. One time, I made friends with a squirrel right before I went to sleep and thought I could keep it with me. When I woke up the next time, it was nothing but bones."

"That's… a really sad story," I said. "Dude, what the *hell*."

"Now you see why everything is about pain," Zero moaned. "No one understands me, not even squirrels who die on top of me and leave their stupid bones for me to find when I wake up. I mean, who *does* that?"

"That damn squirrel."

"Right? That *damn* squirrel. Whatever. I didn't need him. I didn't need anyone. I still don't. I have my trees and flowers. That's all I need."

"I think everyone needs someone," I said quietly. "It helps. In the long run."

He didn't say anything, just looked off into the dark forest around us.

"I need them," I admitted. "The others. Maybe not Ruv, but then I don't know him. He's... not a part of us. And I don't know that he will be." I didn't think that was any slight against him. It just didn't seem like he fit. I thought maybe he needed to find his own path, if he ever decided to break away from Vadoma. But that didn't seem likely.

Zero mumbled something that I couldn't quite make out.

"What was that?"

He sighed the weary sigh of the put-upon. "I said, Kevin seems all right. And the unicorn. And maybe the giant."

"Have you... ever met another dragon before? You didn't seem surprised to see him."

"Aside from the star dragon? No. I don't think so."

I frowned. "What about your parents?"

He chuckled bitterly. "How can you not know anything about dragons when you travel with one? Ask your Kevin. He should tell you."

He had a point, though I wasn't going to let him know that. "What do you think about the knight?"

Zero huffed. "He's full of himself."

"Yeah," I said fondly. "But he's pretty awesome."

"You love him, huh?"

"I do."

He opened and closed his mouth a few times, and I was sure he wasn't going to say what he wanted. But then he blurted, "What's it like? Being in love?" Then he groaned and turned his head to the side, curling his face against his serpentine body, hiding himself away.

I blinked at him. "Um."

"Forget it! I don't know why I asked that." His voice was muffled. "I don't *care* about stuff like that—"

"It's pretty great, if I'm being honest."

"It *is*?" he asked, unfurling himself, eyes wide. He moved closer until I could feel his breath on my arms. "Like, okay. Just... what's great about it? You should tell me. Not that I care about that at all. Or anything."

I tried to keep the smile from my face. I didn't know how well I succeeded. It would be just my luck that my fourteen-year-old emo snake dragon was also a closet romantic. It seemed par for the course. Yeah, he fit. Somehow, he fit. "Well. I guess it's... it's the moment, you know, when you wake up first in the morning. You open your eyes and your thoughts are muddled. You're still partly asleep and you're warm and don't want to move, but you know you have to get up anyway. So you stretch and it feels good, but your arm hits something next to you and you look over and... there he is. Still asleep. And it's the first clear thought you have, and you think, Hello. Hello there. Hi. I'm so glad you're here. I'm so glad you're next to me. And then for some reason, he must feel you watching him, because he wakes up too, you know? And he's blinking and looks all soft and beautiful and then he sees you and he *smiles*. Like all it takes for him to be the happiest he's ever been is to see you there. Next to him. That's… that's what's so great about it. That's what it feels like."

Zero was quiet for a long time. I let us sit there, next to his trees, lost in our thoughts. Me thinking that that's something Vadoma could never understand. The love I had for Ryan. She could never know what it meant to me. What *he* meant to me. I felt sorry for Ruv, sure. But I would never give up something I'd worked so hard for. Vadoma wouldn't win. Not in that respect.

Then Zero sighed and sounded just like any other fourteen-year-old I'd ever known. It was really rather startling. "That's so *cute*," he squealed. "Oh my gods, I *want* that. *That's* what I want. Like, *forever*."

I laughed. "What about your plants? The trees?"

"I can do both! I *could*. I *know* I could. You gotta believe me!" But then, amazingly, his eyes began to fill with *tears*. "But—but…."

"Oh no," I groaned. "Don't cry. Please don't cry. I am absolutely *terrible* when other people cry. I get so damn awkward that—"

"But no one will ever *love me*!" he wailed, throwing his head back and twisting his massive body until he lay on his back. "I'm going to be alone *forever*!"

"Oh," I said. "Noooo. Noooo, of course not." I leaned forward and patted the side of his head clumsily. "There, there. Oh, you. You're just… swell."

"Swell? I'm *swell*? I don't *want to be swell*! I want to be in *love*!"

"O… kay. Uh. It'll happen. When it happens? To you. It's like, um. Your plants here. They. Grow. Like love does?"

"Wow! Thank you so much for the sound advice! Gosh, what would I have done without you!"

"Oh my gods."

"Not that it matters, anyway," he grumbled. "S'not like anything is gonna happen."

"Oh. Come on, you. You got this. Why would you say that?"

"Have you *seen* me? I scare *everyone*."

"Oh," I said. "Noooo. Of course not. That's not—noooo."

He hissed at me, hood unfurling partially, spikes rattling.

I squeaked, "Kill it with fire!" Then, "I mean, wow. You're—if only I was, like, seven years younger. And single. And a dragon. And into that."

"See! I scare *everyone*!"

I tried to be as stern as possible. "You're a little young for that, don't you think?"

"No! No, I am *fourteen years old*. I *know* what I want!"

"I don't think so, Zero. I'm pretty sure you're not thinking very clearly about this."

"I *am* thinking clearly! You just don't understand what it's like to be my age!"

"Uh, I *was* your age once."

"Yeah, when the giant *yaks* roamed the earth. That was like, *forever* ago. You don't get what it's like to be a young person. My feelings are *real* and *valid* and everything I say comes from my *life experience*."

I snorted. "Yeah. Life experience. Okay. Because you have so much of that."

He glared at me upside-down. "Whatever. I don't need this. You don't get to tell me what to do."

I narrowed my eyes at him. "Now, you listen here, young man. I will not sit here and listen to you disrespect me like this. If you think that you're going to talk to *me* like that, you've got another—"

"I don't care! You don't know me. You don't know my *life*. You're not even my real dad!"

"*What*? That hurts, Zero. That *hurts*. Do you know what I've *done* for you? I've—oh my fucking gods. What the fuck am I even *talking about*?"

"You're trying to stifle me as a person!" Zero cried. "I am an *individual*. You need to *respect* that! I will spread my wings and *fly*, and there is nothing you can do about it!"

"No," I said, standing up against the tree. "No, no, no. I am *not* going to turn into Gary and Kevin. I swear to the gods. This is some weird freaky-deaky parental magic shit or something. That's all it is!"

"Maybe I'll go out and find someone right *now*," Zero growled. "Because I can do what I want."

"Oh no you won't," I snapped. "You don't know what kind of *strangers* are out there—how are you making me *do* this?" I slapped my hand over my mouth, trying to keep myself from vomiting more parenting all over the place.

"You can't tell me how to live! I am a free spirit. I go where the wind blows!"

I had to resist the urge to tell him that I knew what I was talking about, that I'd lived a lot longer than he had, and that he should listen to me. But I realized how that *sounded*, and I hadn't *come here* for this. For *any* of this. I didn't need to be a parent to an emo snake dragon, especially when Kevin thought said emo dragon was his little brother while also thinking he was my stepfather.

I really needed to sit down and make a pros and cons list about the choices I'd made to get to this point.

"Look." I dropped my hand, trying to regain control of the situation. "You're… neat. You'll find what you want with *who* you want when it's time. Not before. And not before I ask you for your help."

He cut off his whining almost immediately and opened one eye to look at me. "My help."

I sighed. "You know what I'm talking about."

"Oh. Do I?"

"Zero."

"Mr. Wilds."

I groaned. "My name is Sam. And yes, you know. The star dragon. What did the he tell you?"

"Maybe that's private."

"Zero."

"Your face gets really red when you get mad."

"I'm not mad," I said through gritted teeth.

"You sound kind of mad. Or constipated. I don't know which."

"Look. I just… we need to know."

"What will you do for me if I help you?"

"What?"

He rolled over and laid his head near my feet. "It seems like you need me for this. What will I get if I help you? The star dragon said I had a choice. Said there was another too."

And that… well. That's when I stopped playing games. I told him what Morgan told me. About Myrin. About the end. About why he'd had to lock away his only family into the shadow realm. About what it meant to forsake a cornerstone once found. The corruption in the soul that came from it. The malice in the heart.

Zero remained silent while I spoke, understanding that I was no longer interested in placating him. He looked shaken by the time I'd finished. My voice was hoarse, and it was like I'd heard it all over again for the first time. I hadn't said anything to anyone about this, not even Ryan. Randall and Morgan's secret had become my own, but I was tired of bearing the weight.

It was quiet for a long while after I'd finished speaking.

Then:

"You're serious."

"Yes," I said.

"And you really need me?" His voice sounded small.

"Yes."

"What can *I* do?"

"I don't know yet," I admitted. "But it must be something."

"He told me. That a boy wizard would come. That he would need my help. That I would need to make a choice. That I could choose to help you. That I could choose to help the other. Or I could do nothing."

"And he hasn't been here? The other."

Zero shook his head. "No. Just you."

"Those are some serious choices you have to consider."

"They are, aren't they? I asked him what I should do. What was the right choice to make. Do you know what he told me?"

"No."

"He told me that a dragon's heart is a wondrous thing, capable of love and hatred. Of death and destruction. That there were dragons who had rained fire down from the sky. That burnt lands until they were nothing but ruins. That killed because they could, leaving nothing but wastelands behind them. And even though I was young, even though I didn't know very much about the world, I knew that was wrong. That I could never be a dragon like that. I never wanted to be a villain. I just wanted to make things grow again. So I flew as far away as I could, far away from everyone else, and found a place that looked like a wasteland. That looked like it had already been burned and destroyed. And I stayed here to prove to myself that I could make it beautiful again, even if I could never be beautiful myself."

Ah gods, how my heart ached.

He looked out at the forest around us, the trees swaying in a breeze, the birds that sang melancholic songs, the lights from actual fireflies, blinking lazily in the dark. "It was my gift," he said quietly. "I thought it was my gift to a world that had lost its way. That if I could make a little corner of it better, then I wasn't going to be like one of those bad dragons. That I could be one of the good guys. Does that make sense?"

"More than you could possibly know," I said honestly. "You're very smart. And very brave."

I thought maybe he smiled at me, though it was hard to tell. He could have been just flashing his fangs, the cheeky bastard. "I don't know about all that." He hesitated. Then, "Are there… bad dragons?"

"I don't know," I said quietly. "There aren't many left. You're only the second I've ever met. But maybe. I think that if you're intelligent, if you can form thoughts in your head, there's a chance that you could be a villain. And dragons are smart. So there might be some that are bad."

His tongue flicked out. "I don't want to be bad."

"I don't think you are."

"If I help you, do you think I'd… do you think I'd be doing good?"

"Yes."

"Even though you don't know how yet."

"Yes."

"You're asking me to take this on faith, wizard."

"Yes."

"Do you believe in it? Do you believe in your friends? In your family? Do you believe in yourself?"

And I didn't hesitate when I said, "*Yes*."

"Your eyes," he said. "They're glowing. They're…. It's so pretty."

I felt it coursing through me. "Red, right?"

"Yes."

"Do you know what that color is?"

"What?"

"I think it's the color of your scales."

He gasped. "Really? But it's... it's so. It's so—"

"Beautiful," I finished for him.

He reared up slowly, curling his body underneath him, eyes flashing in the dark. From the earth below that he'd created, those little lights began to glow again, flashing weakly at first, but then becoming stronger and stronger. He towered above me as the lights rose around us. Those musical notes I'd heard when they touched me before were louder this time around, more vibrant. More real. I didn't know if they were in my head or if they echoed throughout the dome, but the song they sang was bittersweet and heartbreaking. I could feel Zero in them, feel his doubts and insecurities, his loneliness and desperation. I thought maybe this was a test, that he was showing himself to me, showing me all the different pieces that made the whole of him, the sum of his parts. And it made me wonder if he was seeing the same in me, if he was getting all of *my* pieces. If he was, what did he see? What did I show?

I was smart.

I did stupid things.

When I loved, I loved fiercely and with my whole heart.

I didn't make friends easy. A lot of people liked the *idea* of me, but that wasn't the same as liking *me*.

Sometimes I thought maybe Morgan had made a mistake and I couldn't be what he thought I was.

I worried that I was going to disappoint my parents.

I was scared that one day Ryan would look at me and think he'd made a mistake.

I was angry at Randall, angry at Morgan, and I didn't know how I was going to get over it. But I had to. I knew I had to and that they didn't deserve my ire. But I didn't know how to get past it, even knowing what Morgan had told me.

I wanted to keep my promise and help Gary find his horn. I didn't know how to do that.

I wanted to keep my promise to give Tiggy a family he could call his own.

I wanted to believe my grandmother, that I was chosen for a reason.

I didn't know how to do that.

I wanted to believe that Myrin could be saved, that he could be the person Morgan and Randall had loved again. That he could be a brother again. A cornerstone.

I didn't know how to do that.

I wanted to believe that I could do this. That I could save Verania. That I could save the world. That the faith the King and his son had in me were not misplaced, that any villain that rose in opposition would be struck down because it was the *right* thing to do, that good would always triumph over evil.

I wanted to do what was right.

I didn't know how to do that.

"You're very conflicted," Zero said, eyes glittering in the light of his magic. "Is that how it is to be human?"

"I don't know," I said. "I've never been anything else."

"You're very brave. Like a hero."

"So are you." Because he was. Yes, he was a pain in my ass, but I had a feeling that anybody worthwhile would always *be* a pain in my ass.

"If I did this," Zero said, "if I helped you, would you help me?"

"To do what?"

"Make the world beautiful," he said. "I want the world to be beautiful again."

I smiled up at him. "I think I can do that."

He leaned forward until his face was inches from my own. His slitted nostrils flared, and he said, "The star dragon told me you would be good. And kind. A little foolish, but that your heart would be as big as a dragon's. Do you know what he told me about the other?"

I shook my head, not trusting myself to speak.

"He told me the other was your opposite. That he would bring this world to its knees. That he would lord over everyone and everything. I don't want that. I just want to grow my trees and flowers. So yes, Sam of Wilds, I will side with you. Because of your dragon heart."

And then he pressed his snout against my forehead, the lights exploding all around us, and——

CHAPTER 20
Tripping Balls Again

I GROANED, HEAD POUNDING, TRYING TO find the will to open my eyes. I wanted nothing more than to sink into sleep, but I knew that wasn't what I needed to do.

I had to get up.

I had to get up.

I had to *get up*—

I forced my eyes open.

Everything was bright and shining, and I brought my hand up to my face to shield my eyes and—

I was made of stars.

My fingers. My hand. My arm.

All of it was stars.

They reminded me of Zero's fireflies, his little lights that brought beauty into this world.

I was in the night sky.

I said, "What the fuck is this shit?"

From off to my left, a voice said, "That's probably the first time I've heard a constellation curse."

I looked over.

The star dragon stood there, watching me.

"You," I said, narrowing my eyes. Or rather, I think I did. It was hard to tell what I was doing. I didn't even know if I had eyelids.

"Hullo, Sam."

"*You.*"

"So you've said."

"Am I dead?"

He snorted. It shot little comets across the sky. "Not hardly."

"Oh. Did you drug me? Is that what's going on? You drugged me so I'm tripping balls again and are now about to have your way with me? Dude, that is so fucked-up. What is *wrong* with you dragons? I do not consent for you to touch my body."

He sighed. "And you're the chosen one. Wonderful."

"Can we not call me that? Or say anything about destiny? I feel like it's creating an aura of expectation that I may not live up to."

"Oh, I'm aware."

"You're mocking me, aren't you."

"Possibly."

"But—but, you're a *god.*"

He cocked his starry head at me. "And you don't think gods can have a sense of humor? Of course we do. We made *you*, after all."

"Hey! That's not very nice! Stars aren't supposed to be dicks!"

"I would have thought you believed the opposite," he said quietly. "Most of the wishes you've made upon us didn't come true."

"Well, yeah. But they aren't supposed to."

"How do you figure that, Sam?"

I shrugged. "It's not how wishing works. If we got everything we ever wished for, we wouldn't have the capacity to be thankful for all the things we'd already been given. I've got so much already. I don't ever want to lose sight of why it's important."

"And you wonder why you were chosen," the star dragon said. "You wonder why, out of everyone, the light has shined down upon you. Sam, it was you because it could only *be* you. You were always meant to be strong and brave. You were always meant to have power unlike anyone else. But it was always up in the air what direction you would go with it. You could have chosen a path that led to the dark. But instead your heart was lightning-struck, and it split and spilled its light upon those around you. You were chosen, Sam, because there was no one else it could have been."

"I still don't know if I'm good enough," I admitted. "And I don't know what will happen if I am."

"What do you mean?"

And I finally said the one thing that'd been weighing on me the most since I'd found out the truth. "It's either me or Myrin, right? There's no middle ground."

David's Dragon said, "Yes, Sam. That's correct. There is no middle ground."

"He won't turn back?"

"Would you turn to the dark?"

"No. Never."

"You seem sure about that."

"I am."

"Because of the path you've chosen."

"Yes."

"Myrin is the same way," the star dragon said. "He has chosen his path. Yes, Sam. There is no middle ground."

"And if I win? If I beat him? What will they think of me?" My voice was small.

"Morgan and Randall."

I looked away.

The star dragon chuckled. "How you could think they would love you any less, I will never understand. Your heart is an astonishing thing, Sam of Wilds. I've never heard one beat quite like it. They will love you as they always have. They have made their choices. They have chosen their paths, like you have. There might be regret, but not the way you think. It was always going to end this way."

"Why?" I asked, suddenly angry. "Why, if you knew about this, if the gods knew this was inevitable, why would you stand by and do nothing? Why would you let this happen? Why wouldn't you stop it?" I knew I was probably foolish, yelling at a god while made of stars in some fucked-up hallucination, but I had no fucks left to give. Turning into a constellation after having a heart to heart with a snake dragon could do that to you.

"Because we do not interfere," the star dragon said.

"Bullshit. You interfere all the time. You interfered with Vadoma. With Zero. With Kevin, and with me right now."

The star dragon looked chagrined. "I still have secrets."

"Do you know how this will end?"

The briefest of hesitations. "It could go either way."

"Fuck you sideways, you vague asshole."

"I like you," the star dragon said. "I always have."

"Are you telling him the same thing? Playing both sides?"

"No. Can I tell you something I've never told anyone?"

"Can I say no?"

"You can do anything you want."

I sighed. "Fine. Tell me."

"I hope it's you," he said. "I hope it's you who overcomes. I'm not supposed to choose sides, but I would choose you, Sam. I have seen you, more than you could possibly know. The life you've led. The decisions you've made. It hurts me, sometimes, knowing what I do. And because of that, I offer you this: the road to triumph is littered with sorrow. It is the way of things. For there to be success, sacrifices have to be made."

I went cold, remembering Ryan upon a slab, eyes closed, sword clasped against his chest. "What do you mean?"

"A warning. All of you will not survive until the end. There will be loss, Sam. And it will burn like nothing has ever burned before. You must remember to keep to the light, even when the dark begins to curl around your feet."

"She showed me," I said hoarsely. "Vadoma. About Ryan. I won't let it happen. I won't let anyone take him from me."

"Open your eyes, Sam," the star dragon said.

"They *are* open."

"Sam! Open your eyes!"

"What the hell are you talking about. I'm *right here*—"

The stars exploded.

VOICES ABOVE ME.

"Move, you dippy little cunts! You obviously don't know how to wake an unconscious Sam. You have to slap the *shit* out of him. And there is *no* one who does a better bitch-slap than a unicorn. This is *proven science*."

"I didn't do it!" another voice cried. "Or if I did, I didn't mean it! One moment we were *talking*, and then there was *magic* and *lights* and *decisions*. I don't even know!"

"You are *not* going to slap him. Do you know how hard your hooves are? I'm not going to let you hurt him."

"*I* know how hard his hooves are, ba-*zing*."

"Kevin, now is not the time to discuss the firmness of my hooves, you disgusting cretin. And now that I think about it, you don't get to talk about my hardness *ever again*."

"Oh, like *that's* a hardship. Ha. Get it? *Hard*ship."

"Is this always how it is with all of you?" yet another voice asked, this one heavily accented.

"No. Wait. Yes. Mostly. Sometimes, I smash things."

"Oh my gods, you guys are so *loud*," I groaned. "I can't even pass out, have visions, and then wake up in peace. Sweet fucking *molasses*."

"He's not making any sense!" Gary cried. "He must be crazed. I can still slap him."

I opened my eyes.

Many faces peered down at me.

"Why does this keep happening to me?" I moaned.

"Waking up on your back without really remembering what you've been doing the night before?" Kevin asked sympathetically. "Invite me next time. Let you find out what a real man tastes like, not some twinky little dragon."

"I am *not a twink*," Zero said. "I refuse to let you *label* me into something I want no part—"

"I didn't have *sex* with him," I growled. "What the hell."

"Hey, no judgments."

"Kevin."

"Yes, Sam?"

"Shut the fuck up."

"Shutting up, Sam."

"You okay?" Ryan asked me, crouched at my side. He helped me sit up, and I closed my eyes against the way my stomach rolled.

"Yeah," I muttered. "I just need a minute."

"What the hell happened?"

"How long was I out?"

"I don't know," Ryan said. "It's almost dawn. I woke up and you were gone. I found you in here, passed out with Zero above you."

"I didn't attack him," Zero said petulantly. "I wouldn't hurt him."

"He didn't," I said before Ryan could follow through with the look he shot the snake dragon. "It was…. I had a vision. I think."

Gary leaned down until we were eye level, his nose almost pressed against my face. "You trippin' balls, son? How many Garys do you see?"

"Too many," I said, shoving his face away as he cackled.

"What happened?"

"Zero agreed to help us, his face touched my face, I passed out and became a constellation and talked with the star dragon who hinted that he's rooting for us but that he can't exactly come out and say that. Oh, and I also called him a dick. You know. The usual."

Everyone gaped at me.

I sighed. "I don't know why you're all acting so surprised. This is the kind of shit that happens to us all the godsdamned time. I'm actually getting kind of sick of it. For once, why can't I just be a normal twentysomething who goes out and gets drunk and ends up having sloppy drunk sex with his boyfriend while eating cake off his ass?"

The gaping continued.

"What," I said, sounding grumpy. "It's a thing."

"I don't want your ass cake," Tiggy said solemnly. "No more cake for Tiggy."

Ryan helped me up, arm wrapped around my waist. The lights of Zero's magic were gone, and the forest around us was dark, but I felt… lighter, somehow. Like a burden had been lifted from my shoulders. I glanced at Zero, who was curled in on himself, looking pensive and nervous, like he'd done something wrong.

"It worked, didn't it?" I asked him.

"I'm sorry," he said quickly. "I didn't know what was going to happen. I didn't mean—"

"Zero."

He flinched.

I pulled away from Ryan and took a slow step toward the snake dragon. He looked as if he was about to flee, but I reached up and touched his face, trailing my fingers along his jaw. I thought he'd jerk his head back, and for a moment, he almost did. But then I pressed my hand firmly against him, and he shuddered before nuzzling into my touch. There was a spark deep within me, and it felt like his firefly lights, like he'd given me part of himself. It was warm and sweet, and it felt *right*, like it was supposed to be there. Like *he* was supposed to be there. But it was still timid, unsure.

"Thank you," I said.

"You really want me?" he whispered.

"I do."

"And you think I can help?"

"Yes. Because you're not a villain, Zero. And when this is over, I will help you make things beautiful again."

And for the first time, Zero smiled at me, a wide, toothy thing that was really rather remarkable.

That spark in me burned a little brighter at that.

"ARE YOU SURE ABOUT THIS?" RYAN asked, watching as Kevin carried Tiggy across the divide. The dragon had already brought Gary and Ruv across, given the stone path had been broken during the mermaid attack. "It just feels… weird. Leaving him here."

I glanced back over my shoulder where Zero lay curled up behind us, tail twitching back and forth. "Yeah," I said. "I'm sure. He needs to stay here for now. He's not ready to leave yet. And I'm not ready for him. There's still work to do."

"The other dragons," he said.

"I don't know how they'll react," I admitted. "And I don't want anything to happen to him."

"Ah, but that doesn't necessarily bode well for the rest of us."

I laughed, leaning over to kiss him on the cheek. "I'll protect you, babe. I got your back."

He rolled his eyes, but I could see the blush on his face. "Maybe I want to protect *you*," he muttered.

"Yeah, yeah, big strong knight. I get you."

"What if Myrin comes for him?"

That name. I felt chilled every time I heard it. "Even if he does, Zero's already chosen. I trust him."

He searched my face for something. What, I didn't know. "And you don't think someone like Myrin could bend another's will?"

"I don't think it's possible for someone to make a dragon do anything they don't want to do."

"You have a lot of faith in that."

"I have to," I admitted. "Because the alternative scares me."

"North, then? To Randall."

Hurray for conversational whiplash. I thought maybe he did it on purpose. "Yes," I said stiffly. "To Randall."

Ryan sighed as he hooked an arm around my shoulders, pulling me close. "You ever gonna tell me what happened?"

Even though I knew what he meant, I played dumb. "With what?"

"Sam."

"Ryan."

"You know more than you're telling me. About all of this. About Myrin and Randall. Morgan."

"I'm still… working through it. It's a lot. More than I thought it would be."

"You need more time."

I nodded.

"And you're not withholding anything that could hurt us?"

That was tougher, but I shook my head anyway.

"Okay," he said. "That's fair. But you know when you're ready, I'll be here, right?"

I knew that. I knew that probably better than anything else. I leaned in and kissed him again, a little desperate, but his mouth opened against mine, and the press of his tongue was light and wet. His arm was still around my shoulders, his other hand cupping my face, and I allowed him to direct the kiss.

"That shit's so hot," Kevin said as he landed. "Oops. Didn't mean to interrupt. Don't mind me, though, if you want to keep going. I could even give you some pointers if you wanted. Sam, lick his—"

I sighed against Ryan's smile. "It's not funny."

"If I didn't laugh, I'd be screaming," Ryan assured me, kissing me on the tip of the nose. He stepped away. "You first?"

I shook my head. "Gonna say goodbye to Zero."

"Great. So I'll just let Kevin carry me across the gigantic divide by hanging from his claws."

"I promise I'll try to not drop you," Kevin said. "And I'm mostly good at keeping my promises. Though if you want, I could always just chuck you across. See how good the old arm is. Sam! Tell your side of beef I've got a good throwing arm. Sam knows. I play ball with my boy. Father-son time, you know."

"Kevin, don't throw my boyfriend across the cavern."

"You sure?"

"Pretty sure."

"You guys are no fun," Kevin grumbled.

"What do you mean *pretty sure*?" Ryan asked me with a scowl.

"Love you," I said sweetly before turning back toward Zero.

"There," Kevin said as I walked away. "You've said your goodbyes. You've had a little lip action. We appreciate you flying Kevin Air, emergency exits are all around you, but I suggest you use them only if you have a death wish. Should there be a water landing, I'm sure your ego could be used as a flotation device."

"Har, har, can we just—*holy fucking gods, why are you going so fast!*"

The sand and dust kicked up around me as Kevin rocketed into the air. I glanced up, lifting my hand against the sun in time to see Kevin catching an updraft and flying far higher than he should have, just to fuck with Ryan. I was going to give Ryan so much shit about the way he was screaming. It was awesome.

Zero was waiting for me, lying in the shade of a crumbling battlement. I hadn't been lying when I told Ryan that it was better if Zero stayed here. I honestly believed that. But I couldn't help but think that I wanted him with us, at my side, so I could keep an eye on him. I'd known him for less than a day, but I already felt protective of him. Maybe it was his mental age. Maybe it was because of his insecurities. Or maybe it was just because for all intents and purposes, he was my dragon, just like Kevin was. I didn't know him as well as Kevin, but I could feel him like I could the other dragon, though I wasn't sure when that had happened. I had my suspicions, but I'd have to ask Kevin about it.

Zero understood. In fact, I thought he was probably relieved that he'd be staying behind, at least for now. It was a lot to take in. And it felt… right, that we had a deadline, given that he'd only be awake for a year. Everything would be said and done by the time the year was over. It had to be. There was no other choice.

"You didn't tell them," he said.

I arched an eyebrow at him. "Tell them what?"

"What the star dragon told you."

This made me pause. "You heard?"

"Bits and pieces. It was… blurred. Like a dream."

"You can dream?" I asked, unsure why this surprised me.

Zero sounded amused. "I *am* alive."

"What do you dream about?"

"Trees. Fire. Flowers. Stars."

"Why do you dream of fire?" I asked.

He snorted, and a little curl of smoke shot from his nose. "I'm a dragon. I was born in fire," he said. "Why didn't you tell them?"

I watched him for a moment, trying to decide what to say. It felt important, like he was testing me. And I wanted to get this right. Finally I said,

"Do you believe the gods are absolute? That they control everything?"

"If you're asking me about free will, I'll remind you that I'm fourteen and really only care about myself."

I couldn't help it: I laughed. "Dude. You're an ass."

He smiled, looking rather pleased with himself. "I like making you laugh. It's a nice sound. Can I tell you something?"

I nodded.

"When I was five, humans came for me. I don't know if they were terrible people. I don't know if they were villains, or if they were just scared of something they didn't understand, but they wanted my blood spilled upon the earth."

My hands twitched to reach out and touch him, but I kept them at my side.

"I escaped, but not before they'd cut me. Broke through some of my scales. I thought about hurting them, about putting my teeth into their flesh, but I couldn't make myself do it. I didn't understand them, and they didn't understand me, even when I cried at them to stop, that I would leave if they just let me. They didn't let me. I got away, but only after I knocked them down. I didn't mean to, but I hurt one of them. A woman. She hit her head on something. A rock, I think. It was scary, because she was bleeding and crying, and I just wanted to go. I tried to tell her that I was sorry, but she thought I was coming to eat her, because she screamed and ran away. So I left."

"It doesn't matter if they were villains or not," I said. "No one should hurt another just for the sake of doing it. Or because they're scared."

"But aren't you scared?" he asked me. "You're scared, and you're going to have to hurt someone. To stop this. Because when a life ends, it hurts."

"My hand is being forced."

"Maybe those people who came for me thought the same thing. That they were being forced."

"Did you hurt anyone?" I asked him. "Did you give them any reason to see you as a threat?"

"No."

"Then what they did was wrong."

"Is that absolute?"

I balked at that, wondering how he'd been able to complete that circle.

"They chose to come for me," Zero said. "They made their decision out of fear. Am I supposed to believe that was the path the gods set them on? That if they'd succeeded, that my life didn't matter as much as theirs did?"

"Dude," I breathed. "So heavy."

"No," he said. "I don't believe things are set in stone. Look around you, Sam. Stone crumbles. Be it from time and age or the minds of men, it still crumbles. But I also think when a dragon god tells you something, you should listen. And maybe you should tell those closest to you about it."

"It's Ryan," I blurted. I winced. "Shit."

Zero's eyes went wide. "What?"

I hadn't meant to say that out loud. I thought voicing it would make it more real. I didn't want it to be real. "Vadoma showed me," I said begrudgingly. "My grandmother. In one of her visions. Sooner or later, Ryan will die."

"Everything dies, Sam," Zero said lightly. "It's the price we pay for being alive."

"Do you believe in me?" I asked. "Do you believe I can do what I say I can do?"

"Yes," Zero said promptly.

"Then you best believe me when I say that I will see that stone turn to dust before I let anything happen to him. I don't care what Vadoma says. I don't care what the star dragon says. He's not going anywhere."

"Chills," Zero whispered. "So many chills. I want someone to love me the way you love him."

I smiled at him. "One day, someone will. They call us HaveHeart, you know. For Sam Haversford and Ryan Foxheart."

Have you ever heard a fourteen-year-old snake dragon monster thing squeal like he's just heard the greatest thing in the world? I have. It was a lot louder than I thought it would be. "Oh my *gods*," he said. "I could just *die*."

A shadow passed overhead as Kevin returned.

Immediately, Zero's smile dropped off his face, and he slumped down when Kevin landed near us. "Everything's lame," Zero moaned. "It's all so lame. None of you understand what it's like to be me."

I wasn't fooled.

Kevin was, but I let it slide. "Little bro, you need to listen to me. You listening?"

Zero harrumphed but said nothing.

"Your big bro is gonna lay some advice down on you. You get me? Some real life-changing shit."

"Great," Zero muttered. "Just what I wanted."

"If you ever want to get some dick, you gotta chill with that whole me-against-the-world thing."

"Uh," I said. "I don't know if that's the best advice."

"Of course it is," Kevin said. "It's coming from me. That means it's automatically the best advice ever."

"See," I said. "I don't think that's a thing. In fact, I would say the opposite is actually truer."

"You'd be wrong. I get laid all the time."

"So do I."

Kevin rolled his eyes. "Yeah, but yours is married sex. That's so boring. Me, I'm not tied down. I've spread my wings, and I'm going to *fly* straight into some butt."

"We're not *married*," I said, wondering yet again how it got to this point. "Don't even *say* that."

"Why not?"

"Because," I sputtered. "You could, like, I don't know. *Jinx* it or something."

"Right," Kevin said, sounding gleeful. "And the only way it'd be jinxed was because you were thinking about it, right?"

The blood drained from my face. "You shut your whore mouth," I said.

"You *have* been! Oh man, I can't *wait* to tell—"

"You breathe a word about this and I swear to the gods, I'll curse your dick off."

"—absolutely no one because it's not their business and I don't even know what we're talking about," Kevin finished. "Zero, it's been fun. It's always good to meet another dragon for the first time in my life. Stay real, little bro."

He scampered off toward the stone path.

"He's… not right in the head, is he?" Zero asked.

I sighed. "That's still up for debate. You gonna be okay?"

Zero rolled his eyes. "I've only been without you for fourteen hundred years. I think I can handle a few weeks until you're ready."

I reached out and pressed my palm on his snout. His eyes fluttered closed, and he hummed a little under his breath. I thought it was probably involuntary, but I couldn't help but smile at the sound. "You need me, you come find me, you hear? If someone comes for you, you run. There is no shame in running, Zero. I'd rather have you safe and at my side than have you fighting alone."

He opened his eyes. "I can handle myself."

"I know," I said. "But you're not alone anymore, okay?"

"You're not going to convince me to come with right now by being mushy."

"Wouldn't even dream about it." I dropped my hand. "See you, Zero."

I started to walk away.

I'd only made it a few steps when he called my name.

I looked back over my shoulder.

"You need to tell them," he said. "Everything. Because secrets have a way of coming out when you least expect it. They deserve to know. He deserves to know. Stone crumbles, Sam. It always crumbles. Remember that."

And then he slithered toward the dome, wings tucked at his sides.

Godsdamn him for getting the last word. I *never* got the last word.

That dick.

Kevin was waiting for me near the edge of the island. He eyed me carefully as I approached. I could see the others on the far side of the cavern, standing on a sand dune, waiting for us so we could head back to Mashallaha.

"Is he going to be okay?" Kevin asked.

"I think so."

"He's... not what I expected."

"Is that good or bad?"

Kevin shrugged. "Neither, I think. It just... is. I always wondered what it would be like. Meeting another dragon. If I would feel any connection to them because of what we were. How few of us are left."

"And did you feel a connection?"

He looked surprised. "Yeah. Just... protective, you know? He's only a kid."

"And yet he's technically older than you."

"It's best not to focus on the logistics," Kevin said wisely. "It's easier to just roll with it."

"I feel like that pretty much sums up our lives."

"Eh. I have no complaints."

Something Zero had said ran through my mind then. "Kevin? Where did you come from?"

He cocked his head at me. "The jungles," he said. "You know that, Sam. Beast from the East and all that. If you've forgotten, I can give you my whole spiel again. I don't mind."

"No, no," I said hastily. "That's okay. And I'm not talking about... that. Who are your parents?"

He blinked at me before he started laughing. "My *parents*? Oh, Sam. Sam, Sam, Sam. You know *nothing* about dragons, do you? Wow. How the hell are we your *destiny*? You poor, poor sexy man-child. I feel bad for you. And slightly aroused. But mostly bad. And aroused."

I scowled at him.

"Magic," he said, wiping his eyes. "Sam, we're born from magic. We don't have parents. We are created when the world needs us most. There's magic everywhere, in the smallest of things. Once there's enough concentration of it, and once the world wills it so, a dragon is born."

"But... but, that's so *stupid*," I exclaimed. "What the fuck is that esoteric *bullshit*?"

"Oh boy," Kevin said. "Hey, champ. You okay? Your worldview expanding because your tiny little mind was just blown? Yeah. You're okay."

"But how do you *know* that if you've never met a dragon before?"

"How do turtles know to head for the sea once they hatch? Instinct, Sam. It's ingrained into us."

"I'll *never* understand dragons," I said grumpily as I crossed my arms over my chest. "They make no sense whatsoever."

"That's because we're amazing."

"That's *not* what I mean."

"Shh," he said. "Shh. It's okay. I heard what you didn't say. I got you.

Your mouth is saying no, but your body is saying yes."

"God, that was so rapey."

"I doubt that. The body wants what it wants."

"You're stupid."

"Says the man who didn't know where dragons came from. Hi, I'm Sam of Wilds. I have a destiny of dragons, but guess what? I don't know a single thing about them!"

"I thought it was supposed to be a fairy tale! And I don't sound that high-pitched and whiny!"

"He said, whining in a high-pitched voice, like the insignificant little speck of dust that he was."

"You ass."

"You love me."

"Yeah, yeah. Ferry me across, Lord Dragon."

He bowed low. "But of course, sweet cheeks." He reached a hand to carefully pick me up and held me close to his chest. But before he could spread his wings, I said his name. "Hmm?"

"I felt him," I said. "After. With his firefly lights."

"So you said."

"It's not the same, you know? Like it is with you. He's a part of us, but not like you are."

"Are you hitting on me? I'm flattered, but I don't know if now's a good time. Oh, who am I kidding, it's *always* a good time. Take off your pants."

"Kevin."

"Sam."

"When did you become mine? When did you know?"

Kevin looked taken aback, like he hadn't expected the question. He opened his mouth once, twice, and then sighed. He held me up until I was eye level with him. His teeth were razor sharp, but I didn't fear them. I didn't fear him. He was my friend, and I would do anything for him, just like he'd do for me. "You remember that night at my keep? After Ryan left with the Prince."

I did. My heart had been broken. Everything felt like it'd been crashing down. I had kissed Ryan, and he'd kissed me back, almost with the same breath he'd used to tell me he couldn't—*wouldn't*—break his oath to Justin. The stars had been bright above.

Where did you come from?

Far away.

What were you looking for?

A place to call my own.

And I remember thinking how this creature—this magical, wonderful creature—infuriated the shit out of me. That even though it felt like I was bleeding out on the stones of the keep, he was being enough of a dick to help me forget how much I hurt.

I've seen things. Many different things. There are lands far away from here that you couldn't even possibly dream of. I've seen cliffs of ice so tall they disappear into the clouds. I've seen flowers deep in jungles that eat everything that happens by them. I've seen the hearts of men, the darkness that lies within. I've been captured by wizards who wanted nothing more than to spill my blood to make their spells. I've seen people cower in fear at the mere sight of me. I've seen a city that floats in the clouds, and the beings that live there have translucent skin and cannot speak for they have no mouths. I've seen a volcano erupting during a lightning storm, ash in the sky as the mountain explodes. I've seen many things, pretty.

And I hadn't understood him. I hadn't understood what that had to do with me.

But he'd known that. Because he was far smarter than I could ever know.

I've seen many things. Both good and evil. Majestic and destructive. Stars falling from the sky and a man whose tattoos moved across his skin as if they were alive before he tried to rip one of my hearts from my chest. I have seen many, many things. But I have never seen one look at another the way the knight looks at you.

One day I'll believe you.

And one day, maybe I could be there to tell you I told you so.

And he'd curled around me that night, holding me together even though I'd wanted to fly apart. I'd told him of the City of Lockes, and that night, when I'd dreamed of home, Kevin had dreamed along with me.

"You made me feel like I could belong," Kevin said quietly. "I told you that I'd left to find a home. To find a place I could call my own. To feel safe for the first time in my life. You told me you wouldn't hurt me."

I smiled faintly at the memory. "Unless you tried to get all up in my business again. Which you totally do. Daily."

"You like it," he rumbled happily. "But I remember seeing how you and Gary and Tiggy were with each other, and I wanted that for my own. Desperately, in fact. I think that's what I wished for. Under all those stars. That I could belong to you. That I could belong *with* you. And I think the stars granted my wish."

"I'm not crying," I said with a sniff. "*You're* crying. Stupid dragon with your stupid fucking stories that make me want to punch your face and then hug you."

"I love you too." Kevin sounded amused. Then, "Do you think it'll be like that for him? For Zero? Can you make him feel safe?"

I looked over Kevin's shoulder back at the dome. I didn't know if Zero heard us talking, but I had a feeling he was listening to every word. "I'll try."

"Good, pretty. That's all I can ask for. Should we vomit more feelings on each other, or should we get back to the others? I'm pretty sure Ryan is about to shit himself with worry."

"Right? He really needs to learn to calm down."

"I've got a few ideas on that. Have you guys ever thought about couple's erotic massage? It works wonders on stress."

"I don't even want to know."

"I'm licensed in the City of Lockes to administer such massages if you wanted to consider it."

"No. You're not. That's not even a real thing."

"It totally is. I have a piece of paper and everything."

"Oh my gods."

"My malt brings all the boys to the vestibule."

"What does that even *mean*? What the hell is you—you know what? I don't even care."

Kevin spread his wings and laughed as we left the island and the snake dragon known as Zero Ravyn Moonfire behind.

CHAPTER 21
The True Cornerstone

RETURNING TO MASHALLAHA WENT QUICKER THAN I expected it to. Maybe it was the fact that we'd succeeded in what we'd set out to do, that something had actually *worked* the first time we'd attempted it, even if it'd been a bit of a bumpy road to get there. I didn't know what it was I'd expected, but I didn't think it mattered. We'd gotten the desert dragon on our side. I had Kevin already. That was two out of the five. The Great White had said I wasn't ready. The star dragon had said there would be a sacrifice. But we'd come out ahead so far. And Zero was right: stone crumbled. We would prove everyone wrong, like we always did. I didn't care if the gods themselves decried us. We would show them. I had faith in those around me. I had faith in myself. I wasn't going to be controlled by Vadoma. I wasn't doing this for Morgan or Randall. I was doing this because it was the right thing to do. And I *would* do this.

Stone crumbled.

Ruv went ahead as soon as we'd gotten into view of Mashallaha, saying he wanted to report to Vadoma as quickly as possible. He snapped open his sailboard and took off down the dunes, the wind at his back. Before he got too far, he turned and winked at me.

"Reporting to Vadoma?" Gary asked. "That didn't sound ominous at all."

"He's probably a spy," Ryan grumbled. "Gathering intel to give to Vadoma."

"You just don't like him because Vadoma wanted him to be my cornerstone," I told him. "If he was anyone else, you'd think he was great."

"No," Ryan said, lying through his teeth. "He rubs me the wrong way."

"I could teach him how to rub if he's doing it wrong," Kevin said.

I ignored him and focused on Ryan. "You know it's nothing, right? There's nothing there."

"Tell your magic that."

I rolled my eyes. "You knew there was more than one. That there could be multiple cornerstones."

"Yeah, but I never expected to *meet* one," he said. "And am I the only one thinking about *how* Vadoma knew that? She didn't know you. She knew *of* you. How could she know who your magic would react to?"

That... was a fair point. "Huh. I never thought about that."

"Knight Delicious Face has brains *and* brawns," Tiggy said.

Ryan preened a little at that. Like a show dog.

"Maybe it was her visions," I said, though I was loath to give any credence to that. I still thought her more of a fortune-teller than an actual seer. Maybe the star dragon had been a fluke, and everything else she'd done was smoke and mirrors. The Great White had said I wasn't ready, but how did I know that had even happened? And the warnings about Ryan's death. For all I knew she'd been manipulating me from the beginning, showing me only what she wanted me to see.

Stone crumbles, Zero had said.

And it did. But not if it was an illusion. Not if it was sleight-of-hand street magic.

"We shouldn't trust her, kitten," Gary said, pulling me from my thoughts. "Nor him, though he seems... enthusiastic. I think he's harmless, but you can't be too careful. We don't know what Vadoma's been feeding him all these years."

Gary was right. Throwing caution to the wind would only end up getting us in trouble.

The problem?

That's pretty much how we operated.

WHEN WE WALKED INTO MASHALLAHA a few hours later, we were greeted quite differently than we'd been the first time. Where we'd initially been met with distrust and derision, the gypsies now welcomed us as if we were the long-lost brothers of the clan. It was rather alarming, this change, because I couldn't prove its veracity. These were the same people who had looked upon me with disdain because my skin wasn't as dark as theirs. These were the people who had shunned my mother because she chose to love outside the clan. These were the people who didn't seem to want to lift a finger to help us in any way.

I didn't know if it had to do with Vadoma announcing that Ruv was my cornerstone before we left, but I thought it was a possibility. My suspicions seemed confirmed when Kevin and Gary and Tiggy had brightly colored scarves draped around their necks, similar to the one around mine, but Ryan was all but ignored. We'd been gone for just over a week. Which meant Vadoma had had eight days to fill her peoples' heads with more of her rhetoric.

Oh man, were we gonna have some words.

To make sure he wasn't separated from us or left behind somehow, I grabbed Ryan's hand tightly, making sure he was at my side. There were grimaces on the faces of the people around us at the sight of him, but they continued to ignore him.

Welcome home, they said.

We knew you'd succeed, they said.

You have tamed the desert dragon, they said.

We've never known such joy, they said.

An illusion.

It all felt like an illusion.

We were herded toward Vadoma's home. I would have preferred to shower and change out of my dusty clothes, to curl up in a bed with Ryan and sleep the rest of the day away, but we weren't even given the option. I went with it, knowing the sooner we saw her, the sooner all of this would be finished. I wanted to leave Mashallaha as soon as possible. Tomorrow, if we could. We had a long road ahead of us to the mountains in the north and Castle Freeze Your Ass Off. Randall would be expecting us before too long.

I also needed to speak to Morgan, to let him know what had happened. And I wanted to hear my parents' voices. To let them know we were alive. That we'd done what we'd come to Mashallaha to do.

So, yes. The very last thing I wanted to do was see Vadoma.

But it didn't matter.

She was waiting for us in front of her carriages, Ruv at her side. He'd cleaned up, face scrubbed, wearing soft-looking trousers. He was shirtless and had a red-and-green band wrapped around his right bicep. He was smiling quietly as we approached.

Even Vadoma looked happy, which was weird. In the time that I'd known her, she'd *never* looked happy. Not like she did now. It was disconcerting, like she knew something we didn't. It reminded me of a predator.

We were ushered to the front of the crowd, the gypsies gathering behind us. I kept my hand in Ryan's, silently daring her to say anything about it. And I wasn't going to be the first one to speak here. If this was a game to her, then I was going to try and maintain the upper hand.

I didn't have to wait long.

"Welcome back," she said, her voice carrying out into the crowd. "I have been informed of your success."

I remembered my training. I bowed my head in deference. Morgan would have been proud. "We did indeed achieve what we set out to do."

"And the desert dragon has committed itself to your cause?"

"*He* has, yes," I said.

She didn't even flinch at the warning in my voice. "Then you have begun the journey that has been placed before you. I have seen this path. I have seen the future and the possible outcomes. This is but one step in your ascension."

"My ascension?" I said, confused. "Into what?"

Her smile widened. "Into the wizard that you are supposed to become." Her eyes flickered over my companions, resting on Ryan briefly before she looked at me. "Though I'm sure the components of your journey can still be... negotiated."

"Oh, is she trying to be undercover salty?" Gary muttered behind me. "Because Gary is starting to feel the need to bring the *pain*."

And because I didn't think Unicorn Rage was something we wanted to deal with right at the moment, I said, "Perhaps you and I can speak in private. To discuss these... components."

"I don't think that's a good idea," Ryan whispered.

"Trust me on this," I said quietly. "I know what I'm doing."

He snorted. "You never know what you're doing."

"Rude," I said. "But mostly true."

"But of course," Vadoma said. "There is nothing more I want than to speak to my grandson about the future. Come, *chava*. As for the rest of you, we have much to celebrate! Let us show our guests how much we appreciate the lengths they go to for the people of Verania."

The gypsies cheered around us.

They sounded bright and happy.

It still felt like an illusion.

WE WERE ALONE WHEN SHE SAID, "You must be tired after your travels. I won't take much of your time." She sat behind her desk and folded her hands in front of her.

I sat in the chair across from her desk. My legs were sore. I had sand in places I didn't want to think of. And so I don't know that I could be blamed when I said, "You can drop the act now. We're alone, and we both know I'm not buying what you're selling."

She chuckled. "Is it so hard to believe I am happy for your return?"

"Anybody else, I would say no. Of course not. But you're not anybody else. You're the *phuro*. The seer. The manipulator."

The smile faded into a more calculating look. It was chilling how quickly it happened. One moment she was the loving grandmother, and the next she was a hardened leader capable of squashing anyone who got in her way. I wasn't concerned. I'd faced worse than her and come off the better. She wasn't a villain, but she wasn't someone I would trust. Not now. Probably not ever.

"I keep having to remind myself you're smarter than they say," she said. "It's... surprising."

I shrugged. "You can't always believe what you hear."

"Oh, I am aware," she said. "But I don't think you realize just *how much* is said about you, Sam of Wilds."

"I am the future King's Wizard. People know my name."

She shook her head. "You mistake my meaning. Yes, they know your name. They whisper it amongst each other. But do you know what is truly said about you?"

"I don't know that I care."

She scoffed. "That's certainly not true. Everyone does, no matter if they speak to the contrary. Especially you, who will be a leader amongst men. How can you say you don't care about the will of the people?"

"I didn't say that."

"You implied it." She sat back in her chair. It creaked beneath her. "Most are in awe of you. Whether it be because of your magic or because of your rise from such... humble beginnings, there is a fascination with you. It doesn't hurt that you carry with you a tongue of silver. There is an irony in calling me a manipulator when you are well-versed in the same, no?"

And as much as I wanted to disagree with her, to shoot her down, we both knew it would have been a lie. Because I *did* manipulate, even if I wasn't thinking of it in that way at the time. I'd talked my way out of many a dangerous situation, turned the tables until I had the advantage. It wasn't as nefarious as she was implying, but I wasn't an innocent party in this.

I said, "I have my reasons."

"I'm sure," she said. "Better alive than dead."

I didn't reply.

"Most are in awe of you," she said again. "But not all. There are... detractors. Those who think you have been given too much power too soon. That you are capable of destruction. Of bending the will of the King." She smiled, but it was a cool thing. "Of murder."

"I haven't murdered anyone."

"I am sure the Darks would disagree with you on that."

"Lartin?" I said, outraged. "He had *captured* us. He was planning on attempting to *ransom* me because of who I was."

"In exchange for?"

"Gold."

"So he deserved to die?"

"I don't—it was him or us."

She frowned. "That's a disturbing mentality to have for someone who will one day be an advisor to a king."

"He was a *Dark*."

"And some think Darks are only those who have lost their way."

I laughed. "Is that what you think? They've made their choices. They've set themselves on a path where they *know* what will happen. There is no one to blame but themselves."

"I wasn't speaking of Lartin, though he does add to my point."

I blinked. "Who the hell were you speaking of? I haven't murdered anyone—"

"Wan. The Dark Hunter."

"Wan," I said. My skin felt cold. "I had nothing to do with *Wan*."

"But you were there."

"How did you—"

She pulled open a drawer of her desk and pulled out a bundled-up newspaper. She slid it across the surface of the desk until it was in front of me. I looked down at it. It was a copy of the *City of Lockes Gazette*, dated a week ago, just after we'd left for the desert dragon.

"How did you get this?" I asked. "They don't distribute the *Gazette* all the way out here."

"I have my ways. And I thought the story on the front page would interest you."

I didn't want to look, because this felt like another of her games. Like this too was an illusion. But curiosity had always been a weakness of mine, and I unfolded the newspaper.

The headline was sensational and accusatory:

DARK DIES IN CAPTIVITY WHILE BEING QUESTIONED BY SAM OF WILDS!

The article was pure speculation, and aside from saying that I was present and that Wan had died, was completely false. It said sources had revealed that Wan was under duress given *the Wizard's apprentice's inter-rogation techniques* and *that Sam of Wilds refused to render aid when it became apparent that there was a medical emergency.* It went on, making sure to skirt that fine line of fact and fiction, saying, *although this has yet to be corroborated, what has been confirmed by the official spokesperson to the Good King is that Wan the Dark Hunter did indeed pass away while incarcerated. "Details will be provided once the investigation has been completed," the spokesperson said. "Given the serious nature of the matter, the King cautions his subjects against conjecture, that the truth will come in due time."*

When reached for a comment on the matter, the president of the We-Hate-Sam-A-Lot Castle Lockes Chapter, Lady Tina DeSilva, said, "It is un-fortunate that yet another person has met their end by the hands of Sam of Wilds. Allegedly. It is also unfortunate that people are just now learning what I've known for years, that Sam of Wilds is a danger to the populace and will stop at nothing until his machinations are fully realized and he has usurped the throne. Allegedly. Since I have my ear to the ground, I've heard that Wan the Dark Hunter met an end similar to that of Lartin the Dark Leaf, violent and bloody, which is no surprise, given Sam's unending rage. Allegedly. And where is Ryan Foxheart in all of this? One might say he is complicit, but one would be wrong. In fact, if one says that at all, one should be dragged out into the street and tarred and feathered for having the audacity to say something so atrocious—ahem. Excuse me. What I meant to say is that an operation to rescue Ryan Foxheart from the clutches of Sam of Wilds should be mounted immediately and performed without regard to Sam's life. Ryan is undoubtedly under some sort of mind-control spell because that is the only reason he would have left Prince Justin at the altar. Ryan must be returned where he belongs, at the side of the Prince, so they can be in love and have babies and hold hands and whisper how much they love each other and give each other forehead kisses, because everyone knows that forehead kisses are the sweetest and most adorable thing that has ever existed. Long live Rystin!"

It should be noted that a petition to have Sam of Wilds removed from his position as the apprentice to the King's Wizard has garnered over ten thousand signatures....

I set the paper down.

I took a deep breath and let it out slowly.

It didn't matter. None of it mattered.

It didn't matter that I was out here, so far from home, working off a prophecy from the gods in order to save the world. It didn't matter that the very people I was trying to protect were apparently turning against me. None of that mattered. It didn't change anything. I would still do what was being asked of me. When this was all said and done, the people of Verania would see that everything I'd done had been to protect them. They'd see. They'd all see.

I ignored the little voice that whispered I was lying to myself. That I'd done this for selfish reasons. That I was here because I couldn't let Ryan die. That I hadn't even thought of the fate of the world.

"I can't control what they think," I said, voice even. "And there's nothing in here based in fact."

"True," she said with a nod of her head. "But since when is the news concerned about truth?"

"Was there a point you were trying to make?"

"My *point*, Sam, is that I am trying to help you become the leader I know you'll be. You may not believe this, but I want nothing but the best for you, *chava*. I want you to succeed."

"But you want me to do it the way you say."

She shrugged. "Can't the same be said for Morgan? For Randall? Are you or are you not following the path they set for you?"

"I trust them. I don't trust you."

"I've never lied to you, Sam. Can they say the same?"

And if that wasn't just a kick in the nuts. "How do I know that's true?"

"I've never had any reason to. Sam, I have a vested interest in seeing the world remain as it is. These people are my people. I am the *phuro* because they placed their faith in me. And it is my duty to protect them at all costs.

Why would I lie, especially if it meant harm could come to them? I would sacrifice myself if it meant the darkness would not fall upon them. They are not meant to live in shadow. The gypsies are meant to bask in the sun."

"You told them that Ruv was my cornerstone," I said through gritted teeth, trying to hold on to any semblance of truth that I could. "You knew full well that I would never accept him. That I had Ryan. That I would *always* have Ryan."

"I am the *phuro*," she said again. "I would protect them. But it also means I am a politician. I curried their favor toward you. They allowed their prejudices to cloud their eyes. I gave you the chance to be seen in a different light. I did what I did for *you*."

"You really believe that."

"Yes."

"And what will you do when they realize I will never be with Ruv?"

"You seem sure about that, *chava*."

I banged my fist on her desk. She didn't even flinch. "I *am* sure about it."

"Well, then," she said. "I will have lied. And I will deal with the fall-out. But tell me, Sam. How can you know what the future holds? You cannot see as I have."

I stood. The chair scraped along the wooden floor. "We leave," I said, "in the morning. Me. Ryan. Gary. Tiggy. Kevin. That is it."

"And the desert dragon?"

"Will remain where he is until I'm ready for him."

"And how will you know when you're ready?"

"When I have them all."

"So you have accepted your destiny because of what I've shown you."

I leaned forward, my hands on the desk. "No. Not because of what you've shown me. Because it's the godsdamned right thing to do. I don't know what you're after, Vadoma. But you would do well to stay out of my way."

She laughed. It grated against my ears. "Oh, Sam. You truly are beyond what I had hoped for. But I must remind you again: I have never lied to you. Can you name someone else in your life that can say the same?"

"I don't have to answer to you."

Her eyes narrowed. "Do you know who I am? Who you're talking to?"

I grinned sharply at her. "Do *you*? Because I'm Sam of Wilds. I'm the apprentice to the King's Wizard. And I will do whatever it takes to keep those I love safe."

"Your cockiness will be your undoing," she said. "The power you wield will not protect you from everything."

"It's a start," I retorted. "And I'll figure out the rest. I mean it, Vadoma. Back. *Off*."

I turned and walked away without looking back.

I was glad she wasn't able to hear the racing of my heart.

I HATED TO ADMIT THAT, ABOVE all else, Vadoma had made a good point. It was easier being in Mashallaha when the people there weren't being racist fucktards. It didn't exactly endear them to me to see how fickle they could be with their affections. That night, as the celebration went on, it was like their previous actions had never happened. They smiled at me. They laughed around me. Men and women grabbed me by the hand and pulled me out to dance, spinning around and around as dresses and feet were kicked up. I had garlands of flowers placed around my neck, beads tied into my hair. They treated me as if I was one of them, as if I belonged.

If this had happened at the beginning, maybe things would have been different. But they hadn't, and I saw through it for what it was: a farce.

Kevin was revered as he always was, regaling the crowd around him with stories that were expectedly untrue, not that anyone else knew.

Gary and Tiggy were given the same welcome I was. Tiggy was pleased, and Gary acted like he was too, but I could see the tightness around his eyes, the calculating look on his face when he thought no one was looking. He didn't trust them in the slightest. After a while, I saw Gary lean over and whisper something into Tiggy's ear that caused him to frown at the people around him, not that they noticed.

Ryan was ignored as if he didn't exist. He was amused by it.

"You just think it's funny because you're the other woman," I accused him as yet another new adoring fan of mine skipped away after not having even acknowledged Ryan sitting next to me.

"Wow," he said. "That's the first time I've ever been accused of *that*."

I scowled at him. "If the high heel fits, you interloper."

"Not one of my kinks," he said easily. "Though I won't tell you no if you want to try it."

"That's not... what are you even... holy gods, *really*? I mean, I don't *think* I would like that, but what do *I* know? If you'd told me a few years ago I'd get off on fucking your mouth and coming on your face while I pulled your hair, I would have—scratch that. I would have believed that in a heartbeat. Holy shit, that's super fucking hot. You know it's—*heeey*, little girl who has apparently been standing in front of me long enough to hear me say something no little girl should ever have to hear. You look... pretty."

The little girl burst into tears and ran in the opposite direction.

"Don't do drugs!" I called after her. Ryan was laughing hysterically beside me, hunched over, arms wrapped around himself. It pissed me off, but it also made my heart thump a bit in my chest that, after all the crap we'd been through, he could still laugh so freely and openly. It really was beautiful to see and hear. I also wanted to fuck him stupid right about now.

"Oh," he said, still chuckling. "You've got that look on your face."

"I have no idea what you're talking about," I said as I drooled a little bit. I wiped my mouth, feeling absolutely no shame. "So, come here often?"

He rolled his eyes. "Not really."

"Would you like to?" I waggled my eyebrows at him.

His smile softened. "You're ridiculous."

"It is part of my charm," I agreed. "Now, what say you and I get out of here and maybe I'll fuck your orifices a little bit."

"With an offer like that, I don't know how I can refuse."

"You seemed like a sure bet," I said, leaning in to kiss him. My skin felt hot, and I wanted to grab hold of him and never let go.

"Smooth talker," he said, and I could feel his breath on my face.

"I'm gonna do so many things to you in like three minutes," I growled and closed the distance to—

"Sorry to interrupt."

I groaned as I missed Ryan's lips and ended up sucking on his nose a little bit. Not the smoothest I'd ever been, but it was all Ruv's fault for even coming over to us when we were obviously about to bone.

Ryan grimaced as he pushed me off him, wiping his face. "That was unpleasant."

"It wasn't *my* fault," I said, looking up to glare at Ruv. He stood a little distance away, hands clasped behind him, looking amused. "*Someone* doesn't know what it means when I'm giving off my *I'm about to get laid* vibes. Not cool, dude. You fucking cock blocker."

"My apologies," he said, though he didn't sound sorry at all. "I was hoping to have a word with you before you became... otherwise engaged."

"That means the sex," I whispered to Ryan.

"I know what it means," he said, shoving my face away. "You dork."

"Just making sure. Sometimes, things get lost in translation."

"You're not translating anything."

I shrugged. "Same difference. Wait, what were we talking about now? Because my erection is getting really uncomfortable."

"I did that," Ryan said to Ruv, sounding smug.

"Congratulations," Ruv said slowly. "You must be so proud. A word, Sam. If you don't mind." He glanced at Ryan, then looked back at me. "Alone."

"Anything you can say to me, you can say in front of Ryan," I said. "I'll just tell him later anyway."

"Yes, I suppose you will. But I'd prefer not to get stabbed."

"Stabbed? What the hell are you—Ryan, put your sword away."

"What? I'm just *holding* it."

"And posing."

"It's not *posing*. It's the proper at-the-ready position."

"You just flipped your hair."

"It was in my eye."

"You just flourished your sword."

"It was slipping from my grasp due to the desert heat, and I wanted to make sure I had a good grip on it."

"You're flexing."

"I am? Oh, I didn't even notice. But thank *you* for pointing that out. I do look rather vascular today, don't you think?"

He really, really did. "You're not going to even be able to walk by the time I'm done with you. I'm going to fuck you so full of my—little girl, *why* do you always come at the worst possible times?"

She burst into tears again and ran away, dropping a garland of flowers.

I almost felt bad but then realized that little girls have the worst timing ever, so I couldn't be blamed. Plus, I figured it was probably better she learned now that boys were gross rather than later. When she got older, I bet she'd think twice before she did something untoward. I had done my duty in protecting the children of Verania.

"You're not going to go away, are you?" I said to Ruv, resigned.

"If you're leaving tomorrow, it's best if we talk now," he said.

"Babe, can you give us a minute?"

"I'm not going to stab him!"

"Babe."

"Okay, maybe just a little."

"You can't stab someone just a little bit."

"Watch me," he said, teeth bared.

"Just… give us a minute."

He groaned. "Fine." He sheathed his sword and shot a glare in my direction before he turned back to Ruv. He took a couple of steps until he was standing right in front of him, only inches separating them. My little dirty lizard brain screamed at them to just *kiss*, but then I realized my dirty little lizard brain was an asshole, and that I'd probably end up punching Ruv in the kidney, so I kept my mouth shut.

Ryan was intimidating as all fuck. He was a big guy, with muscles and scruff and the ability to have a wicked snarl on his face that usually scared the shit out of most people.

The problem was Ruv wasn't most people. In fact, he looked bemused at the posturing before him, like he was dealing with an irate puppy. Ruv obviously wasn't as smart as I'd given him credit for. Or maybe Ryan wasn't as daunting as I thought he was. Since one of those things threatened to change my view of the world, I decided that Ruv just had a death wish.

"I've got my eye on you," Ryan said in a low voice. "You even *look* at Sam in a way that makes him uncomfortable and I'll come back here and shove my sword through your dick until you're shitting it out."

"So violent," I whispered reverently. "I mean, it ignores how the gastrointestinal system works, but *wow*. Also, watch your fucking mouth. There are *children* present."

"I give you my word that nothing untoward will happen to Sam," Ruv said, voice even.

"Darn right, mothercracker," Ryan said. "Ryan doesn't want to have to come back and cut a bro."

"Aaaand that's enough," I said, stepping forward and pushing Ryan out of the way. "When you start sounding like Gary, you lose all credibility. Get outta here, you meathead."

Ryan hooked a hand around my neck and pulled me close, laying a filthy kiss upon my lips, more tongue and teeth than finesse. But it turned out that I'm totally on board with tongue and teeth and gave back just as good as I got. By the time he'd pulled away, my face felt scrubbed raw by the week-old stubble on his face, my lips tingling and warm. He looked smug as he backed away slowly, glancing at Ruv. He brought his hands up, palms toward the sky, and said, "Ryan out." He whirled around and headed toward Kevin, who was demanding even more gold than he'd already been given.

"Stop getting advice from Gary!" I shouted after him, a little dazed. "You stupid, sexy *asshole*."

"He certainly likes to prove his point," Ruv said, once again amused. "I suppose that's a knight, though. Blunt and forward. Lacking in finesse and subtlety."

I stared at him. "Obviously you don't know us at all if you think any of us is subtle. About anything."

"Point," he said. "Walk with me, Sam."

"You're not going to try and touch my junk, are you?" I asked him suspiciously. "Because Ryan will stab you." I frowned. "Not that I need him to. I don't need no man to take care of bidness, if you know what I mean."

"No. I really don't know what you mean. Does anyone?"

"Sometimes. Where are we going?"

"Just away from the noise. There's a dock near where you're staying that—"

"I know," I said. "I was there before we left."

He didn't seem surprised. "Good. It's not far."

I caught Ryan's eye as I followed Ruv through the crowd. I jerked my head, letting him know I'd be right back. He looked like he thought that was the stupidest idea he'd ever heard, but he got distracted by Kevin saying something to him. I was out of his sight before he ever turned back around.

The noise fell away behind us. The wood creaked under our feet, the water lapping against the posts. I had a tendency toward stupidity, but I kept my eyes open, taking in my surroundings, making sure this wasn't some feeble attempt from Vadoma to trap me in Mashallaha. I didn't think Ruv would go along with it, but I didn't really know him. He was the Wolf of Bari Lavuta. His allegiance was to his *phuro*. If it was anything like my bond with the King, I couldn't underestimate what Ruv would do on Vadoma's behalf.

The dock was empty when we stepped onto it. It swayed gently beneath our feet, but not enough to throw me off balance. A dry wind whipped over the water, a faint mist landing on our exposed skin. The stars were bright above. I'd have to remember what they looked like out here in the middle of nowhere when I was back in the City of Lockes. I didn't think I'd come back to Mashallaha. Vadoma wasn't someone I needed. Ruv was a headache I didn't want to have to worry about. When we needed Zero, we could bypass Mashallaha altogether, or I could send Kevin. Either way, I didn't want to come back to this city. It had hurt my family too much.

Ruv sat down on the edge of the dock, feet dangling down into the water. I sat beside him, sitting far enough away that we didn't touch. I didn't like how my magic felt around him, like it was comfortable, like it could be something more. Apparently my magic was a bit of a slut, given how it seemed to curl around him. Ryan felt bright and electric, like lightning. Ruv was smooth and warm, a desert wind. Ryan told me it took a long time before he was able to feel what I did, and even then, it was faint. I didn't think Ruv could feel my magic, given that I hadn't known him for very long, but it still felt... wrong. If this is what it meant to find another cornerstone, I hoped I never had to meet another one for as long as I lived.

"She's worried," Ruv said, breaking the silence.

I didn't need to ask *who*. "Why?"

"Because she doesn't think you're taking this seriously. That this is just a game to you."

I snorted. "She doesn't know me."

"Does anyone?"

"Gary does. And Tiggy. Kevin. Ryan."

"So you say. But I think sometimes you hide behind a mask, even to them."

"Right," I said dryly. "And this is based on...?"

He shrugged. "Observation. It's what I do. I watch. Your sass and snark. You have magic, but you mostly use words as weapons. There is great power within you, Sam, but you choose to hide it away."

"I'm pretty sure you were there when I destroyed all those sand mermaids," I said. "In fact, I know you were there."

"And it was an impressive display. But I think you're scared to show it."

"Great," I said. "It's always fun to be analyzed. Because I don't get enough of that in my life."

"I'm not Morgan," he said, and for the first time, I thought I saw a little crack on the cool façade. "Or Randall. I'm not Vadoma. I'm not trying to control you."

"Then what *are* you trying to do?"

He turned toward me. I didn't move away. "I'm trying to understand my part in this. All my life, I've been told I would be this... this *thing* to you. That I would be by your side and act as your cornerstone."

"I'm sorry," I said. "But I had nothing to do with that."

"I know," he said. "And I don't blame you. But you have to understand. Where your world was changed because of a destiny of dragons, *mine* was changed when the path I'd been set upon ended against a wall."

"How did she know?"

"About me being your cornerstone?"

"Being *a* cornerstone, yes."

He shrugged. "She said it was part of what she'd seen. In her visions."

"And you took her word on that?"

He smiled at me, wide and handsome. "No, Sam. I took it on faith."

"Sometimes faith steers you wrong."

"Maybe. But it'll still be there when I need it. Do you have faith, Sam?"

I thought of my mother and father.

Gary and Tiggy.

Kevin.

Morgan and Randall.

The King.

Justin.

Pete, my guard.

And Ryan. Of course I thought of Ryan.

"Yes," I said. "I have faith. And they have faith in me."

He was close. I didn't know when that had happened. His hand was on mine, pressed against the wood. His eyes were dark, glittering in the starlight.

"I could have faith in you," he said.

"You shouldn't." My magic burned.

"I could be that for you."

"You won't."

"Sam."

"Ruv."

"I'll ask you once. Do you believe that I could be your cornerstone?"

I swallowed thickly. "You could have been. But you won't ever be. Because I found the one who makes me whole. And that's all I have ever wished for."

He smiled sadly... and pulled away. I slipped my hand out from underneath his, thankful that he wasn't pushing this.

"This is where our paths diverge, isn't it?" he asked.

"I think so," I said honestly.

He laughed. It sounded a little hollow, but I didn't blame him. If anything, I blamed Vadoma for filling his head with something that could never be. It was yet another life she'd interfered with, and it wasn't fair. "For what it's worth, Sam of Wilds, I think you aren't what anyone expects you to be."

I smiled at him. "Thank you, Ruv."

He leaned forward, and for a moment, I thought he was going to kiss me. Before I could pull away, he pressed his lips to my forehead, the lightest of touches, and then he was up and walking back down the dock. His footsteps fell away until there were no sounds but the water.

I looked up toward the stars and breathed.

RYAN FOUND ME A LITTLE WHILE later. I'd been planning on using the summoning crystal to talk to Morgan, maybe even Mom and Dad, but the crystal was back in the room I shared with Ryan, and I couldn't force myself to go up and get it. I was too tired, too angry, too worried, too… everything.

I heard someone step onto the dock behind me, felt it shift. I tensed for the briefest of moments but then settled. I knew who it was. I didn't even need to turn around. Soon enough, I felt a hand on the back of my neck, the fingers scratching into my hair. I hummed quietly and leaned against him when he sat next to me. I laid my head on his shoulder, and he rested his atop mine.

"Okay?" he asked quietly.

"Yeah," I said. "Just… a lot. You know. In my head."

"Gets loud, huh."

"A little."

"Need anything?"

"Just you. Just… you."

He chuckled. "That I can do."

He gave me time to parse through my thoughts, to try and put the pieces together and to discard the ones that wouldn't fit. He didn't know everything, but only because I hadn't told him. Given what Morgan had told me before we'd left Castle Lockes, I hadn't been able to work through it all. It'd been swirling around my head, the betrayal of it all, the anger, the anguish. Coupled with the fact that I had no idea what to expect in the desert, I wasn't sure I could have given it the time it needed.

It didn't help that I'd still felt the sting of betrayal. That my whole life had been foretold. That most of the major events that had happened to me, the things that had shaped me to become who I was today, seemed to have been done deliberately. That the man I looked up to almost the same as I did my father knew more about my past and future than he'd ever told me. One of the first things he'd ever taught me was that a wizard had his secrets. I knew that. I understood that.

It still hurt.

Especially to know I was keeping secrets too.

"My head feels full," I muttered. "I don't know what to focus on."

"Okay," Ryan said, turning his face to kiss my hair. "Let's focus on one thing at a time."

"Yeah."

"Did you do what you needed to do here? With Zero."

"I think so."

"Will Zero help us when the time comes?"

I was surer about that. "Yes. He will."

"And where do we go next?"

"North. The mountains."

"Randall. Castle Freesias. The mated dragons."

"Yeah."

"And that's the most pressing concern?"

I have awoken, O human child. In this forest deep, in the dark of the wild. And I have seen what is in your heart. Take heed of my warning: you are not ready.

All of you will not survive until the end. There will be loss, Sam. And it will burn like nothing has ever burned before. You must remember to keep in the light, even when the dark begins to curl around your feet.

I blinked away the burn.

And then I opened my mouth and lied.

"Yes. That, and I need to talk to Morgan."

"Good," he said. "Then we have a plan."

I laughed wetly. He had to have noticed.

He did, of course. "Hey." He lifted his head off mine, put a couple of fingers under my chin until I could look up at him. "What is it?"

I shrugged. "Just… tired. Really, really tired."

"You sure?"

I nodded. "Been a long few weeks, I guess."

"You can tell me anything, Sam. You know that, right?"

I looked into his bright eyes.

And believed him.

"I know."

"All right," he said, sounding regretful. "I distinctly remember a promise of butt sex, but if you're too tired, maybe we should just get you to bed."

I felt lighter because of him. Freer. "That's how you play it?"

He had a wicked smile on his face. "That's how I play it. What are you gonna do about it?"

I narrowed my eyes at him. "Is that a challenge, Sir Knight?"

"It would be, Wizard. Think you can handle it?"

I leaned forward, the weight of the world pushed away, at least for now. I had more important things to focus on. When I spoke, my voice was low and rough. "Tell you what we're going to do," I said, watching as the breath hitched in his chest, because he *knew* that voice. His pupils dilated and his tongue darted out as he licked his lips. "We're gonna head back to our room. You're gonna get undressed. And then you'll be on your knees while I'm still fully clothed. You're gonna take my cock out. You're gonna suck me off. And if you're good, if you can get me nice and wet, I promise I'll eat your ass until you're crying. Then, and only then, will I fuck you. How's that sound?"

"Yeah," he said hoarsely. "That. Please. Let's do that. That sounds good."

"Then get up and get moving."

He did, pulling me up. In his hurry, he almost ended up knocking us into the water but caught us before we went in. I was laughing at him, and he was laughing at me, and there, under the stars, I reminded myself that stone crumbled, and that even if it didn't, I would shatter it until there was nothing left.

"I love you," I said as he dragged me toward our room. "Gods, I love you."

And when he smiled back at me, eyes still blown out with lust, his grip on my hand tightening, I knew no one would take this away from me. Because I would get my happy ending. If it was the last thing I did.

And there, under the stars, he said, "I love you too. You and me, Sam. Always."

Yeah. I had plans, all right.

I could talk to Morgan later.

CHAPTER 22
Something Wicked

SAM.

I'm here.

Sam.

See me.

See me for what I am.

I opened my eyes.

It was dark.

Ryan slept deeply next to me, arm hung heavily over my waist, legs tangled with mine. My skin felt slick with sweat. My heart was in my throat. Magic raced along my skin, and I was *electrified* because of it.

Something was pulling me. That hook in my brain. I thought maybe Zero had come to Mashallaha, but that didn't feel quite right. Maybe it was Kevin. Maybe it was Ruv. I thought about ignoring it. I thought about curling back into the warmth of the man I loved and drifting away. It would be easy.

I didn't.

I didn't because—

"—we loved him, Sam," Morgan told me the day we left for the desert. He sat across from me in our labs in Castle Lockes. I was angry with him. With Randall. With Vadoma. But I was going to hear him out. I owed him that much, at least. "That's something I need you to understand above all else. Regardless of what I tell you, regardless of what you hear, you must know that we loved him." He sighed and looked down at his hands. "And I think it's safe to say we love him still. I can't speak for Randall, but... I've known him for a very long time."

I said nothing. Not because I didn't want to. No, of course not. I had never seen my mentor look so… defeated before. Broken down. I said nothing because I couldn't think of a single thing to say.

"He was kind, but then that's how we were raised. Our parents were powerful. Our father was a wizard. Our mother was… well. I don't know exactly what our mother was. She was magic, yes, but it wasn't like being a wizard. She wasn't a seer. She wasn't a fortune-teller. She was not a mage or a witch or any other form of magical being that I've ever come across. She defied description. I don't know that there has ever been one quite like her before or since. The things she was capable of, Sam. Such beautiful things. You remind me of her, in that way. Magic is stringent. It's governed by a specific set of rules. Those rules didn't seem to apply to her." He looked up at me with a quiet smile on his face. "Or to you. You're alike that way. There is a power in you that I don't know that I will ever understand. Like her. I've often wondered if she knew. If she knew what would become of us. Of what I, as her son, would have to do to Myrin, her other son. If she loved him even though his heart would become corrupted. If she did her all to correct the path he was set upon before she followed my father through the veil. By the time I'd thought to ask her, it was far too late. For all of us."

Gods, how my heart hurt already. I almost opened my mouth to stop him. To keep him from speaking further about deceit and betrayal. I—

—MOVED QUIETLY, TRYING NOT TO WAKE Ryan. It was probably nothing, this feeling I had. I was tired. We'd been through a lot. My mind was probably just playing tricks on me. It was nothing.

It was nothing.

The hairs on my arms stood on end. My skin was covered in gooseflesh. My eyes were wide.

Sam.

Sam.

Sam.

"What the hell," I muttered.

I rose from the bed. Ryan mumbled something in his sleep, moving over to the spot I'd vacated, face pressed into my pillow. Firelight from the lamps around Mashallaha filtered in through the slats of the wall, illuminating his naked back, the blanket pooled at his waist. My heart tripped all over itself at the sight, and I reached down, trailing my fingers along his skin. He hummed quietly, leaning into the touch, eyes remaining closed.

"I'll be right back," I whispered.

And still he slept.

Sam.

I jerked up and whirled around, because *that* voice sounded like it'd come from right behind me.

There was nothing there.

The hook *pulled*.

I told myself to crawl back into bed.

Instead, I moved toward the door and—

"—he treated me as if I was the greatest thing in the world," Morgan said, a far-off look in his eyes. "He was older than me, far older, but he didn't treat me as if I was a burden. Didn't think I was a nuisance. He cared for me, maybe more than our parents did. For all intents and purposes, he raised me. Our parents were... distant, for lack of a better term. Oh, they loved us, and they made sure we had anything we could ever want, but they had other things to focus on. Stretching the boundaries of magic. Defining what it meant to be a wizard. Speaking out against the rejecting of a cornerstone. I never begrudged them for what they did. And I thought Myrin didn't either. I would be wrong about that."

He laughed, but it was a bitter sound. "Randall was everything to him. I was told that even before they were actually... them, you could tell Myrin thought Randall had hung the sun and the moon. Had placed all of the stars in the sky. I told you that Randall was a builder. An architect. That it took him decades to construct his magic, to create the outline for who he would become. He had long since passed the Trials, but it was... different. For him. His magic was theory before it was anything else. By the time he was ready for a cornerstone, by the time he opened his eyes, he was able to see what had been right in front of him the entire time. What Myrin had known all along. That they belonged to each other. That they loved each other. That they were each other's cornerstones. My brother had been a patient man. He knew that one day Randall would see him for what he was. And he did." Morgan wiped his eyes. "Everything was beautiful and nothing hurt."

"Morgan, you don't have to—"

"But I do, Sam. Because you have to know what lies ahead. You have to know what may come down upon us. This is your history as much as it is mine. This is the legacy I will leave to you, and I would have you know it. Will you listen?"

I was helpless, so all I could say was "Yes."

He took a breath, held it for a count, and then let it out slowly, something I knew he did when he was attempting to calm himself. I didn't want to hear how this story ended, even though I thought I knew.

"They... completed each other," he continued. "Unlike anything I'd ever seen before. A wizard's cornerstone isn't usually another wizard. We're taught that there's too much instability, too much of a chance for whatever has been built to come crumbling down. That it's not safe. But it happens. It's rare, but it happens. And even though there were people trying to convince them that they should find another, that they shouldn't depend on each other as they did, they laughed and scoffed and went on as they were. And it was wonderful. I didn't see them as others did. I saw them as something

to aspire to be. Something that I would one day want for myself. Randall was old, far older than a wizard should have been before finding their cornerstone. But the power that they had negated any argument against them.

"Randall became the King's Wizard. They worked here, in the labs, together, every day. They taught me. They taught each other. They laughed and loved and made promises that we all thought would always be kept.

"And then things began to change. I noticed it first, when I—"

—stepped out into the warm night air. The stars were bright above. I immediately sought out David's Dragon, but it said nothing to me, just blinking in the sky as it always had. I wondered if maybe I was dreaming, but it didn't feel like a dream. I did feel awake, but I also felt… more. Like my eyes were open for the very first time in my life. Everything around me felt like it'd come into sharper focus. The crystal clarity of the water around Mashallaha in the starlight. The grain of the wood beneath my feet. The colors of the flags that hung above me.

It was quiet, this late. I heard not a single soul.

Sam.

I took a stumbling step forward as a burst of magic crawled through me. Green and gold and an infected yellow swirled just along the edges of my vision.

I took a breath.

"What is this?" I said. "Who are you?"

There was no one there. Not in front of me. Not behind me.

"I'm losing my mind," I muttered. "That's it. That's all."

The hook *pulled* and—

"—I thought I could handle it," Morgan said. "I thought I could talk to him, and that he would hear me. I didn't know what he was trying to accomplish with the magic he was performing. The boundaries he was pushing. He said that if our parents had done it, then he could too. But that he would stretch it further than they ever had. He didn't want to just push, he told me. No. He wanted to break." He ran a hand over his face, looking more tired than I'd ever seen him before. "I told him that was the path of the Darks. That they had no regard for the rules that bound us to our magic. That anyone who attempted what he was attempting could find their souls cracked, their hearts shattered. Their minds diseased with temptations that should never be considered."

"What did he want to do?" I asked, not sure I wanted the answer.

Morgan looked up at me. "He thought it was possible to bend the will of the people. Verania was… turbulent then. Not everyone agreed with the King in power. There were talks of uprisings. Of coups against the throne. The threat of civil war had hung over the country for years. Myrin wanted to take away their free will. To make the people docile. He said it would prevent death. That it would prevent conflict. That everyone would fall in line, and Verania would not descend into madness.

"I couldn't fault him for thinking that way. I doubt anyone could. Who wouldn't want to avoid war? Who wouldn't want to stop bloodshed? It's seductive, that line of thinking. I truly believe he came to it from the right place, but that before long, it soured within him and began to rot. And that's where he was wrong. That's where the idea as a whole became fetid. Because even if it would have prevented Verania from descending into chaos, even if it would have stopped the deaths of our people, it would still have been wrong. You cannot tamper with free will. You cannot take the choices away from people. They have the right to choose for themselves. Many of them disagreed with their King. They were not wrong. He was a weak man. A coward. Randall had done his very best in trying to counsel him, but he could only do so much. I could see his frustrations, the helplessness that he sometimes showed. And Myrin saw it too. And I think that only fueled him. By the time Randall figured out what was happening, it was too late. For all of us. I—"

—found them sleeping, all curled around each other. It was an old barn of sorts that had lofts that held wheat and oats, rice, sorghum, corn, and barley. It was the only place big enough for Kevin to curl up and sleep at night. Gary had objected (quite loudly and fiercely) at being offered a *barn* to stay in, of all things. Didn't they know how *racist* that was? When Vadoma had told him that it was just for Kevin, Gary had, of course, become even *more* irate, saying that he wouldn't allow Kevin to stay by *himself* in an unfamiliar bed. Didn't they know he had troubles sleeping in places that weren't his home? The *audacity* behind it, the sheer *audacity*, and *yes*, they *were* separated (not that anyone had asked), but that didn't mean he didn't care for Kevin's well-being. Why, anything else would just be *rude*.

Vadoma had looked like she didn't know what hit her. Which, to be fair, most people looked like after having dealt with Gary.

But I remembered the look on Kevin's face as he stared down at Gary, that expression of wonder, like he couldn't believe someone would speak up for him like that. If Gary hadn't, I would have, but I knew he'd do the right thing. Gary always did. He just had to be loud about it. I knew those two crazy kids would make it, once they stopped being idiots.

Kevin lay on his stomach, wings at his sides, head on his hands, taking in low, rumbling breaths and huffing them out in little snores. Gary was sprawled out obnoxiously, tongue lolling out of his mouth, legs and hooves pointed out in all different directions, head on Tiggy's lap. The half-giant was propped up against Kevin's side, rising and falling with the dragon's breathing.

Tiggy opened his eyes as I stood in the doorway. He smiled when he saw me, nodding when I brought a finger to my lips.

"All right?" he whispered.

"All right. Just… checking on you."

"Good. We good."

"I can see that."

"You good?" he said, brow furrowing.

I pulled a smile out of nowhere and said, "Sure, dude. I'm good. I'm gonna head back, okay?"

"I walk with you?"

"Nah. Get back to sleep. We gotta long trip ahead of us."

He blinked sleepily at me. "Castle Freeze Your Ass Off?"

"Castle Freeze Your Ass Off," I agreed.

He yawned, jaw cracking. "Okay. G'night, Sam. Love you."

"I love you too, buddy. Night."

And I closed the door behind me as he fell back asleep. I thought about going back in, letting Ryan hold me close, of being surrounded by those I loved, but the hook was pulling me harder now. It was pulling me away from them.

I left them behind and moved deeper into Mashallaha.

It felt like a ghost town. Like everyone had disappeared and I was all that was left.

I thought about using the summoning crystal to call Morgan, but I'd left it in the room with Ryan.

Besides, I told myself. Morgan would be asleep right now. Like a normal person.

Sam.

My hands shook at my sides. I balled them into fists.

"Who are you?" I said through gritted teeth.

Oh, Sam. I'll show you.

Come to me, and I will show you everything.

And I did the only thing I could.

I went.

I didn't have—

"—a chance against it," Morgan said. *"The King was weak, and Myrin had begun whispering poison in his ear, although we hadn't known it. Or at least that's what I tell myself. Because if I allow myself to ruminate upon it, if I allow myself to give it any more thought than I already have, I'll look back and see that I, like Randall, turned a blind eye to what was happening. I would see that I refused to believe in what was happening right in front of me. That the Myrin we'd known, the Myrin we'd loved, had become lost to us. He had chosen to turn in a direction that we could not follow, no matter how much we wanted to be with him."*

He looked up at me. "Do you know what that's like, Sam? To feel the sting and burn of such duplicity? I know you think you might, that you think that I, and Randall, have betrayed your trust in us. I understand that. I don't repudiate your right to feel that way. I don't. But I ask that you see it from our perspective. To feel what we did. You may not understand why we did what we did, but the choices we made came from a place born of betrayal."

I said nothing, because there was nothing to say that wouldn't make me sound petty.

"The King went mad," Morgan said flatly. "His mind was taken from him because of Myrin. He was nothing but a shadow puppet, a falsity that danced in the firelight. Through Myrin, the King gave orders that led to war. Wizards began to rise from the Dark Woods in numbers that we did not expect, and they looked to Myrin as their leader. Many people died without understanding what they were dying for. Randall and I... we did everything we could think of. But I was an apprentice who didn't yet have a cornerstone, and Randall was a wizard in the process of losing his. Sam, it—nothing can prepare you for that. Nothing can prepare you for how it's going to feel when your other half, the person on which you've built your life, your magic, is tearing themselves away from you while they break themselves apart. Losing a cornerstone to death is always a difficult time for a wizard. But losing your cornerstone to the Dark, it... changes you, Sam. It makes you angry and bitter, it feels like burning oil is in your veins. At least, that's what Randall told me many decades later."

"How did you stop him?" I asked hoarsely. "How did you end it?"

He closed his eyes and said—

SAM.

Come to me.

Come and see what they have made.

I opened my eyes.

I stood at the edge of the dock. The water lapped underneath me. The dock itself swayed gently. Every part of me was electrified.

I looked down into the lake. The water was clear and smooth and echoed the night sky above. It looked as if I was trapped between two mirrors, and I didn't know which cast the true reflection. I was barefoot. I didn't know why that stuck out to me.

A ripple came toward me, spreading wider and wider as it rolled through the water. There came another. And another. And another. The stars were shaking.

I looked up.

A man walked toward me. Each step was deliberate, measuredly paced. He wore a pair of tight-fitting trousers and a jerkin with rows of buttons down the front. It curved up into a collar around his neck.

And he was walking on water.

It shouldn't have been possible.

This had to be a dream.

He was familiar. I could see it in his face. He had the same eyes as the man who'd found me in the alley after I'd turned a group of teenage douchebags to stone. The same beard that curled down the front of him, long and luxuriant. It was such a discordant image that I expected to see pink shoes that curled at the tips on his feet. There weren't. He was barefoot. Each step he took, his feet barely sank below the surface of the water. He even almost looked to be the same age as my mentor, though I knew him to be far older.

I knew this man, though I'd never seen his face before in my life.

He stopped some distance away, a smile playing on his lips. Now that he was closer, I could see the similarities between him and his brother were an illusion. Yes, he had the eyes and the beard, yes, they were from the same blood, but that's where it ended. Morgan's eyes were kind and strong. He held himself high because it was what was expected of him. The power that emanated from him was there because of the sum of the parts that made up his life, both the good and the bad. Morgan was my friend. He was my mentor. I trusted him with my life.

This man couldn't be further from Morgan had he tried. Morgan's magic had always meshed well with mine. It came from our years together. This man's magic tried to do the same, but it felt slick and oily and wrong, and I could only think of how my magic had felt around Ruv, how there was a recognition there since he could have been a cornerstone. But it hadn't been right, because I already had Ryan.

This wasn't right, because I already had Morgan.

There were shadows curling around him like liquid smoke. I wondered if that was his magic. I saw the green and the gold. The colors of the world I'd been brought into.

It looked as if all he saw was black.

"Sam of Wilds," he said, his voice softer than I'd been expecting. It had a lilt to it, almost musically so. It was… calm. Soothing. And oh so wrong. "How lovely it is to look upon your face free from the confines of a dream. I shall remember this moment for an eternity."

"Myrin," I breathed.

ONCE UPON A TIME, THERE WAS a wizard who was loved deeply by two different men.

One was the love of a brother.

The other was the love fated by the stars.

It was a bright and fierce thing, their love. Capable of such wondrous things.

But in the end, it mattered not.

The wizard lost himself on a path that those who loved him could never understand. He descended into the Dark, consumed by the temptation of a magic that should not have existed. But boundaries had been broken;

barriers had been shattered. There was poison in his words, poison that was dripped into the ears of the weak of heart. Follow me, *he whispered.* Follow me and I will show you the way.

And the weak of heart had followed.

The brother begged him when they met in a clearing in the Dark Woods. The brother pleaded with him. Think of Randall! Think of our parents! Think of me! Gods, please, Myrin, I beg you. Think of me.

But the wizard known as Myrin did not.

The love fated by the stars was a great wizard in his own right, and did not beg. He did not plead. Instead, Randall gave an ultimatum, though it broke his heart: Turn away. Turn away and renounce your magic. End this nonsense, Myrin, and I will see to it that you are brought home.

And for a moment, it looked as if Myrin would consider it. There was a flash in his eyes, a crack of the mask. The brother saw the man that had once been before all of this. He saw his brother before him, and he thought it'd be enough. That this would end here as the Dark Woods burned around them and they wouldn't have to go through with what they had planned.

Stone crumbled. It always did.

But Myrin did not.

I cannot do that, *he said.* I am too far gone to ever return.

Then so be it, *Randall said.* Morgan.

And Morgan said, I can't.

The air stilled around them.

Myrin cocked his head. Second thoughts, little brother?

But Morgan only had eyes for Randall. Please. There has to be another way.

There isn't, *Randall said.* You knew it would come to this.

But—

Morgan. As my pupil, I am commanding you.

Morgan hung his head.

Myrin laughed. What's all this, then? You think you can defeat me? Oh, Randall. Love. You have no idea what I'm capable of.

And Randall looked into the eyes of his cornerstone and said, I know. I know what you're capable of. That isn't the problem. The problem is that you underestimated what *I* am capable of.

There was a crack in the sky.

A crack in the air.

A crack in the earth.

Randall's hands were raised before him, palms toward Myrin.

And with a song of sorrow in his heart, Morgan did the same.

At first, Myrin laughed.

He said, This is nothing. You both are *nothing.* You won't kill me. You don't have it in you.

And in that, he was right: they did not have it in their hearts to kill him. They couldn't find it in themselves to destroy the one thing they both loved most in the world. Call it a weakness. Call it their undoing, but they could not kill Myrin.

Myrin, for all that he'd become, underestimated the one thing he should not have: Randall's and Morgan's love for the man he once had been.

It was this love that tore a hole between the worlds. That opened the gateway to a realm steeped in shadows. Magic such as this hadn't been seen in the real world before. And it took a piece of their soul to do it. But as the gateway widened, as the shadows whipped out and curled themselves around Myrin's legs, knocking him to the ground, they knew in their soul-struck hearts that they had made their choice, just as Myrin had made his.

He screamed at them to save him. He told them he could change. Don't do this, he begged them. And when he saw they were not coming to his aid, he stopped his pleadings and snarled at them both. I will return. I will have my revenge. And this time, you won't see me coming. I will take everything precious from you. Everything you hold dear will be torn away. This I promise you.

And then shadows enveloped his body and pulled him from this world to the next.

The gateway closed with a furious crash.

The clearing in the Dark Woods fell quiet, the only sound being the great heaving sobs of the younger brother.

Eventually, they left.

Eventually, Randall pulled the King of Sorrows from madness by the sheer force of his will alone.

Eventually, the name Myrin was wiped from the memory of Verania. As if he had never been at all.

"YES," MYRIN SAID, SOUNDING AMUSED. "QUITE the sad story, I know. It's just so... *melodramatic*, isn't it? If it hadn't actually happened to me, it would be one of those things that's hard to believe. Alas, I don't have problems with belief. Do you, Sam? Do you have problems believing?"

"You're standing on water after having broken your way out of the shadow realm," I said. "I'm really not having a problem believing right now."

He tossed his head back and laughed. It sounded so much like Morgan, and the dissonance caused blood to rush in my ears. "Oh, Sam," he said, chuckling. "I know now what he sees in you. Honestly, it took me a while. I mean, hearing from a *god* that a *child* would rise against me? Can you *imagine* what that must have felt like?"

"Um. No? Wait. Yes. Because a god told me that another villain would come here and blah, blah, blah and then I would have to kick his ass and then all would be right with the world. So I guess I could imagine that after all."

He cocked his head at me. "That easy, is it?"

"Yes."

"Really. Well. I hate to break it to you, kiddo, but that couldn't be further from the truth. Would you like me to tell you why?"

I rolled my eyes. "Oh *gods*. This is it, isn't it?"

"What?"

"This is where you *monologue*. For fuck's sake. We already *had* that moment. I thought we were *past* this. What the fuck, man? Don't you remember? You were all like, hey, you, I'm your opposite, and, oh, look at me, gods and partiality and death and destruction and what the fuck *ever*. I am so *sick* of villains like you. What the fuck is your *deal*?"

He looked taken aback, but he covered it up quickly. "Sam," he said. "Believe me when I say you have *never* faced someone like me. It will be an education like you've never before experienced. But first, a chance for you. To end this all now."

"Let me guess," I said, trying to sift through the green and the gold. My magic was running through me, thrumming just underneath my skin. They had to feel it. Ryan. Gary. Tiggy. Kevin. Maybe even Zero. They *had* to. And if they did, we could end this now. We *could*. "You're gonna give me the chance to join you—*again*, by the way—to be by your side, to learn how to be a Dark douchebag. Sound about right?"

"Yes," he said slowly. "That sounds about right."

"Because—oh, whaddya know—there's never been someone like you, but oh *look*, there's never been someone like me either. Sound about right?"

"Quite."

"And if I don't join you, you're going to kill everyone and everything I love. And if I *do* join you, you'll spare the others and you and me will live happily ever after in some cave in the Dark Woods while you continue my wizard training to make me into a fucking dickbag who monologues with the best of them."

"I wouldn't say it's a *cave*. I mean, there's a house and everything. And you're sort of monologuing right *now*. I don't know how much more training in that you would need."

"Okay, let me stop you right there. No."

"No?"

"No. I will not. I won't ever. You can just cut that shit out of your diabolical scheme right now."

"My diabolical scheme," he repeated.

I squinted at him. "You do *have* a diabolical scheme, don't you? I mean, you're a villain, right? The big bad? It's kind of in the job description, dude."

"Oh," he said. "Is it now?"

"Wow, you sort of suck at the whole villain thing. Am I going to have to tell you how to do this too? Yikes. I think the star dragon might have seriously overestimated your abilities. That's… slightly depressing. Oh! Don't get me wrong. I'm super glad that you're… like that. I just thought there would be more of a challenge." And why the *hell* could I not feel any of the others? Why couldn't I at least get through to Kevin?

"I think there may have been a bit of a misunderstanding," he said.

I snorted. "You're telling me. Are you going to need a moment to shift your worldview back to being a bottom feeder?"

"You talk too much."

"Eh. I've been told that before. Still my thing. Dude, just listen, okay? Can you do that? Okay. So. You won't get the dragons. I already have two of them. I know the star dragon had to come to you and whatever—which, let's be honest, as far as prophecies go, that's really sort of lame—but you won't get what I have. Kevin is mine. Zero is mine. The other three will be mine. You won't have them."

"You're a bit of the cocky sort, aren't you?"

I shrugged. "Prophecies from the gods will do that to you."

"You forget," he said, taking another step forward, and this time I *felt* it. The water didn't ripple, it fucking *cracked* under his feet, like it was something solid. It reverberated through me, like it was a physical thing, rattling my bones and causing my skin to vibrate. "The prophecy wasn't just about *you.*"

I took a step back. I didn't mean to. It showed weakness. It would lend credence to the idea that I was *afraid.* I couldn't show him that.

Even if it was true.

Because I was alone and facing Myrin, the dark man in shadows.

"The dragons—"

"Here's a hint, *Sam,*" Myrin said, smile dropping from his face. "It's *never* been about the dragons. I don't *want* the dragons. Those are all yours, kiddo. Gather them. Don't. I don't give a *fuck* what you do with them. In the end, it won't matter. For them. For you."

"What? Then what hell is your plan?"

"I thought you said you hated it when villains monologue?"

"Wow, way to throw my words right back in my face—"

He took another step, and it was like I was getting *assaulted* by his magic. It wasn't the *morganhomesafe* melding that happened with my mentor. This felt like it was *forcing* itself on me, like it was trying to take me over. The hook in my head *pulled* sharply, causing me to groan as I was enveloped by him. By everything about him. I'd never had this before. Never felt strength like this before. Not even when Randall had given me his all that day in the field when he'd brought the lightning down upon me.

This was more.

"You have no idea what it's been like," he said, eyes blazing. "What I've learned in the shadow realm. It was hell, it was pain and torture, but it was an *experience,* Sam. It *changed* me in ways I never expected. It made me more than I ever thought I could be. And when the star dragon came to me? When he told me *my* destiny? That was the day I knew, the day I transformed. The seal was cracked, and I began to slip through. They didn't even notice. Randall and Morgan *didn't notice.* It took a long time, but I did it, Sam. *I slipped through.*"

"Monologuing," I said through gritted teeth. "You're... still... *monologuing.*"

"They can't feel you," he said. "If that's what you're wondering. The others. Your little cabal. Your *cornerstone.* None of them can feel you. I've cut you off from them so that we could have this little... chat."

"Gods, shut *up*," I snarled at him as I was forced to my knees. The weight of his *everything* bore down upon me, and it was rust and shadow, harsh and biting. I pushed through it, searching for the gold and the green. Searching for my way back home.

The smile on his face was a nasty thing. "Don't you want to know why? Don't you want to know what this is all about?"

"Fuck... *you.*"

"Sam. Sam, Sam, Sam. Don't you see? No. I am your *father.*"

"*What?*"

The smile widened. "Just kidding. I've always wanted to say that."

I'd had enough. Of him. Of this. Of a history that I didn't want but that I was *mired* in. He was no different than the others that had come before him. And I had bested them.

I would do the same to him.

I pulled my hands back at my sides, then thrust them forward, crying out at the pain it caused to burst through the layers of shadows wrapped around me. Lake water snapped frozen in a split second as it rose into a wave of razor-sharp spikes of ice. They hurtled toward him, and I felt no regret at the thought of him being pierced from head to toe. Death would mean an end to all of this. I could go home.

He didn't die.

Instead, before he was run through, he held up a hand and the ice *shattered* into thousands of pieces, glittering in the starlight. He snapped his fist closed, and the ice swirled around him, gathering into a single large piece, sharpened to a point.

"Well fuck me sideways," I muttered as I turned to run.

And then the fucking dickbag *threw* it at me.

My feet pounded against the wooden dock. I felt the burst of magic behind me, that infection and shadow, and I swung my arm up in an arc over my head without thinking complete thoughts about what I was doing. I glanced over my shoulder in time to see the end of the dock snap upward, bursting into flames so hot that the skin of my back felt flash burned. The large bolt of ice smashed into the burning dock, crashing through it, breaking apart as the fire melted it away. The dock swayed sharply under my feet at the impact, and

I almost lost my footing and fell into the lake.

I jumped the remaining distance and landed on solid ground just as the dock broke apart completely. I hit the ground roughly, smashing my knee. A bright flare of pain shot through me, but I pushed it away as best I could as I picked myself up and turned around, chest heaving.

The dock burned on the water, smoke and steam rising into the air.

And Myrin still stood atop the water, as if he hadn't a care in the world.

"You're good," he called out. "I'll give you that. But, Sam. You must know how much better I am than you. You may have power, but it's untamed. And I have *years* of experience."

"Oh, would you just *stop* already? I'm getting sick of your—what the fucking balls of shit!"

The last came out as a squeak because he began *running* toward me, each step making a large splash on the surface of the lake. He moved faster than any man should have been able to, but since he'd been *walking on water*, I figured he could be the exception. He ran at me, and so I did the natural thing that *anyone* would do when being charged at by a formerly good wizard who had been banished to a shadow realm and then escaped: I took the fuck off in the opposite direction.

I could hear him laughing behind me as I ran along the water's edge, trying to get away from the center of Mashallaha where it was more populated. I couldn't take the chance of there being any collateral damage from this asshole's vendetta against me.

Of course, any thoughts of outrunning him faded when I felt the ground beneath my feet begin to bend and crack. I glanced over my shoulder to see him running *just behind me* in the water, and I put on a burst of speed, lungs screaming as I jumped over pieces of the wooden walkways that began to snap up around me.

I thought I was going to make it.

I really did.

I was the good guy.

The good guys always won.

That's what I'd been taught.

That's always how these stories ended.

The good guys *won*.

And I *knew* I was the good guy.

But even before I could reach the end of the walkway, even before I could have any hope of escape or, at the least, getting as far away from Mashallaha as possible, I was knocked off my feet when the ground exploded underneath me. I went end over end into the lake. As my feet hit the water, my head rapped against something solid, and stars shot across my vision as I went under, the breath knocked from my chest.

I was dazed. Confused. Unsure of what had happened or where I was. I choked before I stopped trying to breathe, a small amount of awareness flooding back. I didn't know which way was up. My head was throbbing. Everything felt sluggish. Slow. I tried to gather as much strength as I could, and there was green and gold, and it—

A hand closed around my throat, and I was pulled up and out of the water.

I sputtered as I was held high, toes skimming along the surface of the lake. I tried grabbing at the hand on my neck, but the grip was strong. I kicked out, but the impacts were weak. I opened my eyes, blinking away the water.

Myrin stood on the surface of the lake, water dripping down off me and onto his arm. His face. His body.

He was smiling.

"Sam," he said, clucking his tongue. He sounded *disappointed* in me as I struggled to get a breath in. "That was... underwhelming. *This* is supposed to be the great Sam of Wilds? *This* is who the Dark wizards are supposed to fear? That was *nothing*. You are a *child* playing at a man's game."

"Wait till I get my second wind," I managed to choke out. "We can go again. Next week work for you? Just leave your information with my secretary and—" His grip tightened, cutting me off.

"You still make jokes," he said. "Even in the face of death. It would be admirable if it wasn't so pathetic."

"Hey, man, jokes are what I've got. You've kind of got me by the balls here."

He chuckled. "Indeed I do. And I think a lesson in humility is in order." He lowered his arm, bringing my face closer to his. I was able to grip his forearm with my wet hands. "Even now, the Darks march toward Meridian City where the people sleep unaware of the fate that awaits them. At my word, the city will be razed. It is truly a sinful place, so I doubt it would be missed too much. And they will have my word, Sam. As an example to you." His teeth were bared, his eyes narrowed. "This will be to show you that you are on the wrong side. That you cannot win. Morgan and Randall were weak. They still are. There will be a new order, one that will begin with you and end with me. You can either join me or watch as I tear your whole world apart." And then I felt another *pull*, like he was *sucking* my magic from me, and I thought I was going to split right down the middle.

"You wouldn't," I managed to grit out.

"Oh I would, Sam. You're playing with the big boys now. The stakes are a little higher than what you're normally used to. Their deaths will be on your head, every man, woman, and child in Meridian City. I told you once that I would rip the lightning-struck heart from your chest. Trust me when I say I will do just that."

I began to laugh.

Because it was so godsdamned obvious.

He frowned. "What's so funny?"

"You," I wheezed, lake water still dripping down onto him. "Gods, you think you're so different. You think you're better than all the others that have come before you. I've got news for you, dude. You're a fucking idiot, just like the rest. It's *incredible*."

He brought me close to his face, his nose almost touching mine. I could see the fury in his eyes. "An idiot? If I'm such an idiot, what does that make you, seeing as I have the upper hand?"

I grabbed the front of his jerkin, completing the connection between us. "Oh, man. You have no idea what I'm capable of." I leaned forward, straining against his grip. It must have looked like I was going in for a kiss. Instead I said, "You want to see just how lightning-struck my heart is? You've got it. By the way, water conducts electricity."

His eyes widened.

And because I'd probably never have a more perfect moment, I grinned and said, "I think you're going to find the results quite... *shocking*." Catchphrase for the motherfucking win, asshole.

And then I screamed in his face as my magic exploded out of me. From the very first day that I'd been lightning-struck, from the moment it had curled around my heart, I'd known that nothing would ever be the same. That things would change. That I could become something more than what I already was. And I'd given that heart away to the ones I knew could keep it safe. Tiggy. Kevin. Gary. Ryan.

I would do anything to keep them safe.

The lightning didn't come from above.

It came from within me.

The snarl of lightning burst from my chest. From my mouth. My eyes and fingertips and toes. It was white hot and almost *sentient*, following along the path I'd set for it. It rolled from inside me with an electrical *snap*, pouring out and crawling over Myrin. It jumped along the water covering his skin, his wet clothes, striking down into the surface of the lake through his feet.

The entire lake became electrified beneath us. The world took on a bluish hue as the lightning spread through the water, arcing off in different directions. It glowed so brightly, it was almost as if the sun had risen.

Myrin's jaw was clenched as his body seized. The grip around my throat tightened, but it was a flexion of the joints more than anything else. His eyes were beginning to roll back into his head, and I *pushed* as hard as I could, filling his body with everything I had. My own skin felt like it was on fire.

"You... won't... win," he stuttered out, jaw clenched. "This is the beginning... of the end."

I smiled at him, knowing my eyes were glowing brightly. "Dude, go fuck yourself."

And then I went boom.

The grip around my neck was torn as we were thrown away from each other, the shock waves rippling the air around us. I had a moment to think how much this was going to fucking hurt before I slammed into the side of a building, the wood cracking behind me before giving way and sending me through the wall.

It got dark real quick after that.

"SAM? SAM!"

"Whazzit."

"I need you to open your eyes. Sam, listen to me."

"Whodat."

"What?"

"I think he just asked *who dat?*"

"Thank you, Gary. That helped me with absolutely *nothing*."

"Yikes, someone woke up bitchy today. And that someone is named Ryan Foxheart."

"He sad 'cause Sam go boom?"

"Yes, kitten."

"I sad 'cause Sam go boom?"

"We'll be sad if he dies. And after an acceptable period of mourning—say, three and a half days?—we'll start to divide up his stuff. I get mostly everything, and the things I don't want will be thrown away. Or donated to charity. Most likely thrown away."

"I get his brooms."

"I don't know where this broom fetish came from. I had absolutely nothing to do with that. You are a strange, wonderful half-giant who I love dearly."

"It's because he stole them from my keep. Everyone knows that brooms are part of any good hoard. It's just common sense is what it is. I mean, why *wouldn't* you have brooms?"

"Shuddap," I said. "Tryna leep."

"What the hell is he saying?"

"Shut up. Trying to sleep. Oooo, I'm like the Sam whisperer. My thighs are tingling. That's a good thing, especially since he seems to get knocked out a lot lately."

"I am going to slap the shit out of him if he doesn't open his eyes."

And since that voice sounded serious (and slightly frantic), I did just that.

I blinked blearily at the faces staring down at me.

They all looked immediately relieved.

And because I couldn't pass up the opportunity to be an asshole, I said, "Where am I? Who are all of you? Why can't I remember anything, such as my own name or country of origin or the people in my life who I am supposed to love?"

Gary burst into tears and started wailing. "Oh my gods, he's lost his *memories*. Why, gods, whyyyyy would you do that to us? How can he remember how splendid I am if he doesn't know *who* I am? Do you know much *work* I put into him? Why? Whyyyyyyy!"

"Oh no, Sam!" Tiggy said, bottom lip quivering. "'Member me? Old pal, Tiggy?"

Yeah. You try having a half-giant on the verge of tears staring at you and saying something like that. "Just kidding! Oh my gods, I'm *kidding*. Sweet molasses, that *face*. Gaaah, I want to hug it and kiss it, what are you *even*?"

Gary immediately stopped shrieking, eyes dry. "You fucking motherfucker fuck," he snarled, sounding rather impressed. "You should go live under a bridge, that was such good trolling. I am going to *murder* you."

"Not if I get to it first," Ryan said, grinding his teeth together.

"Uh-oh," Kevin said, face stuck through the large window. "Either Sam's about to get kissed or punched in the butt, I don't know which—oh, he's getting kissed. Personally, I would have gone for the butt punch, but what do I know?"

I couldn't respond that Kevin knew absolutely nothing because I had a mouthful of knight. Not that I was complaining.

Okay, I was a little bit, because that *hurt*. Everything *hurt*. "Ow," I said against his mouth before I shoved him away. "Dude, your face on my face does *not* feel good right now."

"You fucking asshole," he snarled at me, eyes wide and frightened. "Do you have *any* idea how scared I was?"

"You know we've talked about cursing, Ryan. You can't fucking talk like—okay, you're right. Now's not the time. Stop looking at me like that." I sat up, groaning as I did so. I put my hand to my head, which was pounding something fierce. Somehow I was back in the room Ryan and I were sharing, wearing only a pair of what looked like Ryan's trousers. My body felt like it was covered in bruises. I looked down at my bare chest, expecting to see mottled blues and purples, but was surprised instead to see a raised red scar that looked like tree roots stretching along my skin, curling down toward my stomach and over to my right arm.

"Uh," I said. "Did I get drunk and make the unfortunate decision to get tattooed? I *told* you guys to never let me get shattered and make decisions involving needles. You *know* how I get."

"Unfortunately," Gary said, rolling his eyes.

"It's a *mulani*," another voice said. "A ghost scar."

I looked up to see Vadoma standing in a corner, Ruv at her side. She was watching me with a look of what I could have sworn was fear on her face, but it was gone before I could pin it down. That didn't bode well for what was to come.

"Come again?"

"The lightning," Ruv said for her. "It came from you. From your heart. It scarred your skin."

"Suuuuck," I said, wincing as I pressed against it. It looked odd on my darker skin. I thought it would eventually fade white, but I didn't know.

"I dunno," Gary said, sounding chipper. "I think it looks really badass. And look at it this way: if you ever think of scaring us like that again, a chest scar will be the least of your worries because I'll be bathing in your blood."

I gulped, because when a unicorn sounded that happy while threatening you, you had to take it seriously. Unicorns were bloodthirsty creatures who would bring the pain. "Got it. What the hell happened?"

"We found you inside a collapsed building," Ruv said. "Along the edge of the water."

"I didn't do it this time," Kevin said, head stuck through an open window. "It would have felt a little repetitious. Lord knows people hate repetition." He frowned. "But then they'll also complain when something wasn't exactly the same as it was before. I really don't get humans."

"Shit," I groaned, wincing as I tried to swing my legs off the bed. "Myrin."

And that pretty much sucked the air out of the room. "Myrin," Ryan said. "Are you trying to tell me that the bad guy—the *main* bad guy, the one who wants to kill you—was *here*?"

"Um, yes?"

"And you faced him alone."

"Hey! It's not like I went *looking* for him. Mostly. He was sort of... in my head? Maybe?"

"Gary! Get me my sword."

"Do I *look* like a little servant girl? Wait. Don't answer that. I don't think my ego can take—"

"You didn't find anyone else out there?" I asked, grabbing Ryan by the arm to keep him from going off half-cocked. If Myrin was still out there, I didn't want Ryan anywhere near him. He was dangerous, and he needed to be dealt with as soon as possible. I felt a pang in my chest that had nothing to do with the scar. I didn't know what it said about me that I could think of killing someone without hesitation.

"No," Ruv said. "The night guards said there was a great storm within the lake. They'd never seen such a thing before and thought that the gods had been angered. That they were bringing down the heavens in penance. They came to me, but by the time I got outside, the lightning was fading. And it was only then we heard the building collapse on the water's edge." He looked away. "We found you in the rubble. You weren't breathing."

That... wasn't something I expected to hear. "Oh."

"Oh," Ryan said mockingly. "*Oh.*" He stood and started pacing, something he only did when he was really angry.

Yeah. I felt like shit.

Even though I didn't think I'd technically done anything wrong.

"Ruv got you breathing again," Gary said quietly. "Chest compressions."

"How long?"

"Since we found you?"

"Yes."

"Six hours," Gary said.

"Shit," I muttered. That explained the daylight filtering in through the windows. It didn't help either that I felt like I was forgetting something, something important, but it was lost in the fog of pain in my head.

"He was here?" Vadoma said, voice trembling.

I looked up at her. She was pale. Shaking. "Yeah. He said... he didn't need the dragons for what he had planned. That he—" I shook my head. "I don't know. It's all a blur."

"If he doesn't need the dragons, then what does he want?" Gary asked.

"I am okay with this turn of events," Kevin said. "I would prefer not to be the bitch of some evil wizard. He might make me do things I don't want to do. *Sexual* things."

"Kevin, there is nothing sexually you don't want to do," Gary said. "Remember that time we tried docking?"

Kevin smiled down at Gary. "I'll never look at that church the same way again. Hey. So. I was thinking. Um. Maybe after all of this is over, we could—"

"Everybody out," Ryan growled.

"Yeah," I said. "Let's all just go out and—"

"Not you," Ryan said, hand on my elbow holding me back.

"Save me," I hissed as Gary walked past me.

"Oh, girl," Gary simpered. "You gonna need to save yourself on this one. Go easy on him. He had a scare, and you know he doesn't deal well with that."

"Yeah," I said to Ryan. "Go easy on me. I had a scare."

"I was talking to you," Gary said as he walked out the door.

"You bitch!"

"Love you, kitten!" And the door closed behind them.

I was doomed.

"So," I said nervously. "What are the chances we can just forget all about this and—"

Ryan kissed me, gripping the sides of my face tightly. His teeth clacked against mine, and he swallowed my gasp down. His tongue was warm and slick, and I groaned, forgetting about the pain for at least a moment.

We were both panting as he broke the kiss, pressing his forehead against mine. My hands were on his waist. He still cupped my face, brushing his thumbs over my cheeks, arms folded between us.

"You can't do that to me," he said, sounding angry and broken. "You just *can't*."

"I didn't mean—"

"I don't care. Sam. Promise me. You can't do that. You can't die."

I gave him a trembling smile. "I can't promise that. None of us can. You know that, Ryan."

His eyes were wide and a little manic. "Promise me."

I meant to say *You don't have to worry about that.* I meant to say *I love you so, so much.* I meant to say *We're gonna do this together.* I meant to say so many things.

But I was young and foolish. I'd just met Myrin face-to-face and I'd survived. I'd tamed the desert dragon. So much was up in the air, but I knew I could do this. I could end this. I could beat back the dark.

I said, "I promise. Ryan, I promise. Nothing's going to happen. To either of us. Any of us."

He kissed me again, desperately so.

All of you will not survive until the end. There will be loss, Sam. And it will burn like nothing has ever burned before.

Fuck the star dragon. Fuck the gods.

I wouldn't let anything take him away from me.

And just when I was about to lead him back to the bed, to take what he was offering to me so freely, I remembered what it was I'd forgotten.

Indeed I do. And I think a lesson in humility is in order. Even now, the Darks march toward Meridian City where the people sleep unaware of the fate that awaits them. At my word, the city will be razed. It is truly a sinful place, so I doubt it would be missed too much. And they will have my word, Sam. As an example to you.

"No," I breathed against Ryan's lips.

I felt Ryan frown. "What?"

I pushed him away. "We have to get to Meridian City. We have to—"

In the corner, where our packs lay on the ground, something rattled sharply.

Ryan took a step back. "Is that the—"

"Summoning crystal," I said, brushing past him. "It's gotta be Morgan." I groaned as I crouched, my back screaming at me, the lightning-struck scars on my chest on fire. I dug through my pack until my hand closed around the crystal. I pulled it out and saw the little burst of light shoot off deep inside it.

There was that little tug in my head, that old familiar pull, and the crystal lit up in my hand.

"Morgan?"

"Sam," he said. "Thank the gods. Where are you?"

"We're in Mashallaha still. The dragon is ours. He's—"

"Sam."

"No," I said. "No. No."

But I knew. I already knew.

He said, "You must listen to me."

He said, "For we don't have much time."

He said, "The Darks are heading toward Meridian City."

He said, "The defenses will hold, but we don't have much time."

He said, "Randall is coming for me."

He said, "We'll do everything that we can."

He said, "Sam. It's begun."

"I understand," I said, swallowing thickly. "We can—"

"No," Morgan said firmly. "I want you to go north."

"*What?*"

"Listen to me. There's nothing you can do. You can't make it on foot. Your magic cannot transport you there."

"But Randall can take *you*? I'm getting real sick of your godsdamned rules, Morgan. I can *help*—"

"Don't you think that's what he wants?" Morgan demanded. "Don't you think you'll play right into his hands?"

"He was already here. Myrin was already here."

Silence. Then, in a whisper, "What?"

"He came for me. I held him off."

"You *what*? How in the name of the gods—"

"And he almost died doing it," Ryan growled down at the crystal. He stared at me defiantly, as if daring me to speak against him. "Myrin almost killed him."

"North, Sam," Morgan said. "Don't make me tell you again. You have a job to do."

"Morgan—"

"*Sam.*"

"What about the King? The Prince? My parents?"

"They'll be safe here. The Castle Guard is on it. There is no stronger hold than Castle Lockes. We'll—"

"Blast it, Morgan, are you *still* blathering on to that thing? We have to *go.*"

"It's Sam," Morgan said to Randall. "Myrin's already found him. They escaped."

"Hey!" I barked. "We didn't *escape*. I kicked his motherfucking *ass*."

"Aren't you just a special snowflake," Randall said, and I could picture the constipated look on his stupid face. I was going to turn so many things of his into dicks the next time I saw him. "You have your orders. North, Sam. Don't tarry. Mind me now. We'll meet you at Castle Freesias."

And then the crystal went dark.

"That motherfucker *hung up* on me," I snapped. "That... *that... I* can't even think of an awesome insult because I'm so pissed off!"

"You heard them," Ryan said. "We should head north."

"Damn right we should. But we're not going to."

Ryan sighed. "I was afraid you were going to say that."

"Dude. You know me. There's trouble. And I need to be smack dab in the middle of it. Mama's there. I have to help her."

Ryan was already throwing our clothes into the packs. "I'm sure she's probably already leading an army of whores as we speak."

"Dude," I breathed. "That is the best army *ever*."

Ryan grinned wildly at me. It really was a breathtaking thing.

"We're gonna kick so much ass," I said.

"Damn right."

"Kiss my face," I demanded.

He did just that.

Then, "Wait."

I frowned, because I was feeling badass and was having a great mack sesh with my man. "For what?"

"Meridian City is on the other side of Verania."

"I know. Do you think we have time for blow jobs?"

"Sam."

"Right. Let's just jack each other—aw, crap, Meridian City is on the other side of the country. How in the fuck are we going to get there in time?"

And then I had the most awesome idea in the history of ideas.

EPILOGUE
Taking Flight

I BURST OUT INTO THE SUNSHINE. A crowd had gathered outside. They took a step back, a look of fear on their faces when they saw me. There were probably a million different rumors being whispered about me, but I didn't have time for that. Or them.

"Kevin!" I bellowed.

"Damn right," the dragon said. "Screaming my name and shit. Lord Dragon is *allll* about that."

I glared up at him.

He didn't look intimidated at all, the bastard.

"Do you trust me?"

He cocked his head at me. "What's this, then?"

"Do you trust me."

His nostrils flared. "Yes."

"And you know I would never hurt you."

"Yes."

"Sam?" Gary asked, Tiggy at his side. "What's going on?"

I ignored him, staring up at the dragon. "I need to ride you."

Kevin grinned. "Yeah you do, baby boy. What are your thoughts on role-play? Since I'm your stepfather, we can always go with you coming home with a bad report card and I'll be there to help you get your grades back up. With my penis."

"We did that once," Gary said to Tiggy. "I went from failing to graduating with honors."

"Ick," Tiggy said.

"The Darks are heading toward Meridian City."

That shut everyone up right quick.

Kevin didn't look away.

"And I need you," I told him. "I know you've been hurt in the past. I know you don't trust most humans. I know you don't trust most wizards. But you're my friend. And I would never do anything to hurt you."

The air around us began to feel electric, as if we were both leaking magic all over the place. He lowered his head until we were eye level, and I wondered if my eyes were darkening, like they'd changed colors with Zero. They'd been red, for Zero's scales. Kevin was black as the night. There was a bond between us. I didn't know why I'd never felt it so strongly before.

His tail twitched dangerously. He looked more animal than I'd ever seen him before.

He said, "Will you use your magic against me? If I say no? To force me to do your bidding?" His voice was deeper than it'd ever been before.

And I said, "*No.*"

"Then yes, wizard. I will help you."

I reached out and touched his face. He pressed back into my hand. "We have to be quick," I said quietly. "People are getting hurt. We have to help them."

"Leave it to me," the dragon said, breath hot against me. "I'll show you just how fast I can fly."

"HOLY FUCKING BALLS OF FUCKING SHIT!" Gary screamed as we rocketed up into the sky, the wind snapping around us. "THIS IS NOT WHAT I HAD IN MIND FOR—OH I'M GOING TO BE SI—" I looked down from my spot on Kevin's back just in time to see Gary vomit rainbows from where he sat in the clutches of Kevin's hands against his chest. I could sympathize with the vomiting. At least he hadn't been eating corn.

Ryan sat behind me with Tiggy behind him, arms wrapped around us both, holding us in place as we left the desert behind and rose toward the infinite blue. It was frightening. It was exhilarating.

But I had no time to enjoy it.

Because the Darks were coming.

And I was going to make them pay.

You are not ready, the Great White had said.

There will be loss, the star dragon had said.

Fuck them.

Fuck them all.

I was Sam of Wilds.

And I was going to face my godsdamned destiny.

ABOUT THE AUTHOR

TJ KLUNE is a Lambda Literary Award-winning author (*Into This River I Drown*) of over twenty novels and an ex-claims examiner for an insurance company. His novels include *Wolfsong*, *The Lightning-Struck Heart*, and *Bear, Otter and the Kid*. Being queer himself, TJ believes it's important—now more than ever—to have accurate, positive, queer representation in stories.

www.tjklunebooks.com
twitter.com/tjklune
www.facebook.com/TJKlune
www.instagram.com/tjklunebooks

OTHER WORKS BY TJ KLUNE

THE BEAR, OTTER AND THE KID CHRONICLES
Bear, Otter and the Kid
Who We Are
The Art of Breathing
The Long and Winding Road

TALES FROM VERANIA
The Lightning-Struck Heart
A Destiny of Dragons
The Consumption of Magic
A Wish Upon the Stars

GREEN CREEK
Wolfsong
Ravensong
Heartsong
Brothersong

AT FIRST SIGHT
Tell Me It's Real
The Queen & the Homo Jock King
Until You
Why We Fight

HOW TO BE
How to Be a Normal Person
How to Be a Movie Star

IMMEMORIAL YEAR
Withered + Sere
Crisped + Sere

STANDALONES
Burn
Olive Juice
Murmuration
Into This River I Drown
John & Jackie